TREASURE COAST Legacy

EMERALD BAY
BOOK 6

LEIGH DUNCAN

Treasure Coast Legacy
Emerald Bay, Book #6

Copyright ©2024 by Leigh D. Duncan

This book is a work of fiction. The characters, events, and places portrayed in this book are products of the author's imagination and are either fictitious or are used fictitiously. Any similarity to real person, living or dead, is purely coincidental and not intended by the author.

Digital ISBN: 978-1-944258-38-2
Print ISBN: 978-1-944258-39-9
Gardenia Street Publishing

Published in the United States of America

Welcome to Emerald Bay!

After a lifetime of running the finest inn in Emerald Bay, Margaret Clayton has to make a decision…sell the Dane Crown Inn to a stranger or put her hopes for the future in her family's hands. For most people, the choice would be simple. But nothing about her family is simple…especially not with her daughter and four nieces whose help Margaret needs now more than ever.

The five cousins know the inn as well as Margaret does. As young girls and teenagers, they spent every summer keeping the cottages and suites spotless, and enjoying the gorgeous beach as a tight knit family. Thirty years later, though, these five women have complicated, important, distant, and utterly packed lives. The last thing any of them can do is drop everything and save the inn. But, when it comes to family, the last thing is sometimes the *only* thing.

As the once-close cousins come together on the glorious shores of Florida's Treasure Coast, they learn that some things never change, but others can never be the same. And the only thing that matters is family which, like the Dane Crown Inn, is forever.

To get the most enjoyment from the Emerald Bay series, start with *Treasure Coast Homecoming* and read the books in order.

Margaret

en million dollars?

That couldn't be right. Her lips pursed, Margaret leaned back in her chair and waited for the punch line. Because this had to be some kind of colossal joke, didn't it? Diane couldn't be serious.

When no one in the room cracked a smile, she treated her niece to the kind of hard-eyed stare that had never failed to stop a much younger version of the girl in her tracks. A glare that wasn't nearly as effective now that the girl in question was nearly middle-aged. With children of her own. Though Margaret supposed she could hardly call Nick a child anymore now that he was in his twenties. As for Caitlyn, the girl was bright, articulate, polite…traits every parent wanted their teenagers to possess. Not that Diane's children had always been perfect little angels. No, sirree. They'd thrown their fair share of tantrums when they were toddlers. To say nothing of the trouble Caitlyn had gotten herself into last year. Taking all that into consideration, Margaret had no doubt that Diane had perfected her own version of *the look*.

Did that give her niece some kind of immunity?

It must, she decided, when Diane patently ignored Margaret's glower and went on talking utter nonsense with the rest of the family.

Which was what it had to be, right? There couldn't be any truth to Diane and Nat's story of how they'd dug up a buried treasure worth more than a king's ransom. The numbers they were batting around were preposterous. Yet, as strange as it might seem, no one had questioned their outlandish tale.

Why was that?

Surely her nephew Scott, a true legal eagle if there'd ever been one, ought to ask a pointed question or two. Having been married to a con man, Kim should be saying, "This can't be true." But neither did. She hadn't heard a peep of protest from Amy or Jen, either. Instead, they all sat there with tears in their eyes and gushed over the things they'd do with their share. Even Belle—one of the most levelheaded people she knew—was dreaming up ways to spend the unexpected windfall.

Well, she, for one, was not going to get sucked in. She refused to believe a word of the yarn Diane was spinning. Not without proof, she wouldn't. Why, the amount of money being bandied about the room was enough to buy the Dane Crown Inn ten times over.

Ridiculous.

She'd spoken to enough of those pushy real estate agents over the years to have a pretty good idea of the current value of her home. Land had been cheap back when her dad bought the twenty-acre parcel that had been in her family for well over sixty years. Not so much these days. Especially if you factored in the roomy, two-story house, with its thirteen guest suites, airy wraparound porches and the family quarters that had been her home for most of her life. Along with the six cottages her brother-in-law had built out back, the property would fetch a pretty penny when she sold it later this year. She'd get top dollar for the place, considering all the improvements she and the girls had made over the last six months. Once she paid the bills, there'd be enough left over to care for all her needs in whatever time remained to her, along with a small sum she could pass on to Belle.

But the amount she'd get for the inn paled in comparison to the kind of money Diane and Nat were talking about. That kind of money changed lives. Changed generations.

Her eyes drifted closed as she considered how differently her own life would have turned out if her father had discovered a stash of gold and gems from a ship that wrecked off the coast of Florida some three hundred years ago. Much as her parents had dreamed of running the inn, they'd faced some pretty daunting challenges when they decided to build along the beach in the Sixties. If their pockets had been filled with gold doubloons back then, would they have stuck it out? Would they have battled the heat, the ever-present mosquitoes or the threat of hurricanes and built here at all? Or would they have piled her and her siblings, along with all their belongings, back into the station wagon and headed for someplace cooler...with better schools...better opportunities? How would her life have differed if she'd grown up in, say, Myrtle Beach? Or if her parents had chosen to build their inn on the shores of Lake Placid in the Adirondacks?

Margaret frowned. If she'd lived anywhere else but Emerald Bay, she might never have met Eric, never married the love of her life, never had Belle. She shook her head. No amount of money was worth giving up the life she'd led.

Others, though, might not feel the same.

Take her brother Edward, for instance. He'd wanted nothing to do with running the inn. After several heated discussions with their parents, he'd demanded his share in the family business, which he'd spent on tuition, books and lodging at a prestigious four-year college. After graduation, he'd moved to Houston, where he'd gotten a job with the space program. He'd lived there until he died from a heart attack before his fiftieth birthday.

Would he have made different choices if someone in their family had found the treasure a generation earlier? *Would he still be alive?*

And what about her sisters?

Margaret swiped the dampness from her eyes. Lord, how she missed Liz. It had been five years since the accident that had taken her sister's life and left Margaret dependent on a cane. Not a day had gone by since then that she hadn't wished she could ask Liz's advice. Evenings, when the two of them used to take their glasses of sweet tea out onto the deck, where they'd sit and talk for hours, those were the worst.

Would Liz be alive today if they'd grown up in New York or North Carolina instead of Florida?

What about Shirley? Would doctors have found the cancer in time to treat it if they'd lived in a bigger city?

She blotted her cheeks. *Phooey*. It did absolutely no good to play the "What if?" game. She couldn't change the past. Couldn't keep Edward from following his own dreams. Couldn't go back to the fateful night of the accident and slip behind the wheel of the car herself, rather than letting Liz drive. As for Shirley, her older sister had lived her life on her own terms. Margaret seriously doubted that growing up someplace different would have changed that. No. Dwelling on what could have been was a waste of time and energy. Both of which were better spent on the here and now.

She opened her eyes and studied the people seated in the family quarters' living room. She couldn't blame her daughter or her nieces or her nephew for their excitement. Practically every-one who lived on the Treasure Coast had heard the tale of a French galleon and eleven heavily laden Spanish treasure ships that set sail from Havana in the summer of 1715. From Miami to

St. Augustine, schoolchildren could recite the story of how all but one of those ships had been lost in a hurricane off the Florida coast, their precious cargo scattered over the ocean floor. In recent years, salvagers had located several of the wrecked ships and recovered much of the gold, silver and gems that had been bound for King Philip's court more than three centuries earlier. A substantial amount had never been accounted for, though. Which explained how—every blue moon or so—some lucky soul out for a morning walk along the beach would find a gold doubloon, a silver real, or an emerald washed up on the shore by a passing storm. So she understood why her closest family members might believe Diane and Nat's tale of buried treasure.

But if it were true—not that it could possibly be, but if it were—did they have any idea how much such a discovery would change their lives? Once the word got out, curious lookie-loos and treasure hunters would descend on the Dane Crown Inn from every corner of the globe. To keep the trespassers at bay, they'd have to install fences and hire guards to patrol the grounds. A line of people looking for a handout or a contribution to one cause or another would stretch from the front door all the way down the length of the coquina driveway to the main road.

And that's not all.

Each member of her family would need to consider the changes such sudden wealth could cause in their own lives. Even divided equally among the people in this room, they were talking about a lot of money. More than most of them had ever hoped to see in their lifetimes.

One by one, she scanned the faces of her immediate family. She had no doubt that Belle, Diane and Scott could handle an unexpected windfall with common sense. Her daughter had already lived the life of the rich and famous without letting it all go to her head, hadn't she? Belle would surely handle a new influx of cash in the same thoughtful and gracious manner as she'd handled it before. As for Diane, in her job as an accountant, she dealt with large estates all the time. And Scott didn't have a foolish bone in his body—he never had.

Margaret took an easy breath. At least she wouldn't have to worry about those three. But what about the others?

Turning to Amy and Kim, she supposed she should be thankful that no one had found the treasure—if it existed—while Amy was still married to Connor or Kim to Frank. Those good-for-nothing leeches would have bled their wives dry in no time. Now, though, both women had new men in their lives, men who were a huge improvement over their earlier partners. Max's family were builders and, from all she'd gathered, quite successful ones, at that. And Craig certainly wouldn't let money turn his head. His forebears had owned some of the first citrus groves in Florida. Thanks to a whole lot of luck and a few wise investments, they'd amassed a fortune. Enough of one that Craig refused to draw a salary as mayor of Emerald Bay. If either Amy or Kim needed help staying on the straight and narrow, Margaret was sure Max and Craig were the right men for the job.

She scanned the rest of the room. What about Jen? Her breath grew ragged with worry. Ever since Shirley's youngest daughter had surprised them all by showing up at Christmas, Margaret had been hoping against hope that her niece would finally put down roots in Emerald Bay. For a while there, it had seemed like she might.

In no time, Jen had taken over most of Margaret's hostess responsibilities—tracking reservations, greeting their guests by name, seeing to their needs like someone who'd been doing it all their life instead of just a few short months. But then she'd met Caleb, and something about that man had triggered Jen's wanderlust. The only thing that had kept her here, at least as far as Margaret could tell, was money. Or, to be more precise, the lack thereof. If Jen received a sudden influx of cash, would they all wake up one morning to find her bed empty, her closets bare, and nothing but tire tracks in the spot where she'd parked her car?

Not that all this talk of riches and treasure could possibly be true, Margaret reminded herself. Any minute now, Diane would grin broadly and shout, "Gotcha!" Then Nat would spring out of the corner she'd tucked herself into for the last little bit and hand everyone a gold coin. Only, the ones she gave out would be the kind of foil-wrapped chocolate *coins* she and her sisters used to buy at Mr. Wallaby's Grocery.

Hadn't this little joke of theirs gone on long enough?

"What do you want to do with the money, Mama?" Belle asked from the chair she'd pulled up beside Margaret's Queen Anne, the one with a cheery print that showed too much wear and tear for use in one of the guest suites.

Waiting for Diane and Nat to finally admit they'd been pulling everyone's leg for the past hour, Margaret ignored the touch of her daughter's hand on her arm and the slight hint of worry in her voice. Her focus unwavering, she stared expectantly at Nat.

"Mama?"

"Aunt Margaret?"

Out of the corner of one eye, Margaret caught movement as Diane stepped nearer. As if she'd signaled the others, everyone else surged closer. The tension in the room tightened until it was practically palpable. Whispered phrases filled the air.

What's wrong...a stroke...an ambulance...

"Aunt Margaret," a man's voice demanded. "Aunt Margaret, are you all right?"

When Scott's deep timbre broke her concentration on Nat, Margaret blinked slowly and gazed into a circle of worried faces. She jerked upright.

"Go on, now." Making shooing motions with her hands, she bought some time to gather her wits about her. Which, she realized, she needed to do pretty quickly before the expressions of concern her nieces and her daughter wore deepened into downright panic. "I was lost in thought there for a minute," she admitted, "but I'm fine."

"What were you thinking about, Mama?"

Margaret fought the urge to grind her teeth in frustration when Belle slowly and carefully enunciated every word, like people did when they were talking to someone who wasn't quite all there. Eager to prove she was still in full possession of all her marbles, she said, "I was thinking of all the ways our lives might have changed if my dad had made this discovery. Or if you'd stumbled across it on one of those treasure hunts you kids used to go on." While she spoke, she made eye contact with each of the people who'd rushed to her side. Relief spread through her when their worried frowns gradually faded.

"I hadn't really thought about it, but things would have been different," Belle mused.

Margaret straightened her shoulders. "This will change them, change us," she predicted. She eyed Diane. "Unless you've been pulling a fast one and this is all some kind of joke you and Nat are playing on us."

"No, ma'am," Diane insisted. "I would never." She glanced at Nat. "We should have brought one of the coins or necklaces with us tonight."

Nat, who'd abandoned her spot in the corner and joined the rest of the group, shook her head. "Wyatt cautioned against it."

"Wyatt?" Margaret frowned. "Who's Wyatt?"

"He's the coin expert who's been helping us identify and trace the history of the pieces we found," Diane said quietly. "He owns the East Cove Trading Post in Sebastian. He told us to stick everything in a safe deposit box and leave it there."

"So you can't prove any of this?" She enjoyed a joke as well as the next person, but it was time to put this one to rest.

Nat's expression brightened. "I have pictures on my phone." She whipped the device out of her back pocket.

Seconds later, Margaret's mouth went dry as Nat flipped through a series of photos.

"These are the rocks I nearly tripped over," the young woman explained, pointing to a bunch of stones that were barely visible in a field of tall grass.

"Here's one of Aunt Diane starting to dig the hole." Nat flipped to a picture of her aunt plunging a trowel into the dirt.

"I took this one of the first piece of jewelry we found. We learned it's called a money chain because, in the olden days, people used the links to pay their rent or buy a cow." Several other pictures followed in quick succession.

Margaret thought her heart might beat its way right out of her chest when she stared at the final image. Despite the sand and dirt that clung to the pieces, bright gold glittered from an impressive pile of coins and necklaces arranged on one of the inn's ratty old bath towels.

"What are these?" she asked, unable to keep her finger from shaking when she pointed at a stack of some blackened disks that were roughly the size and shape of a half-dollar.

"Those are Spanish reales," Diane said. "They're solid silver. They don't look like much in this picture because they'd built up three hundred years' worth of tarnish. But trust me, once Wyatt cleaned them up, they sparkled."

"So this is all real?" Margaret peered up at Diane. "You swear?" Surely they couldn't blame her for doubting the story that sounded like something straight out of a fairy tale. At her niece's solemn nod, she added, "And did I hear you right—the entire collection is worth over ten million dollars?"

"Ten point four. Maybe more, depending on how things go at the auction."

Margaret resisted the urge to hold her head in her hands and settled for running her fingers through her hair instead. She wished she'd paid more attention earlier when they were talking, but the whole idea of discovering buried treasure on the inn's grounds had sounded so far-fetched, she hadn't given it any mind at all. Nat's pictures, though—those had convinced her the women were telling the truth. Now questions buzzed in her brain like hornets around a nest. "The auction. You mentioned that earlier." She paused. "When is it?"

If she minded having to repeat herself, Diane didn't show it. "That's one of the things I'd planned to discuss with everyone tonight." She took a breath. "Scott pointed out that it really isn't a group decision. The inn and the land around it belong to you. That means everything we discovered, the whole kit and kaboodle, is yours. You have to decide what becomes of it."

Margaret sucked in a breath as the weight of responsibility for the not-so-small fortune crashed onto her shoulders. She swung an imploring look at Scott, practically begging her nephew to say that she didn't have to carry this burden alone. That the money—however much it turned out to be—would be equally divided between the people in this room.

But no.

Scott barely nodded as he met her gaze. "It's true, according to Florida law. Whatever they unearthed, it belongs to you."

"Do you want me to go over your options, Aunt Margaret?" Diane asked. "I'd be glad to tell you all about the different auction houses and what each one of them brings to the table. You probably ought to pick one soon, before word of the discovery gets out."

Margaret rubbed her fingers over her chair's worn fabric until she gripped both armrests. "I think that might be rushing it," she said. "This whole thing is more than a little overwhelming. I'm going to need some time to think about it." She leaned forward, intending to retreat into her room to think and pray about the decisions she'd have to make in the coming days. Before she had a chance to get to her feet, though, Scott cleared his throat.

"If you don't mind waiting just a minute longer, Aunt Margaret, there is one thing I need to make clear."

Margaret shrugged. A minute or two wasn't going to make much difference.

She watched as Scott scanned the room, his sharp gaze narrowing in on one person after another. At last, he said, "It's critical that we keep this tightly under wraps. I know it's going to be mighty tempting to share this news with the people we love and those we'd trust with our deepest, darkest secrets. I want to run home and tell Fern. I'm sure each of you has a special confidante, too. But we can't breathe a word of it to our boyfriends, our fiancés, our spouses or our best friends. There's too much at stake. The last thing we want is for a horde of money-grubbing treasure seekers to start digging up the property. Or worse." He let that thought hang for a minute, allowing everyone the chance to define exactly what *worse* might be.

Margaret stifled a groan. She could think of a thing or two that qualified. The thought of kidnappers and ransom demands pushed the idea of beefing up security higher on her list of things to do.

"One more thing, and then we'll let Aunt Margaret get her beauty rest." Scott's eyes filled with compassion as his focus dropped to the diamond ring his cousin Kim wore. "Anyone even remotely thinking of getting married needs to have their betrothed sign a prenup. I know that sounds harsh but…"

"Not at all, Scott," Kim interrupted. "It's smart. I'm not saying Craig is anything like Frank. I like to think I learned from my mistakes. But I've seen firsthand how greed can ruin lives and marriages. You draw up a prenup for me — an ironclad one — and I'll see that Craig signs it before I walk down the aisle."

Margaret scooted forward on her chair but stopped when Kim's gaze pinned her in place.

"Not that I think I deserve or even want any part of this treasure, Aunt Margaret," she said.

"My kids and I are closer than we've ever been. I have my own business, and it's doing well. And in a few weeks, I'll marry the man of my dreams. Whatever you decide about the treasure, I already have everything I ever wanted."

"That goes for me, too," Amy blurted. "I've been blessed with so much. There's nothing else I need."

"Me, too, Mama," Belle whispered.

Margaret patted Belle's hand when her daughter squeezed her shoulder.

"A fortune would be wasted on me," Jen declared. "As long as I have a roof over my head and food in my belly, I'm perfectly content."

"I couldn't agree more," Diane put in.

"Thanks, girls. And Scott," Margaret said while fatigue settled over her like one of those weighted blankets she saw advertised on TV. She yawned and stood. "I have a lot to think about over the coming days. But for now, I think I'd best get these tired old bones to bed."

Not that she'd sleep a wink, she added to herself as, leaning heavily on her cane, she bid her family goodnight.

Two

Diane

cooting back in her chair on the inn's wide front porch, Diane took a minute to listen to the low rumble of the ocean. Beyond the dunes, foam-capped waves rushed ashore before retreating once more into the depths. Seabirds rode the thermals, soaring high above the water. Closer at hand, the fronds of tall palm trees filtered the rays of the setting sun and dappled the lawn with shadows. A distinctive, briny smell floated in the air, and she drank in the scent that always reminded her of home.

"This is my favorite time of day," she announced to no one in particular.

"Really? I prefer mornings. I like listening to the birds sing their wake-up calls while I drink my coffee." Amy stretched her arms over her head before letting her hands plop down into her lap. "By this time of day, I'm usually exhausted."

No surprise there, thought Diane. By the time the sun peeked over the horizon, her sister usually had a dozen loaves of bread in the oven. Unless Amy had changed her schedule, she drank her first cup of coffee while they baked.

"How about you, Belle?" Diane chanced a glance at the redhead who sat cross-legged in a chair on the opposite side of the table.

"Favorite time of day? Whenever I've finished my workout and get to take a shower." Belle grinned. "I do love a hot shower."

"Tell us something we don't already know," Diane teased. When they were younger, they'd all raced to get into the bathroom before Belle used up all the hot water.

"So many cold showers." Amy clutched her fists to her chest and gave an exaggerated shiver.

"That's why I lobbied so hard to put tankless water heaters in all the suites," Belle said.

Diane nodded. Though she'd nearly had heart failure at the price, even she had to admit their guests had been pleased with the upgrades they'd installed during the renovations.

The sound of footsteps drawing nearer came from inside the house. Seconds later, Kim appeared in the doorway carrying an oval platter.

"Is Nat joining us?" Diane peered past her cousin's shoulder, hoping to spot the niece she'd grown closer to over the last few weeks.

"Not tonight." Careful not to tip over the tall tumblers Diane and Amy had brought out earlier, Kim stepped onto the porch, where she slid the plate and a stack of napkins onto the center of the rattan coffee table. "She's helping Samuel with the evening service." While the morning sessions followed a traditional format, the Sunday night services featured a praise band that was popular with the younger crowd.

"Hmmm. Never took Nat for the kind to become a preacher's wife," Amy mused.

Belle swiped an apple slice from the selection of fruits, cheeses and crackers arrayed on the platter. She nibbled on the piece before she asked, "What type is that, exactly?"

"C'mon." Amy held out her hands. "You have to admit, it takes a special person to marry a minister." When Belle lifted a challenging eyebrow in response, she continued. "Look at Pastor Dave's wife. No matter where she goes, Claudia is always put together. Hair, makeup, jewelry, clothes. All sensible, nothing cut too low or too high. Nothing too flashy or ostentatious. Nat likes more flair."

"True. But I don't think her personal style is a

deal-breaker. After all, Samuel seems to like her as she is."

"I suppose." Amy sighed, but she clearly wasn't ready to let the subject drop. "Being a preacher's wife takes commitment with a capital C. Claudia's involved in every committee and study group in the church. Always has a kind word for everyone. Knows her Bible front to back."

"True," Belle allowed. "But she and Pastor Dave have been married forty years. She wasn't nearly as involved in church activities when their kids were younger."

Diane quietly counted the calories she'd eaten that day. Deciding she was still under her limit, she helped herself to precisely three crackers, which she topped with thin slices of sharp cheddar. All this talk of preacher's wives was a little premature, wasn't it? She posed the question. "What makes you think Nat and Samuel are serious in the first place? Nat told me they were just friends."

"They're *just friends*." Amy made air quotes. "Until they aren't."

"In this case, Diane's right." Carrying a tall pitcher, Jen elbowed the screen door aside and joined the others on the front porch. "Nat told me the same thing a couple of days ago. She said

Samuel kissed her when he brought her home the other night. She said it was like kissing her brother."

"Eww! That does it. No sparks equals *no* relationship," Belle announced. She wiped her fingers on a napkin as if that settled the matter.

"I guess," Amy conceded.

"That's a shame," Kim murmured. "I like Samuel. He's a sensible young man with what Aunt Margaret would call good prospects."

"Yeah, but if he's not her guy..." Diane didn't bother to finish the sentence. She didn't need to. At one time or another, each of them had kissed a frog and tried to convince themselves they'd found their Prince Charming. It never worked.

She cast a speculative look at Jen. "Do we have the house to ourselves?"

Jen nodded. "The Coopers were the last to leave, and they've been gone since noon. No one else is due to check in until tomorrow."

Diane drummed her fingers on her leg. The gardeners rarely worked weekends. The maids, however, were another story. She'd heard the vacuum running earlier and knew the house-keepers had been whipping the recently vacated suites into shape for the next guests. "How about Irene and Eunice?"

"They came through the kitchen an hour

ago," Kim offered. "Said to tell everyone they'd be back tomorrow to finish the laundry and tackle the downstairs."

"Good." A breathy sigh escaped Diane's lips. With no guests to worry about and the staff gone for the day, she slipped off her deck shoes and tucked her feet beneath her on the rattan chair's plump cushion. "Tim and I spent all day yesterday and most of today packing up the house in Tampa. I'm beat."

"You didn't want to spend the night?" Amy nudged her sister.

Not in the mood to discuss her sex life, Diane ignored the playful gesture. "Caitlyn has a soccer match tomorrow. I didn't want to miss it. Besides, I have a lot to do to get ready for the movers."

"When do they come?" Belle scrunched her napkin into a ball.

"We're supposed to sign the final papers at five on Tuesday. Tim says the moving van will be here first thing Wednesday." She swept her gaze over the porch. Much as she'd looked forward to turning the new house into a home, she'd miss the close companionship she shared with her cousins and her sister at the inn. Not to mention the treasure she and Nat had recently discovered. That complicated *everything*.

"I'm surprised that you're going ahead with the house. You didn't want to wait and see what happens?" Jen asked.

Diane frowned. "With what?"

"You know. With the fortune." Jen pantomimed digging for buried treasure.

"Oh, hush," Diane chided. "What if somebody hears you?"

Jen cast a furtive glance over her shoulder. "I just said we're the only ones here," she reminded them.

"I know, but still." It couldn't hurt to be extra careful. Hadn't both Wyatt and her brother cautioned them to keep their find under wraps for the time being?

Kim flexed her fingers. "I have to admit, I've been dying to talk about it."

"I've hardly been able to think of anything else," Amy added.

"But no one's said a word until now," Belle said, speaking for everyone gathered around the coffee table. "Mama and I haven't even discussed it. Neither of us wanted to take the chance that a guest or one of the staff might overhear us."

Diane treated the walkways and the lawn to a searching gaze. Satisfied that no one lingered behind the palmetto bushes and that the only cars in the parking area belonged to the women on the front porch, she leaned forward. Her voice low and conspiratorial, she asked, "What if we came up with a code word?"

"Ohhh, good idea!" Jen clapped her hands together. "Didn't the map lead you to the old oak? We could use *oak*."

"That's a little too on the nose." Belle tapped hers. "Plus, if anyone did overhear us talking about it, they might put two and two together and start digging holes in the ground up there. Or cutting up the tree's roots." She shuddered. The oak's health depended on leaving its massive root structure intact and undisturbed.

"I didn't think of that." Jen's shoulders slumped. "That tree has been there forever. I'd hate to see anything happen to it."

"The jewelry we found was listed on the manifest of the *Nuestra Señora del Carmen*. What if we referred to the discovery as just Carmen?" Diane suggested.

"I like that. Then if anyone overhears us, they might assume we're talking about a guest," Belle said.

"Or, if they make the connection to the 1715 fleet, it wouldn't seem unusual for us to discuss the shipwreck they found right off Vero Beach. After all, it's not all that far from here." Jen tipped her head toward the south.

Surprised to learn her cousin knew that salvagers had located the wreckage or that it lay so close by, Diane shot Jen a puzzled look.

"What? I didn't have anything better to do, so I stopped at A Likely Story and picked up a book about local shipwrecks." Jen rubbed her temples. "I haven't studied so hard since I left high school."

"I hear ya." Diane aimed a sympathetic smile at her cousin. In her quest to learn as much as she could about their discovery, she'd spent the last two weeks soaking up the history of the 1715 fleet like a sponge soaked up water. She felt a pang of sympathy for her cousin. A lot of the accounts had been poorly translated from Spanish. No wonder Jen had struggled with them. "I found a few websites that are pretty easy to understand. I'd be glad to give you a list." She glanced at the others. "That goes for any of us. As long as we don't discuss them where anyone can overhear."

"We can talk now, though, right? 'Cause no one's around?" Amy questioned.

Without waiting for an answer, Jen poured generous servings of a fruity sangria into five tall glasses. "Here's to Carmen," she said, lifting her glass. "And Aunt Margaret's good fortune."

Glasses clinked, and they all took a sip or two.

"I hate to bring this up, but I've been wondering what to do about Sweet Cakes 2," Amy confessed once they'd complimented Kim on the fruity concoction and helped themselves from the snack tray. "We've made plans for a soft opening in a little over two weeks, with a ribbon-cutting on Saturday, May 18th. With all this treasure business to contend with, though, I'm wondering if we should cancel it."

"I'd be lying if I said I hadn't had any qualms about closing on the new house," Diane admitted.

"I thought you'd fallen in love with the place. The pool. The big backyard. It sounds perfect. Why would you pass it up?" Belle wanted to know.

"It's exactly what we want—what I want. But with the tr—with Carmen," she corrected quickly, "I don't know. Maybe we need something more secure. But if we back out, we'd forfeit the deposit. I'd hate to lose that money. And Tim would be furious. Especially if I couldn't give him a good reason for backing out of the deal."

"Let me stop you right there." Belle's clear and emphatic tone cut through the static that buzzed in Diane's brain. "We need to maintain the appearance that everything is perfectly normal. At this point, we don't want to do anything out of the ordinary."

Belle singled out Amy. "You should go ahead with Sweet Cakes 2."

Diane stilled when the redhead turned to her.

"You need to close on your house and move in. We'll all be there to help out, just like always."

"Yes, ma'am." Happy to have the decision taken out of her hands, Diane gave her cousin a mock salute, which Belle ignored.

"Until the matter of Carmen is settled, we all need to go about our lives," she said with unblinking firmness. "I'm still going to visit Emerald Oaks with Mama soon. The Emeralds will keep all their gigs. And we'll hold the reunion just like we planned."

"Whew!" Kim wiped a bead of invisible sweat from her forehead. "I, for one, am thrilled to hear this. I didn't want to have to postpone my wedding."

"Not on your life." Apparently done giving orders, Belle took a long pull from her glass.

"Speaking of which, we need to take you on a shopping spree." Amy aimed her comment at the bride.

"Why? I already have the dress. Thanks to

Belle." Pressing her hands together, Kim bowed to the cousin who'd graciously lent her a gown from her private collection of stunning designer dresses and outfits.

"Shoes. Lingerie. Clothes for your honeymoon." Amy ticked off items on her fingers. Her brows knit. "Where is Craig taking you?"

"I'm not sure exactly. He just said someplace tropical."

"You'll need a new bathing suit, then. And a cover-up. And…" Amy eyed the ragged hem of the cut-offs Kim wore. "Sundresses and capris."

"I don't know," Kim hedged. "Royal Meals is operating in the black, but money's still tight."

"This is your wedding we're talking about. You let us worry about the cost," Diane chided. She wasn't exactly swimming in spare cash—not with one kid in college and one in high school, to say nothing of the expense involved in getting her accounting business off the ground and buying a house—but she'd kick in her share toward Kim's trousseau. "We haven't had a wedding in this family in ages. You have to let us pull out all the stops for yours."

"Yeah. So pick a date, and we'll make a day of it," Jen said.

"Okay." Though Kim's face colored slightly, excitement shone in her blue eyes. "Any Monday or Tuesday works best for me. That way I'll have the rest of the week to get ready for my deliveries." Her Royal Meals subscribers expected to receive their freshly prepared, heat-and-serve meals each Friday.

"I'll put together a list of dates and check with each of you," Jen volunteered. Grabbing the pitcher, she topped off everyone's glass. "Now that that's settled, can we get back to this, um, Carmen thing? I have so many questions."

"You're not alone," Amy commiserated. "Any idea what Aunt Margaret's going to do? Has she said anything to you, Belle?"

"No." The edges of Belle's kewpie doll smile drooped. "I can tell it's been weighing heavily on her, though. I think that's why she insisted on going to church with Nat tonight."

Diane unfolded the legs she'd stuck beneath her and stretched. In the interest of full disclosure, she reported, "Aunt Margaret called me last night. She wanted to know about the auction houses and how they'd handle the sale."

"Speaking of which, have you spoken with Harold Carstair?" Belle's curls bounced as she leaned forward to take a handful of grapes from the tray. When Diane shook her head, the onetime superstar said, "He handled the sale of the Twombly for me. I was very pleased with his work." The funds from selling the pricey piece of art had settled all Belle's debts, with enough left over to help with the renovations of the inn. "I can put you in touch with him, if you'd like."

"Definitely talk to your mom about it, but I like the idea of working with someone one of us can vouch for personally. Apparently, the coin business can be pretty cutthroat. Who knew?" The underhanded tricks some dealers had pulled was enough to curl her normally straight hair. She'd have been lost without Wyatt's guidance.

"I will." Belle popped a grape in her mouth and chewed slowly. "What else did Mama want?"

Diane cracked her knuckles. "She wanted to know more about Wyatt." She shook her head. "Of all the coin dealers in Florida, I thank my lucky stars he was the one we talked to first. Do you know he waived his usual percentage just for the privilege of handling what he calls 'such an important discovery'?"

"That's pretty amazing," Kim acknowledged.

"The whole situation is exactly that— amazing," Belle agreed.

When no one seemed to have anything to add, Diane and the others sat in silence, enjoying the breeze and the sound of the ocean while the sky gradually darkened.

The monk parakeets slept in their nests, their tiny heads still curled into their feathers, when Diane told Jen she'd meet her in the car and walked from the main house to the inn's parking area. Other than the ever-present rumble of the ocean, only the sound of her sneakers on the crushed coquina broke the stillness of the predawn morning. The soft click of her car lock cut through the quiet like a rifle shot when she pressed the key fob. After storing her purse and a large duffle in the back seat, she slid behind the wheel and settled a to-go cup in the holder between the bucket seats. The car purred to life at the touch of a button. With sunrise an hour away, her headlights illuminated the hedge that ran between the parking spaces and the house. Seconds later, Jen climbed into the passenger seat beside her, placed her own coffee in the holder, and buckled her seat belt.

"You're sure you don't mind leaving this early?" Diane backed the car slowly out of her spot. "I hate to ask you to give up the entire day." The two of them were headed to the new house, which they'd begun cleaning shortly after the

Realtor handed Diane the keys at last night's closing. Today, they'd pick up where they left off, hoping to finish before the moving truck arrived at nine.

"Puh-leeze. I'd rather clean than hit the gym. Even if muscles I didn't know I had are complaining about it."

"I know, right?" At the end of the long driveway, Diane checked carefully in both directions before she turned onto the main road. "I had to take ibuprofen last night. I'll probably need to take more tonight." She walked two miles every morning and worked out with weights three times a week. What was it about sweeping and mopping floors that made her bones ache? She pressed her shoulders into the backrest.

"Before I forget, Kim said to give these to you." Jen placed a pad of yellow Post-its in the center console's tray. "She said to label the cabinets with what you want in them, and she'll organize the kitchen as soon as she gets back from the grocery store this morning."

Gratitude spread through Diane's chest like warm syrup spread across pancakes. No doubt, her cousin would have her kitchen whipped into shape in time for dinner.

"Amy promised to make the beds and unload

the wardrobe boxes once the bakery closes," Diane reported. With her sister's business partner supervising the final preparations at Sweet Cakes 2, Amy needed to spend the day at her shop in Emerald Bay.

"We should be fine. Belle will be along once Aunt Margaret's friend Maude arrives." The octogenarian duo had plans to spend the day together. "Between the two of them, our guests are in good hands."

"Tim had a couple of patients to see first thing this morning, but he said he'll be here by lunchtime. He can help out with the heavy stuff." Though Diane had a clear vision of where she wanted the furniture to go, the movers would only place each piece once. She suspected a few adjustments would be required and had no doubt that her husband's strong back would come in handy.

"It sounds like we have a plan." Jen reached for her coffee and took a sip.

"You don't think we'll be tripping over each other, do you? With the five of us, plus Tim, I'm worried that we'll end up with too much help." Diane made the final turn into a development where widely spaced homes sat on one-acre lots.

"Nonsense. Many hands make light work," Jen quipped.

The saying had been one of her mother's favorites, and Diane smiled as she followed a circular driveway to the front of a two-story house.

"Sweet," Jen said, eyeing the columns on either side of a double-door with etched glass panes. "I'll get started upstairs in my room. When can I move in?"

"What?" Diane's thoughts stuttered. She and Tim and Caitlyn hadn't even spent one night in their new home. They weren't ready for houseguests, much less tenants.

"Relax. I'm just kidding about that moving in part. But anytime you want company, I'll be glad to come and hang out by the pool." Jen popped her door open and swung her feet out onto the pinkish pavers. "Where do you want me to start cleaning?"

Diane considered the question while she grabbed her things from the back seat. Though the previous owners had left the place in pretty good shape, she'd insisted on scouring the entire house from top to bottom. Last night, after they left the Realtor's office, she and Jen had scrubbed each of the bathrooms until they gleamed and wiped down the shelves and counters in the kitchen. "I guess we'll need to go room by room. Wash windows, wipe off surfaces, vacuum."

"Works for me. I'll start in Caitlyn's bedroom."

"Let me drop this stuff off in the kitchen." Diane hefted the duffle bag, which held a special gift from Amy. "I'll start a pot of coffee and join you in a minute."

A high-pitched beeping startled Diane the second she turned the key in the lock and opened the front door. Hurrying to the alarm panel, she punched in the four numbers the sellers had provided once the papers had all been signed. A ripple of unease shot through her when the beeping stopped, and she knew she wouldn't sleep until she'd changed the code. Might as well have all the locks rekeyed while she was at it, she thought. After all, who knew how many people—housekeepers, dog walkers, maintenance workers—had been given access to the house over the years? She sighed and added the tasks to a growing list of Harry Homeowner chores.

Once the aroma of freshly ground coffee filled the large, airy kitchen, Diane took the boxes of rolls and pastries out of her duffle. After arranging those on the counter, she grabbed two boxed cakes, which Amy had nestled into the bottom of the bag. These, she slid into the fridge while she whispered a nearly silent thanks for her big sister's generosity.

She'd drained her travel mug on the short

drive from the inn, so while she waited for the coffee to brew, she hastily scribbled labels for the everyday dishes and glasses on Kim's Post-its and stuck them on the appropriate cabinets. She was nearly finished when her cell phone buzzed with an incoming call from Tim. Without even trying, she smiled.

"Hey. Going for a run? You're getting an early start." Though her husband regularly ran several miles before breakfast, he usually waited until full sunrise. It was only five, according to the clock on the microwave.

"I'm skipping it today. I suspect I'll get my exercise toting boxes and hanging curtains. The sooner I go into the office, the sooner I can leave for Emerald Bay."

Diane frowned. Nothing less than a Category 3 hurricane kept her husband from his morning run. "What else is going on?" she asked.

"You know me too well," Tim said, sounding grouchy and out of sorts. "I didn't sleep a wink last night. I used to think the house felt empty without you and Caitlyn here. Boy, was I wrong. With so little furniture in the house, every little noise bounces off the walls and the floors. It's louder than I expected."

"I'm sorry." Sympathy wrinkled Diane's brow. She couldn't imagine herself rattling around in the big house alone for the next four years, but Tim had decided to split his time between his practice in Tampa and with the family in Emerald Bay. It was a plan they'd both committed to. With that in mind, she'd done her best to make his stay in the house as homey as possible. Together, she and Tim had hauled Nick's bedroom furniture into the downstairs office and arranged enough leftover chairs and love seats in the family room to create a cozy sitting area. Barstools around the kitchen island took the place of the dining table and chairs that workmen had loaded into the moving van. "I guess that's going to take some getting used to, huh?"

"The noise didn't bother me as much as the air conditioner. The compressor clicked on every fifteen minutes all through the night. I kept thinking about all the money we're wasting by cooling a practically empty house."

Trying to be helpful, she asked, "Do you think it would help to close the doors and vents upstairs?"

"Actually, I don't think this is going to work out at all."

The little hairs on the back of her neck prickled. "What isn't going to work out?" she asked cautiously.

Their marriage?

Diane squeezed her eyes shut tight. Steady now, she ordered. Tim wouldn't leave her. Not again. They'd both worked hard to fix what was broken in their relationship. And they'd succeeded. They'd recommitted themselves to each other. Their marriage was more secure than it had ever been.

"Me living here on my own for the next four years," came an answer that wasn't much better than the one she feared.

She stifled a groan. With Tim's blessing, she'd closed on the new house last night. It was too late to back out of the contract. Even if she could somehow cancel it, she'd sunk nearly every dime of severance pay from her old job into the purchase. She couldn't—*they* couldn't—afford to lose that much money. Plus, even as they spoke, a moving van filled to the brim with their furniture and belongings was on the road to Emerald Bay. She couldn't stop that if she wanted to…which she didn't.

Concern threatened to turn into full-fledged panic at the thought that Tim might consider upending all their plans for the future. Would he ask her and Caitlyn to spend the next four years in Tampa after all? Postpone the timetable for opening her own accounting firm? She shook her head. She had no intention of returning to her old life on the other side of the state. Even more important, their daughter had found her niche in Emerald Bay. She wouldn't, couldn't uproot Caitlyn again.

"I think we ought to put this house on the market as soon as possible," Tim said smoothly.

The announcement surprised her, and Diane blinked several times in rapid succession. At least he wasn't asking her to move back to Tampa, she told herself. That was a plus. But he wanted to sell the house they'd lived in for most of their married life? Where they'd raised their children? The house with pencil marks on the kitchen doorjamb where she'd tracked Nick and Caitlyn's height each birthday? With the bay window overlooking the yard where their daughter had learned to kick a soccer ball? And the putting green where Tim had taught their son the basics of his favorite sport?

She wasn't ready.

"I thought we'd agreed to hold on to it for the time being," she reminded Tim. "So Caitlyn and I would have a place to stay when we come to visit."

Tim countered her protest with cool, calm logic. "You and I both know that's not going to happen very often. Between school and soccer and spending time with her friends, our daughter will want to spend as much time as possible in Emerald Bay. So will you. I get it. You're opening a business there. You have friends and family there. Besides, I doubt seriously if either of you would be comfortable sleeping on air mattresses or camping out in the family room when you do visit."

Her chest tightened as objections swirled in her head. "What about this summer?" she asked. "Isn't Nick spending it in Tampa with you?" Their son had lined up a job caddying at Tim's club for the season.

"Nick tried out for the golf team at Virginia Tech," Tim said, tossing out another huge surprise as lightly as if he was throwing candy from a float in the Christmas parade. "He made it! Can you believe it? It means he'll have to stay in Blacksburg and take summer classes this year. But imagine that, our son, playing for Virginia Tech."

She could practically read her husband's thoughts. In the aftermath of his breakup with his high school sweetheart, Nick had turned down an athletic scholarship at the University of Florida and switched schools. Tim had been bereft. It appeared that all those Saturday tee times and weeknights at the golf range were going to pay off after all.

"I'm thrilled for him," she gushed. "And for you. Give me all the details."

For the next few minutes, Tim explained that Nick hadn't said a word about tryouts until after he'd been offered a spot on the team. The Hokies would play their first match against Knoxville the weekend after classes resumed in the fall. Until then their son planned to spend every spare minute with a club in his hand.

"I think we should fly up for the tournament, don't you?" Tim asked. "That's something we could do if we weren't making two mortgage payments."

"Of course." She'd no more miss her son's first collegiate appearance than she'd miss one of Caitlyn's soccer games. But she had other concerns, and she forced herself to voice them.

"Does that mean you'll sell the practice to Warren ahead of schedule? Move here, now?" She winced at the impact that would have on their finances.

"No. I'll still need to live in Tampa part-time. But if we sell the house, I can move into the apartment behind the practice."

Diane bit her lower lip. Over the past year, Tim had converted the back half of his office building into a one-bedroom apartment. The night he'd walked out on their marriage, he'd moved there. Though Diane had never seen it, Caitlyn said it had all the comforts of home.

She placed her hand on the counter to steady herself. Everything was happening too fast. She had to slow things down. Summoning a calm despite her roiling emotions, she asked, "Is this a done deal? Or do I get to think about it for a minute?"

Tim fell silent for a long beat. At last, he said, "I know I'm springing this on you. We can talk about it."

Diane took a breath. Tim was scheduled to arrive before noon. That didn't give her much time to wrap her head around this change of plans.

Three

Diane

"Ugh!" Diane swore under her breath at the grains of sand that dotted the bricks surrounding the pool. She'd swept the patio from start to finish twice already and stil' couldn't get up all the sand. The long side͏ where the bottom rail of the screened porch the pavers—those dirt magnets were the She'd spent at least an hour attacking with a whisk. As for the corners, dor her started. It had taken a putty kr more time to dig all the gunk ou for what? So far, she was losin' grit and grime. Putting some task, she swept furiously.

"Hey! What'd those bricks

Diane kept sweeping despite the accusation that drifted over her shoulder. "Take over if you think you can do a better job," she snapped.

Instant regret froze her in mid-sweep. Belle hadn't deserved the sharp edge of her tongue. It wasn't her cousin's fault that she was in a bad mood. Letting the broom clatter to the tiles, she spun around. "I'm sorry. I shouldn't have said that. I don't know what's gotten into me. I've spent the last two hours out here sweeping up sand. In Florida. How ridiculous is that?" A heady mix of laughter and tears threatened to overwhelm her. Seconds later, Belle's comforting arms wrapped around her.

"Hey. It's okay," Belle soothed. "Moving is stressful. I get it. Why don't you come inside and have something to drink? You should take a break."

Diane let herself be led one step toward the open door before she forced her feet to stop moving. "I can't. I need to finish this." Her lower ‍ trembling, she waved a hand at the nearly ‍tless area around the pool. "The movers will ‍ere any minute."

‍Yeah. That's part of the reason I came out ‍ Belle said softly. "Your phone's been ‍g up with text messages. The movers got ‍ traffic on Route 60. Something about an overturned dump truck. They're running an hour behind schedule."

Diane automatically patted the pockets of her shorts without finding her phone. Of course. She'd propped the device on the kitchen counter while she talked with Tim earlier and had been so upset afterward that she'd left it there. Her gaze shifted to the sun that had climbed halfway up the sky while she wasn't paying it any mind. "What time is it?"

"A little after nine."

She'd spent the last four hours sweeping the patio?

"Oh, good gracious! I can't believe I wasted so much time out here. I have so much more to do!" Escaping Belle's embrace, she grabbed the broom.

"Relax. Jen, Kim and I have it covered. We just finished running a damp mop over your gorgeous wood floors." Belle aimed a thumb over her shoulder. "Whoever designed this house made some excellent choices, by the way. I absolutely love the Brazilian koa they put down."

Diane felt some of her irritation ease. The beautiful wood, with its distinctive stripes of light and dark, was one of the things she loved most about the house. She glanced at the pavers.

Those, not so much, she decided.

Giving up on the patio for the time being, she followed Belle inside.

"Look who I found," Belle announced as she stepped from the pool enclosure into the roomy family room. Beyond the empty space, Kim and Jen stood at the kitchen island drinking coffee out of paper cups and eyeing the array of pastries Amy had provided.

"Can we have some of these? Or are you, like, saving them all for the movers?" Jen asked as Diane brushed her shoes on the threshold before she stepped onto the freshly mopped floor.

Diane shrugged. "Help yourselves. There's cake in the fridge for later, too. Belle tells me you earned whatever you'd like. Did you really go through the entire house while I was outside?" It certainly appeared so. Everywhere she looked, gleaming floors and sparkling windows met her gaze.

"Yeah." Kim chose a glazed doughnut from the box. "Jen and I finished the upstairs while Belle tackled your suite. Then we all worked on the rest. We got done about twenty minutes ago."

"Why didn't you come get me?"

The question prompted a flurry of raised eyebrows and concerned faces. At last, Jen reached for a cinnamon bun.

"You looked like you were, um, working through something. We thought maybe you needed your space." Having said her piece, Jen broke off a chunk of the pastry and dunked it in her coffee before she popped it in her mouth. "Oh, man. These are good! You should try one." She angled the box toward Belle.

"None for me, thanks." Belle patted her hips lightly and turned to Diane. "So what's up? What had you scouring those pavers within an inch of their lives?"

"Yeah. Is it something we can help with?" Kim wanted to know.

Diane felt her heart melt. This, she told herself, this was why she never wanted to leave Emerald Bay. No matter what troubled her, her family was ready and willing to wade in with advice, comfort and rolled-up sleeves. Still, she refused to take advantage of their generous spirits. "I'll never be able to repay you for what you've already done."

"The day is young. We've barely begun." Having finished one roll, Jen reached for seconds. "We'll be opening boxes and putting things away until the cows come home."

Diane's eyes crinkled. Jen had definitely been hanging out with a certain farmer a lot. She wondered if her cousin was even aware of how much she was starting to sound like Caleb.

"It's Tim," she admitted when the others continued to look at her expectantly.

Jen's hand hovered like a helicopter over the box of sweet rolls as a guarded silence filled the room.

"What about Tim?" Belle asked, her words slow and measured.

"You two aren't having problems again, are you?" Kim asked hesitantly.

"No. Nothing like that." Diane rushed to reassure her cousins. "He and I are good. It's just that, we had this plan. Caitlyn and I would move in here. I'd open my own accounting firm. For the next four years—until Warren is ready to buy out Tim's share of the practice—he'd live in our old house in Tampa. He'd drive over on Thursdays after his last patient, and we'd spend the weekends together."

Kim stirred her coffee with a plastic spoon. "I've heard of worse arrangements."

"It's not ideal," Diane admitted. "But it's doable. At least, I thought it was. Tim, though—it hasn't been a week, and already he wants to change things."

Belle lifted her cup. "How so?" she asked over the rim.

"When we spoke earlier today, he said we

should list the house in Tampa, put it on the market right away."

"Wait. Didn't you say he couldn't retire for another four or five years?" Jen rubbed her lower back.

"Right." Diane nodded. "That part of the plan wouldn't change. But he says he wants to move into a furnished apartment he owns in the same building as his dental practice. It's sitting empty, and he was planning to rent it out. Except, now he says it doesn't make any sense to stay at the house if he's going to be the only one living in it, so we should sell it."

"And you disagree?" Belle arched an eyebrow.

"Well, yeah." Seeing the confusion on her cousin's faces, she hurried to explain. "That was our dream house. When we finally saved enough money to buy a house in Parkland Estates, I thought we'd live there forever." The neighborhood was one of the most sought-after areas in Tampa. "Nick was just a baby when we moved in. It's the only home Caitlyn's ever known."

"I'm not as good with numbers as you are," Kim said quietly, "but it sounds like a smart move. I assume he wouldn't have to pay rent for the apartment?"

Diane hesitated. As much as she hated to admit it, her cousin had a point. Tim owned the building, free and clear.

Kim dug a little deeper. "And the house? Is it paid off?"

"Not completely. We have another ten years left on the mortgage."

"That's what, a couple of grand a month? Which would stop if you sold the house? Plus, I'm assuming you have quite a bit of equity built up in it?"

"It's worth a lot more than we paid for it." Homes in Parkland Estates rarely went on the market. When they did, they fetched premium prices.

Jen whistled softly. "What are you waiting for? Sell the place already."

Diane squeezed her eyes closed. Home ownership involved more than just dollars and cents. She and Tim had poured their hearts and souls into the Parkland house. She'd spent months selecting the right fabric for the drapes in the living room. Tim had labored over the putting green in the backyard like it was a third child. Together, they'd hand-stripped and refinished the railings, newel posts and each of the precisely fifty-five spindles that made up the staircase. How could she make her cousins understand how much those labors of love meant to her?

Belle tapped a perfectly groomed fingernail on the granite countertop. "It sounds to me like maybe you're not ready to let go of your life in Tampa." She paused. When she spoke again, her voice was a mere whisper. "Is that what I'm hearing?"

The question delivered a punch straight to Diane's gut. Her lungs suddenly emptied. Her eyes widened, and she stared at Belle. Was this what it felt like when someone pointed out the obvious? She'd literally been pounding sand for hours while she scoured her brain for some reasonable excuse to hang on to a house she no longer lived in. In all that time, she hadn't once asked herself why it mattered so much.

"So you're saying I should take a closer look at myself. That I'm still emotionally attached?"

Maybe she was.

She'd assumed that, because she was moving on with her life, building a new future here in Emerald Bay, she'd severed all her ties to Tampa. Had she, though?

Tears welled in her eyes. She'd spent years climbing the corporate ladder at Ybor City Accountants. Finally, she'd had it all—the corner office, the perks, the great salary. And she'd walked away from everything the night she'd tossed suitcases and duffle bags into the trunk of her car and driven at breakneck speed to Emerald Bay. That night, though, she hadn't been thinking about her job, her career. She hadn't even been thinking about the decisions she was making. That night, she'd had one thing on her mind: Caitlyn. Her daughter had messed up royally by throwing an unsupervised party where minors drank alcohol. That had gotten the teen kicked off the soccer team and, in turn, suspended from school. The only fix, as far as Diane could see, had been to bring her daughter to a place where she'd be surrounded by women who'd made their own fair share of mistakes and risen above them. So she'd ordered her belligerent teen into the car and brought her home to her family.

The decision had proven to be a wise one. Caitlyn had thrived in Emerald Bay. Of equal importance, Diane and Tim had rectified their differences and healed their broken marriage. She'd embarked on a new career, bought a new house, started a new life here.

But had she ever fully let go of the old one? Was it time to snip the cords that tied her to Tampa?

She swiped at her cheeks. "You guys sure

know how to ask the hard questions," she said, staring at the women who'd given up their day to help with the move. "It's a lot to think about."

Thinking, however, would have to wait because, at that moment, the doorbell rang. Less than five seconds later, someone pounded on the front door with a heavy fist.

"I guess the movers are here." Belle's announcement stirred a ripple of anticipation.

"Coming!" Diane shouted in response. Already in motion, she sent up a silent prayer that the day would go smoothly.

"Places, girls. It's showtime!" exclaimed Jen. Snagging another pastry, she cut through the living room to the stairs and trotted up the steps. Meanwhile, Belle sped to her assigned position, while Kim remained in the kitchen to handle the unpacking of the dishes, pots and pans.

For the next few hours, Diane barely had a moment to think, much less stray from her post by the front door. From there, she directed a steady stream of furniture- and lamp-toting movers to various sections of the house.

"Those go in the master bedroom," she said after glancing at the ivory-colored headboard one burly character carried. She pointed past the double doors that opened into the downstairs suite. Silently, she thanked Belle for picking up the job from there by showing the workers where to assemble the bed or place the dresser.

She hardly had time to catch her breath before the next mover crossed the threshold wheeling a large wardrobe box on a dolly. She peeked at the label. "In the girl's room upstairs," she directed, knowing that Jen would be sure Caitlyn's clothes ended up in her room, rather than in Nick's or the guest room.

"We're going to put the table over there by the window," she overheard Kim tell another mover who'd wheeled past Diane with the polished wooden top strapped to a hand truck. A little while later, she smiled when she caught a glimpse of her cousin arranging chairs around the reassembled table.

And so it went until, just before noon, Diane spied Tim's dark SUV pulling to a stop behind her car on the circular driveway. As pleased as she was to see him, she couldn't completely ignore the twinge of anxiety his presence stirred in her chest. She'd been so caught up in directing the movers that she hadn't had a moment to think about what to do with their home in Tampa. But one glimpse of Tim's car served as a reminder of the weighty decision that faced them both.

Moments later, work ground to a halt as her

husband called, "Who wants lunch? I brought subs." Hefting a couple of ice chests from the trunk of his car, he handed one to a workman who hustled to his side. While the moving crew retreated to a shady spot beneath the trees that lined the edge of the property, Tim followed the pavers toward the front door.

The tension in Diane's shoulders ratcheted tighter with every step he took. Fearing he'd want an answer she wasn't ready to give, she blurted, "I haven't had a chance to think about what you asked me earlier."

Puzzlement deepened the cleft between Tim's brows. "I wouldn't expect you to. Not with all this going on." He motioned to the moving van parked on the street.

Diane felt her insides go soft. She rose on tiptoes and brushed a quick kiss on Tim's cheek. "Have I told you lately how much I love you?" she whispered.

"Yes. But I'll never get tired of hearing it. Now," he said, meeting her gaze, "I don't want you to worry about the house. I know I said I thought we should list the house right away, but there's no hurry. Besides..." Stepping back, he gave the handle of the container he carried a playful jiggle. "I stopped at Bella's on my way. Are you hungry for an Italian?"

"With hots?" Tim knew her so well, she thought, her mouth watering. Thick with no less than four varieties of cold cuts, drenched in oil and vinegar, and topped with chopped hot peppers, the sandwiches were her absolute favorite.

"It wouldn't be Bella's without them." Tim surveyed the sofas and chairs, lamps and end tables that crowded the living room. "Whew!" he said. "You're making good progress."

"I'm ready for a break, though. It's been hectic." She'd been making decisions and directing traffic for hours. Now that she'd stopped for a moment, fatigue swept over her. "I don't remember it being this hard the last time we moved." Of course, that had been before Nick had started kindergarten. Soon he'd begin his junior year in college.

"We didn't have this much stuff back then." Tim pointed to the matching sofa and love seat Diane had purchased with her Christmas bonus two years ago. "C'mon. You'll feel better after you eat. Who else is here?"

"Belle, Kim, Jen." Diane didn't object at all when Tim slung an arm around her shoulders and steered her toward the kitchen.

"Practically the whole crew," he mused. "Good! I brought plenty."

"Amy and Nat are at the bakery," Diane added. "They'll be along after it closes."

Kim had unearthed a disposable tablecloth from somewhere and draped it across the table. The others filed in while Tim pulled napkins, bags of chips, the subs and a selection of sodas from the cooler. Though Diane wanted to savor every bite of the delicious sandwich, she and the others polished off their lunch in record time. Even then, they'd barely gathered up the trash before the foreman of the moving crew was knocking at the door again.

"Ma'am?" he called.

"Be right there." Diane blotted a tiny bit of tangy dressing from her lips. She moved swiftly to the front of the house.

"Thanks for lunch. The men and I really enjoyed the food. Y'all ready to get back at it?"

"Yeah. I think so." The break, however brief, had worked wonders.

"We got most of the furniture unloaded and in the house already. We hope to be outta your hair by two." He and his team would need to make the return trip to Tampa before their day ended. He flattened a work-worn hand atop the stack of boxes on his dolly. "What's left are mostly boxes. They'll go pretty quick. So, where do you want these?"

As she'd been doing all morning, Diane gave the labels plastered on the cardboard a quick glance. "Those go right around the corner here." She pointed toward the master suite.

When the man and his load had trundled past, Tim asked, "What would you like me to do?"

"I've been sending a lot of stuff out to the garage, but there's no one out there to organize it," Diane suggested.

"Say no more. I'm on it."

Certain that by the time they stopped work at the end of the day, every hammer, screwdriver and wrench in her husband's tool arsenal would be hanging from the pegboard racks in the garage, Diane chuckled as, whistling one of his favorite show tunes, Tim skirted around a workman pushing a fully loaded hand-truck and disappeared. She, meanwhile, returned to her job of directing what seemed to be an endless parade of boxes toward the correct rooms. Eventually, the last mover carried a final box into the house and announced the truck was empty.

By the time Tim had tipped the movers and wished them godspeed on their trip back to Tampa, Amy and Nat had reported for duty. Though the pair had spent all day at the bakery, they set to work creating order out of the family room's chaos of misplaced furniture and accessories.

Not long after that, a familiar voice called, "Did someone say they needed help assembling beds?"

Diane peered around the tall cardboard wardrobe she was opening to find Max standing in the doorway of the master suite, toolbox in hand. "Seriously?" she asked. "You're here to help out, too?"

"Sure am. Amy said you might appreciate an extra set of hands."

"You're exactly what the doctor ordered," Diane said. "I thought we'd be sleeping on mattresses on the floor tonight." She motioned to the box springs and mattresses the movers had propped on their sides against the wall.

"We can't have that, can we?" Max asked with a grin. He strode into the room. "Start in here?"

Diane gave her own disassembled bed a wistful glance but shook her head. "Much as I'd love that, I'd rather you put Caitlyn's bed together first." The teen would be home from soccer practice within the hour. "Her room is upstairs. End of the hall."

A short time later, she wondered if she should replace the front door with a revolving one when, one after another, friends and family members showed up to lend a hand. Shortly after she finished transferring her clothes from the wardrobes to the roomy walk-in closet, Caleb stopped by with a welcome basket of fruits and vegetables fresh from the organic farm he owned on the outskirts of Vero Beach. Before she could thank the man who'd driven thirty miles to help them get settled, Caitlyn arrived. Soon, loud music reverberated from behind her closed bedroom door as she unpacked boxes and stowed her belongings.

By six o'clock, all the beds had been assembled and made up with fresh linens, Kim had the kitchen in hand, and the house had been transformed into a home filled with familiar furniture and well-loved accessories. Sure, lots remained to do—pictures to hang and shelves to mount along with dozens of other tasks—but towels filled the linen closets, and the washer and dryer had been hooked up. All in all, not bad for the first day in a new house, Diane thought as she joined the others who crowded around the island, scarfing down fragrant slices of the six tasty pizzas Craig had toted into the house a few minutes earlier.

Looking at the gathering of people who'd all given so freely of their time and efforts to help out today, she brushed away the dampness that had spilled onto her cheeks. She wouldn't trade her life here in Emerald Bay for anything. Not the corner office or the big salary…or the house she'd left behind.

Silently, she reached for Tim's hand and gave it a squeeze. "Put the Parkland house on the market as soon as you want," she whispered.

She was ready, at last, to cut the final cord to her old life in Tampa and fully embrace her fresh start in Emerald Bay.

Four

Jen

The click of heels accompanied by the louder thump of heavy footsteps on the front porch interrupted the quiet afternoon. Jen looked up from the name badges she'd been lettering for the reunion in time to spot a man and a woman wheeling matching suitcases through the inn's front door.

"Welcome to the Dane Crown Inn. How can I help you today?" Rising from her seat at the reception desk, Jen favored the thirtysomething couple with a warm smile.

"I'm Dallas Evers." A raven-colored curl fell onto a forehead so pale Dallas must not have seen the sun all winter. He brushed the errant strand aside with milky-white fingers before he slipped one arm around the woman at his side. "I have a reservation."

"Of course, Mr. Evers." Mentally checking the name off the list of guests she expected to greet today, she turned to the brunette at Dallas's side. "I'm Jen Passel. My Aunt Margaret owns the inn."

"Mandy Stevens," the younger woman said.

"My fiancée," Dallas added, as if the situation required an explanation.

Oh, just kill me now. Another happy pair of lovebirds.

Jen tucked a clenched fist behind her back. Lately, it seemed like she couldn't turn around without running into one couple in love or another. If it wasn't Kim and Craig billing and cooing at each other while they roped her into helping out with decorations for their wedding, it was Belle asking her to pretty-please sit in the back and let Jason drive them to their next gig. Or Amy and Max who, just last night, had suggested she and Caleb join them on a double date.

Like that would ever happen. The last thing she needed was those two putting ideas in Caleb's head. He had enough ideas of his own.

For a while there, she and Diane had had their single status in common, but no longer.

Not since her cousin and Tim had patched things up. Now it looked like even Nat was deserting her. No matter how much her niece protested that they were *just friends*, it sure looked like she was getting serious about Samuel. If that kept up, Nat would soon turn just as saccharin-sweet as the rest of the women in the family.

Well, not her. She wasn't going to fall for a man, any man. Not again. She'd tied—and untied—the knot twice already and had no interest whatsoever in repeating that painful mistake. Particularly not with Caleb, no matter how he got her motor purring. That man had marriage written all over him. And she was not marriage material.

"A-hem."

"Oh!" Jen flinched when the man on the other side of the desk cleared his throat. Belatedly, she realized that Dallas Evers stared at her, his dark eyes expectant. Quickly, she reran the conversation back to the point where she'd drifted off.

"Congratulations," she gushed, hoping against hope that she sounded far more sincere than she felt. "When's the wedding?"

"Next winter. We're hoping to firm up the date while we're here." Mandy extended her hand, ring-side up.

"Lovely!" Jen pronounced, taking a minute to admire the diamond that was considerably larger and brighter than one of the stars that sparkled in the night sky. When something she refused to call envy stirred within her, she dropped Mandy's hand like a hot potato.

"Um, let's get you both checked in, shall we?" she suggested. "I believe you booked online and requested the Emerald Suite." A handy printout sat in the desk drawer, but Aunt Margaret had taught her well. She'd committed the particulars about their incoming guests to memory.

"Yes, if it's available," Dallas answered.

"You're in luck," Jen assured the young man before she walked the couple through the check-in process. When they'd finished, she retrieved their keys. "Let me give you a quick tour while I have someone take your bags to your rooms." She glanced through the open door at the shiny blue sedan that sat just beyond the front steps. A rental, no doubt. She made a mental note to ask Dallas to move it to the parking area. "Do you have more luggage in your car?"

"No." Dallas pumped the collapsable handle on his suitcase. "This is it."

As if they were good friends, not complete strangers who'd only just met, Mandy cupped one hand at her mouth and stage-whispered,

"He insisted I only bring one carry-on, so all I packed were bikinis."

There was no denying the spark of interest her comment generated, though Dallas chided gently, "I hope you brought more than that. We can't spend all our time at the beach."

Mandy smiled lovingly up at her fiancé. "Tsk-tsk. Always so literal. Don't worry. I managed to squeeze in a sundress or two."

Jen stared at her phone, silently rolling her eyes at the couple's playful banter while she sent a quick text to Nat. In the time it took her to show Dallas and Mandy where they'd get their morning coffee, Nat would deliver the couple's bags to the Emerald Suite and give the rooms a last-minute walk-through, opening the drapes and plumping the throw pillows.

Once Nat replied that she was on her way, Jen launched into a well-practiced introduction to the inn her family had owned and operated for more than sixty years. She didn't bother to hide her love for her current home as she pointed out the game room and the library, the sitting rooms and the sunroom.

"And right through here is the dining room," Jen said, leading the newcomers down the hallway. "Coffee and water are available twenty-four-seven." She motioned to the sideboard, where insulated carafes kept each beverage of choice piping hot. "My cousin Amy owns Sweet Cakes, a fabulous little bakery in downtown Emerald Bay. She provides us with a delicious assortment of freshly baked sweet rolls and coffee cakes each morning. In addition, we serve lemonade and cookies at four every afternoon."

Nodding her approval, Mandy patted the roomy bag she wore over one shoulder. "We stopped at a fruit stand on our way in. Will there be a refrigerator in our room?"

"No." Jen gave the woman a sympathetic smile. "But we do have one you can use just around the corner." After finding improperly wrapped food in the Sub-Zero she used for her catering business, Kim had insisted on purchasing a separate refrigerator specifically for their guests to use. "It's right through here."

Stepping into the kitchen, where a shiny new side-by-side stood opposite the Aga range, Jen skidded to a halt when she spied Kim and Craig sitting at the table. Not that finding her sister in the kitchen was a surprise—between preparing meals for the family, as well as for her catering business, Royal Meals, Kim spent most of her waking hours bustling between the stove and the sink. Craig, however, was another story. He normally spent the day in his Town Hall office.

"Hey, Kim! Craig!" Jen put a little extra *oomph* into the greeting. She edged sideways, blocking the view in case she and her guests had walked in on this particular pair of lovebirds fooling around.

"Hey, yourself." Kim looked up from the papers spread across the table in front of her. "Craig and I were going over some last-minute plans for the reunion next month." Her gaze lifted over Jen's shoulder to the couple behind her. "Welcome to the Dane Crown Inn," she said.

Jen gave her sister a quick once-over. Unmussed hair? Check. Unsmudged lipstick? Check. Satisfied, she breathed easier as she handled the introductions. "This is Mandy Stevens and Dallas Evers. They're staying in Emerald through the weekend. I was just giving them the grand tour." She turned to their guests. "And this is my sister, Kim, and the mayor of Emerald Bay, Craig Mitchell."

Once the usual greetings had been exchanged, Kim asked, "What brings you to Emerald Bay, Mandy? Dallas?"

The dark-haired man snugged an arm around the woman at his side. "We're looking at wedding venues. We'd like something near the beach, since most of our friends and family will be flying in from up north, and we're planning to get married in February."

Mandy tilted an adoring face to her fiancé. "What better excuse to visit Florida in the winter, right?"

"I take it you're not from around here?" Craig hinted.

"No." Dallas shook his head. "Chicago."

"Brrr." Kim gave an exaggerated shiver. "No wonder a Florida venue sounds so appealing. Will it be a big wedding?"

"Not huge." Mandy shrugged. "Maybe two hundred? Including the immediate family and our attendants."

"That's not small." Kim tapped her finger against her chin. "St. Helen's in Vero Beach could handle a wedding that size. It's a beautiful church." Over a hundred years old, the stately cathedral was also the oldest Catholic church in the area.

Dallas nodded. "We have an appointment there tomorrow."

Mandy's expression faltered. "I'm not sold on the idea of such a big church, honey. It would be so expensive. The floral arrangements alone could run five figures."

Clearly under the spell of the woman he'd asked to be his wife, Dallas gazed down at her. "If you want to cross it off the list, that's what we'll do. We could get married on the lawn right here, if that makes you happy."

Jen froze. Although they could easily accommodate an outdoor event of that size, they couldn't commit to hold it. Not with ownership of the inn in limbo.

Fortunately, Craig distracted the couple when he smiled at the bride. "That's one smart man you have there, Mandy. Hang on to him," he advised.

"Oh, I will." Grinning from ear to ear, she slipped her hand in her fiancé's.

If she heard one more word about weddings, Jen thought she might be sick to her stomach.

"Moving along," she said, interrupting before Kim and Craig could begin comparing notes on their own upcoming nuptials with their guests. "Didn't you want to put some things in the fridge?" she asked hopefully. She pulled open a drawer filled with press-apply labels and plastic containers and told Mandy to help herself to whatever she needed.

While Mandy was busy storing pints of fresh strawberries and blueberries in the crisper, Jen showed Dallas the storage unit filled with an assortment of beach chairs, umbrellas, and boogie boards. A row of sturdy beach wagons whose wide, thick tires moved easily over sand stood beside the unit. "Feel free to use whatever you want. We just ask that you put everything back when you're finished with it." Since this was turtle nesting season, she also gave him the standard warnings about protecting the nests of the loggerheads, leatherbacks and green turtles that laid ninety percent of their eggs on Florida beaches.

Once she'd covered the basics, she and Dallas backtracked through the kitchen, where they retrieved Mandy and bid goodbye to Kim and Craig. Two minutes later, Jen led the guests around a final turn and into the large corner suite where the afternoon sun filled the sitting room with an ethereal light.

"Oh!" Mandy gasped. The young woman stared out the picture window, her gaze following the trail that led through the dunes and on to the beach beyond. "This is beautiful. I can't wait to lie out and get some sun. Our friends will all be so jealous when we go home!"

"The weather should be great this week," Jen assured the pair. She eyed the young woman's complexion, which was only slightly darker than her fiancé's. "Just be sure to wear sunscreen. You don't want your trip to get ruined by a bad sunburn. We keep SPF 40 on hand if you didn't bring your own."

His eyes fixed on his bride-to-be, Dallas asked, "What about the beach itself? Is it private?"

Jen stifled a groan. It didn't take a genius to understand that the man was picturing his girlfriend in one of those bikinis she'd mentioned. Though she wanted to tell their guests that sex on the beach was not nearly as much fun as people thought—the sand got *everywhere*—she guarded her expression.

"Not that private," she answered. "The closest public accesses are about a mile away in either direction, which makes our little spot in the sand relatively secluded. But we do share it with treasure hunters and their metal detectors or fishermen who'll spend hours waiting for a bite. Plus, you're likely to run into other guests from the inn and possibly some of the staff."

Dallas gave a sheepish grin. "I guess we'll just have to behave ourselves then, won't we."

"Oh, you!" Mandy pushed playfully on his chest. "You hush, or you'll give Jen the wrong impression." Her face rosy, she turned away from her fiancé. "Don't mind him. He's just teasing."

Whether he was or not, Jen decided it wasn't any of her business. After making certain the couple was happy with their accommodations, she left Mandy and Dallas to get settled in and returned to the reception desk. She'd no sooner picked up her pen and returned to work on the name badges than her phone rang.

Seeing Caleb's face on the screen, she did her best to ignore the way her insides quivered. Okay, so she was attracted to the big farmer. Who could blame her? The man had been half in love with her the moment she climbed out of her car at Moss Meadows. Hadn't he called her "the one who got away"?

Too bad she hadn't had the slightest inkling of how he'd felt about her in high school, she mused. If she had, she might have been tempted to stick around.

But no.

Even back then their lives had been headed in different directions. He'd been one of those smart fellas—the kind that took all honors classes. President of the debate club. Member of the geek society, though they'd called it Moo Alfalfa Theta or some such nonsense.

By comparison, thanks to her mother's rather lax philosophy toward school attendance, none of her teachers thought she had the brains to put two and two together, much less handle complicated algebraic equations. They'd stuck her in the dummy classes, where she'd done her absolute best to prove them right—skating by with barely passing grades, skipping school as much as she attended it.

The night of graduation, though, she and Caleb had both walked across the stage to get their diplomas. Him, wearing all those colorful braids around his neck as proof of how he'd excelled. Her, holding her breath until the principal actually handed her that rolled-up slip of paper, determined not to let anyone see how scared she was that he'd change his mind at the last second.

She'd lost track of Caleb after that, but she'd always figured he'd spent the summer getting ready to go off to college and, from there, onto a bright future that included his dream job, marriage and all the good things that came with it. She, on the other hand, had struck out on her own with barely enough money in her pocket to get her across the state line. There, with the help of a fake ID and a brazen independence, she'd landed her first job waiting tables in a run-down honkytonk. Taking a page out of her mother's playbook, she'd spent the next decade bouncing from one town, one job, one relationship to another until, two failed marriages later, she'd landed in Biloxi as a cocktail waitress.

That's when she'd finally figured out she wasn't as dumb as her teachers had thought she was. It took skills to remember who, on the vast casino floor, had ordered which drink, how to tease and flirt with the customers just enough to earn the best tips without putting ideas in their heads, and how big a cut to give the bartenders so they'd always fix her orders first. Best of all, waitressing gave her the flexibility to pick up and leave whenever her feet got itchy, content to know she could always land another job in another city.

Or so she'd thought, until a string of really bad breaks had sent her home to Emerald Bay. Where, for a while, she'd considered herself a one-of-a-kind failure. Or she had until she'd looked around and realized that, from Belle on down to Kim, each of the women in her family had faced a setback of one kind or another. And, thanks to grace, luck and the support of women who'd grown up together, they'd overcome whatever had gone wrong in their lives.

Being surrounded by family, working at the inn, had given her a sense of belonging and purpose she hadn't ever known before. Which, when she thought about it long enough, she realized was awfully strange. She hadn't thought she'd ever be content to stay in one place for any length of time. She was, after all, her mother's daughter, and Mom hadn't exactly been the kind of woman who stayed put. But she would have considered making the Dane Crown Inn her permanent home...if her aunt hadn't already decided to retire and sell the place.

Ironic, right?

Once Aunt Margaret moved into the local assisted living, though, she still might have stuck around. She'd actually given more than two seconds' thought to getting a job at one of the hotels out by the Interstate, buying herself a little house and living out the rest of her life in the same town as the rest of her family. However, running into Caleb at Moss Meadows had crushed that fantasy flatter than a pancake. One glimpse of the smoldering sexiness in his hazel eyes, the waves of dark hair that fell to his broad shoulders, the legs as thick as tree trunks below a narrow waist, and she'd felt her motor rumble. She'd fallen head over heels for the guy before he'd even said two words to her.

And then...

Then he'd filled her in on what had happened in his life since the last time they'd seen each other. How he'd earned his degree, just as she'd known he would. How he'd landed the great job and the fabulous wife and started building the kind of future she'd pictured him having back in the day. And how he'd lost his wife to cancer, walked away from the career he hated, and started over as a farmer.

Talk about opposites. Caleb was so settled, so stable, so *grounded,* it absolutely scared the bejeezus out of her.

He deserved better. He didn't need someone like her in his life. Someone whose first fifteen years on this earth had been the very definition of *in*stability. Who couldn't be counted on to stick around. Who—with the sole exception of the period when her Aunt Margaret and Aunt Liz had taken her and her sister in after their mother died—had never spent more than six months in one place in her entire life.

Speaking of which, she was perilously close to breaking that record now, wasn't she?

She counted back to the day she'd arrived in Emerald Bay. That had been at Christmas, and here it was, May already. Five months had flown by, and though she'd loved every minute she'd spent with Aunt Margaret and Belle, Diane and Amy, Nat and, most of all, with her sister, she told herself it was time to hit the road.

Oh, she'd stick around for Kim's wedding, of course. She wouldn't miss that for anything in the world. But as soon as the final Dane Family Reunion drew to a close, once they'd toasted the last marshmallow over the firepit, when the newlyweds flew off to parts unknown for their honeymoon and the big old For Sale sign went up in the front yard, she'd pack her bags and head out.

Would the fortune in buried treasure Diane and Nat had discovered change things?

She scoffed at the idea. "Pie in the sky," her mother would have called it. There was no way a few coins and a couple of necklaces were worth over ten million dollars. Nobody hit a jackpot like that, not even in Vegas. She could see a million, maybe. At that, once the government took its cut, there'd be just enough left over to provide for her aunt's retirement. So, no, there was no life-changing windfall in her future.

Besides, much as she'd hate to leave her family behind, she didn't have any choice. *Caleb* didn't give her any choice. If she cared about the big farmer—and she did—she had to put as much distance as possible between the two of them before she broke his heart. Because that was the only possible outcome if she let their relationship deepen into anything more than friendship, and the man who'd lost his wife to cancer had already been hurt enough.

Her phone buzzed again, jolting her back to the present. She glanced at Caleb's picture and, despite the tears that threatened to fill her eyes, she managed a wan smile.

"Hey," she said, tamping down a pang of

regret for what was not to be while she accepted the call. "What's up? We weren't supposed to work in the garden today, were we?" She gulped. The garden she and Caleb had started was another thing she'd regret leaving behind when she left.

"Nah. I got weedin' to do here at the farm."

The image of Caleb's muscular arms bending and flexing as he wielded a hoe sent another thrill through her midsection. "Whew!" she managed.

"But I was wonderin'…"

"Yeah?" Jen deliberately thumbed the stack of blank name cards.

"Um, how 'bout I pick you up and we grab a bite at Pirate's Gold and then catch a movie in Vero? There's a new action flick I've been wantin' to see."

Startled by the suggestion, Jen jolted. The move scattered cards across the tabletop. She lunged for them before they could fall to the floor. Was Caleb asking her out on a date?

That would be a first. Sure, they'd danced together at the Spring Fling, but well aware that her entire family was also in attendance, Caleb had been a perfect gentleman. Honestly, it was like his hands were glued to her waist, his fingers not straying so much as an inch up or down.

Since that night, they'd spent plenty of time together, but she'd made sure they always had one project or another to accomplish. One that required all their attention. Like sorting the late-season strawberries for Moss Meadows' fruit and vegetable stand. Or planting and tending to the young seedlings in the garden down by the old grove.

But going to dinner and seeing a movie together—that sort of thing sounded romantic. It was the kind of thing that led to goodnight kisses...and, if she wasn't very careful, broken hearts. Wasn't that exactly what she'd been trying to avoid?

He must have sensed her hesitation, because his voice lowered to a deep timbre that sent chills down her spine.

"It's just the diner in town. No big deal. We can skip the movie if you want."

Jen squeezed her eyes tight. She supposed no harm could come from having dinner with Caleb at the Pirate's Gold Diner. The man certainly wasn't going to profess his love for her over meatloaf and potatoes. Or propose to her over a dish of apple cobbler. Not even if he splurged and ordered it à la mode.

Besides, if she was going to leave, there were certain preparations she had to make. She'd been out on her own in the big wide world before. This time, with few prospects and no particular destination in mind, it was likely to be a bumpy ride. If she was going to survive it, she'd need to stockpile as many good memories as she could make between now and the day she drove her car down the driveway of the Dane Crown Inn for the last time.

"I like action movies," she said softly. As memories went, she was determined to make this a good one.

"You do, huh?" Caleb asked, his tone a mix of surprise and delight. "I'll pick you up at six. I gotta run. Those weeds ain't gonna pull themselves."

She barely had time to register the smile in Caleb's voice before she sat, listening to dead air. And with that, Jen clicked the tip of the pen. Like Caleb's weeds, the name cards weren't going to write themselves, and with only a few weeks left before the family reunion, her sister's wedding and her departure, she had a lot to do.

Five

Jen

"You're wearing that?" Seated at the desk where she was filling in for the evening, Nat curled her lip into a sneer.

"What's wrong with it?" Jen smoothed her hand over a pair of wide-legged jeans while she glanced in the mirror that hung near the stairs. Okay, maybe the outfit hadn't walked off the pages of the latest fashion magazine, but the straight lines of the oversize jacket she'd pulled on over a plain white T-shirt made her look taller than she was. Better yet, the blousy fit helped disguise the "assets" she'd been known to flaunt when working the floor of a major casino.

"Nothing…if you're headed out for lunch at the senior center." Nat, being Nat, refused to pull any punches. "I thought you and Caleb were going out on a date. Your *first* date. You go dressed like that, it'll be your *last* one."

"I don't want to give him the wrong idea."

"Mission accomplished." Nat smirked.

A long-suffering sigh hissed between Jen's lips. Most of her limited wardrobe consisted of shirts with plunging necklines and pants that were either too short or too tight. In other words, perfect for serving cocktails in dimly lit bars where making enough money to pay her rent depended on giving patrons a glimpse of her hips or breasts or maybe both. She'd spent hours trying on one outfit after another, judging each as far too revealing for a casual date with a man she was trying to keep at arm's length. As the mound of rejected clothes grew higher on her bed, frustration made her head ache. She'd been on the verge of canceling altogether when she'd pulled the jacket and pants from the very back of the closet. The items had been a spur-of-the-moment purchase nearly two years ago when she'd gotten the not-so-bright idea to apply for an office job. Why she'd thought anyone would hire her, a woman with absolutely no qualifications, to sit at a desk and answer phones was anyone's guess. Needless to say, the company had hired someone else, and she'd forgotten about the outfit.

"Fine. I get that. But would it hurt to show a little bit of cleavage?" Nat refused to back down. "I'm not saying you have to put all the goods on display, but what you're wearing is...how should I say this? Old and frumpy. Not even Aunt Margaret would be caught dead in those clothes."

Okay, that definitely wasn't the look she'd been going for.

Jen pulled her cell phone from the pocket of her jeans and checked the time. "It's too late for me to change. He'll be here in fifteen minutes."

As if she'd waved the checkered flag at the start of a race, Nat bolted from her chair behind the receptionist's desk. "Last one up the stairs has kitchen duty for a week," she challenged. Her long legs gobbled up the steps. At the landing, she called, "Come on! Show me what you've got."

Not certain whether her niece meant her speed or her wardrobe, Jen took the stairs as fast as her shorter legs would allow. In the hallway outside her rooms, she warned, "It's messy inside."

"You don't say." Taking in the pile of discarded clothes on the bed, Nat whistled. She rubbed her palms together like people did when they were trying to warm them on a cold winter night. "All right. We don't have time to be too picky, but I got this."

And she did.

Jen watched in near awe as her niece retrieved one item after another from the stack of clothes Jen had tried on and abandoned. In a matter of minutes, she'd traded the baggy jeans for a pair of stretchy leggings. A patterned number that dipped just below her collarbones replaced the round-necked T-shirt. Last, but not least, a long cardigan tied everything together.

"See?" Nat smiled her approval when Jen modeled the new outfit. "The sweater minimizes your chest while, at the same time, it shows off your other curves."

The girl certainly knew fashion, Jen admitted as she marveled over clothes that gave off an entirely different vibe than the ones she'd chosen. "I can't believe all this came from my closet. I would never put these pieces together the way you did, but it definitely works. Thanks, girlfriend."

Nat doffed an imaginary hat and took a deep bow. "My pleasure. Now I need to get back downstairs. Mr. and Mrs. Turnbull should be here any minute." Retirees from Oklahoma, the couple had flown to Orlando, where they'd rented a car for the week they'd spend at the inn.

It's times like these I'll want to remember later, Jen told herself as she trailed her niece down the wide staircase. A sudden awareness of how much she was going to miss hanging out with Nat or helping Kim in the kitchen pierced her like an arrow straight to the heart. Her legs threatened to buckle as the rest of the things she'd miss piled on. All the evenings her sister and her cousins would spend out by the firepit, laughing and sharing stories about their days. The birthday parties and anniversary celebrations she wouldn't be here for. Good Lord, would she even be in town when Fern and Scott had their baby?

The thought that she might not be a part of such a momentous family occasion took her breath away. She clutched the banister with one hand while she dabbed her eyes with the other. Maybe she was being too hasty. Maybe she should stick around after all.

But no. Whether she stayed or went didn't matter. Big changes were on the horizon. Regardless of what she did, the inn was going on the market. That decision had already been made. Eventually, new owners would take over the Dane Crown Inn, and once they did, her family would scatter. Diane and Caitlyn had been the first to go when they moved into their own home. The others would follow. Kim would move in with Craig once they'd tied the knot. If Aunt Margaret hadn't picked out her room at the retirement home, she would soon. Oh, the rest might stay in Emerald Bay for a year or two. Before long, though, they'd move on, too. The Emeralds were undoubtedly on the path to success. When they made it big, Belle would jet off to parts unknown. As for Nat, her niece was far too worldly to stick around their sleepy little beach town for long.

So, no, it didn't matter whether she left now or waited until the new owners changed the locks on the doors. As much as she hated the idea, her family would be like a million others— spread from one end of the country to the other, relying on the occasional phone call or Christmas letter to keep in touch, seeing each other only at weddings and funerals.

That left Caleb as the deciding factor. In order to protect his heart, she needed to get out of Dodge as soon as possible. And, squaring her shoulders, she marched to the bottom of the stairs, resigned to making enough memories with the man to sustain her for the rest of her life.

Standing at her side, Caleb eyed the battered pickup truck that sat in the parking lot of the Dane Crown Inn. He made a sound like the clicking of his tongue against the roof of his mouth. "Shoot," he said. "Don't know what I was thinkin'. I should have brought the SUV."

Jen stopped short of asking him if he'd lost his marbles. She'd never seen him drive anything but the pickup and couldn't quite figure out which surprised her more—that the farmer owned more than tractors and tillers or that he thought what he drove mattered to her.

"Your truck is perfectly fine," she assured him. "You've seen the hunk of junk I drive, haven't you?" Duct tape and bailing wire had literally held the front bumper in place ever since an unfortunate run-in with a cement curb.

Caleb ran a hand through a shaggy mop of dark hair. "Sorry. It's been a while since I've taken a woman out on an actual date."

Jen latched onto the statement as a conversation starter. "How long has it been?" she asked, curious as to how a man like him hadn't been snatched up already.

"No one since Willa," he admitted.

"You're kidding, right?" More than a dozen years had passed since Caleb's wife had succumbed to leukemia. "Good-looking guy like you? I'm surprised every single woman in a hundred miles hasn't lined up outside your front door."

"Nope. For a little while, a couple of widows hovered around like bees in a clover patch. They flew off to greener pastures once I chucked the aerospace job and went to work at Moss Meadows full-time. Turned out, they were more interested in my paycheck than me."

She laughed, trying to make light of a matter that was anything but laughable. "There had to be others, though. I can practically hear the grocery store's PA system squawking, 'Single man in the produce section.'" Abandoning their carts, women from every corner of the store would hustle toward the bananas and tomatoes like moths drawn to a flame.

Caleb chuckled. The door of the pickup truck issued a loud squeal when he opened it for her. "Have you forgotten what I do for a living? I don't shop for lettuce and cucumbers."

Of course he wouldn't. The man owned a vegetable farm, after all. "Church then," she said, ignoring the little zing that shot through her when Caleb boosted her onto the high seat. "How many women have insisted on having you over for a home-cooked meal after Sunday service?"

"Hmmm. Let me think. Yep. None."

Jen scoffed. "I hardly believe that." They said the way to a man's heart was through his stomach. What woman in her right mind could resist the opportunity to tempt Caleb with her best pot roast?

"The casseroles I bring to the potluck suppers are pretty darn good. I think some are intimidated by that." The shy smile he wore as he shut her door warmed her heart.

Giving the matter more thought, she buckled her seat belt while Caleb circled the hood of the truck. No chance run-ins at the grocery store, and he didn't need anyone to fix his dinner. The man couldn't be a better catch if he tried. How had the women of Indian River County overlooked him?

"You mean to tell me you've never had to fend off a flirty salesclerk? Or had a single mom push an adorable toddler at you while you shopped for a new shirt? A pair of shoes?" she asked when the truck dipped slightly as Caleb took his place behind the wheel.

"Six days out of seven, I'm in the fields by

sunup," he said, sticking the key in the ignition and giving it a twist. "It's usually close to dark by the time I finish. Mostly, I order what I need online. When I do shop, which isn't often, I'm in and out of the store in ten minutes."

"You sure don't make it easy, do you?" she grumbled over the throaty engine.

"I guess not." Shifting the truck into gear, Caleb shrugged. "I never saw the point in starting something when I wasn't interested."

And that was the problem, wasn't it?

Caleb, the man who hadn't been on a single date in the dozen years since his wife had passed, was interested...in her. Under other circumstances, she'd be thrilled. But not now. Not when she'd made up her mind to put Emerald Bay in her rear view. In a month, give or take a week or two, she'd head out. Her car would bump along the long coquina driveway that led from the Dane Crown Inn to the main road. When she reached the highway, she'd flip a mental coin to choose the direction she'd take next. Whichever option she picked, she knew one thing—her path would not lead back to Caleb.

She had no doubt whatsoever that he deserved to have someone special in his life again. A woman who'd sit beside him in an old rocker on the front porch in the cool of a summer's evening. Who'd share his bed, cuddling into his side when he stole all the covers. A partner to keep his dinner warm for him on the nights when he worked late in the fields, ask about his day, and delight in the monotony of planting, tending, harvesting. Rinse and repeat. Year after year.

As much as she longed to be that girl, she couldn't fit into Caleb's life any better than a square peg fit into a round hole. She was a tumbleweed, one that didn't stay long enough in one place to put down roots. He, on the other hand, was an oak. Tall, strong, with roots that went on forever. In a picture dictionary, they'd put his image under the word *permanence*.

Oh, sure, she and Caleb could have fun together for a week, a month, maybe even a year. But eventually, the wind would blow and she'd go with it. In that regard, at least, she took after her mother. And, like a leopard and its spots, she didn't see that changing anytime soon.

Jen drew in a big breath. The sooner she told Caleb they had no future together, the better. Before his feelings deepened, before both their hearts got broken. Determined to get the conversation over with as soon as they got to the diner, she stared out the window, gathering her courage while the palm trees and palmetto scrub on the outskirts of town gave way to houses with manicured lawns and then, finally, to the shops and stores in the heart of Emerald Bay.

"Looks busy for a weeknight," Caleb observed as he pulled off the road onto an asphalt lot. "Fried chicken must be the special of the day." He narrowly avoided a large pothole that threatened to eat the truck for dinner and pulled into the last available spot. "The Border sisters might want to think about repaving." He unbuckled his seat belt.

Jen eyed the crowded parking lot and groaned. She had planned to wait until they were inside before bringing up their future—or the lack of it—with Caleb. So much for that idea. All it would take was for the person in the next booth to overhear their discussion and, by the time they finished dessert, the news that she'd dumped him would spread from one end of Emerald Bay to the other. She couldn't let that happen.

She laid her hand on his wrist. "Can we talk for a minute?"

"I guess."

The frown flickered across Caleb's features so quickly that Jen barely caught it, but she couldn't miss the guarded note that crept into his voice, any more than she could ignore how his muscles tensed under her fingertips. The man might be out of practice, but he'd been around the block a time or two. He didn't need a road map to know where their conversation was headed when a woman said, "We need to talk."

She plunged ahead anyway. "I want to make sure we're on the same page, is all. After Aunt Margaret puts the inn on the market later this summer, I won't be sticking around."

"Okay." His hazel eyes darkening, Caleb turned toward her. "Why are you telling me this?"

Jen took a breath and let it out quickly. "I just, I didn't want you to think this could lead to anything." She wagged a finger back and forth between them. "I like you, Caleb. I don't want you to get hurt. Not on my account."

"You may not have noticed, but I'm a big boy." Caleb blew out a forceful breath. "I can take care of myself."

"Duly noted. So we're good?" Jen let the question hang.

"Yeah. We're good." He reached for the door handle. "Do you mind if we eat now? I'm hungry for some fried chicken."

"Sure." Her heart ached. His brave front hadn't fooled her for a minute. Hoping Caleb hadn't noticed the tears that sparkled in her eyes, Jen swiveled toward her door.

The clanging of a ship's bell and the aroma of fried foods greeted them when they stepped into the diner's small entryway. Jen glanced at the larger-than-life wooden statue of Captain Hook that had been a fixture of the restaurant for as far back as she could remember. Sure enough, the list of daily specials scrawled across the chalkboard in the pirate's hands included fried chicken.

A teen who bore a slight resemblance to the Border sisters greeted them. "Two for dinner?" she asked. When Caleb nodded, the slim redhead slipped a couple of menus from a stack under the hostess stand. "A booth? Or would you like to sit in the back?" She inclined her head toward the row of stools at the lunch counter.

"Booth."

Jen nodded in agreement when Caleb glanced down at her.

"Follow me." The teen started off at a good clip.

"Don't look now, but we're going to be the talk of the town tomorrow," Caleb growled in her ear as neighbors and friends in various stages of their meals nodded greetings.

Considering the number of raised eyebrows and speculative smiles she counted as the two of them passed between the rows of booths that ran the length of the diner, Jen couldn't disagree. She supposed the very fact that Caleb towered a good foot or more over her would have earned them a second glance on its own, but she knew that wasn't the real reason their presence caused a stir. No, by the time their waitress brought water to their table, the grapevine would already be humming with the news that she and Caleb had been on a date. She forced a smile and wished, for his sake, that they'd chosen to have dinner in Vero or some out-of-the-way spot where her presence on his arm wouldn't set tongues wagging.

They caught up with the hostess, who stood, tapping her toes, in front of an empty booth at the very back of the restaurant. Sliding menus and silverware wrapped in paper napkins onto the table, she assured them, "Your waitress will be right with you."

Despite the crowd, she was right. Less than thirty seconds passed before Silvia, who'd waited tables at the diner when Jen was in her teens, hustled toward them. The gray-haired matron plunked down glasses of water without asking, grabbed a pad of order forms from her back pocket and retrieved a pencil from over her ear. Standing with one hip cocked at the edge of their table, she asked, "What can I get for you to drink?"

"Sweet tea," Caleb answered. He looked at Jen.

"Same for me."

"Two sweet teas coming up." Silvia scribbled on her pad. "You know what you want to eat?"

"I'll have the fried chicken special," Caleb said with a wide grin. "What's that come with?"

"Sorry, hon. We're out of fried chicken." Silvia's expression shifted into a sad smile. "Just sold the last one five minutes ago. We still got the meatloaf," she said, mentioning the other special from the list up front. "It comes with mashed potatoes, gravy and green beans."

"Outta chicken." With a sigh, Caleb retrieved the menu he hadn't bothered to study. "I'm gonna need a minute. Jen?"

She hesitated. Farmers had a reputation for pinching pennies till they screamed. With that in mind, she'd intended to order something that cost less than whatever Caleb ate. A plan that wouldn't work if he made her choose first. "I'll have the meatloaf," she said after a pause. The dish wasn't her favorite, but it was definitely reasonably priced.

"Chicken-fried steak for me," Caleb said. He gathered their menus and held them out for Silvia. "Instead of potatoes, can I have applesauce and a fruit cup?"

"You got it." In a move so fluid, she'd probably done it a million times during her long tenure at the diner, Silvia grabbed the menus, tucked the order pad in her pocket and returned the pencil to its usual spot behind her ear. Less than a second later, she slipped from sight.

Curious about her date's choice of sides, Jen tilted her head. "Applesauce and fruit salad?"

Seated across from her, Caleb gave her a cockeyed smile. "I get enough vegetables at home."

Jen would have asked more, but she spied one of the deacons from their church on the approach. "We're about to get company," she whispered.

Despite the warning, Caleb craned his neck. He started to rise to greet their visitor. A hand on his shoulder kept him in his seat.

"Hey, Caleb. Jen." Ron Power's blue eyes peered out from a round face. "You're both looking mighty nice tonight. You mind if I interrupt? I promise this won't take but a minute."

"Of course not," Jen assured the man. Not that she had much choice. Ron served as a greeter on Sunday mornings. The man had a kind word for every person who walked through the doors and took one of his church bulletins. His generous spirit had earned her respect.

"Thanks." Shifting his stance slightly, Ron leaned toward Caleb. "I wanted to thank you for all the support you've given the food bank. It means a lot to the community."

"Happy to do it," Caleb said with the smooth acceptance of someone who was used to being singled out for a good deed.

Curious, thought Jen. She'd heard people say Caleb helped out around town, but she'd had no idea what that entailed. Apparently, it involved regular donations to feed the hungry.

"I hate to ask," Ron continued, "but I was wondering if you could see your way clear to giving us an extra bushel or two of tomatoes each week. We've been getting them from another source, but it dried up."

"The Bucher farm, you mean." Caleb nodded. Including Jen in the conversation, he explained, "That's the land adjoining mine. Todd Bucher died of a heart attack in the middle of his turnip field last year. His estate's still in probate."

"Darn shame about Todd. He was a good man," Ron interjected.

"That he was," Caleb acknowledged. "As for the tomatoes, I could probably do two bushels a week. More if they don't need to be perfect."

"We'll take as many as you can spare. I'll sort out the bruised ones and take them to Doris."

Ron's wife, Doris, regularly volunteered at a soup kitchen on the mainland.

"In that case, I'll be sure to load them on the truck next Tuesday."

"Thanks. Bless you." Ron clapped Caleb on the back. "You couldn't find a man with a more generous heart than this one," he said, aiming the comment over his shoulder at Jen.

"He's definitely one of the good guys," she agreed. But then, Ron was no slouch in the good deeds department. He definitely stood high on the ladder to sainthood, in her book.

She waited until the deacon had returned to his own booth before she turned to her date. "You regularly donate to the food bank?"

"What little I give is not as big a deal as Ron makes it out to be." Caleb reached into the plastic basket at the end of the table and took the saltshaker from among the bottles of pepper, hot sauce and ketchup. He pushed the tiny glass jar back and forth between his hands as he spoke. "The fruits and vegetables we sell at the stand have to be fresh or people will find someplace else to shop. So, at the end of each day, we box up all the leftovers and put them in the walk-in cooler. The church sends a truck by to pick it all up once a week."

Jen resisted the urge to scratch her head.

According to every news story she'd seen, farmers across the nation teetered on the brink of bankruptcy. It made her wonder. "And you can afford to throw in a bushel of tomatoes? No. Make that two bushels of tomatoes."

Caleb raised and lowered one shoulder. "People have been good to me. When I can, I pass it on."

"Like how?" Jen had a sneaking suspicion that the farmer was deliberately minimizing his involvement.

"There's the food bank, but you already know about that one. And I support the soup kitchen whenever I can." Caleb passed the saltshaker from one hand to the other. "Like a lot of the guys at church, I pitch in whenever they need help at Habitat for Humanity." He caught the saltshaker and held it. "My favorite thing, though, is the gleaning."

Jen felt both her eyebrows hitch upward. "Wasn't that a horror movie?" Did Caleb have a mean streak she'd hadn't noticed?

Caleb grinned. "This is nothing like the movie." His expression turned serious as he returned the shaker to its holder. "You and I have worked on that little garden out at the inn enough that I know farming's not your strong suit."

"To put it mildly." He'd shown her how to plant green beans, tomatoes, cucumbers and melons in neat rows near the old orange grove. Beyond that, she knew precious little about what made things grow.

"Let's talk about my corn. I don't plant a lot of it—ten acres, more or less."

"That's all?" When she'd traveled through the Midwest, cornfields had crowded both sides of the highway for miles and miles of unbroken monotony.

"I raise sweet corn, not feed corn. Mostly, I sell to local stores and restaurants, plus what people buy at the vegetable stand. Around here, ten acres is about all the market will bear. So harvest time rolls around. I instruct my crew to pick three out of four ears. We leave the rest for whoever's in need and doesn't mind investing a little sweat equity."

A quarter of his crop?

"That's awfully generous," Jen observed.

"Aw. I can spare it. Like I said, I've been blessed."

The simple, heartfelt statement amazed her. Caleb was one of those rare few who'd suffered a great loss without letting himself grow hard and bitter. Instead, he'd hung on to the capacity to lend a hand to others who might not be as fortunate as he was. He was, as Ron had pointed out, one of the good guys.

Her throat tightened with emotion. She cleared it. "Tell me more about this gleaning thing," she said, wanting to know more about what made him tick.

"I wish you could be there for one," Caleb said. "As soon as we know the final day of the harvest, word gets around that the next day will be the gleaning." His whole face brightened as he spoke. "Boy, do we make a day of it. I bring in a bounce house for the kids. Lacy—you met her at the vegetable stand—she practically buys out the Dollar Store, gets all these little trinkets and toys for the little ones. The last couple of years, the migrant workers' wives have set up a table where they sell tamales and empanadas. That morning, whew, there's a line of cars waiting at the gate. We line up the adults, one person per row, hand out bags and off they go. They fill as many bags as they can carry with ears of corn."

Jen pictured herself in that line. "Aren't you afraid they'll ruin the plants?"

Caleb's grin widened until it threatened to split his face in two. "That's the beauty of it—it doesn't matter. Corn's an annual, like those green beans we planted at the inn. When they're finished producing for the year, you pull 'em out and plant fresh next year."

Jen felt her face warm. She had a lot to learn about growing things. She reached for one of the glasses of iced tea Silvia had dropped off at their table while she wasn't looking. When she'd taken several deep gulps, she set the glass aside.

"The gleaning sounds like fun," she announced. "When's the next one? I'd like to be there for it."

Sadness gathered in Caleb's eyes like storm clouds. "This year's corn crop is already in. We won't have another one till late spring next year." His words slowed. "And by then, you'll be…"

Gone. Long gone.

She drew in a thready breath, thankful for the distraction when Silvia approached their table, her hands full. Jen eased back as the waitress slid a piping hot dish loaded with not one, but three thick slices of fragrant meatloaf in front of her. Steam rose from the well of dark gravy that sat in the middle of a mountain of fluffy white potatoes. Bits of ham and onion flecked the green beans tucked along the side, almost as an afterthought. She stared in disbelief at more food than she normally ate in a week.

Across the table, Caleb unrolled his napkin,

spread the wafer-thin paper in his lap and placed his knife and fork on either side of his plate. Like a general preparing a battle plan, he studied the platter-size serving of crispy steak smothered in thick, white gravy and the accompanying bowls of chunky applesauce and chopped fruit.

"Dig in," he said, picking up his knife and pointing it toward her dish. "That looks good. What do you think?"

"It's a lot," she said, inhaling the tantalizing steam. She eyed the slab of meat that hung off either side of his plate. "Did they serve you the whole cow?"

"Maybe half," he admitted with a wry smile. "But I like a challenge."

"No way will I be able to eat all this," she warned. "I'm going to need a box." Not that it would matter, she thought with a guilty pang. Her leftovers were sure to spoil by the time the credits rolled on the movie Caleb wanted to see.

While Caleb attacked his meal, she tried a bite of the meatloaf. It was decent, she decided. Not as good as her sister's, but then, every cook had their specialties, and meatloaf was one of Kim's. She dug into the mashed potatoes next and dipped a forkful into the well of gravy. It remained suspended midway between her plate and her mouth when she spied one of the diner's co-owners covering the distance to their table in purposeful strides.

"Uh-oh. Here comes Denise," she whispered to Caleb. "I wonder what she wants."

"Must be you." Caleb swiped his mouth with his napkin. "I usually eat my meals in peace when I come here by myself."

The teasing smile that bowed his lips made Jen's heart skip a beat. She stared for a moment, wondering how those lips would feel against hers. By the time she looked away, Denise stood at the end of their table in a bright red apron that sported the restaurant's logo in gold thread. Her boisterous greeting rose above the hubbub of the crowded restaurant.

"Caleb! Always good to see you." Her gaze sped across the table and landed on Jen. "You, too, Jen. When did you two start seeing each other?"

"We're just two friends having dinner," Caleb said, managing to sound like a policeman directing traffic around a fender bender.

Nothing to see here, folks. Move along. Move along.

"Uh-huh," Denise said flatly as she continued to eye them for several long seconds before drawing her own conclusion. Whatever that was, she didn't share it with them. Instead, brushing back one of the curls that framed her face just like it had when they were in high school, she homed in on Jen. "As a matter of fact, I was hoping to run into you. We need to talk."

"Oh, really?" Jen lowered her fork. As far as she knew, she hadn't done a single thing worthy of the gossip queen's attention.

Did Denise hope to pry the details of Kim and Craig's wedding from her? Determined not to provide a single shred of information, she did her best not to squirm under the other woman's intense scrutiny.

"People are starting to wonder what's going on out there at the inn," Denise said, sounding concerned. She leaned one arm against the built-in hat rack at the end of the booth like someone who was settling in for a lengthy visit.

Of all the topics Denise might choose to discuss, renovations at the inn hadn't even occurred to Jen. She blinked in confusion. "We've been sprucing up the place a bit," she said slowly. "I'm not sure why anyone would care."

"Well, you know I'm not one for telling tales out of school, but I can't help it if I overhear people talking from time to time." Denise's sharp eyes belied the mask of innocence she'd pulled over her face. "I think you should know that people say you all have been pouring a lot of money into that old place. All that carpeting and wallpaper." She counted items off on her fingers. "Refinishing all those old wood floors. Then there was that painting crew out of Vero. They came into the diner for lunch every day for a solid week. They said they were repainting the entire exterior." Denise's eyes narrowed slightly. "Work like that don't come cheap."

"I wouldn't know," Jen hedged. "I didn't hire them." That last bit was true. As for the rest, how they paid for things was nobody's business but their own. She certainly didn't intend to tell Denise that Belle had sold a priceless piece of art to pay for the new carpets. Or that Diane had dipped into her retirement account to make sure the insurance premiums got paid.

Jen saw an edginess in Denise's expression that warned her to shut this conversation down as quickly as possible. Knowing full well that the woman was aware of the event they'd planned over the long Memorial weekend, she asked, "You do know we're hosting a big family reunion at the inn later this month, don't you? It's only natural that we'd want the inn to look its best."

"Uh-huh." Denise gave a derisive huff. "I'm just telling you what I've heard. People are wondering where all the money came from."

"Really?" It seemed odd that their friends and neighbors would hold such lengthy discussions of the Dane family's finances behind their backs. "I tell you what—next time you hear someone asking that question, you just send *those people* to me." Jen made air quotes.

"It's not just the inn." Accusation crept into Denise's tone. "Everybody knows Max has been working round the clock on another Sweet Cakes location up in Sebastian. It's the talk of the town, I tell you."

"It is, is it?" Jen countered.

"It most certainly is." Denise's chin jutted out.

At a loss for how to react, Jen glanced across the table at Caleb while she reached for her glass of iced tea. To her chagrin, the big man only lifted his palms slightly and gave his head a nearly imperceptible shake. He wasn't going to be any help. He didn't understand what the woman was driving at any better than Jen did.

Denise's voice dropped until she could barely be heard above the clatter of dishes and silverware, the low buzz of conversation. "There's a rumor going around town that someone found a large cache of coins and jewels from the 1715 fleet. I've heard it's worth millions."

What the…?

The abrupt shift of topics startled Jen so badly that her hand shook. The ice in her glass of tea jittered. She lowered the drink to the table.

"You wouldn't know anything about that, would you?" A speculative gleam filled Denise's eyes.

"Wha-what?" Jen sputtered a protest. "How would I?"

"That's what I'm asking. Are you the one who found it? Or someone else in your family? Is that how you're able to afford all those expensive changes at the inn?"

In the barrage of rapid-fire questions, Jen struggled to gain traction. Her thoughts churned like the legs of a cartoon character in a self-propelled vehicle. At last, they caught, and when they did, she resorted the one surefire method she'd used whenever an insistent—and usually drunk—customer got too handsy.

She laughed.

"Oh, my," she said, slapping one hand on the table and pressing the other to her chest as if Denise had told the funniest joke she'd ever heard. "That's hilarious. I have to give it to you, that was a good one." She fanned her face, hoping against hope that the nosy woman would buy the act.

Apparently, she did, because the owner protested, "Well, you don't have to go and get hysterical. The idea wasn't that far-fetched."

"No. No, I guess not." Jen grabbed her glass and downed half the sweet liquid like people did when they were trying to quell either laughter or tears. Tucking her hands beneath the table where no one could see her crossed fingers, she schooled her features into an earnest expression. "I assure you," she said, forcing herself to stare at Denise with her own unwavering intensity. "No one at the Dane Crown Inn found a single doubloon."

Lying didn't count if you crossed your fingers, did it?

Not that she'd lied, exactly. Her cousin and niece hadn't found a single coin—they'd found a great big pile of them.

Despite the doubt that flickered in Denise's eyes, she must have decided to take Jen at her word because she said her goodbyes and retreated as quickly as she'd come. Jen held her breath and dared not move until the last of the woman's red curls disappeared through the doorway that led to the kitchen.

"Whoo!" On the other side of the table, Caleb let out a breath. "She really had a bee in her bonnet, didn't she?"

"Yeah." Deciding she'd better wait until her hands stopped shaking before she tried to eat, Jen glanced down at food she'd barely touched. Food that, judging from the thin ribbon of grease that now outlined the meatloaf, had grown cold. A skin had formed atop the gravy. Her stomach turned over at the thought of biting into one of the bits of cold bacon in the green beans. Fighting tears, she turned an imploring face to Caleb. "Do you mind if we leave?"

His answer delivered another surprise in an evening that had been filled with them. Reaching across the table, he cupped her hand in his. "I think we should stay a little while longer. If we rush out, Denise will think maybe there was some truth to her story, after all."

She couldn't deny it—he was right.

"What do I do about that?" She gestured toward her uneaten meal. Neither of them had taken more than a bite or two or was fool enough to think no one would notice. Leaving their food untouched was bound to raise questions.

A smile softened the corners of Caleb's eyes. "What'd you do when you didn't want to eat your vegetables when you were a kid?"

Dinner had most often consisted of mac 'n' cheese prepared by her sister, but she got his drift. "I hid them."

"Yeah. Like that." Picking up his own knife and fork, he deftly cut his steak in two and stacked the layers, one on top of the other. Next, he spilled half the fruit salad onto the larger plate and scattered it about. The results looked like he'd at least made a fair-size dent in his meal.

Copying his movements, Jen stirred a fork through her mashed potatoes. The dam holding back the lake burst, and cold gravy spread slowly over her plate. She couldn't do much about the meatloaf—there was too much of it and no place to hide it. Instead, she tossed her crumpled napkin down on top of the whole mess and hoped it would suffice.

"I don't suppose we're going to make it to that movie tonight, are we?" Caleb asked while they waited for Silvia to return with his change a few minutes later.

"Do you mind if I take a raincheck?" Jen asked. She appreciated how well he read her mood more than he knew.

"Nope. Not if it means we get to do this again sometime soon." He circled a finger over their discarded meal.

"Hmmm." Jen pressed her lips together briefly before she suggested, "Maybe we could try someplace different next time?"

Caleb's face crinkled into a smile. "Sure

thing," he assured her. "You trust me?" he asked, his hazel eyes meeting hers.

In that minute, there was no one she trusted more, and she said as much.

"Then follow my lead." Standing, Caleb wrapped his arms around her in a possessive hug the instant she slipped from the booth. He leaned down, his dark hair forming a curtain around her face while he spoke gruffly into her ear. "Let's give these good folks a reason why we're hurrying out of here."

Before she had a moment to think, much less react, he moved in for a kiss. The instant his lips touched hers, Jen swore the world stopped spinning. Nothing else mattered. Not the fact that they were standing in the middle of the Pirate's Gold Diner. Or the collective gasp that rippled through the restaurant. Or that word of Diane and Nat's discovery had spread. No. The only thing that mattered was the feel of Caleb's lips against hers. The warmth of his hand cupping her cheek. The steady thudding of his heart when she rose on tiptoe and pressed into the kiss for all she was worth.

When they finally parted, she was glad for his support when he slipped his arm around her waist as if it was the most natural thing in the world. Truth be told, Caleb's kiss had left her so weak in the knees that she didn't think she was capable, in that moment, of making it to the door under her own steam. She didn't mind a bit when Caleb continued to hold on to her until he'd guided her outside as if they truly were a couple who had better places to be, better things to do than spend another minute at the diner.

"When did you get to be such a good kisser?" she asked as they walked, arm in arm, to his truck.

"I could ask you the same thing," he said, helping her into the cab. "Where to next?" he asked, sliding behind the wheel. "My place?"

The playful grin Caleb wore didn't fool her for a minute. His voice carried the sheer disbelief of a child who heard there was a pony in the barn but hadn't traipsed out in his Christmas pajamas to see it yet. She understood. She felt much the same way. Unfortunately for both of them, she couldn't let anything interfere with warning her sister and her cousins about the gossip going around town. Not even the chance to spend more time with Caleb.

"I think you'd better take me home," she said, never regretting the words more than she did at that moment.

Six

Belle

"*G*ood grief, Jen. Where's the fire?" Belle struggled to keep from breaking a heel while she hurried behind her cousin, who power-walked up the pavered walkway that led from Belle's makeshift studio in one of the cottages to the main house.

"C'mon, slowpoke." Jen motioned, urging her to pick up the pace. "The others will be here any second."

Twin sets of headlight beams briefly cut across the grounds as two cars pulled into the parking area behind them.

"You called Diane and Amy?" Belle's voice rose. "Was that absolutely necessary?" It was bad enough that Jen had interrupted her practice session. Especially now when every minute she spent behind the mic was more important than ever. But to make the others drive out to the inn after dark on a Friday night seemed overly dramatic.

Jen practically ran onto the steps that led to the back deck. Her words coming in puffs, she said, "I'll...get the wine...while you...go wake Aunt Margaret."

Was she nuts?

Margaret had retired to her bed over an hour earlier. By now she'd read her Bible, said her prayers and fallen sound asleep.

"I'm not waking Mama." Belle folded her arms across her chest. She refused to disturb her mom without good cause. So far, Jen hadn't given her one.

Jen huffed. "I suppose we can break the news to her in the morning." At the French doors that led into the kitchen, she tossed more directions over her shoulder. "Light the citronella candles then, so the mosquitoes don't eat us alive out here."

Enough was enough. If she had to risk getting bitten, she was going to sure as heck know why. Belle let her voice drop into the diva tone she hadn't used since her career as a pop star had crashed and burned. "Hold on there just a moment. What is this all about?"

"Carmen."

The single word Jen flung over her shoulder before she ducked inside gave Belle pause. Her jaw clenched briefly. *What about Carmen?* She stood, watching her cousin dash about the kitchen like one of the monk parakeets flitting about its nest. She'd get no more answers from Jen until she lit down somewhere.

In the meantime, she could practically feel an army of mosquitoes forming up, ready to descend on the unwary and unprotected. Grabbing the electric wand they kept on hand for the candles and the grill, she lit the tiki torches and the tiny buckets of repellent scattered about the deck. The air soon filled with a citrusy scent that kept all but the most insistent insects at bay.

By the time Belle put the lighter away, Kim was stepping onto the porch in her pajamas. Her slippers made scuffing noises on the wooden slats as, wine stems dangling from her hands, she sauntered across the deck.

"Do you know what this is all about?" she asked while she arranged the glasses on the table.

"She didn't tell you? She's your sister," Belle said, her tone implying guilt. "I asked, but all I got out of her was, 'Carmen.'"

"Huh. I guess it's important then. It better be." Cinching the belt on her robe, Kim sank onto a chair. "My alarm is set for five. Craig's picking me up at seven so we can go to the rental place in Orlando and get the tents for the reunion." Her fiancé had gotten a deal on them, thanks to his many business connections.

Footsteps hurried toward them on the path from the parking area. Amy's distraught voice floated in the still air. "At least there wasn't an ambulance parked out front. That's something to be thankful for."

Seconds later, she and Diane sped around the corner of the house.

"Is Aunt Margaret all right?" The flickering candlelight spilled onto Diane's face, where it highlighted the worry lines that crisscrossed her brow.

"Mama's fine," Belle assured the new arrivals. "Everyone is fine."

"This is about Carmen," Kim said, using their code word for the treasure Diane and Nat had unearthed on the inn's property.

"Whew. That's a relief." Amy collapsed into a chair with a sigh.

"What about Car—" Diane's head swiveled. "No one's going to overhear us," she declared. "What about the treasure?"

"That's what we all want to know," Belle answered. "Jen's the one with the answers."

As if that were her cue, Jen stepped onto the porch trailed by Nat, who immediately moved to the table and began filling glasses from one of the two bottles she carried.

"Okay, Jen. We're all here. What's going on?" Kim challenged her sister.

"I have bad news," Jen whispered breathlessly. "The word about Carmen is out."

Nat's hand jerked. Wine sloshed onto the table. "You told Caleb?"

"Honestly, Jen?" Belle snatched a wad of napkins from the dispenser. "Why would you do that?" Shaking her head in disbelief, she helped Nat mop up the mess.

"Where were you? Did anyone else overhear? Is the Channel 2 news van going to be parked outside my door tomorrow?" Diane scanned the skies as if she thought the station's helicopter might appear.

"No—wait. That's not what happened," Jen protested.

"Maybe we can swear Caleb to secrecy." Kim either hadn't heard her sister's denials or chose to ignore them. "I don't know him well myself, but Craig vouched for him. I'm sure if we explained to him how important it was to keep the news under wraps, he'd help us."

"I don't know," Amy said doubtfully. "If we

can't keep the secret, how can we expect an outsider to?"

"He would, but Caleb's not the problem." Jen rapped her knuckles firmly on the glass tabletop. "Caleb's not the problem," she repeated when she had everyone's attention. "Denise Borders is the problem. And it's not just her. To hear her talk, everybody in town knows."

Belle hardly thought that was true. If the discovery of a ten-million-dollar stash of gold coins on the Dane property had been the hot topic at the Pirate's Gold Diner, hordes of reporters would already be camped out on the front lawn. Her sense of urgency fading, she suggested, "Maybe you need to back up a step and tell us exactly what happened."

She held her glass without drinking while they all let Jen take a moment to gather her thoughts. Belle noted that her cousin's breath came evenly now that she'd had a chance to slow down after rushing around so much. Her dark eyes were clear and focused. Though a tiny frown marred her otherwise smooth features, Jen didn't look guilty. At least, she didn't look like someone who'd spoken out of school and was trying to justify her actions.

Standing at the head of the table, Jen took a sip of wine and set her glass on the table. "Okay," she said in a calm, steady voice. "Here's what happened. Caleb and I were at the Pirate's Gold Diner when Denise…"

For the next ten minutes, they listened closely as Jen gave a blow-by-blow account of the ill-fated dinner date. When she finished, no one spoke for a long minute. Wondering if the others didn't know what to say any more than she did, Belle scanned the expressions on the faces of her cousins. As near as she could tell, they were all in various states of shock.

At last, Kim blinked slowly, like someone might if they were waking from a nap. "So the word is out, then?"

"According to Denise," Diane corrected. Her worried expression deepened. "That woman loves to spread gossip."

"True." Amy swirled the wine in her glass while she spoke. "Remember last year when the whole town thought I was putting Sweet Cakes up for sale?" The rumor had put a serious dent in her sales. No one wanted to order a wedding cake from a bakery that might go out of business. "It didn't take much effort to trace the story back to Denise. She was the only one who knew I met with that real estate broker from down south."

"Samuel told me Denise waited on him when he stopped at the diner for lunch the day he arrived in Emerald Bay," Nat said. "By Sunday, when he was introduced to the church as the youth pastor, everyone already knew his entire life's story."

"Let's not be too hard on Denise. Sure, she's the go-to person for juicy gossip," Kim acknowledged. "But look at all the good she does. She organized a meal train when Aunt Margaret came home from the hospital. I think there still might be a casserole or two left in the freezer."

Amy's mouth slanted to one side in grudging respect. "If Habitat for Humanity needs volunteers or the Little League wants to start a scholarship program for kids who can't afford the registration fees, they only have to contact one person—Denise. Before you can blink twice, she'll have a collection jar at the cash register and people all over town will be signing up or pulling out their wallets."

Wondering aloud, Nat shifted in her chair. "Who started the rumor about the treasure, though?"

"Gossip usually starts from a kernel of truth and grows from there," Jen observed.

"I know." Grinning, Diane snapped her fingers. "Denise overheard someone talking about the treasure hunt we held at the gender reveal party. Someone else questioned the renovations we've made at the inn lately. She put two and two together. Voilà! A rumor was born."

"We'll probably never know," Belle interjected before anyone could heap unnecessary blame on Denise. "I can name at least ten people who know about the treasure. More, if we count the auctioneers who are vying for the privilege of handling the sale." Her gaze shifted between Amy and Diane. "I suspect your brother would have a very difficult time keeping such a huge secret from his pregnant wife. And rightfully so."

Her tone bordering on defensive, Diane said, "I promised not to say anything to Tim. Not until the deed, as they say, is done. I've kept that promise, but..." She took a breath. "But it's one of the hardest things I've ever done."

Kim twisted her engagement ring. "I haven't told Craig. I don't plan to, not until he signs the prenup."

"Our situation is different, but I'm not telling Jason." Belle folded her arms across her chest in a protective gesture. "We're still finding our way in this relationship. At this point, discussing our finances would only cloud the issue."

"If Max has heard anything about it, he hasn't mentioned it to me. I'd like to keep it that way," Amy said.

"My point is," Belle continued, "it doesn't really matter who spilled the beans. Word was bound to get out."

Jen tugged on one earlobe. "What are we going to do about it, though?"

Belle shrugged. "There's not much we can do. The coins and jewels are safe right where they are for now." She looked to Diane for confirmation.

The accountant nodded. "I'd say a bank vault ranks right up there with Fort Knox."

"And I'd say that's pretty safe," Amy agreed.

Belle quickly reviewed where they stood as far as the sale. "Wyatt has finalized the provenance." Not only had the coin dealer matched the coins and jewelry to bills of lading for the *Nuestra Señora del Carmen*, he'd also documented their recovery using Diane's notes and the pictures Nat had taken. "Mama has narrowed the auction houses down to two. She'll make a final decision this week. They'll take possession of the coins and jewelry right away. Then all we have to do is wait to see what the collection brings at sale."

Diane tapped her fingernails on the tabletop. "When do you think they'll hold the auction?"

"Any day but the eighteenth works for me," Amy said. Turning to the others, she said,

"That's the opening day for Sweet Cakes 2."

"We haven't forgotten." Not that they would, Kim assured her. The whole family planned to turn out in support of the event.

"About the auction, though," Belle said, addressing Amy's concern. "It will probably take several months to get the collection listed in the house's catalogue. I'd say late June at the earliest."

"That's a long time to keep a secret." Kim pursed her lips. "In the meantime, what do we say if anyone asks us about it?"

"The treasure, you mean?" Belle faced Jen. "How did you handle it with Denise?"

"She took me completely by surprise," Jen said, looking slightly stricken. "I didn't know what to say so I, uh, I laughed out loud. I told her that was the best joke I'd ever heard."

Laughter built in Belle's chest. "Oh, my goodness, Jen. That's brilliant." She chortled. "I bet that shut her down."

"Yep. She swelled up like a puffer fish and stormed off." The tiny speckled species could inflate to nearly twice its size whenever it felt threatened.

"I'm not sure I could actually laugh in someone's face," Amy said.

"Sidestep, then. Or hedge," Diane suggested

quickly. "These are our neighbors and friends we're talking about. Sooner or later, they're going to know the truth—the whole truth. So we probably want to avoid telling out-and-out lies, if we can."

"Smart," Kim declared.

"Then we're all agreed. We'll be like the three wise monkeys." Belle cupped her fingers over her eyes. "See no evil." She moved her hands to her ears. "Hear no evil." Covering her mouth, she finished, "Speak no evil."

At the head of the table, Jen picked up her glass and held it aloft. "To keeping our secret a little longer," she chimed.

Glasses clinked softly. They sipped and absorbed all that had happened for a few minutes before Belle stirred.

"Um, speaking of secrets..." She paused to give the others a moment to mentally shift gears. "I need to tell you all something I've been keeping under my hat for a few days. This..." She shot Jen a quick smile. "This definitely falls into the good news category."

"Oh?" Jen leaned forward.

Refusing to make it sound like a bigger deal than it already was, Belle said, "The Emeralds— Daclan and I—have been asked to appear on *The Newsy Morning Show*."

Amy gasped audibly. At the same time, she pressed one hand over her heart. "The one with Saundra Carter and Wilton Weathers?"

"The very one." The nationally syndicated show was currently ranked as the top morning news show in the country.

"I *love* Saundra Carter," Amy gushed. "I watch the show every morning while the bread is baking and I'm getting ready for work." In recent weeks, she'd let her other bakers take over responsibility for the white and whole wheat loaves that were the mainstay of the bakery. A few of her recipes, however, had taken years to perfect. Those, she made herself, drinking in the rich, nutty scent of the seed bread or the slightly sweeter aroma of her buttermilk rye before the sun came up each day.

"That Wilton isn't hard on the eyes, either," piped Jen.

"Simmer down, Jen," Belle teased, though she had to admit, the host's good looks were at least partially responsible for the show's great ratings.

"Oh, my goodness, Aunt Belle. That's fabulous news." Nat's excitement glowed in her eyes. "When do you go on?"

"They wanted us this month, but I put them off until after school lets out." She thought Nat's eyes would pop out of their sockets at that, so she took a moment to remind her niece and the others. "I promised Daclan's mom I wouldn't let his playing interfere with his schoolwork. So, jaunting off to Nashville for a week isn't going to happen until summer break."

"Ding-ding! Shopping trip!" Amy squealed. "You need a stunning new outfit to wear on TV."

"I hardly think so." Though she'd given her previous assistant an armload of dresses, she could open her own upscale consignment shop with the designer originals that remained in her closet. Still, she couldn't help it when doubt nibbled at her smile. "To tell the truth, I've been so focused on choosing the songs Daclan and I will perform on the show that I haven't given our clothes much thought." She turned to Nat. "Can you help me sort through my wardrobe and find something appropriate?"

"I'll do you one better than that," the younger woman replied earnestly. "I'll go through everything and pull together a few outfits. You can choose the one you like best."

"Whew." Belle swept the back of her hand over her forehead. "That's a load off my mind." She grasped Nat's hand and gave it a quick squeeze. "I don't know what I'd do without you."

But as the others plied her with more questions about the upcoming show, Belle couldn't quite shake the feeling that something she'd said was responsible for the strained expression on her niece's face.

"Knock, knock." Belle peered through the open door into the suite Nat shared with her mother. Her niece sat at the small secretary, where she'd apparently been sorting correspondence into tidy stacks.

"Oh, hi, Aunt Belle." Nat leapt to her feet like a jack-in-the-box. "Are you ready?"

"Girl, I am bushed. And I'm so, so sorry I couldn't get here sooner." Nat had texted her that morning, asking if they could meet at lunch to look over the outfits she'd assembled from an admittedly extensive wardrobe. But here it was, nearly five o'clock. Between practice sessions, her stepped-up exercise regimen—the camera really did add ten pounds—and the new song she was writing, she'd completely lost track of the time.

"It's okay, Aunt Belle. I know you're busy." Nat gave a nervous laugh. "I haven't exactly been sitting around, twiddling my thumbs." As if she needed to prove herself, she ran down an agenda that included making the deliveries for Sweet Cakes, covering the front desk while Jen took a lunch break, preparing press releases for The Emeralds and juggling the group's schedule to accommodate the upcoming appearance on *The Newsy Morning Show.* "I was just finishing up with your fan mail." She waved a hand at the stacks of letters and glossy color photographs of Belle on stage with Daclan.

"All that, plus you pulled some outfits for me to look at? Where do you find so much energy?" Belle asked when Nat finished.

"Must be something Mom puts in the tea." She glanced at the pitcher that sat on a nearby dresser. "Want some?"

"No, thanks. My dad always said that stuff made his ears wiggle." Much as she loved it, Belle stuck to plain water, preferring to limit her sugar intake to a single glass of wine at night. Which didn't stop her from eyeing the sweat that beaded on the outside of Nat's glass.

Oh, to have the metabolism of youth again.

Aware that she only had an hour before Daclan arrived for their evening practice session, she scanned the room. Four zippered bags hung from the back of Nat's closet. "Are those the outfits you wanted to show me?" she asked with a nod.

"That's them," Nat said in a rush. "If they're not right, I'll try again. Let me pull them down for you." In her haste, she bumped the desk hard enough to rock her glass. She stopped to steady it.

"Don't bother," Belle said, wondering what made Nat so jumpy today. "I can see them just fine right where they are."

She strode across the room. Unzipping the first bag, she pushed the black plastic aside to find an A-line leather skirt that ended at mid-calf, a short denim jacket with a beautifully embroidered collar and cuffs, and an emerald-green shirt.

"This color will pop under the TV studio's bright lights," she murmured, studying the blouse. She ran her fingers over the sleeve of the jacket she'd spotted on display in Saks shortly before her fortunes shifted. She'd fallen in love with the piece and had to have it despite the half-dozen similar ones already hanging in her closet. Other than modeling it for the women in the alterations department, though, she'd never even had it on. Seeing how the shirt and jacket complemented the leather skirt, she had to ask why. Paired with low-heeled boots and a few simple jewelry pieces, the outfit conveyed exactly the right look for a rising star on the Christian music scene.

"Nat, I swear, you hit a home run on your first try," she declared. Satisfied that her niece had chosen the perfect outfit, she prepared to hurry back to the music studio.

"I appreciate that, but hold up." Nat twirled a finger through a loose curl. "Don't you want to look at the others?"

Belle tilted her head, considering. Her niece seemed overeager to have her look at the remaining selections. And, seriously, what harm would it do? It wasn't like she'd have to waste time trying things on. Every item she owned had been altered to a perfect fit before she added it to her collection. More to humor her niece than for any other reason, she tugged on the zipper of the next garment bag.

"Oh!" she exclaimed. If she'd thought Nat couldn't do better than her first choice, she'd been wrong. The cobalt blue Carolina Herrera shift was simply stunning. Better still, the finely woven, cream-colored wrap Nat had draped over the dress provided a necessary ingredient Belle hadn't even known was missing. She shook her head. As with the previous outfit, Nat had factored in both the harsh studio lights and her own coloring. The result was sheer perfection.

When the sides of the third bag parted to reveal an ivory shirt and sage-green Ralph Lauren slacks, she gasped, "My goodness, Nat. You have a flair for this!"

The high-waisted pants with their loose fit would add an illusion of height to her short stature, while a batwing wrap by a designer whose name escaped Belle would lend the entire ensemble an air of sophistication. Nevertheless, she frowned. "I'm not sure..." she began.

Nat's face colored. "I thought you could wear the pants to the studio and bring one of the first two outfits to change into for the actual taping," she hurried to suggest.

"Of course you did. That's an excellent idea." Belle smiled her approval. So far, Nat had chosen three winners. Curious to see what else her niece had in store for her, she moved on to the last bag.

"Just so you know, that one's not to wear on air," Nat said before Belle had a chance to tug on the zipper. "I thought you might want something more traditional in case you took meetings while you were in Nashville."

Belle wished she shared her niece's optimism. Record executives weren't exactly beating down her door these days. Deciding it couldn't hurt to be prepared, she looked inside the final bag.

Speechless, she stared at a peach blouse that would work beautifully with her coloring. Beneath that lay a charcoal business suit by Prada that had long been one of her favorites.

"Did I guess wrong?" Nat asked hesitantly.

Belle started. "No. Not at all. I was actually thinking that you know my tastes and preferences even better than I do. These four ensembles are exactly what I need. I'll take them all with me to Nashville."

"Oh, good," Nat whispered. Obvious relief rounded her shoulders. The faintest stutter marred her usual self-confident manner when she said, "I'll, um, I'll pack the jewelry and shoes for each outfit separately and mark it so you know what goes with what."

Belle felt her brows knit, something that happened far too often now that she no longer followed her old regimen of Botox injections. Turning from the closet, she studied her niece. To say Nat looked slightly disheveled would be an understatement. Her blond curls, which she normally tamed into softly falling waves, stuck out in tufts. She must have grabbed clothes at random this morning because her plaid shorts absolutely did not go with that tie-dyed T-shirt any better than the mismatched flip-flops she wore. Now that she thought about it, Nat had seemed ill at ease ever since she'd stepped into the room.

Her concern mounting, she asked, "Is something wrong?"

"No." Nat exhaled an unsteady breath. "Yes. Um…" She blew out another breath. "Do you mind if I ask you a question?

"Of course not. Shoot." Belle twisted her wrist to check the time on her watch. Though she needed to run through her music once more before Daclan arrived, she had a few minutes to spare.

"Well, I was wondering…" Nat blinked several times as if she was trying to come to grips with something important.

"Yes?" Had she done or said something to upset the girl? Wracking her brain, she hoped not. So far, she and Nat had worked together like a well-oiled machine. She'd hate for anything to disrupt their flow.

"I have to ask, um, how did the people on *The Newsy Morning Show* hear about The Emeralds? I'm almost positive I didn't send them one of your press releases. I probably should have, but I didn't. Do you think one of the staff stumbled across your new website?"

The questions seemed to come from out of nowhere, and Belle pressed her lips together while she tried to figure out what had prompted them. She'd certainly been happy with Nat's efforts to promote The Emeralds. The publicity she'd generated had landed the group several gigs throughout the state. As for the awesome website she'd designed, it was drawing more and more traffic every week. As successful as those efforts had been, though, none of them had captured the news show hosts' attention.

She toed one of the floorboards. "It was just a lucky break. So much about the music business is, you know? You drop in during a telethon for a cause you support. A year later, one of the other—better-known—performers asks you to tour with them." That had happened to her once, and several years later, she'd returned the favor.

"I get that, but do you know what, exactly, stirred the pot, so to speak, this time?"

Not sure why the answer seemed so important to her niece, Belle nodded. "I do. It was Jason. He's a regular guest on *Today's Top 10*." The radio show, hosted by Carly Adams, was hugely popular. "Two weeks ago, as the segment was winding down, Carly asked Jason what music he tuned into for pleasure. He said he'd been listening to Christian rock lately and mentioned The Emeralds. He didn't think much of it at the time, but that afternoon, staff from *Newsy* contacted him, wanting more information about us. And the rest, as they say, is history." Belle's nose scrunched. "Why do you ask?"

"That's what I was afraid of." Nat sank onto her chair as if she didn't have the strength left to stand. "I've been thinking you and Daclan deserve more than what I can do for you. This proves it."

"What?" Belle's voice climbed an octave. She took a second to regroup. Not only was her niece the best personal assistant she'd ever had—and she'd had plenty—but Nat was a skilled publicist. Why would she doubt it?

Belle's thoughts stuttered. Back in the day, when she'd moved in fame and fortune's upper stratosphere, she'd been surrounded by people who jumped to do her bidding, often before she even asked. Though things were different these days, maybe she'd taken her niece's help for granted. If so, that was a mistake she'd fix right here, right now. "You know I'd be absolutely lost without you, don't you?

A small, wan smile tugged at Nat's lips. "I've loved working with you, too. I even think I helped get The Emeralds off to a good start."

"You most certainly did." Belle's hand found her hip and rested there. "We'd still be begging

Pastor Dave to let us sing at the Wednesday night prayer services if it hadn't been for you."

Of The Emeralds' first ten gigs, Nat had lined up nine of them. Word of mouth had spread after that, and their calendar had begun to fill as if by magic. But those first few appearances had been crucial. In fact, Nat had done such a great job that, if they were in New York, she'd worry about losing the younger woman to another celebrity.

The thought chilled her. A good assistant was hard to come by, but the young woman wouldn't be the first to leave for greener pastures. Not sure she wanted to know the answer, she eyed her niece. "Have you gotten a better offer?"

"No."

The answer rolled so effortlessly off Nat's tongue that Belle had to accept it as truth. That still didn't tell her why the girl would even consider leaving. "So why would you quit?"

"Duh." Nat blew out a breath. "Because you're on the cusp of hitting the big time. Everybody knows it. Once you and Daclan appear on *The Newsy Morning Show*, the offers are going to pour in. All the other morning shows will be begging you to come on air with them. Record deals are sure to follow. Don't you think you need someone more experienced to guide you through all that? I know I would." Nat's eyes watered.

Belle sank onto the guest chair beside the desk. "That's what's bothering you? You don't think you can do the job?" Which was ridiculous. So far, Nat had handled every challenge with poise and grace. There was no reason to think she wouldn't continue to do so.

"I can handle it." Showing more of her usual spunk, Nat swiped her eyes and crossed her arms across her chest. "I just think you might want someone better. Someone who knew to send your press releases to the people at *Newsy* in the first place. Someone who would have already contacted all the morning talk shows. Someone who *knows* people at those stations. I'm not that person. I don't want to be the one who holds you back."

"You wouldn't be. That's my job," Belle assured her niece.

"Say what?" Nat's blue eyes widened. "Aunt Belle, you're great. Your voice is as strong as it ever was. You're not going to hold anyone back."

"Oh, but I am," Belle said firmly. "I have to." When confusion swam in Nat's eyes, she wondered aloud. "How can I put this?" Bowing her head, she took a minute to ask for the right words to explain her role as the gatekeeper.

When she looked up, she met Nat's gaze head-on.

"I don't sing for the fame and the fortune anymore. I've had all that. The high-powered agent. The record deals. The yes-men and the sycophants. That's not the future I see for The Emeralds. I mean, yeah, it'd be nice to make a little money. I'm not going to lie—this past year has been tight. But I'm doing a little songwriting on the side. With any luck, I'll make enough from that to keep a roof over my head. To be perfectly honest, though, I almost turned the people at *Newsy* down."

Shock rippled across Nat's features. "Why on earth would you do that?"

Belle lifted her hands, palms aimed toward the ceiling. "To protect Daclan. He's young and so impressionable. He needs time to decide whether or not a career in music is really what he wants. And if so, the kind of music he wants to play. See, the thing about making it big is you get locked in. Everybody—your agent, your producer, your fans—they all demand the same thing from you. Over and over and over again." Belle rolled her eyes. She'd been there, done that.

"Another 'Jimmy, Jimmy, Oh'?" Nat asked.

"Exactly." The girl was quick. Belle gave her

that much. "I was only a couple of years older than Daclan is now when I cut that record. It was the best and the worst thing I ever did," she said wistfully. "After that, it didn't matter if I could sing 'Casta Diva' like Maria Callas or 'Tiptoe Through the Tulips' like Tiny Tim. After 'Jimmy,' pop was the only thing people wanted from me."

Nat cupped her jaw in her hand and thought for a moment before she said, "I can see that. Didn't Mr. Medford want you to sing 'Jimmy' at the Spring Fling?"

"That he did." Belle chortled. Daclan's father had been quite insistent. She cleared her throat. "Right now Daclan loves Christian rock, and I'm ever so thankful for the chance to work with him. But I have to ask—how much of that is his parents' influence? As he gets older—when he goes off to college—will he develop other interests? Take his music in a different direction? It's important to give him the time and freedom he needs to make his own choices. And that means not letting The Emeralds get too big, too fast. 'Cause that money? That success?" She shook her head and sighed. "They're stronger than the bars of any jail cell."

"So you don't want The Emeralds to be successful?" Doubt filled Nat's voice.

"Well, who doesn't want some success?" Belle smiled. "But not at Daclan's expense. Which is why we'll only perform on weekends and school breaks. And why, if and when we're offered a recording contract, I'll refuse to sign a multi-album deal." One that would lock Daclan in for the foreseeable future.

Nat ran a hand through her hair. "Why go on the *Newsy* show at all, then? Why didn't you turn them down?"

Belle shrugged. "Christian rock isn't exactly mainstream. This is an opportunity to bring our music onto the national stage and, by doing that, to bring people closer to the Lord. Which is what it's all about, isn't it? Believe me, though. I really had to pray about it." She paused.

Nat's gaze drifted to the garment bags. "Well, at least you have the right clothes for the show."

Belle smiled. "That I do, thanks to you." She clapped her hands together. "Now can we forget this nonsense about quitting?"

"If you're really sure..." Nat's voice still sounded doubtful.

Sensing the girl needed more reassurance, Belle reached out. Grasping her niece by the shoulders, she stared into Nat's blue eyes. "If I haven't said it enough, I appreciate everything you do for me personally, as well as for The

Emeralds. I really, really want you to stay on," she insisted.

"Well, if you really, really want me to, I guess I will," Nat said with a warm grin.

"Excellent!" Seeing her niece's usual buoyant nature reappear, Belle breathed a sigh of relief. Then, straightening, she checked her watch. Aware that Daclan would arrive soon, she added, "I have to get back down to the studio for a practice session, but I'll let you know as soon as I firm up the date with the *Newsy* people. In the meantime, be thinking of travel arrangements and hotel accommodations for…" She stopped to count. "I think there'll be five of us. Daclan and one of his parents. Jen—she'll need to work with their sound engineers. You. And me, of course."

"Me?" Nat's brow wrinkled. "You want me to make the trip to Nashville?"

"Of course," Belle said, her voice firm enough to eliminate even the slightest doubt. "You're part of the team."

"Okay. Got it." Nat's smile widened slightly as she jotted something down on a notepad.

Glad to catch a glimpse of her niece's usual take-charge attitude, Belle said goodbye and hurried out the door. On her way to the cottage she'd turned into a music studio, her footsteps slowed. She refused to kid herself into thinking that Nat would stick around forever. Sooner or later, her niece would want to strike out on her own, forge her own way in the world. When that day came, Belle promised she'd offer all the encouragement the girl needed to spread her wings and fly.

Seven

Amy

"Whew," Amy said. She waved her hand, trying to dispel the paint fumes and the smell of sawdust that floated above the tongue-and-groove flooring of the former Bath Cottage in Sebastian's shopping district. "We need to give this place a good airing out before we bring in the first cookie or cupcake." Otherwise, the baked goods she'd worked so hard to create would absorb the odors like a sponge.

"Don't worry. We will." A sharp zip sounded as Max's measuring tape retracted into its holder. "We'll open all the doors and windows as soon as I get the display cases installed. By the time you're ready to fill them, you'll never know this place was a construction zone."

Amy cast a worried glance around the shop. Would they really be ready on time? Less than two weeks remained before the soft opening, yet the display cases hadn't even been delivered. Drop cloths still covered the floors. Behind a wall lined with racks that would eventually hold the day's selection of breads and rolls, the break room stood empty except for the commercial refrigerator where she and Deborah planned to store extra cakes, eclairs, Danishes and fruit tarts.

She eyed the beach scene that had ever so slowly and surely taken shape on the white walls. Because the new shop didn't have the square footage to accommodate a café, she'd asked the artist to forgo the treasure chest and sunken ship that kept children enthralled at the Emerald Bay location. Here, they'd kept the design simpler, with gulls and pelicans soaring through clear blue skies while sea creatures dotted the turquoise water beneath foamy white waves. She studied a dolphin that was so lifelike, Amy swore she could almost hear its high-pitched whistles.

"You're never going to be ready on time," it seemed to say.

"When...when will the cabinets get here?" she asked hesitantly. She hated to push Max. He'd been going practically nonstop ever since she and Deborah had signed the contract. Each evening, after he finished working for his regular clients, he'd driven to Sebastian and put in another day's work on the new storefront. He had to be exhausted.

"I was hoping to surprise you but..." Max pulled his cell phone out of a back pocket. After scrolling through several aps, he punched two buttons in quick succession. A pulsing red dot appeared on a map on the phone's screen. "The truck is crossing the causeway as we speak. It should be here in, oh, fifteen minutes?"

"Really?" A thrill shot through Amy. She tugged her lower lip between her teeth. "Maybe I should stick around. To, you know, make sure they sent the right ones this time." She didn't know which of them had been more disappointed—her or Max—when the first delivery had contained the wrong cases.

"Relax. Everything's under control. I stopped in at the plant and looked over your order when I was in Orlando last week. I just double-checked the measurements." Max pulled an inch or two of metal tape from the dispenser and let it snap back into place. "These will fit. I guarantee it."

Amy hesitated. "Won't you need help unloading them?"

"That's why the good Lord gave me muscles."

Chuckling, Max struck a he-man pose. "Besides, weren't you planning to introduce yourself to the neighbors today?"

Amy slapped her palm to her forehead. In her worry over getting things shipshape in time and her added excitement over the arrival of the much-anticipated display cases, her plans had flown straight out the window. But Max was right. She'd intended to spend the better part of the day visiting each of the two dozen stores and offices clustered around the lake in the center of their little shopping district. It'd be a shame to let the trays of goodies she'd prepared for her neighbors go to waste.

"Tell you what," Max said. "You go play nice with the other business owners while I take care of the display cases. With any luck, we'll both finish up about the same time."

She couldn't really find any fault with his plan. If she stuck around here, she'd only be in the way. "Have I told you lately that you're the best?" She rose on tiptoe and kissed Max's grizzled cheek.

With a low growl, he pulled her closer. "We can do better than that," he said, his eyes going dark.

When his lips met hers, she had to agree. She relished the protective grip of his two strong arms, the softness of her breasts pressed against the firm planes of his muscular chest. He tasted of coffee and mint, a blend she'd come to love and could never get enough of. She clung to him until a soft beep from his phone drove them apart.

"That's the driver. They're five minutes out," he said, breaking the kiss. "I have a few things to finish up before they get here." He gently kissed the tip of her nose.

"I'll go, then," she said, though leaving was the last thing she wanted to do. "I'll have my cell phone. Text me if you run into any problems."

Aware that Max stood in the open doorway watching her go, she put a little swing in her step on her way to the van she'd left at the curb. She felt suddenly adrift when, by the time she'd reached the double doors at the back, he'd ducked back inside. Seconds later, she heard the whir of a belt sander and knew he'd returned to work. She blew him a kiss anyway—just in case—and retrieved one of the trays she'd slid onto the delivery van's shelves before she left Sweet Cakes this morning. Beneath its plastic cover, blond and chocolate brownies wreathed a selection that included several of the bakery's most popular cookies. The bright red bow she'd placed on top anchored a business card for Sweet Cakes 2 to the lid.

Satisfied that all was in order, she stepped smartly toward the store next to hers. The cottage, like most of the buildings in the popular shopping area, had once been someone's home, and the exterior displayed a cozy charm. A few minutes later, the tray balanced in one hand, she pulled open the door of the women's clothing store. She grinned, getting a quick impression of a place she'd like to visit before embarking on a weekend cruise from one of Florida's many ports.

"Welcome to Sea Togs," called a cheery brunette from a checkout counter that, with its tin sides and rough wooden planks, looked like it might have come straight out of a tiki hut. "Have a look around. I'll be with you shortly. Here you go, Ms...."

The brunette's voice faded into the background while Amy admired the faux thatched roof above the counter. Just beyond it, the fronds of a large fern dripped down from atop a sunglass display shaped like a palm tree. She spotted two more palm trees among clothes racks that held bikinis, brightly colored casual wear and sundresses. The racks had been spaced far enough apart on the shiny wood floors to give customers plenty of room to browse. Sandals and colorful beach bags were displayed along one wall. Near the back, a selection of floor-length dresses provided options for last-minute shoppers who needed gowns for the formal dinner onboard ship.

"I love your decor," Amy said after the customer left, carrying her purchases in a turquoise blue bag tied off with a coral ribbon. "It makes me eager to book my next trip to some exotic tropical island."

"Thanks. It's a work in progress, but I like it." The brunette's focus narrowed on the tray in Amy's hands. "I'm sorry, but we don't allow solicitors in here," she said in a not unkind tone.

"Oh, no. These aren't for sale. They're a gift. For you." Amy thrust the platter forward.

"Why?" Her hands remained at her sides while confusion clouded the brunette's gaze.

Amy felt her cheeks warm. This wasn't going at all as well as she'd hoped. She took a breath and tried again. "I'm sorry. I should have intro-duced myself first. I'm Amy. Amy Peterson, your new neighbor. My business partner and I are turning the old Bath Cottage into a storefront for our bakery."

"Hmmm." The salesclerk's lips pursed. "I had noticed someone working over there." She stared in the direction of Sweet Cakes 2 as if she could see through the walls into the other building.

"I'm sorry. I don't mean to be rude, but I sure hope you know what you're doing. This will be the third business that's gone into that location since I've been here. They've all failed," she said flatly.

Amy tensed. She understood her neighbor's concerns, but she was no rank beginner. "This will be my second bakery. Our main store is in Emerald Bay. Maybe you've heard of it?" She hated the uncertainty that had crept into her voice when she said, "Sweet Cakes?"

The name had no sooner left Amy's lips than the woman reeled back a step, her entire demeanor instantly undergoing a change for the better.

"Seriously! You own Sweet Cakes?" Her dark eyes turned dreamy. "You have the best fruitcake. My Christmas wouldn't be complete without one. I wish you made them all year round."

"That's always good to hear." Amy relaxed. Lowering her voice to conspiratorial levels, she said, "Next holiday, buy two and stick one in the freezer. Properly wrapped, fruitcake will stay good for up to a year. And take this." She reached into her pocket and drew out a coupon. "It's good for fifteen percent off any purchase you make at either Sweet Cakes location. Special orders are included, and there's no expiration date, so hang on to it until next Christmas."

"Oh, I definitely will." After taking the slip of paper, the woman tucked it into her pocket. Only then did she extend her hand. "Sorry if I wasn't all warm and fuzzy at first. We get a lot of first-time business owners in Sebastian. They rarely last. I'm glad someone with a proven track record bought the place next door. I'm Rebecca Hold, by the way. I own Sea Togs. I've been here going on ten years."

"It's so nice to meet you, Rebecca." After they shook, Amy held out the tray. Her smile widened when the owner of the clothing store accepted her gift.

"Oooh!" Rebecca peered through the clear plastic cover at the selection of goodies. "Let's see. I'll save one of those brownies for my dessert tonight and give the rest to my customers." She gave Amy a chagrined look. "If I eat these all myself, I'll gain ten pounds."

"At least you know the best place to shop if you need to *expand* your wardrobe." Grinning at the play on words, Amy gestured toward a rack of capri pants and tops similar to the ones Rebecca was wearing.

Rebecca's answering laugh rang through the store as she carried the tray to the counter and left it there. She was on her way back to the spot where Amy stood when, her brow furrowing, she looked in the direction of the new bakery.

"Hmmm," she said again. "You know, I considered your building before I bought this one, but I needed more space. Are you sure it's big enough for a bakery?"

"Yes and no," Amy said. She'd anticipated the question and hurried to explain. "We'll offer cookies and sweet rolls and breads here, but we'll continue making everything in Emerald Bay. I'll mostly hold down the fort there, while Deborah—she and I run Sweet Cakes together—she'll stock this location daily. And if anyone wants a cake decorated for a birthday or special occasion, she'll be able to do that here, too."

"That sounds absolutely ruinous for my diet." Rebecca patted a slim hip. "When's the big day?"

"Week after next," Amy said. "We'll hold a soft opening Wednesday through Friday. The Grand Opening will be on Saturday the eighteenth. The mayor suggested we hold a ribbon-cutting ceremony before he declares us officially open for business."

"Hmmm," Rebecca said in what clearly had to be a habit. "Our mayor does love his publicity. Don't be surprised if the local news van is there."

"That'd be awesome," Amy said while

making a mental note to give the rest of her family a heads-up. "We'll have live music and giveaways throughout the day. We'll also give free cupcakes to the first hundred people who walk through the doors."

"Sounds like fun." Rebecca's brows rose. "You know what? I'll hold a sidewalk sale that day, too. In fact, we should get all the businesses around the lake to do the same. Really make a day of it. I'll talk to Clara Whitley—she's the president of our little business association. She'll spread the word to all the others."

"Gee. That's awfully generous of you," Amy said. A stop at the property office was on her agenda today, but it never hurt to have an established member put in a good word. As for Rebecca's sidewalk sale, the more foot traffic they could generate for the opening of Sweet Cakes 2, the better.

"What can I say?" The shop owner raised her shoulders in a graceful shrug. "Us small business owners have to work together. You know what they say, 'A rising tide lifts all boats.'"

And, as she left the shop a few minutes later, Amy could only pray that Rebecca was right.

The next shop on Amy's list was so different from Sea Togs that she wondered if the owners had designed it that way on purpose. Where the dress shop definitely had a tropical vibe, no one in The Glass Monkey had paid much attention to the overall décor. Opposite the rickety checkout counter, plywood sheets divided the shop into a rabbit warren of tiny cubicles separated by aisles barely wide enough for customers to walk down in a single file. Each cubicle housed the work of a different artist or crafter, but if there was a rhyme or reason behind who got which booth, Amy couldn't decipher it. The result was a confusing mix of crocheted doilies and doll clothes across from beaded jewelry, of stark, black-and-white prints displayed next to a collection of hand-thrown pottery.

She tore her gaze from the disorganized layout, plastered a cheery smile over her concerns and turned to the elderly couple who hadn't looked up from a crossword puzzle that occupied their attention. So thin that their clothes seemed too big for their bony frames, the duo perched on tall stools while they bickered over a seven-letter word for *foundation*. Wondering if the incense that smoldered from a holder at the end of the counter had suppressed their appetites, Amy waited until the woman filled the squares with *bedrock* before she cleared her throat.

Determined to avoid the mistakes she'd

made at Sea Togs, she said, "I'm Amy Peterson, your new neighbor. I own the Sweet Cakes bakery in Emerald Bay, and next week, my business partner and I will be opening a second shop, Sweet Cakes 2, where the old Bath Cottage used to be. I'm visiting all the shops in the area today to introduce myself and also to drop off these free samples of the baked goods we'll carry." She slid the tray onto the counter between an old-fashioned cash register and a modern credit-card reader.

"Oh, look, Carl. Brownies. My favorite." The woman stuck her ink pen in a plastic cup that bristled with a dozen more. A second later, she ran her long, red fingernails along the tray's lid, trying to pry it open.

Carl slid aside the newspaper that had been folded to reveal the crossword puzzle. Adjusting the glasses that threatened to fall off the tip of his nose, he peered intensely at the contents of the tray. "Are any of those peanut butter?" he asked.

"Of course! Who doesn't love a good peanut butter cookie? There are snickerdoodles, frosted sugar cookies and oatmeal raisin, too." When Carl's partner continued to struggle with the lid, Amy tugged the ribbon securing it loose. A sweet, spicy scent warred with the musty smell of the incense when the top slid free.

"I do love a good brownie." The woman chose the largest and took a bite.

Carl leaned closer. "Which one is peanut butter?"

"These three." Amy pointed to cookies that bore the traditional cross-hatched mark.

Carl grabbed one with a shaky hand. Meanwhile, the woman scarfed down her chocolate brownie in three bites. While she helped herself to a blond one, she eyed Amy. "Who did you say you were again?"

Already half in love with the elderly couple, who apparently had big appetites for sweets and little else, Amy chuckled. She quickly ran through her spiel while she tried to ignore the crumbs that littered the craft shop's counter.

"Welp, welcome, Amy," the woman said around a mouthful of brownie. "I'm Agnes, and this here is Carl Byrd. It'll be nice to have a good bakery so close by. That coffee shop down the way only has prepackaged stuff." Agnes's nose wrinkled in disgust. "Nobody wants a scone that's been wrapped in plastic for who knows how long."

"You won't find anything prepackaged at Sweet Cakes 2," Amy assured her. "We plan to stock our shelves with freshly baked items from our main store in Emerald Bay."

"That was mighty fine." Finished with his cookie, Carl smacked his lips and dipped into the tray a second time, this time choosing a sugar cookie covered in swirls of pink icing.

"How long have you and Carl been here?" Amy asked, trying to get a sense of the nearby businesses. From the hodgepodge behind her, she guessed running The Glass Monkey was something of a hobby for Carl and Agnes.

Carl squinted one eye. "Five years? Is that about right?"

"Six, this October," Agnes corrected. "We're both artists. I work with textiles." She pointed to a half-completed piece of needlepoint in a round frame that sat at the end of the counter. "Basketry is Carl's forte. Those are his, right over there."

Amy followed Agnes's nod to a booth where intricate scenes had been woven into baskets made of seagrass and pine needles. Both the weavings and the needlework were so stunning, Amy had no choice but to reevaluate her initial opinion of the shop and its owners.

"The textile museum up in Melbourne used to display our work. It closed a few years ago. More's the pity," Agnes explained. "We opened this space to showcase the work of local artists and, hopefully, help them earn a little bit of money. We also offer classes in the back."

Another nod indicated a doorway Amy hadn't noticed before.

"It's a very, uh, interesting store," Amy said after a brief search for the right word.

"Oh, honey. You might as well be honest. You're not going to hurt our feelings. Is she, Carl?"

"Nope." Carl, who was working on his third cookie, smacked his lips. "One man's Picasso is another man's finger painting." He laughed at his own joke.

"Hey. If you've been here six years, you must be doing something right." Amy smiled at the pair of octogenarians.

"It's a mishmash, but we love it." Agnes's lined face hardened just enough to let Amy glimpse the shrewd businesswoman beneath the facade of folksy good humor. "We've built up a loyal clientele. Members of our little co-op change their displays frequently, so there's always something new to see. That's what brings people in. They're afraid they might miss something." Agnes slipped another brownie from the tray. "Why don't you tell us what really brings you into our store today, sweetheart?"

Amy held up her hands in a sign of innocence. "Just introducing myself and Sweet Cakes 2." She gestured at the tray the pair had plundered. "We'll open unofficially next Wednesday, but our Grand Opening will be that Saturday, the eighteenth. We'll have a lot going on that day. I think some of the other shops might hold a special sale or something then, too. You know Rebecca at Sea Togs?"

Carl sucked his teeth. "We do. She's good folks, Rebecca. When we had that hurricane blow through two years ago, she helped us haul our storm shutters out of the storage unit."

"Bob—he owned The Bath Cottage back then—he helped Carl hang them. But what a waste that was," Agnes complained. Plastic crackled as Agnes replaced the lid over what was left of the brownies and cookies. "By the time we got all the shutters hung, the storm had veered off to the east. We had to take them all back down and store them away till the next time."

Amy let out a long, slow breath. Mid-westerners lived with the threat of tornadoes. Californians built their houses to withstand earthquakes. People up north kept well-stocked pantries in the winter. Prepping for a hurricane was a fact of life in Florida. Personally, she'd rather get ready for a storm that never made landfall than fail to prepare for one that did. But that was just her.

On the other hand, the idea of a shaky Carl standing on a stepladder while he bolted storm panels over his windows was enough to give her nightmares. At least it sounded like Rebecca and the other business owners in the area helped watch out for their elderly neighbors. Silently, she pledged to do her part, as well.

"I think Rebecca's going to hold a sidewalk sale during our Grand Opening."

"Oh, yeah?" Agnes broke off a chunk of brownie and popped it in her mouth. "Looking to drum up more business, is she? That sounds like a good idea." She turned to her partner. "What do you think, Carl?"

"I don't know. Saturday is already our busiest day of the week," the older man mused.

"Can't argue with that." Agnes swept a few crumbs into her hand. They rained into a trash can behind the counter.

Amy might have said more, but the door swung open just then. Carrying large totes, two fashionably dressed women entered the shop.

In an instant, Agnes's attention riveted on the new arrivals. "Good morning, Deidre, Elaine," she called. "Go on in the back and get set up. I'll be with you in just a minute."

When Amy turned back to Agnes to say her goodbyes, the remaining baked goods had disappeared from view, hidden, no doubt, beneath the counter. She managed not to laugh as, reaching into her pocket, she retrieved another coupon, which she slid across the rough plywood surface. "I won't hold you up. I just wanted to give you one more thing. In case you decide to give Sweet Cakes 2 a try," she added, her smile warm.

"Oh, you can count on it," Agnes said. "Those brownies were better than mine, and that's saying something. Mind the store now, Carl," she said, slipping from her perch on a tall stool. "I'll be in the back."

Amy caught a whiff of a musty scent as Agnes, dressed in a flowing caftan, floated by. The smell was unmistakable, even for someone who didn't partake. The mystery of the elderly couple's healthy appetite for sweets solved, Amy swallowed another laugh.

"Where do you want the eclairs?" Amy asked, eager to put down the tray she'd carried from the van parked behind Sweet Cakes 2 through the building to the front of the store. Though six pounds of the cream-filled pastries arranged in neat rows on a parchment-lined sheet of thick, black plastic didn't sound like a lot of weight, she'd kneaded and shaped and baked more loaves of bread in the last twenty-four hours than she usually handled in a week. Not to mention lending Mary and the rest of the bakers a hand with the cookies, pies and other delectable treats they'd prepared for today's Grand Opening.

Tempted to choose one of the empty spaces at random, Amy held herself in check while Deborah and Jen finished arranging the cakes in another case. After all, Sweet Cakes 2 was her business partner's bailiwick. Though they'd worked together on the overall design and features of the new storefront, Deborah would run the shop on a daily basis. It was up to her whether the eclairs went next to the Napoleons or the cinnamon buns.

"Right there, beside the fruit tarts," Deborah said, indicating an empty spot in one of the two refrigerated cases. "That way, we'll have our bestsellers right next to each other."

Glad to put down the pan that had grown heavier with each passing moment, Amy slid it into its assigned space. It fit perfectly, as if the cases had been designed to hold precisely four trays per row. Which they had.

"What's left?" she asked. She eyed the plentiful supply of sweet treats, much of which had been taken straight from the bakery's ovens in Emerald Bay, placed onto rolling racks and immediately loaded into delivery vans. Most of the rolls and bars had still been warm when Amy or Deborah or one of their helpers had unloaded them in Sebastian.

"Just these cookies," Nat called. Carrying a tray filled with six different types of cookies, she rounded the corner from the back of the shop. "Mom is putting all the extras in the fridge. Aunt Jen said to tell you she'll be outside. She needs to help Belle and Daclan with their gear." Once the mayor officially declared Sweet Cakes 2 open for business, The Emeralds would take the stage beneath a canopy Max had erected.

"Great. Has anyone seen Aunt Margaret?" Amy wanted to make sure her aunt was comfortable during the festivities.

"Not yet," Nat said as she slid the cookies into their assigned spot in the display case. "Aunt Diane is supposed to give her a ride. Aunt Belle said they were right behind her."

Amy made a mental note to have Diane escort their aunt to the seat reserved for her in the first row of folding chairs they'd lined up in front of a makeshift stage constructed of wooden pallets.

Now that the last tray was in place, Amy

went down the line of display cases, snapping each one closed. "I think we're all set," she announced.

"I still need to..." Deborah started toward the back of the shop.

Amy caught her partner by the hand as she hurried past. "Hold up a sec."

"Oh, but..."

"It can wait," she assured Deborah with a smile. Threading their arms together, she steered them to the front door, where she spun them in a slow half-circle without breaking contact.

"It's not every day we get to open a new location," Amy said. "For the last few weeks we've both been moving at warp speed to get ready for today. I think we need to take a minute and just drink it all in before it gets too crazy. Don't you?"

"But there's so much left to do," Deborah protested.

"Relax. We still have thirty minutes." Ordinarily, the bakery would open at seven so they could catch people on their way to work. But for today's Grand Opening, they'd delayed the start of the day until ten.

"This is a once-in-a-lifetime experience. We need to savor it. Close your eyes." Amy waited to make sure Deborah did as she'd asked before she let her own lids drift shut. "Okay," she said, "on the count of three, open them. One, two, three."

Tears stung Amy's eyes as she studied the final results of all their planning and hard work. The first time she and Deborah had seen the old Bath Cottage, they'd been convinced that the wooden beams overhead added to the building's charm. Though it had been a challenge, they'd retained them, as well as the wooden floors, which gave the shop a cozy, homey vibe. Shallow baskets mounted on the back wall held loaves of fresh bread that perfumed the air with the enticing aromas of wheat, oat and rye. And here, as in Emerald Bay, dozens of mouth-watering treats tempted visitors from behind rounded glass cases. Brass fixtures, colorful seascapes and a glowing neon sign above the bread baskets reminded customers of its connection to the larger bakery.

"Oh!" whispered Deborah. "It's so beautiful, I could just cry."

"I think it's worth a tear or two." Amy swiped at her own damp cheeks. She hugged Deborah closer. "I could never have done this without your help. I'm so glad we decided to join forces."

"To think I almost passed this up to work at

Ocean Grill." Deborah shook her head. A salaried position in the larger corporation had seemed tempting, but it hadn't compared to the chance to have a stake in Sweet Cakes.

Another long minute passed before Max rounded the corner from the break room into the front part of the bakery. "Can I interest either of you in some coffee?" He brandished a drink caddy filled with tall takeout cups.

"My hero." Amy's face broke into a grin. She'd long since drained the last drop from the thermos she'd brought from Emerald Bay. "You're right on time. Deborah and I were just admiring your handiwork," she said as she took one of the cups for herself and handed a second one to her partner.

"I'm amazed," Deborah said, her gaze traveling over the space Max had completely transformed. "I never in my wildest dreams thought it could turn out like this. You did a fantastic job."

"Thank you both." Max gave a mock bow.

"You, sir, have earned yourself a lifetime supply of sweet rolls." After planting a light kiss on Max's cheek, Amy drank deeply from her coffee cup. Even without cream or sugar, the dark brew tasted smooth and almost chocolaty. She sighed. "Mmmm. Where did you get this?"

Max pointed toward a line of stores closest to Sebastian's main street. "At that little coffee shop, Beans and Things. They're doing a brisk business, what with all the shoppers milling about."

"Is there a big turnout?" Amy shivered in anticipation. It had been dark when she'd unloaded her van in the alley behind Sweet Cakes 2. After moving the vehicle to make room for the next delivery, she'd been working nonstop to get ready for the Grand Opening. Hours had passed since she'd even considered looking outside.

"It looks like all the businesses in the area are holding special events." Max traced a circle in the air to indicate the dozens of stores clustered around the small lake. "I counted at least six sidewalk sales. The shop with all the purses in the window is giving twenty-five percent off every purchase. The coffee shop is offering a buy-one-get-one special. That cute place two doors down?"

"The Glass Monkey?" Amy asked, though "cute" wasn't exactly the word she'd use to describe the eclectic mix of arts and crafts.

"Yeah, that's the one." Max paused long enough to take several swallows from his cup. "They have a bunch of local artists stopping by at various times throughout the day. They even have a billboard out front listing who will be here and when they'll sign autographs or hold demonstrations."

"Wow," Amy whispered. She didn't know if she was more thankful or surprised that Agnes and Carl had decided to get in on the fun. Either way, the sweets-hungry couple had earned another basket of goodies.

Max drained the last of his coffee and pitched the cup into a nearby trash can. "Belle asked me to set up a few more chairs out front. Do you need anything before I go?"

Amy looked to Deborah, who shook her head. "No. I think we're all good here."

"In that case…" Max moved closer.

Amy's breath caught when Max whisked her into his arms. She melted into him, letting the press of his lips against hers banish every thought except how much she loved the feel and touch and taste of him. All too soon, though, they parted, and with a silly grin, he marched out the door.

"Mmm-mmm-mmm," Deborah said. She stared after Max until the door swung shut behind him. "That man is a goner. Tell me you'll let me make your wedding cake."

"Phhhhh." Feigning an indifference she definitely did not feel, Amy blew out a breath.

"We're not getting married. At least, not anytime soon," she amended. As much as she looked forward to spending more time with Max once things with Sweet Cakes 2 settled into a routine, she couldn't think about commitment and marriage. Not yet. Between the reunion and the sale of her childhood home, not to mention the impact a recently discovered treasure would have on her future, her plate was more than full. Besides, today wasn't about her and Max. Today was about the Grand Opening of Sweet Cakes 2.

To that end, she straightened. "C'mon," she said to Deborah. "I have a gift for you. It's in the office."

A few seconds later, they squeezed into the tiny room wedged between the bathrooms and the rear exit. Removing two emerald-green chef's coats from a hook mounted on the wall, Amy handed one to Deborah. "I want you to have this."

Deborah's mouth gaped open. Her fingers traced the word "Owner" Amy had had embroidered between the Sweet Cakes logo and the pocket. "I—I don't know what to say."

"You don't have to say anything. You just have to put it on." She prodded her partner gently. "I can't think of anyone who deserves this more than you do." She and Deborah had both been putting in long hours at the new store after they finished their usual shifts at the bakery.

With shaking hands, Deborah slipped the coat on over her T-shirt. For several long seconds, she stood, staring into the mirror Amy had hung on the back of the door. "None of this seemed real...until right this minute," she whispered. Her lips trembled. "Six months ago, Don and I didn't think we'd ever be able to afford a house of our own. Or send Danny to college when the time comes. Now our future is filled with possibilities."

Memories of the day Amy had decided to open a bakery came back in a rush. She'd stood in Deborah's shoes; she knew how it felt. "With hard work—and a little bit of luck—there's no telling what you'll accomplish."

"Hey." Deborah turned away from the mirror. "Do you think one day we'll own a chain of bakeries all over the state?"

"We can dream, can't we?" Amy grinned. To be honest, she hadn't considered anything beyond the success of their current two locations. But Sweet Cakes 4? Sweet Cakes 6? With her experience and Deborah's fresh ideas, she wouldn't rule them out.

Stepping from the office in their new green jackets, they hurried through the final preparations for the Grand Opening. Fifteen minutes before the big event, Amy herded everyone out the back door and around to the front, where a large crowd had gathered. Even though Max had warned her, seeing the number of people who'd gathered to wish them success sent a nervous shimmy through her insides. She squeezed Deborah's hand, knowing the young mother felt just as overwhelmed by the turnout as she did.

Side by side, they moved through the gathering, taking the time to thank both old friends and new ones for coming to the celebration. As they neared the front, Amy spotted most of her family in one of the rows of chairs. Touched by their steadfast support, she broke away from Deborah long enough to give her aunt a heartfelt squeeze and worked her way down the line from there. Turning, she shot a quick wave to Jen, who gave her the thumbs-up sign from her spot behind a board crowded with dials and switches. Relieved that the sound system was in her cousin's capable hands, she rejoined Deborah just in time to greet the mayor of Sebastian, who, along with his assistant, waited in the shade of the canopy.

"Mr. Mayor," Amy said, covering the final two steps. She extended her hand to the portly man who sported snowy white fringe around his shiny bald head. "Thank you for coming to the Grand Opening of Sweet Cakes 2," she said as they shook. "I'd like to introduce Deborah Jones, co-owner of the bakery. Deborah, the mayor of Sebastian, Gerald Grimshaw."

"Mr. Mayor. It's an honor, sir," Deborah gushed.

"The honor is all mine," said the man who looked like he'd stepped straight out of a Norman Rockwell painting. "We are very fortunate, indeed, that you chose to expand your bakery here in Sebastian." He cleared his throat. "I don't want to rush you, but the news people are on a deadline." Pointing to a gangly fellow with a bulky camera perched on his shoulder, the mayor harrumphed. "Here's how it'll go. I'll introduce you and say a very few words about your enterprise. Then you can each say a few words. We'll cut the ribbon. And that'll about do it. Sound good?"

When Amy and Deborah agreed, Mayor Grimshaw hooked his thumbs under a pair of bright red suspenders and snapped his signature braces. "Shall we get to it then?"

"Just a sec." Deborah motioned her husband and son to join them.

Amy's heart melted the tiniest bit when the pair swiftly moved into position, the youngster clinging to his father's hand as if it were a lifeline. Once they were all in position, the mayor tapped the mic and launched into his talk.

"Greetings, friends and neighbors. I'm Mayor Grimshaw, and I'd like to officially welcome you all to the Grand Opening of Sebastian's newest business, Sweet Cakes 2." He paused for applause and, sure enough, the crowd responded.

When the clapping died down, the mayor leaned toward the mic again. "Purely in the name of research, I stole one of Sweet Cakes' cupcakes earlier, and let me tell you, folks, it was hands down the best cupcake I've ever eaten. I have no doubt you'll be as happy as I am to have Sweet Cakes 2 here."

Following another burst of applause, the mayor turned to Deborah. "This here is Deborah Jones, one of the owners of Sweet Cakes 2. I'm going to turn the mic over to her for just a minute before we get on with what you all came here for...the ribbon-cutting." Taking two steps away from the mic, the mayor prodded Deborah to step forward.

Amy wondered if she should step in when panic flashed in her partner's eyes. Time seemed to stand still while she prayed for the younger woman to find her bearings. At last, Deborah grasped her husband's hand in her own and gave the crowd a tremulous smile.

"This is such an exciting day for us here at Sweet Cakes 2," she said in a shaky voice.

Amy glanced at Jen, but her cousin was already twisting knobs on the sound board.

Her words sounding somehow stronger, Deborah continued. "As most of you know, we own the original Sweet Cakes bakery in Emerald Bay, and we're thrilled to be able to share our freshly baked products with a whole new audience here in Sebastian. I personally want to thank my business partner, Amy Peterson, for this wonderful opportunity, and my husband, Don, and our son, Danny, for helping to make this dream come true."

As if she'd run completely out of steam, Deborah stared at the crowd without saying another word. Figuring that was her cue, Amy stepped to her partner's side and slipped a hand around her waist.

"Thanks, Deborah," she said as smoothly as if they'd practiced the move. "And many, many thanks to all our friends and family members who helped make this day possible, and to the new friends we hope to make right here in the great town of Sebastian."

The mayor took the next round of applause as his sign to rejoin them at the mic. At his urging, they stepped off the wooden pallets and covered the short distance to the emerald-green ribbon Max had hung from two temporary stanchions on either side of the bakery's front door. There, the mayor's assistant handed the big man an oversize pair of shiny scissors.

Amy hardly had time to catch her breath, much less enjoy the moment, before Mayor Grimshaw coached, "Slip your hands into the loops with mine."

They'd no sooner done so when he said, "Big smiles now!"

Almost before she knew what was happening, cameras flashed and, with one snip, the ribbon parted. The instant the two ends of the green strip fell to the ground, a cheer erupted.

The next seven hours passed in such a blur of activity that, later, Amy remembered only brief snippets of time that played across her mind's screen like the highlights from a football game. A game for which Belle and Daclan provided the soundtrack. In one scene, Caitlyn and one of her school friends took up positions on either side of the main entrance, where they handed out cupcakes decorated with the bakery's logo. In another, Aunt Margaret and Diane replenished empty trays at the table in the break room. Kim made frequent passes through the store, picking up discarded cupcake wrappers, wiping down door handles and erasing fingerprints from the glass-fronted display cases. Employees on loan from the main store in Emerald Bay waited on customers. Manning the cash register, Deborah rang up sale after sale while, standing beside her, Amy bagged and boxed purchases.

By five o'clock, when only a handful of broken cookies and one sad, slightly squished slice of Danish remained, Deborah announced that Sweet Cakes 2 was closed for the day. Ushering the few stragglers who remained in the store to the door, Kim handed each a discount coupon and encouraged them to come back when the store reopened on Tuesday.

"Woof." Amy brushed the back of her hand over her forehead. "I'm beat."

"I'm not," Deborah said with far more enthusiasm than anyone should after such a hectic day. She punched buttons on the electronic keypad that handled credit-card sales. "Do you have any idea how much business we did today?" She turned the screen so they could both see the impressive line of numbers. "And that doesn't even count the cash sales. I had to empty the till twice. At this rate, we'll open Sweet Cakes 3 in no time."

"Not so fast." Placing a hand on her partner's shoulder, Amy laughed lightly. "Today was not exactly a normal day. Next week, we might only have a dozen customers a day." Keeping the shelves stocked with freshly baked products could prove expensive until they understood the ebb and flow of traffic in the new store. For a while, they might actually lose money.

"But still…" Deborah tapped the number on the screen again. "Isn't this awesome?"

"It is," she said, happy to share Deborah's excitement. Not that the number came as any surprise. She knew the profit margin of each brownie or cookie to the penny. Calculating the potential earnings based on the number of cakes and tarts in the display cases was just part and parcel of owning a business.

As was cleaning up after even the longest days and making sure everything was prepared for the next opening. Another hour passed while they wiped down the display cases, relined the bread baskets with fresh parchment and emptied the refrigerator. At last, they loaded the empty trays into the back of Deborah's car.

"We'll drop these off at the bakery on our way home," Deborah promised. Her energy finally flagging, she yawned as she slipped onto the passenger seat beside her husband. Her sleepy little boy dozed in the back seat. "You're leaving, too, aren't you?"

Amy leaned on the doorframe. "I won't be long," she said in answer to her partner's quizzical gaze. Stepping away from the car, she waved. "I'll just take one last walk-through before I lock up."

Minutes later, her footsteps echoed in the otherwise silent shop as she double-checked that the refrigerator and counters were spotless, the bathrooms adequately stocked, the cash register emptied, its drawer sitting open. An uncommon restlessness crept over her as she moved from place to place. At last, she stopped to ask herself where the feeling had come from.

She didn't mind being alone in the shop, did she? Pulling her shoulders straight, she rejected the ridiculous idea. She was used to doing things on her own. After all, her days in the bakery often started long before the other staff arrived and continued well past the time the last of her assistants departed. Going to the grocery store, running errands, gassing up her car by herself never bothered her. She even lived alone, except for Socks. So, no, loneliness wasn't the issue.

Still, she couldn't ignore the fact that she felt a sudden weight on her shoulders. Spotting a stray crumb on the hardwood floors, she tried to shake the feeling while she ran a push broom back and forth across the floor. When she finished, she pressed her hands to the small of her back and arched, stretching muscles that had grown so tight, she might as well be carrying the weight of the world.

She sighed, finally accepting the obvious. She was unsettled. Blue, even.

But why?

She supposed the letdown was normal. After all, she—along with Max and Deborah—had spent months focused on the opening. Now that it was over, what did she have to look forward to?

The family reunion was right around the corner, of course. But she wasn't in charge of it, and besides, once the weekend ended, then what? Selling the inn and moving her aunt into a retirement home were next on the agenda. Neither of those items sounded like much fun. In fact, when she considered the top ten things she'd least like to do, breaking her ties with the Dane Crown Inn rated right up there at number one.

As if that wasn't bad enough, there was the not-so-little matter of the fortune in gold and coins Nat and Diane had discovered. She smoothed one hand over the bun at the nape of her neck. Whether Aunt Margaret decided to give all the money to charity or spend it on a lavish trip around the world, Amy worried how it would impact her family.

Feelings were bound to be hurt. How could they not be? The elation that had swept through the room when Diane and Nat announced their find had ignited a firestorm. Everyone had started talking at once, most making plans for what to do with their share of the windfall. But then, whoa! When Scott announced that, legally, the entire find belonged to Aunt Margaret, it had knocked the wind out of everyone's sails.

Hers included, much as she hated to admit it.

Not that she needed the money or even wanted it. Even if a sudden windfall landed in her lap, she couldn't imagine changing her life. Why should she? She already spent her days doing what she loved to do—baking bread, providing tasty treats for customers who appreciated them, visiting with the friends and neighbors who frequented the café at Sweet Cakes, spending time with Max. One day, if and when they decided to take their relationship to the next level, she and Max might need a bigger house. One they could afford to buy on their own. No buried treasure needed, thank you very much.

She wouldn't fool herself, though. Not everyone in her family would see things the same way as she did. After all, ten million dollars was not pocket change. It was what some would call generational wealth. Money that, if invested properly, would make life easier, not just for their own lives but for their children and grandchildren. Diane had Caitlyn and Nick's futures to worry about. Scott had to consider Isabella, Sophie and the new baby. No one, certainly not her, could blame Kim for being concerned about Nat and Josh. As for Belle and Jen, they might not have children, but a boatload of money would go a long way to securing their own futures.

A terrible fear swept over her. She'd read the horror stories about lottery winners whose lives and families had been destroyed by the sudden influx of wealth. Would her own family end up squabbling over the treasure? Would it ruin their closeness? She squeezed her eyes closed to block out the thoughts, but her concerns didn't fade until she took several long, calming breaths. Even then, they wouldn't disappear completely.

Determined to be on guard against any signs of discord among the people she loved most in the world, she finally resumed the process of double-checking that the doors and windows were closed and locked. At last, she cut through the empty rooms to the back, where she set the alarm.

As she stepped out onto the graveled parking area at the rear of the building, she spied Max's long, lean form propped against the side of the bakery's delivery van.

"Max?" she called, feeling the familiar jolt of pleasure that cut through the layers of fatigue that had settled over her as she pulled the door shut. "What are you still doing here? I thought you left to take the chairs and tables back to Emerald Bay ages ago."

"Tim volunteered to drive my truck so I could wait for you." His smile warmed his eyes. "I thought we could ride back together. You've got to be exhausted after today."

"I am," she admitted.

Even though he'd put in a long day, too, Max insisted she sit in the passenger seat. In no mood to argue, she handed him the keys and buckled her seat belt.

"It was a good day?" he asked as he backed out of the parking area.

"A very good day." Despite her fatigue, she smiled. "We sold out completely. Best of all, everyone seemed very happy with their purchases."

"Why wouldn't they be? It's the same great stuff they'd get at the original Sweet Cakes."

"Many of these people have never visited us in Emerald Bay." She crossed her fingers and held them up for him to see. "Fingers crossed that we turned a lot of first-time buyers into loyal customers."

She stared out the window while Max slowly drove past several of the nearby businesses on his way to the main road. She blinked, surprised that the wide grassy areas around the little shops were completely free of litter. She'd been certain the throngs of customers had left a mess behind.

Suspicious, she turned to Max. "Did you clean up the outside? I was planning to come back tomorrow and do that."

"Not me." Max briefly lifted the fingers of one hand off the steering wheel. "You have your Aunt Margaret to thank for that. While Caleb and Tim and I were taking down the tent and stacking the folding chairs, she organized a cleaning brigade. She handed out trash bags and lined everyone in the family up six feet apart like people searching for a lost kid. They went from the bakery all the way to the lake picking up trash. When they finished, there wasn't a speck of paper left anywhere."

"Everyone?" Amy pulled the tie from her hair and shook her curls loose. "Not Belle, though, right?"

"Oh, no. Belle was right there with them. Daclan, too," Max assured her as he steered onto the main road that led south to Emerald Bay.

Tears stung Amy's eyes as she pictured the many ways her close-knit family had pitched in to help make the launch of Sweet Cakes 2 a success. It would take more than the discovery of buried treasure to break those bonds. And, wiping away her tears, she put her fears of an impending rift to rest.

Eight

Belle

"I wish I could be there with you today." Careful not to ruin the makeup the stylist had spent the last hour applying, Belle pressed the earbud tighter into her ear. "You don't know how much I'd like that." Her breath hitched. Though she longed to see Jason, they'd decided that having him standing in the wings during The Emeralds' appearance on *The Newsy Morning Show* would send the wrong message.

"What if I fly down over the weekend? We could spend some time at the beach, grab a bite to eat."

The suggestion lifted her spirits. They plunged just as quickly when she pictured her calendar. "Mmmm. Next weekend, maybe? We perform in Jacksonville on Sunday. We'll have to leave by six sharp to make the eleven o'clock service." The state's largest city was two hundred miles north of Emerald Bay.

Disappointment flooded Jason's voice. "I'll be in California that weekend."

Belle let out a long, slow breath. Between his busy schedule as a high-powered record executive and The Emeralds' increasing popularity, it grew more and more difficult for her and Jason to schedule time together.

The young intern who'd guided them to the makeup department reappeared in Belle's sight. "Ms. Dane? I'll take you to the Green Room now."

Belle held up one finger, signaling the young woman that she'd only be another minute. Into the phone, she said, "We'll work something out. Maybe I can fly up during the week sometime soon." Jason would be at the office during the day, but they could at least spend an evening or two together. "I have to go. They're calling us."

"Give my best to Daclan," Jason said. "How's he doing, by the way?"

Belle cupped her hand protectively around her mouth. "Could be better," she admitted with a glance at the teenager who remained in the stylist's chair. Her young guitarist's eyes had gone impossibly wide the instant they'd stepped inside the television studio. Since then, he'd grown paler by the moment. She'd hoped having his parents accompany them to the taping would settle his nerves. So far, it wasn't quite working out as planned. While Tom Medford gruffly admonished his son to "hang tough" and "buck up," Mrs. Medford looked like she was on the verge of bolting...and taking her son with her.

"You've worked with nervous young performers before. You've got this, Belle."

"Thanks. That means a lot." Jason's encouragement never failed to bolster her confidence. Ending the call, she determined that, come what may, she could indeed handle it. Signaling Daclan to join her, she stood and breathed a sigh of relief when the boy jumped to his feet.

"Right this way, Ms. Dane. Follow me, Ms. Dane." In a tight red sweater above a navy skirt that clung to her curves, the long-legged intern who'd introduced herself as Miranda strode down the corridor in a pair of four-inch heels.

Her own sensible—and much more comfortable—low heels tapping out her footsteps on the tiled floor, Belle ran her fingers over the buttons on her denim jacket as she checked on the others in their little entourage. Nat brought up the rear, her focus locked on her phone, her thumbs in motion as she updated their fans on The Emeralds' appearance on *The Newsy Morning Show*. No doubt hoping to catch a glimpse of one of the stars, Jen's head swiveled left and right as they passed the dressing rooms of the show's hosts. Daclan's parents marched straight ahead, their twin gazes focused with such laser-like intensity on their son that Belle wondered if they'd leave marks on the back of his neck.

"You okay there, Daclan?" she asked, keeping her voice to a low whisper.

"I'm sorry, Belle." The teen licked his lips. "I'm not going to be able to do this."

Belle stopped so suddenly that Jen and Daclan's parents nearly ran into one another while, never looking up from her phone, Nat neatly sidestepped the train wreck.

Ignoring them, Belle asked, "Not going to be able to do what? Accompany me?" The Emeralds were a team. She'd have no choice but to cancel their appearance entirely if Daclan wasn't able to perform.

"Nah. I can play." Daclan's grip on the handle of his guitar case tightened until his knuckles turned white. "But I can't talk to Saundra and Wilton. What if one of them asks a question I can't answer? I'll embarrass myself in front of millions of people. You gotta get me out of it,

Belle. Please?" His eyes turned to bottomless black holes as he pleaded with her.

"Young man, you are not—"

Belle shot the grumbling father a stern look. The last thing Daclan needed was more pressure. Especially from his parents. Eyeing the boy, she swallowed. Daclan had been visibly nervous when they'd run through their interview and performance earlier...and that had been with stand-ins for the hosts of the nationally syndicated show. She'd hoped his nerves would settle while the studio's stylists had fussed with his appearance, applying the thick pancake makeup that would stand up under the hot stage lights. Apparently, that hadn't happened. If anything, he looked like he was two beats from passing out.

"You're sure you can play?" she whispered. The opportunity for this kind of exposure didn't come along every day. She'd hate to miss it.

"Yes, ma'am," he said without hesitation. "That part I can handle."

"Okay, then," she said with far more reassurance than was probably wise. "I'll tell Miranda we need to move to Plan B and you'll be fine. Just..." She paused. More than almost anything, she wanted Daclan to treasure this day. "You're so talented. You'll probably make hundreds of guest appearances throughout your career, but this will always be the first time you were on national TV. Just try to relax and live in the moment."

Lifting her chin, she placed one hand on Daclan's shoulder and addressed the boy's parents. "Everything's fine," she said, her tone insistent. "Just making some last-minute adjustments with my awesome guitarist." Without saying another word, she turned forward once more and strode toward Miranda, who stood at the end of the corridor, waiting for them to catch up.

"Is everything all right, Ms. Dane?" the young woman asked when Belle reached her. A tiny line creased the forehead of her otherwise flawless face.

"Oh, yes." Belle plastered a confident smile over her doubts.

Miranda didn't press for details but swung open a door that led to a roomy area where she and Daclan would wait until their portion of the program. "Right in here, then, Ms. Dane. Please help yourselves to the beverages and snacks. Do you need anything else?"

Belle surveyed the room. While not as posh as the Green Rooms in some of the other studios she'd visited, this one was nice enough.

Comfortable-looking couches and club chairs provided plenty of seating options. On one wall, previous episodes of *The Newsy Morning Show* rotated through four TV monitors. At the far end of the room, a long table held platters of bagels, doughnuts and assorted breakfast treats. She studied an array of bottles and cans closely, noting that, per her request, there wasn't a single alcoholic beverage in sight.

"This will do quite nicely," she assured the assistant.

"In that case..." Miranda consulted the clipboard she carried. "One of the other interns will take the Medfords and your assistants to their seats out front in fifteen minutes. Your appearance comes at the end of the show, so I'll be back in about an hour to escort you and Daclan to the set. When Saundra announces that the special guests today are The Emeralds, that'll be your cue for you and Daclan to walk on stage. Saundra and Wilton will take it from there."

"That sounds great." Waving the others into the room, Belle singled out her cousin. "Jen, can you help Daclan and his parents get something to eat? I'll join you in just a minute. Nat, hang back here with me."

Momentarily halting the flood of posts and texts she'd been sending out to fans, Nat moved in beside Belle while, like a mother duck tending to her brood, Jen sprang into action. Belle waited until her cousin had guided the trio toward the snack table before she closed the door to the Green Room behind her. Motioning Miranda to one side, she said, "We need to implement Plan B." She didn't need to explain any further. They'd run through the contingency plan during the earlier rehearsal.

Miranda's face froze. "Do I—do I need to find a replacement?" she asked in a horrified whisper.

"No, we're still going on," Belle hurried to reassure the young woman before the problem of finding someone to fill in for them at the very last minute put a permanent crease in her forehead. "It's Daclan. This is all very new for him. He doesn't want to do the interview."

"Just that part, though?"

"Yes. He'll handle the rest." Though Belle kept her tone light, she'd promised Daclan she'd never push him to do more than he was comfortable with. It was a promise she intended to keep, even if it meant losing out on an appearance as important as this one.

Miranda nodded. "Okay," she said, switching gears like someone who was used to dealing with last-minute changes. "You're sure you can handle the interview portion on your own?"

"I'm sure." A tiny snicker escaped Belle's lips. If she had a nickel for every talk show she'd visited in her thirty-plus years of performing, she could treat her entire family to dinner at the very best restaurant in town. She could definitely handle a quick chat with Saundra and Wilton.

"Well then, Plan B it is. I'll see that Mike and the rest of the house band know Daclan will stay with them during the show," Miranda promised. "He won't have to say a word. When it's time for your songs, you'll introduce him. He'll bow and launch right into the first number."

"Perfect." The plan was exactly as they'd discussed earlier. Belle released a breath, hoping the arrangement would put Daclan at ease.

An hour later, Wilton Weathers propped an elbow on the arm of his chair on the set of *The Newsy Morning Show*. "Christian music. That's quite a departure from 'Jimmy, Jimmy, Oh,' the song that launched your pop career, Belle. Are you sure you won't regret it?"

Knowing Wilton had lobbed her a softball, Belle shook her head. "Not for a single second, Wilton. When you know, you just know."

Wilton's eyebrows rose dramatically. "But how did it come about?" he asked, leaning forward almost as if he was issuing a challenge. "How did you *know*?"

Belle fluffed the mass of red curls that trailed over her shoulder and let her smile deepen. "It is a change," she acknowledged. "It was time for one. I tried country. I failed miserably at it." Poking fun at herself, she shaped her lips into a moue while she stared briefly into the camera. Her attention shifted back to Wilton. "I was searching for what came next, really praying about it, you know?"

Belle didn't know whether Wilton was a believer or not, but she felt a tiny flicker of ease when he nodded as if he knew exactly what she meant.

"One night, I took my Mama to the potluck dinner at church. The music minister—"

"Oh, how sweet," Saundra Carter broke in. "Isn't that sweet?" She turned toward the largely empty studio beyond the cameras as if waiting for an answer. "Belle Dane taking her mama to the church potluck." Sighing, she held one hand over her heart, though she was careful not to actually touch the silky fabric, which might rustle against the mic hidden under her blouse.

Belle silently waited a beat for Saundra to finish. America loved the woman's folksy personality. It made the perfect foil for Wilton's straightforward interviewing technique.

"Don't let me interrupt you," Saundra said,

giving her head the tiniest shake, which made her glossy blond hair sway. "You were telling us what made you change course."

"Right." Belle brightened. "The music minister wasn't able to attend that night, so our pastor asked if I'd sing the Lord's Prayer. I don't want to stick a label on what happened next, but in the middle of that song…" Reliving that moment, she studied her lap for a long second. Looking up, she didn't have to manufacture the tears that shimmered in her eyes. "It was like a bolt from above, a thunderclap. In that instant, I knew what I was supposed to do."

Wilton's voice deepened. "And the rest, as they say, is history."

"Right." Belle nodded. "I discovered a fabulous young guitarist in our small town. Together, we formed The Emeralds. We've been blessed to be able to perform in churches all over Florida. Thanks to you and Saundra, we're able to bring our music to an even larger audience." Her answer provided the perfect segue into their first number, and Belle uncrossed her ankles, prepared to rise and walk to the mic.

Saundra, though, had something else in mind.

"The Emeralds," she mused aloud. "That's such an interesting name for a band. Does it have some special meaning or significance?"

The question definitely had not been on the list of topics the studio had provided ahead of time, but Belle was an old hand at dealing with questions that came out of left field during an interview. Happy to handle Saundra's, she recrossed her ankles and relaxed into her chair.

"The scriptures do mention emeralds several times," she explained. "In the Old Testament, emeralds adorned the breastplate of the high priest. In Revelations, the heavenly throne is surrounded by an emerald-colored rainbow." She smiled crookedly. "But there's also the fact that Daclan and I come from the same small town, Emerald Bay."

Wilton chuckled. Taking back the reins of the interview, he said, "So you'd say the name of your group is based in both religion and personal experience."

"That's right, Wilton," Belle agreed. "That's why it's perfect for us."

"I, for one, can't wait another minute to hear you perform. What do you say, Saundra? Are you ready for The Emeralds?"

"Oh, I am!" the perky blond hostess gushed. Staring straight into the camera, she added, "I think everyone at home wants to hear them, too."

Correctly interpreting the comment as her cue, this time Belle stood. Crossing to the mic, she looked to her left, where Daclan stood beside the band leader, his guitar at the ready. Smiling widely, she gestured toward him. "Please join me in welcoming the other half of The Emeralds, Daclan Medford."

Just as he'd been coached, Daclan gave a small bow. When he strummed the opening bars of "The Old Rugged Cross" with a sure and steady hand, Belle sent up a quick prayer of thanks. Trusting her young guitarist to play the hymn exactly as they'd done in practice, she started the first verse on precisely the right note. The song brought back memories of the nights she and her cousins had sung it in the big, airy kitchen of the Dane Crown Inn, which added an extra layer of emotion to her performance. When they finished, Wilton applauded with far more enthusiasm than Belle had anticipated, while Saundra sat looking slightly bemused.

"Excellent! That's one of my favorite songs." Wilton sprang to his feet when Saundra, who was supposed to introduce the next number, remained rooted to her seat. "You have to have another one for us, don't you?"

"We do, Wilton," Belle said, veering off script just as he'd done. "This next song is one I wrote. Daclan and I are honored to introduce 'Night Talk' to the world on *The Newsy Morning Show*."

"I'm sure our listeners will be just as thrilled as Saundra and I are to be the first to hear 'Night Talk.' Isn't that right, Saundra?"

Rousing at last, his co-host responded with a cheery, "Absolutely, Wilton!"

With that, Wilton retreated to his usual chair while the band played the opening bars of their final song. In contrast to the soft, steady rhythm of the previous number, this one featured an upbeat tempo. Swaying a little to the beat, Belle belted out the tune.

Who do I turn to in the middle of the night
When troubles come from the left and right?
I turn to You. I turn to You.

Together, she and Daclan sailed through the first verse. At the end of the chorus, he launched into a short instrumental break designed to let him show off his considerable skills with the guitar. When he'd finished, they moved into the second verse and closed with a soaring chorus that called upon every bit of Belle's impressive vocal range.

As the director yelled, "Cut!" and then, addressing the rest of the crew, added, "And that's a wrap, folks," Saundra dabbed at her eyes with a tissue. She hurried to Belle's side.

"I've never..." Saundra's voice caught, and she looked away, struggling to maintain her composure.

This, Belle told herself while she waited for the woman to continue. This was what it was all about. If the only person she and Daclan had reached with their music was the TV show host, then it was worth it.

Several deep breaths later, Saundra said, "I've never felt like a song touched my heart like that one did. Tell me you have an album. I need more music like 'Night Talk.'"

Belle gave her head a sad shake. "I'm afraid you'll have to wait a while for that. Daclan and I do have several other pieces, but we haven't been in a recording studio." Studio time cost money which, for the time being, was in short supply. "Maybe one day."

Though disappointment clouded Saundra's eyes, they were interrupted before she could say anything more.

Nat murmured, "Our car is waiting."

At almost the same moment, a young woman who could have been cut out of the same piece of cloth as the intern who'd been assigned to The Emeralds stepped to Saundra's side. "Time for your wardrobe change, Ms. Chase," she announced.

"I'm sorry. I have to go." The talk show host extended a hand. "We film a whole week's worth of shows on Mondays, so they have me on a tight schedule. But thank you. I'd love to have you and Daclan come back and visit us again sometime soon."

"We'd like that," Belle assured the other woman as they shook hands. Guided by the slightest press of Nat's fingertips at her elbow, Belle turned toward the exit in time to see Wilton Weathers slip a business card into a beaming Daclan's hand.

"Hmmmm," Belle mused. Much as she wanted to, she resisted the temptation to ask Daclan about the exchange. They'd had numerous talks about the importance of transparency among band members. This, she decided, was as good a time as any to learn if her lessons had sunk in.

She waited expectantly when the boy hurried toward her, but instead of brandishing the business card, he asked, "Did I do okay, Belle?"

Remembering what it was like in the early days, when her own confidence level depended on how many dollar bills were in her guitar case at the end of a long day of busking on street corners, she smiled warmly. "More than okay, Daclan," she reassured the boy. "You were phenomenal." She leaned her head down to his, "How do you think I did with that last song?"

Daclan's eyes grew round. "Are you kidding me? You nailed it!"

Laughing together, they exchanged high-fives as the rest of their group joined them. She smiled at Mrs. Medford, who clasped her hands together in a prayerful gesture and whispered a quick, "Thanks!" before turning her attention back to her son. Meanwhile, Tom Medford clasped Daclan's shoulder and proudly told anyone who'd listen that the teen had just finished taping a show for national television, as if they weren't still standing in the middle of the studio, surrounded by people who worked for the network.

Moments later, with Jen at her side, they followed Nat through the studio's halls. At the door, Nat had them pose for a quick photo beneath the station's logo before they covered the short distance to the shiny, oversize van that sat, its engine idling at the curb.

"You have our bags?" Belle asked the driver, who stood ready to lend a helping hand as his passengers mounted the steps into the van.

"Yes, ma'am. I stopped at the hotel on the way here and picked them up at the bellhop stand."

Belle nodded. The ever-efficient Nat had told everyone to leave their luggage with the bellman before they left for the studio this morning. Her phone buzzed while she was fastening her seat belt in one of the cushy leather captain's chairs.

Certain Jason wanted an update, she accepted the call without looking at the screen.

"Ms. Dane."

Belle's brows knitted at the booming, effusive voice that was so not Jason's. "Who is this?" she asked, her thumb hovering over the End Call button.

"This is Bob Morely, president of Sunshine Records. I wanted to be the first to congratulate you on an absolutely stunning performance today on *The Newsy Morning Show*."

Though she'd been expecting some interest following their appearance on the talk show, the call took Belle's breath away. Bolting upright in her chair, she slashed one hand across her throat, signaling for silence while she cupped a finger over the microphone and mouthed *Sunshine Records* to the others. Throughout the van, conversations cut off as if someone had thrown a switch. With the possible exception of their driver, every single person present was familiar with biggest name on the Christian music recording scene. With only the low rumble of the engine providing background noise, Belle took a steadying breath and put the call on speaker.

"Thank you so much, Bob. I must say, your call caught me off guard. We only finished taping the segment a few minutes ago."

"Yes, well, Saundra is a very good friend of mine." Bob's hearty chuckle didn't quite ring true. Perhaps realizing he only had a few seconds to make a good impression and, so far, was striking out, he added, "We attend the same church, as a matter of fact. Whenever she happens across an impressive talent, such as yours, she lets me know."

Belle filled the pause that followed with a noncommittal, "Uh-hum."

"Saundra mentioned you hadn't taken this new song of yours into the recording studio," Bob continued. "We at Sunshine Records would be happy to help with that. Why don't you stop by my office this afternoon and we'll discuss what Sunshine can do to take your music to the next level?"

Whoa! In her experience, an invitation to the head honcho's office was tantamount to a contract offer.

In the seat behind her, Tom Medford gave an excited, "Yesssss!"

Muting her phone, Belle made a chopping motion with her free hand. "Hush," she ordered sternly. "We have a lot of homework to do before we sit down with *anyone* in the recording industry." Quickly, she explained the need to look into the company's policies, talk to a couple of their artists and, most importantly, study the way they treated younger talents like Daclan before either she or the boy's parents would be ready to sit down and discuss terms.

"Sorry," Tom murmured, looking thoroughly abashed when he'd absorbed the fact that Belle was only looking after his son's interests.

Certain there'd be no more outbursts from the back seat, Belle put the phone back on speaker. It was time to nip the conversation with Sunshine Records in the bud, and she said, "I'm afraid Daclan and I are actually headed to the airport at the moment, Bob. Perhaps we could talk some other time?"

"I really think we should talk today. How can I change your mind?" Bob demanded.

Belle remained firm, even though she could practically hear the man's teeth gnash together. Clearly, Bob was used to having both new and established talent ask, "How high?" when he told them to jump.

"We'll put you on a different flight. As a matter of fact, you can use Sunshine's jet to fly home whenever you're ready," he said, sweetening the deal.

"Thank you so much. That's a kind and very generous offer. I wish I could take you up on it. I do. But we have plans that require us to be in

Emerald Bay tomorrow, so it's just not possible to meet today." Even though Bob couldn't see her expression, she smiled warmly.

"Whatever your plans are, I can't believe you wouldn't put them off for one more day." Bob sounded aghast at the idea that she wouldn't do his bidding. "Not when it means the chance to work with the largest producer of Christian music in the world."

"No, sir. They cannot." Belle drummed her fingers on her leather skirt. Schools in their county had been closed today for a teacher work day, but Daclan needed to be in class tomorrow, and she'd promised to take her mother to lunch. So, no. She couldn't, wouldn't, simply shift gears to accommodate Bob. Besides, the kind of pressure he was exerting was exactly why she'd been reluctant to consider working with a huge company like Sunshine Records. "I have your number," she said, wrapping things up. "We'll talk again soon."

She barely had a moment to picture Bob's shock and dismay when she ended the call before her phone rang again. This time, an executive from Mainline Music spoke on the other end of the line. The conversation echoed the earlier one with Sunshine Records and ended nearly the same way. Belle fielded two more calls before they reached the airport. Deciding she'd had enough, she put her phone in Do Not Disturb mode for the rest of the way home.

Belle leaned over the keyboard in the studio she and Jen had cobbled together in one of the cottages. She struck the same chord over and over. The sound rang true to her, even though it had a bluesy dissonance rarely heard in Christian music. Harmonizing with it, she sang the words to a tune that had been running through her head ever since they'd returned from Nashville. Since before that, even.

She scratched out notes on a nearby sheet of staff paper and wrote down new ones. After running through the song again, she made a few more changes and repeated the process. Laying aside her pencil, she played the tune from the top, putting her all into the words and music.

The moon is full, and the night birds sing.
No one listens. No one hears.
In the dampness of my tears,
silence echoes. Silence rings.

Belle closed her eyes. The song evoked feelings of loss and longing for something beyond her reach. In that way, it was perfect. Her teeth captured her bottom lip and held it. Okay, so *perfect* wasn't the right word. Not by a long shot. The perfect song would praise the Almighty. This one certainly did not.

Slowly, she opened her eyes and stared at the words. Could she change them? Massage the lyrics to fit the Christian music genre?

She gave her head a sad shake. No matter how she unraveled this pretzel, at its heart, the verses would always retain a trace of their original meaning. Meaning to crumple it into a ball and pitch it on top of the dozen or so other songs in a nearby waste can, she reached for the sheet music. A sharp rapping on the cottage door derailed both her thoughts and her actions.

It couldn't be four thirty already, could it? One glance at the clock furrowed her brow. Daclan was earlier than she'd expected, but where had the day gone?

Intending to work for only a couple of hours, she'd come to the studio straight from her morning run. Instead, she'd gotten lost in the music. Here it was, late afternoon, and she was still wearing her workout shorts and a grubby T-shirt, her hair in a tangled mess of a ponytail.

Well, it would have to do, wouldn't it?

After the busy trip to Nashville, they'd taken a much-needed break on Tuesday. They'd resumed their practice schedule yesterday, but things had not gone well. Daclan had seemed distant, distracted even. Which made the rest of their sessions leading up to an appearance in Jacksonville this weekend all the more important. Given that, she couldn't very well leave the teen alone in the studio, cooling his heels while she showered and changed, could she?

"Door's open, Daclan," she called.

Door hinges squeaked. Something struck the floor with a soft thud. "I'm not Daclan," announced a voice that definitely did not belong to the teenager. "Can I still come in?"

Hearing the deep timbre, Belle leapt to her feet. "Jason?" She blinked owlishly. "Jason, what are you doing here?"

"I'll take that as a *yes*." The door clicked shut behind him. In four long strides, he closed the distance between them.

Belle let herself be swept into Jason's embrace, and when he bent to kiss her, she rose on tiptoe to meet him halfway. For several long, delicious seconds, she relished the feel of his strong arms around her, the press of his lips against hers, the steady beat of his heart beneath the palm of the hand she placed on his chest.

All too soon, though, he was holding her at arm's length, his puzzled gray eyes meeting hers. Belle felt her cheeks flame. "Don't look at me. I'm a wreck!" she protested. She covered her face with her hands.

"Stop." Gently, Jason captured her fingers in his. "I wouldn't care if you greeted me wearing an oatmeal mask and your hair in curlers. You'll always be gorgeous."

"You have to at least let me go change into something respectable." She stared down at the ratty T-shirt she'd tugged on this morning. Thank goodness, she'd at least brushed her teeth before she'd hit the beach for her usual five-mile run.

"Dress later. First, tell me what you were singing when I got here. It sounded different! Haunting. Beautiful."

"Oh, that." Belle made a dismissive gesture. "I was working on a song, but it didn't turn out right." She tsked, dissatisfied with her efforts to come up with new material for The Emeralds. "I have to scrap it and go back to the drawing board, I'm afraid."

"Hold on. What's the rush?" Jason's gaze shifted to the sheet music filled with pencil marks and scratched-out words. As if drawn by a magnet, he crossed the room to the keyboard. Retrieving the scrap of paper from its stand, he hummed the opening bars.

"F-flat?" he asked, naming the key.

"I know. It's awful, isn't it?" Belle felt her cheeks warm. Nothing about the song—not the key and certainly not the words—fit into The Emeralds' repertoire.

Jason slid onto the piano stool, propped the paper up in front of him and ran through the music. His fingers flew over the keys, picking out the bluesy notes with ease. "Sing it for me?"

Belle shrugged, unable to turn down his request even though she and Daclan would never perform the piece. She counted off the beats and launched into song, matching Jason's accompaniment as perfectly as if she were playing the piano herself. When they reached the end, Jason finished with a flourish and swung around to face her.

"You know who'd pay an arm and a leg for this?" He didn't wait but answered his own question. "Sammy Fasta. He and one of his writers had a, um, falling out over artistic interpretation. It's left him short one song for the album he's been working on. I think he'd love this." Jason flicked the paper.

"Sammy?" Belle crinkled her nose in disbelief.

Not about the falling out. She had no doubt Jason was telling the truth about that. As a vice-president at Noble Records, he made it his business to keep his fingers firmly on the music industry's pulse. But Sammy was the premier R&B artist of the decade.

"He must have a whole team of writers," she protested. "They wouldn't appreciate me sticking my nose in his business." While she'd be the first to admit the piece she'd written contained many of the elements Sammy regularly included in his music, she was better known for her vocals than her songwriting talents.

Jason rolled the paper into a cylinder and tapped it on one knee. "This is too good to end up in the waste can," he said firmly.

"You really think so?" Belle chewed on one nail while she considered the possibility.

"If you'd like, I'll reach out to him for you," Jason suggested.

"I can't let you do that." Her head shook from side to side before he even finished the sentence. From her own time at the top of the heap, she knew that even stars at Sammy's level considered it an order when the head of the record label *suggested* a song. "If anyone's going to call him, it needs to be me."

If being the operative word, she added silently.

"No time like the present," Jason pressed. "He's in the recording studio today."

"Grrr," Belle growled playfully. The man knew her too well. Left to her own devices, she probably would have *forgotten* all about calling Sammy the moment Jason dropped the subject. Something that, from the way he continued to stare at her, wasn't going to happen anytime soon.

"All right," she gave in with a sigh. "I'll do it. Give me Sammy's number."

She had no doubt Jason had it, and she wasn't wrong. After whipping out his phone and scrolling through a couple of screens, Jason rattled off the digits. Belle dutifully punched them onto her own keypad and listened while, somewhere in the towering forty-story headquarters of Noble Records, a phone rang.

"Yah." Sammy's deep voice rumbled through the speaker.

"Hey, Sammy. It's Belle." After a pause, she added, "Dane," in case more than one Belle had his number. Knowing he wouldn't have answered if he'd been in the middle of a practice or recording session, she didn't bother asking if she'd caught him at a good time.

"Hey, girl." The warm greeting carried with it a mix of surprise and curiosity. "Where you keepin' yourself these days? I missed you at the Grammys."

Belle smiled into the phone. She and Sammy had presented the award for Best Song of the Year a while back. "Oh, you know. Here and there. These days I'm at my mom's place in Florida."

"Hey, that's dope. Gotta love your mama. Whazzup?"

Taking the single-word question as a sign that Sammy was done with chitchat, she plunged straight into the reason for her call. "I hear you're looking for a song. I might have something for you."

"Yah?" A man of few words, Sammy had mastered the art of expressing emotion in a single syllable.

Belle couldn't blame Sammy for the caution that filled his voice. She could list a dozen reasons why he'd doubt her ability to craft a song he'd want to perform, beginning with the teensy little fact that R&B wasn't her jam and ending with her passion for Christian music.

"Tell you what, I'll shoot you a demo," she said, surprised by how much she wanted the chance to prove herself. "If you don't like it, delete it. If you decide to use it, all I'll ask for is the standard rate. Deal?" The offer was a good one. At worst, Sammy would waste five minutes listening to a song that wouldn't work for him. At best, he'd get a Belle Dane original at a bargain-basement price.

"Sounds good, girl. I'll give it a listen."

For the next half hour, Belle buzzed around the room, setting up recording equipment and running through the song with Jason several times. She refused to get bogged down by her usual drive for perfection. The demo was, by its very nature, just that—a demonstration. Assuming he accepted it, Sammy would no doubt put his own spin on the melody as well as the lyrics until both suited his personal style.

"Okay, that's it," she announced a moment after they'd recorded their fourth iteration. Judging it *good enough*, she sent the song on its way through cyberspace to Sammy's phone. She remained focused on the screen until the single word, *Delivered*, appeared beneath the text. With the matter out of her hands, she drew a thready breath.

"Thank you," she said, feeling the tension seep from her shoulders. "I'm not sure I'd have ever thought to call Sammy on my own."

"You're welcome." Warmth glinted in Jason's gray eyes. "Happy?"

"I am now that you're here," Belle murmured. She tugged the hem of her T-shirt lower. "I just wish I'd known you were coming. I would have cleared my schedule so we could spend more time together." A glance at the clock confirmed what she already suspected—Daclan would arrive any minute for their practice session.

Jason's smile widened. "I like that you're busy. Much as I enjoy looking at you, we'd have a pretty dull life if all we did was stare at each other every day." He eyed the small bag he'd dropped by the door earlier. "I should probably head on over to the main house and get checked in. I have a few calls to make this afternoon." He leaned down.

For an instant, Belle thought they were about to kiss again. But Jason only brushed a gentle touch on the tip of her nose.

"Dinner tonight?" he asked, lingering close. "Beach tomorrow?"

"Mmmm. Sounds good," she agreed. "Waldo's at seven?" The zany restaurant, with its cedar-paneled walls and odd mix of knickknacks, had become their favorite haunt. Jason could make an entire meal out of the smoked fish dip and fried green tomatoes, while she appreciated being treated like any other local by the staff.

"Perfect. I'll go see about a room. But first…"

Jason trailed tiny kisses across her cheek until he possessively captured her mouth with his. By unspoken agreement, they deepened the kiss, and Belle gave herself over completely to it, loving the taste and feel of him, hoping they were at the beginning of something that would last forever. As time stretched out, though, a yearning for more than mere kisses stirred within her. At last, she drew back, ending things before they crossed a line neither of them had committed to cross.

Barely five minutes passed between the time Jason strode out of the cottage bag whistling the tune from Belle's demo before Daclan walked in carrying his guitar.

"Hey." Belle blotted her skin with a towel as she emerged from the bathroom, where she'd splashed cold water on her face. "Ready to get to work?"

The teen's feet shuffled nervously on the floor. "Uh, not really. You got a minute?"

"For you? Always." Warmth flooded Belle's chest. Daclan reminded her so much of herself as a teen that she often prayed his music would take him as far as he wanted to go. Studying the lanky young man over the edge of the towel, though, she sobered while she slowly mopped the last few drops from her cheeks. Usually quick to smile and eager to please, the other half of The Emeralds wore an uncharacteristic frown.

"What's going on?" Had the boy decided to give up the guitar and take up a tennis racket instead? Or had Wilton Weathers made him an offer he couldn't refuse when they were in Tennessee earlier in the week? Hanging the towel over the back of a nearby chair, she braced for bad news.

"I've been thinking about all those phone calls you got while we were in the van. The ones from the record companies?" Daclan's voice lifted at the end, as if he wondered whether she'd know the ones he meant.

"Sunshine Records. Mainline Music. Bethany Vocals," Belle counted off the first three. "What about them?"

"Why'd you want all of us to listen in?"

Huh. That wasn't at all where she'd expected the conversation to head. She gave the matter a minute's thought before deciding that keeping Daclan or his parents out of the loop had never occurred to her. Puzzled as to where his questions were leading, she countered with, "Why wouldn't I?"

When he remained silent, she wagged a finger back and forth between them. "You and me, we are The Emeralds. You have just as much say in which performances we accept or turn down and which songs we pick as I do. If and when we go that route, I'll want your input on the contracts we'll sign."

Daclan scuffed one foot against the floor. "My dad says I'm too young to sign a contract. He says it wouldn't be legal till I'm eighteen, that he and Mom would have to represent me till then."

Belle nodded. "He's right. You need all the facts, though. I wanted you—and your folks—to listen in. And voice your opinion," she added.

"You wanted to know what I thought?" Running one hand through his hair, he seemed surprised.

"I did," she assured him. "I still do."

"Okay." Daclan's chest swelled. "I thought that Bob guy..."

"Bob Morely. Sunshine Records."

"Yeah. That's the one. My dad liked him. He wanted to stay in Nashville. Visit him and all those record companies."

Belle nodded. "I can see why he'd want to do that." It was pretty heady stuff to have the president of a recording company reach out to you personally. Tom's reaction had been normal for someone who was new to the music business. "What'd you think?"

"I thought he was pushy." Daclan must have replayed the answer in his head because he said, "Bob. Not my dad."

Belle grinned. The kid had instincts, she'd give him that much.

"I did, too," she confided. "The thing is, once a guy like Bob Morely has you sitting in his penthouse office overlooking Music Row, it's too easy to believe all his promises of instant fame and fortune. Later you might find out you signed away your life for a handful of magic beans."

The first hint of his usual smile appeared on Daclan's face. "Like that kid in the fairy tale."

"Exactly." Belle let her own expression mirror Daclan's. "Before we sit down with Bob or any of those other bigwigs, we need to learn more about their companies. We need to find out what they've done for other recording artists. Are they, like you said, pushy? Or will they let us grow and develop on our own time?"

That and so much more went into the decision about whether or not to work with a major record company. Along with the usual questions about advances and royalties, they had

Daclan's schooling to consider. She wasn't willing to sign with a company like Sunshine Records, no matter how much money they offered, if doing so put the boy's education at risk.

Noting that Daclan had fallen silent, she wrapped things up. "Once we have all the information we need, then you and your folks and I can decide which company—if any—we want to work with. Or we could decide to remain independent." She held her hands up as if she were catching raindrops while she added, "Which is all a very, very long answer to the question of why I wanted you to listen in on those calls. I want everything to be open and aboveboard between us."

With just a little more prodding, would Daclan mention the secret she knew he'd been hiding since their appearance on *The Newsy Morning Show*? She studied the young man. "If there's anything else we need to talk about, now's your chance."

She paused, but when Daclan didn't volunteer anything more, she crossed to the keyboard. It was time to confess her own secret. "In that case, I have something I need to tell you. You know I've been working on some new material for The Emeralds. In the process, I also wrote a song that isn't right for us. Before you got here, Jason and I cut a demo of it and sent it to a friend of mine. He might use it on an album he's recording."

"Yeah? That's lit," Daclan said, using his current favorite term for all things wonderful. "Who is it?"

"Sammy Fasta," Belle said, dropping the name of the well-known performer with an unassuming shrug.

Daclan's face scrunched. "Don't know him."

Belle couldn't prevent the laughter that bubbled up inside her. Here she'd been thinking to impress Daclan by being on a first-name basis with one of the top performing artists of the decade...and the boy hadn't even heard of him. The gap in their ages had never felt wider, and she sank onto the bench in front of the keyboard. "You should look him up," she suggested. "You might like his music." Slapping her hands on her knees, she said, "If that's all, we should probably get to work."

All signs of humor fled from Daclan's face. His gaze dropped to the floor and stuck there. "There is one more thing," he mumbled.

Belle's own tension flared. She took a calming breath and waited.

"When we were in Nashville on Monday, Mr. Weathers gave me this." Digging around in the pocket of his jeans, Daclan handed her a crumpled business card. "He said I should call him. He wants to fly me up to play with his band."

"On the show?" Belle swallowed. She could understand why Daclan would be excited at the prospect, but what would that mean for his schooling? His involvement with The Emeralds?

"Nah. Him and some of the guys get together to play for weddings and birthday parties. Mostly old stuff. Hits from the Seventies and Eighties."

Belle let air seep through her lips. "Is that something you're interested in doing? Joining a cover band?" Several well-known musicians had gotten their start playing songs previously recorded by other artists. Was that what Daclan wanted to try?

"Maybe?" Daclan shrugged. "I don't know." His mouth slanted to one side. "I was kinda happy that he asked me."

"You should be." Belle chose her words carefully. She didn't want to rain on Daclan's parade, and she certainly wouldn't stand in his way if that was the direction he wanted to take.

"Yeah, but I, uh…" Daclan's eyes rose to meet hers. "I've been thinking about it. A lot. And, uh, I don't want to mess things up. I, uh, I like what we're doing. The Emeralds, I mean. My dad says I can learn a lot from you."

At that last bit, Belle's estimation of Tom Medford rose a couple of notches. She'd butted heads with Daclan's father often enough that she'd begun to wonder if he really wanted his son to work with her. Apparently, he did.

She cleared her throat. An opportunity to work with and, perhaps, mold a talent like Daclan's didn't come along often. Grateful she'd been given this chance, she said, "I like what we're doing, too, Daclan, and I really, really enjoy working with you."

She'd meant the statement as a compliment and was surprised when the teen's face fell. "What?" she asked.

"The thing is, I don't want Mr. Weathers to be mad at me."

"He won't be," Belle assured the boy. If need be, she'd contact the TV host herself to make sure of it. "Wilton's a smart guy—he knows your paths will cross again. The next time they do, maybe you'll take him up on his offer." She glanced around the studio. Though they needed to get ready for their upcoming performance in Jacksonville, this discussion was important, too.

"I want you to know how much I appreciate that you told me about Wilton. It's always better to get stuff like that out in the open. I mean, you'd expect me to tell you if someone like Bob Morely asked me to sign a solo contract, wouldn't you?"

"Wait." Daclan frowned. "That wouldn't be any of my business."

Belle pulled the band from her hair and refashioned her curls into a rough ponytail. Before they went too much further, she supposed she needed to provide Daclan with more insight on how musicians worked together. Taking a deep breath, she said, "A relationship with a band is like a relationship with anyone else who's special in your life. As long as you and your girlfriend agree that you're not exclusive, it's okay to see other girls or for her to see other guys. But once you make a commitment to each other, you don't see anyone else on the side. And you don't start a new relationship until you end the one you're in. Got it?"

"I think so," Daclan said, but he didn't sound convinced.

"Okay, let me put it another way. You know I'm seeing Jason. We haven't made any secret of how much we care for one another. But what if someone else came along and he started to get interested in her? Would it be right for him to see her before he broke things off with me?"

Daclan gave his head a vehement shake. "I can't imagine anyone doing that to you."

"You'd be surprised." She'd had her heart broken by a cheater or two over the years. Not that Daclan needed to know those details. "When my last tour got canceled, one of the hardest things I ever had to do was to break up my old band." She still got teary whenever she thought about the day she'd broken the news to them. "But afterwards, one of the guys landed with BTK," she said, mentioning a group that was so famous, even Daclan had heard of it. "If he'd done that earlier, while we were still performing together, I would have been furious. But he made sure we'd ended our relationship before he took BTK up on their offer."

"So you're saying I needed to tell you about Wilton's offer before I agreed to play with him."

Close enough.

She nodded. "I've said it before; I'll say it again—you are incredibly talented. Wilton might be the first, but he certainly won't be the last to ask you to join his band. Just make sure that you're always open and aboveboard with the rest of your team." Satisfied that she'd given her young charge enough to think about, she dusted her hands together. "Now, I think we'd better get to work, don't you?"

While they set up the mics and got ready for their practice session, Belle refused to kid herself. She had to be realistic. For a boy with his talent, Daclan's involvement with The Emeralds was a stepping stone that led to bigger and better things. At most, they'd work together for a few years before he moved on to a future that wouldn't include her. But until that happened, she'd do her best to help him become the best musician—and the best person—he could possibly be.

Nine

Kim

"I'll be outside with the rest of the crew." Hoping the smoke would ward off the mosquitoes, her sister and daughter had decided to hold their nightly gabfest with their cousins by the firepit.

With her shoulder hunched, Kim propped the phone to her chin while she surveyed the ingredients for the tasty bruschetta she'd fix for this evening's treat. She gave the items arrayed on the counter the barest nod and returned to the phone call. "Just honk when you get here. I'll meet you in the parking area."

"Beep my horn like some teenager who can't wait to get you in the back seat of my car? I don't think so." Craig managed to sound both insulted and amused by her suggestion. "Besides, I want to say hello to everyone. It's been nearly a week since I've seen your family. I have a serious case of FOMO."

"Right. Five whole days." On Sunday, he'd sat beside her at church. Afterward, he'd come along like any other member of the family for their traditional post-service lunch at the Pirate's Gold Diner. Though she couldn't account for every minute of the others' time since then, she was pretty certain no new crises had arisen. She could practically assure Craig that he hadn't missed out on any exciting news. Instead, the rest of her family had been going about the business of daily living, like she had.

"What can I say? Now that you've whipped the inn into shape, I don't get to see you all as much as I did when I was working there every weekend."

"Which do you miss more—wielding a paintbrush? Or exploding Shop-Vacs?" Kim's light teasing served to remind them of the day her sister had mistakenly plugged the hose into the wrong port on the industrial-size vacuum, which then proceeded to coat Craig—and the freshly washed walls—in a layer of dust and dirt.

"I miss stealing kisses with my favorite girl while we hang wallpaper in the upstairs bedrooms," Craig confessed. "I miss sitting beside you on the deck while Tony and Caitlyn kick the soccer ball around the backyard."

Kim brushed a loose strand of hair behind one ear. She missed those things, too. "How is Tony?" she asked. "Is being a Florida Gator everything he'd hoped it would be?"

"I know I helped move him into the dorm, but it's hard for me to believe that he's already a college freshman." Summer classes had started a week earlier at the prestigious university, where Craig's nephew had landed a full academic ride. "It's a big adjustment. He might be a little homesick."

"Good. He'll be here for the wedding, then."

"He'd better. I'm counting on him to be my best man."

Kim took a breath. As much as she looked forward to the day she and Craig would begin their lives as husband and wife, one hurdle remained to their happiness. Tonight, she planned to discuss it with him. "What time will you pick me up?"

"We have a short agenda. The meeting shouldn't drag on too long," he said hopefully.

"Or we could wait until tomorrow night," Kim suggested. Spooning diced roasted tomatoes and olive oil over the toasted baguette slices, she eyed the manila envelope that lay beside her purse and fought down a shiver of nervous energy. Ordinarily, she'd want to see Craig no matter how late he was tied up with the town council meeting. Tonight, though, she was willing to make an exception. Especially if it meant putting off any discussion of the prenup for at least one more day.

"No. I'll be there by nine. If the council members get too long-winded, I'll just have to shut them down. I *need* to see you."

When Craig's sexy chuckle didn't follow the comment, Kim felt a flutter of concern. "What's one more night when you'll have me all to yourself in two weeks?" she asked. It wasn't like Craig would sweep her off her feet and into the bedroom before the wedding. After his proposal, they'd agreed to wait until they said their "I do's" before they slept together again.

"I need to go over some paperwork with you." He hurried to add, "It's family business."

"Whose family?" Kim felt her back stiffen. Had Craig somehow learned of the discovery Diane and Nat made? Of the millions in gold and gems that belonged to her Aunt Margaret?

"Mine. I'll explain it all when I pick you up. Nine okay?"

"I'll be ready," she said, ending the call.

While she scooped portions of buttery burrata cheese on top of the tomatoes, she wondered if she should have mentioned the agreement her own family wanted him to sign. But no, she needed to see Craig's reaction in person, to gauge it for herself.

She drizzled a balsamic reduction over each of the pieces of bruschetta and rocked back on her heels to study the results. The snack had eye appeal, she'd say that much for it. The dish combined the crunchy goodness of toasted bread with the sharp, nearly acidic flavor of the tomatoes. Offset by the creamy cheese and the tangy reduction, the treat would taste every bit as good as it looked.

After retrieving the manila envelope from where it lay, she slipped it into her purse and slung the strap over one shoulder. Picking up the snack tray, she headed out to join the others around the firepit, where, no doubt, a glass of much-needed wine waited to calm her nerves.

The distant sound of an incoming tide provided a soothing background as Kim crossed the wooden deck. At six in the evening, sunset was still hours away, and trees and bushes cast long shadows across the lawn. A breeze carried smoke from the firepit. The smell of burning wood grew strong enough to drown out the ever-present briny smell of the sea while she traveled down the path.

"Hush, now. Here she comes."

Belle's stage whisper rose over the light scuffing noise Kim's sandals made against the pavers. She decided to play along.

"Too late. I already know you're talking about me. What is it now?" They hadn't resurrected the idea of a bachelorette party, had they? She'd already vetoed those plans. Reaching the circle of chairs, Kim handed the snacks to Amy before she took the empty seat beside Jen.

"Nothing much," Amy said. The glow of the flickering flames bathed her face in innocence. She slid a slice of bread onto a napkin and passed the tray to Diane.

"Just a little shopping trip tomorrow," Belle said. Leaning forward, she placed her glass of wine on one of the flat stones that ringed the firepit.

"Shopping?" Kim made a face.

"Who doesn't like shopping?" Jen shifted in her chair, her ankles crossed.

"Craig and I don't need a thing," Kim argued. "His house is already fully furnished. Plus, I have all my stuff from the apartment in Atlanta. We could probably outfit two kitchens between us." Sorting through the duplicates and disposing of the extras was one of the first tasks that faced them as a married couple.

"Not that kind of shopping," Belle interjected. "You need a few things for the wedding."

"New shoes," Diane suggested around a bite of tomato and cheese. "This is yummy, by the way," she added.

"Sexy lingerie," Jen suggested with a sly smile.

"A couple of outfits to wear on your honeymoon." Amy broke off a piece of her bruschetta.

"We've decided to put that off till later," Kim demurred. "Between Royal Meals and his schedule, neither of us wants to take time away right now. We'll go in the fall."

Amy shrugged. "That's understandable. But where will you go?"

"Not sure. Someplace tropical, though." None of Kim's efforts to pry the destination out of Craig had been successful.

"You could use a new bathing suit anyway, Mom," Nat said from her chair on the other side of the pit.

Kim let her frown deepen. "Much as I appreciate the offer, shopping isn't on my agenda for tomorrow." She didn't have to look far to find an excuse to get out of the excursion.

"The reunion is only a couple of weeks away. I'm trying to prepare as much food as I can ahead of time. I'll probably spend the day cooking."

"C'mon." Having gobbled down her piece of bruschetta, Jen eyed the lone slice that remained on the tray. "You know good and well the freezer is packed to the gills with food for the reunion already."

"Yeah, 'fess up." Amy nudged the tray toward Jen. "What's the real reason you don't want to go?"

Kim sighed and drank deeply from her wineglass. When she'd first come to Emerald Bay, she'd expected that living day in and day out surrounded by her family might get on her nerves. It hadn't. Instead, she'd come to rely on her cousins and her sister as much as, if not more than, they turned to her. The only drawback, as far as she could tell, was that the very closeness she cherished also made it all but impossible to keep secrets from each other.

"I've put off asking Craig to sign that prenup, and I've run out of time. Scott called earlier. He absolutely demanded I get it signed tonight. I'm worried about how Craig will react. He may ask for his ring back." Kim centered the gorgeous diamond on her finger.

"Are you kidding me?" Nat straightened so

quickly that she nearly tipped her wineglass over. Steadying it, she continued. "That man loves you more than life itself. He's not going to cancel the wedding."

"Maybe not." Craig really did love her, Kim admitted. But was that enough? "Sometimes I think I should beat him to the punch and cancel it myself." Not that she wanted to end things between her and Craig. Never that. But they could at least postpone the wedding until her aunt decided what to do with all the money from the treasure Diane and Nat had discovered.

"Why would you do something like that?" Amy stared at her with wide, disbelieving eyes.

Did she really have to spell it out for them, Kim wondered. From the confused expressions on the faces gathered around her, she guessed she did. Putting it as succinctly as possible, she explained, "I don't think it's a good idea to start our marriage with a lie between us."

"You wouldn't be lying, Mom. You just wouldn't be telling him the whole truth."

"Isn't that the same thing, though?" Kim countered. "I feel like it is."

"I hear you," Diane said, wading into the conversation. "I felt the same way with Tim. We're in a better place with our marriage than we've ever been. I worried that asking him to sign a prenup—or, in our case, a postnup—might jeopardize that."

"But you did? And it worked out?"

"Tim was a lot more open to the idea than I thought he'd be." Diane ate the last of the tomato and cheese from her bruschetta and carefully wrapped the toast in her napkin while she talked. "I told him I didn't know all the details but that I might come into some money when Aunt Margaret sells the inn, and I wanted to keep that separate from our household and business accounts."

Kim tapped thoughtfully on her chin. Her cousin's explanation had covered all the bases while being just vague enough to avoid telling an out-and-out lie. And really, she didn't have much choice, did she? Not with her cousin Scott waiting in the wings, threatening to stand up and object in the middle of the ceremony if she tried to marry Craig before he signed an ironclad prenup.

"I don't think we have to worry about Carmen." Amy used the code word they'd chosen for the treasure. "Scott said that money belongs to Aunt Margaret."

"Is that why you haven't talked to Max?" Diane asked, voicing the question that had been on all their minds.

"Puh-leeze. Max and I aren't even talking about marriage. By the time we get to that point, if we get to that point, Aunt Margaret will probably have donated the bulk of the treasure to charity."

Not sure how she felt about that, Kim swung to face Belle. "Is that what she's going to do? Donate it?"

"Don't look at me." Belle held out her palms. "This is the one thing—the only thing—Mama and I don't talk about."

Only the crackling of the flames in the firepit broke the silence that settled over the group like a thick layer of fog. Maybe a large charitable donation would be for the best, Kim thought. So far, the treasure had only piled more worries on top of what was already her usual, substantial load. She wondered if any of the others felt the same way. She'd scooted forward, the question forming on her lips, when the sound of a car door closing, followed by the distant chirp of a key fob, intruded on her thoughts.

"We have company," Belle announced. "Are we expecting guests?"

"No," Jen and Nat chorused almost in unison.

"We're full, every room taken," Nat added.

Kim fumbled in her purse until her fingers wrapped around her cell phone. She checked the time and relaxed. Regardless of Craig's prediction that tonight's meeting would be a short one, she knew from experience that town council meetings never ended early. Their newest arrival—a man, judging from the sound of his footsteps—couldn't be Craig.

And yet, there was no doubt that the long, lanky form striding down the pavered walkway toward them belonged to none other than her fiancé.

"Craig?" she asked, unable to mask the surprise in her voice. "I didn't expect you until nine."

"Hey, honey." Bending over her chair, he placed a chaste kiss on her cheek before he addressed the others. "Sorry if I'm early. We didn't have a quorum. Bill Doherty's wife has the flu, so he stayed home. And Tom Medford is out of town on business." Craig's gaze circled around the fire to land on Belle. "I was hoping to see Jason, Belle. I heard he was in town."

"He is, but he had a business thing in Vero tonight." Belle propped her elbow on one of her knees. "I'll tell him you were asking about him when I see him later."

"Do that." Craig nodded. His focus shifted to Diane. "How's the house? Are you and Caitlyn all settled in?"

"Just about." Diane stretched languidly. "We only have a few more boxes to unpack."

His attention turned to Amy. "I don't have to ask how things are going at Sweet Cakes. The line was so long at lunch today that by the time I placed my order, you were all out of chicken salad." The item was a staple on the café's menu.

"I thought business would die down when we opened the second shop," Amy said. "If anything, we're busier than ever. I'm sorry you missed your sandwich."

"Not to worry," Craig said with a nonchalant grin. "I had the tuna. It's my second favorite." Turning to Jen and Nat, he said, "I hope you won't mind if I steal Kim for the evening."

"As long as you don't keep her out too late," Jen cautioned. "We're taking her shopping tomorrow." When Kim started to object, Jen overruled her. "It's not all for you. We've invited Fern to join us, too. She needs to get out, spend a little time with the grown-ups before this new baby arrives."

Kim ran out of excuses. "You could have led with that," she chided. The newest member of the Dane family was due in six weeks or so. "Of course, I'll come. What time are we leaving?"

"Stores open at ten, so nine thirty." Belle reached for her wineglass.

"I'll be ready," Kim assured the rest of the crew. Already looking forward to the prospect of spending the morning shopping for teeny tiny baby clothes, she slipped her arm in Craig's.

"We're not going to the diner?" On the nights the town council met, they usually stopped in for a quick bite after the meeting. Tonight, however, Kim stared out the passenger window when Craig passed the restaurant without stopping.

"Like I said, we need to go over a few things. This is one time I'd rather not have everyone in Emerald Bay looking over our shoulders while we talk." His turn signal blinking, Craig steered off the main road and into a neighborhood of older homes that sat on wide lots along the river.

"Works for me," Kim agreed. She couldn't remember a time when she and Craig had made it through an entire meal without a well-meaning citizen or two stopping by their table.

"What smells so good?" she asked when she stepped into the living room of Craig's house ten minutes later.

"Crock-Pot chili," Craig answered after he'd punched buttons on the alarm panel. "I started it this morning before I left for work. I hope that's all right."

"Smells delicious." Kim followed her nose into the kitchen, where bowls and silverware sat at the ready on the wide island. "Want me to dish it up?"

"Sure. Just give me a second to change." He ran a hand down the jacket of the suit coat he'd worn in honor of the meeting that didn't happen. "Chopped onions, jalapenos, and cheese are in the fridge."

"I'm on it." Kim crossed to the sink, where she washed her hands.

She'd just finished arranging the glass bowls of toppings on the counter and had ladled out bowls of the fragrant chili when Craig emerged from his bedroom looking much more relaxed in jeans and a blue polo shirt that brought out the color of his eyes.

"Want to sit out on the back porch? We can watch the sun set. Might even see a dolphin or a manatee."

"Sounds like my kind of heaven," Kim said. She could use an hour or so of listening to the water lap against the sea wall, watching the birds fly to their roosts and enjoying the sunset with the man she loved. In all likelihood, it would ease the tension that held her shoulders in its viselike grip. Ease it but not erase it completely. She wouldn't be able to fully relax until she and Craig discussed the papers in her purse.

In minutes, they were seated on comfortable padded chairs at a round, glass-topped table while the setting sun painted the clouds on the horizon in various shades of pink and gold. Kim blotted her lips.

"This is very good chili," she said. "Where'd you learn to make it?" Craig's refrigerator rarely held more than takeout cartons and condiments.

"It's my grandmother's recipe. I use all the same ingredients, but I cheat some by cooking it in the Crock-Pot instead of on the stove."

"I don't think I've had anything quite like it." Kim speared a chunk of melt-in-your-mouth pork. "Do I taste chorizo?"

"Yes." A wide grin broke across Craig's face. "Grams's family came from Spain. Legend has it they brought the dish with them when they came over in the 1800s."

"That's nice." Kim chewed thoughtfully.

"What is?"

"Being able to trace your family back several generations." She scraped the last bite of chili from the bottom of her bowl. Though she knew almost everything there was to know about the Spanish treasure fleet of 1715, she'd never had much interest in tracing her own roots. "My mother's parents moved here and built the inn in the 1960s. I know very little about them before that and practically nothing about my father's side of the family." When asked, her mom sometimes said Kim's father had been an astronaut. On another day, she might say he'd been killed in the war. Whoever he was, if her mom had known his name, she'd carried that secret with her to her grave.

Changing the subject, Kim asked, "When did your folks move to Florida?"

"In the early 1900s. They raised cattle and grew oranges." Craig pushed his empty bowl aside. "I guess that brings me to what I wanted to talk with you about tonight."

"Yes?" The tension came back in a rush and brought friends, Kim discovered as she crumpled her napkin.

"It's not something we flaunt, but between the cattle ranches and the orange groves they inherited from my great-grandparents, my dad's folks were pretty well off. Then canker struck in the late Sixties, and they were forced out of the citrus business. Things got so bad that my dad had to leave school. Later, somebody up north decided that Florida made a nice place to retire. Grams and Poppy sold the useless groves to developers and made a killing. Enough that they established a trust to protect our holdings."

"Really?" She glanced through the sliding glass doors into Craig's updated but otherwise modest living room. Her fiancé's understated style was a far cry from that of the few uber rich she'd dealt with in the past. Those people had dripped furs and gold chains, while Craig's attitude was humble and unassuming.

Now that she knew his family had what some called old money, she realized she'd overlooked some telling clues. For instance, the engagement ring that sparkled on her finger had to have cost as much as a used car. Then there was New Year's Eve. Craig had hired a limo for the entire night, wined and dined her at a posh restaurant and even taken her to an exclusive rooftop party. Nights like that one came with hefty price tags. She'd known all along that Craig didn't draw a salary as the mayor of Emerald Bay, but she'd assumed he viewed the role as his civic duty.

"You're...wealthy?" she asked, needing confirmation.

"Not me, per se," he corrected. "I get annual stipends from the family trust. It's enough to live on. But here's the thing—because we're getting married, I have to ask you to sign a prenup."

She sat back. What were the odds of both of

them choosing the exact same night to spring this kind of surprise on their prospective spouse, she wondered. The two of them had been seeing each other for nearly a year, engaged for over a month. Why was he just now bringing up the fact that he was wealthy? Substantially so?

Her heart sank. The answer was so obvious, she should have thought of it much earlier.

"It's because of Frank, isn't it. You weren't sure you could trust me?" Her ex-husband was a con artist, a man who'd bilked millions from unsuspecting investors in one Ponzi-flavored scheme after another.

"No." Craig's answer was as emphatic as it was firm. "The prenup is a requirement of the trust. Anyone marrying into the family has to sign one. As for the fund itself, I didn't earn that money, so I always feel a little conflicted about it." His voice softened. "In the event of my untimely demise, agreement or not, you'll be well taken care of. I promise."

"Oh, sweetheart." The idea of losing him brought on a flood of tears. She blotted them with her balled-up napkin. Grabbing the glass of iced tea she'd poured to go along with supper, she took a long drink. Not a big believer in liquid courage, in this case, she wished she'd asked for something stronger as she drew in an unsteady breath that did nothing to settle her nerves.

"I don't want your money," she said when she was able. "I'll be glad to sign anything you'd like. As a matter of fact, I have a prenup of my own. You don't have any idea how upset I've been about asking you to sign it."

Her tears gave way to a ripple of nervous laughter.

"I know you aren't very well-off." Craig's eyes narrowed, but humor danced in their gray-blue depths. "I was there when you were scraping up the money to start Royal Meals, remember?"

Kim smiled sadly. "I do." Early on, there'd been days when she didn't know how she could afford to buy the groceries she needed for the catering business. Thankfully, the list of customers who wanted weekly deliveries of her ready-to-cook meals had grown faster than she'd ever dreamed possible. "Royal Meals is on solid financial footing now." She took a breath. "But that's not the reason I had Scott draw up the papers."

"No? Are you the long-lost heir to some Austrian prince? You own a castle I don't know about?"

"Not exactly." Her nerves were getting the best of her, forcing her to suppress an ill-timed giggle. "It's Aunt Margaret. You know she's agreed to sell the inn."

"Right after the reunion." Craig nodded as though he'd discovered the final piece of a jigsaw puzzle lying on the floor at his feet. "I get it. She's going to divide the proceeds between you and your cousins."

"And Jen," Kim said, not forgetting to include her sister. She took a breath and tried not to squirm. No matter what Diane and the others thought, she simply did not feel comfortable with skating this close to a lie. Settling for giving Craig the broadest possible hint, she said, "It could be a sizable amount."

"I understand," Craig said as he clasped her hands in his. "It's only right that you'd want to protect Josh and Nat's interests. If I were in your shoes, I'd do exactly the same thing."

Kim had absolutely no doubt that he meant what he said. Which didn't help the situation, not one bit. If anything, his kindness made her feel even guiltier for not being completely honest with him. But she'd promised Scott and the others that she'd keep their secret, and she always kept her promises.

"What do you say? Should we get this over with so we can enjoy what's left of our evening together?"

At Kim's nod, Craig rose. He gathered their dinner dishes while she carried their empty tea glasses into the kitchen. Going through the motions of cleaning up as if they'd spent years together instead of months, they loaded the dishwasher. After the leftover chili went into the fridge, they retreated to the living room, where they spread their paperwork in neat piles on the coffee table.

Craig plopped down on the couch beside her, pen in hand. "Where do I sign?" he asked, eyeing the papers Scott had prepared. Once he'd jotted his signature on the dotted line, he handed the pen to Kim.

As much as she'd fretted over asking Craig to sign a prenup, sliding the signed paperwork into her manila envelope felt anticlimactic, Kim thought a few minutes later. Nevertheless, she vowed to tell Craig the truth—the whole truth—the minute Scott and the others gave their okay.

"Music or TV?" Craig slipped one arm around her shoulders and pulled her close.

"Mmmm, music, I think." Night had fallen. She'd have to leave soon, and they still had a few things to discuss about the wedding.

Craig pressed a button on a remote. A second later, the smooth sounds of soft rock drifted from hidden speakers.

"I can't decide between sliced fruit and fruit salad for the wedding breakfast." Kim rested her head on Craig's wide chest. "What do you think?"

"I think we've done entirely too much talking and not enough kissing."

Angling his head toward hers, he sought her lips, and when they met, his touch banished all her concerns.

"Oh, my goodness, will you look at this adorable outfit?" Yellow flowers adorned the pink onesie Kim held up by its shoulders in the chic children's boutique tucked into one of the many shopping plazas in Vero Beach.

"It's too small," Amy complained. "Socks wouldn't even fit into that, and he weighs about the same as a baby. Does it come in a bigger size?"

"That cat will look like a giant next to a newborn," Kim countered. "He's what? Ten or twelve pounds? Our new niece won't weigh nearly that much."

Amy moved farther down the row of hangers until she reached the section for slightly older infants. Flipping through them, she selected a similar item with purple flowers instead of pink ones. She held it up. "Which one do you like, Fern?"

Fern, who'd just emerged from the restroom in the back of the store, pressed one hand to her lower back while she waddled closer. She flipped the size tag of Kim's choice. "Zero to three months. That's about right. And it's super cute. Yours is, too, Amy. For later, when she's bigger. Ooof." Her hands shifted from her back to her belly as she bent slightly.

"Are you okay?" Concern thickened Kim's voice.

"Uh-huh," Fern said through thin lips. "Braxton-Hicks contractions. Give me a sec."

Kim's stomach clenched in sympathy. She'd suffered through months of false labor pains with Josh. Not so much with her second, though. Was it normal to have them with a third, she wondered.

"Whew!" Fern straightened a few seconds later. "I know these are warm-ups for the real thing, but seriously, they're the worst. They won't let you take anything for them. Once I'm actually in labor, I'll get an epidural and bye-bye, pain."

"You're sure you're okay?" Amy asked doubtfully.

"I'm fine. I wouldn't say no to a glass of iced tea and putting my feet up. Are my ankles swollen?" Fern peered down but couldn't see over her big belly.

"They're not too bad," Kim said, inwardly wincing at the sight of the sandal straps that pressed into Fern's puffy skin.

"You're not ready to call it quits, are you?" Nat fretted. "We're just getting started. We're going to hit the outlet mall after this." The discount center boasted two of the better-known children's clothing stores.

Setting the onesie she'd chosen aside for the moment, Kim slipped her arm through her daughter's. "When a woman who's eight months along says she needs to sit down, you don't argue. You find her a nice comfy chair," she whispered. "Where are we having lunch?"

"I reserved the back room at Too Jays." Nat looked longingly at the stacks of neatly folded baby clothes arranged by color and size in the upscale boutique. "Are you sure we can't shop for just a little while longer?"

"We brought two cars. I can take Fern and a couple of the others to the restaurant. Aunt Margaret is probably ready for a break." She scanned the small store without spotting several members of their group. "Where are Aunt

Margaret and Belle? And Jen?" she asked.

"Jen and Belle wanted to go to the gift shop next door. They said they wouldn't be long," Amy volunteered.

"Aunt Margaret insisted on stopping at the bookstore we passed on our way here. Diane is with her," Nat added.

"Oh, dear." Fern pretended to moan. "If your aunt keeps buying books, I'm going to have to buy another bookcase for the nursery. I swear she's already bought out the children's section of A Likely Story."

Kim laughed. A stop at the independent bookstore was mandatory whenever she took her aunt to lunch in Emerald Bay. Margaret usually emerged an hour later weighted down with her purchases.

"We'll grab Aunt Margaret on our way out," she offered. Turning to Fern, she said, "Unless you'd rather have me get the car and come back to pick you up?" With spaces limited, she'd been forced to park in a public lot two blocks away.

"Walking actually feels better than just standing. Gets the circulation going. Or so I've been told." Fern cast another glance at a stack of blankets on a table next to the racks of baby clothes. "If anyone wants to buy something for this little one"—she patted her bulging stomach—"she could use a couple of lightweight blankets." She let her hand drop and grinned. "I'm just saying."

Kim dug a couple of twenties out of her wallet and handed them to Nat along with the onesie she'd had her eye on. "Get this for me, will you? And one of those blankets? Shop for another fifteen minutes, and then start herding everyone to the car. We'll see you at the restaurant."

"Sounds good." Nat pocketed the cash. "There's so much to choose from, I'm sure I can find something nice pretty quickly."

Finding something wasn't going to be the problem. Not with the wide selection the shop had to offer. Narrowing her choice down to one, possibly two items, that could take Nat all day.

"Don't dawdle over your decision," Kim warned. "We can always exchange it later if we need to." With that, she headed for the door, intent on collecting her aunt and cousin for the short ride to the restaurant.

"Oh, my. How pretty," Margaret said, standing in the doorway of the private dining room at the back of Too Jays restaurant a scant twenty minutes later.

Kim gaped at the mix of pink and white balloons that floated above the table. "Bridal

Shower," a festive banner proclaimed from one wall. Opposite it, another banner read "Baby Shower." In front of one chair, a white baseball cap with an attached veil rested on the table. "Baby Time" read the embroidery on the pink cap that sat atop a "cake" made of tightly rolled diapers held together with pink ribbons.

"When did you have time to do all this?" Kim asked no one in particular.

"You can thank Nat for all of it," Diane answered. She held a chair for Margaret. "She organized everything."

"Ooof," Fern said, lowering herself gingerly onto her own chair. Removing the pink hat from the top of the cake, she plunked it on her head. "This is too sweet. Take my picture. I have to send it to the girls."

While Kim slipped her own hat on her head and adjusted the veil, Diane flitted around the room taking pictures until their waitress appeared in the doorway.

"Oh! Two guests of honor. Well, that answers that question."

"Say what?" Kim asked.

The waitress chuckled. "Everybody in the back has been trying to figure out if the bride and the mom-to-be were one and the same. So when's the big day?"

"Memorial Day," Kim said with a smile.

"June 26th," Fern said at the same time.

She paused for a second before she homed in on Fern. "Are you sure, honey? You look like you're ready to pop at any moment."

"I'm sure." Fern ran her hand in circles over her baby bump. "Six more weeks to go."

"If you say so." The waitress looked doubtful. "I'm Vandy, by the way, and I'll be taking care of you today. Can I get you all started on something to drink? A mimosa for the bride-to-be? Maybe an Arnold Palmer for the little mama?"

"Sweet tea for me, thanks," Kim said. Although the mimosa sounded tempting, she had to drive Fern home later and wouldn't risk even a little champagne.

"Mmmm, I'll have regular lemonade," Fern said. "I have to avoid caffeine." She patted her belly. "Makes this little one all squirmy."

"I'd like a Dr. Brown's Cream Soda." Margaret looked up from her menu. "With extra ice."

"Just water for me." Diane pressed a few buttons on her cell phone. "There. I just sent the pictures to your phones."

"Sweet tea, lemonade, cream soda and water. Got it." Vandy jotted notes on an order pad she'd pulled from the short black apron she wore around her waist. She looked around as if just realizing some of the chairs were empty. "Are we still waiting for more people?"

"Yes," Diane assured the woman. "Four more. They should be along very shortly."

"Great." Vandy exhaled a breath. "I'll get started on these drinks, then."

When she'd left, Fern's expression crumpled. "I must look like a cow."

"You most certainly do not," Kim protested. "From the back, no one can even tell you're pregnant." Despite the photos of rail-thin models sporting tiny baby bumps in all the maternity wear catalogues, she'd never known another woman who could pull off a figure-hugging, striped dress this close to term. She certainly hadn't. Not with Josh or Nat.

Margaret turned to Fern. "She was right about one thing, though. You look like you're about ready to have this baby."

"Six more weeks, and we need every minute of it." Wincing, Fern shifted her weight to one side. "Scott hasn't put the crib together yet. Or painted the nursery. I'm sorry, but I need to go to the restroom. Seems like I have to go every ten minutes these days." She hauled herself to her feet and ambled off to find the ladies' room.

Watching Fern's waddling gait, Kim sent a

questioning glance toward Diane. "Has the baby dropped already?"

"I wondered the same thing, but it's too early, isn't it?" During first pregnancies, the baby lightened, or settled into position for delivery, up to a month before the mom went into labor, but it was rare for a second or third child to drop until birth was imminent. "What do you think, Aunt Margaret?"

"I think Scott needs to hurry up and get that nursery ready." Margaret pursed her lips.

"Hmmm. Maybe you could ask your brother if he needs any help," Kim suggested.

"Or we could just tell him we're coming over after church on Sunday." Diane's fingers were already punching buttons on her phone. "I bet it wouldn't take more than a couple of hours for all of us to whip the nursery into shape."

"Count me in," Kim said agreeably. "I'm sure Craig will help out, too. He was just saying how much he missed the work parties we held at the inn."

"You sure picked yourself a good one," Margaret observed. "That man is beyond helpful."

Diane's cell phone dinged with an incoming message. She eyed her brother's one-word response. "He says yes, with three exclamation points," she announced.

"Then it's settled. Sunday afternoon work party at Scott and Fern's. I'll text the others."

While Kim was notifying everyone about the plans, Vandy stepped into the room carrying a tray of beverages and plates. "Here you go," she said, doling out drinks and bread plates. "I thought you might like an appetizer while you wait for the rest of your party." She placed small bowls of applesauce and sour cream on the table on either side of a platter of bite-size potato pancakes.

"Thank you, Vandy. That was very sweet of you," Margaret noted.

"Yes, ma'am. I'll check in with you in a few minutes. Or flag me down when the rest of your group arrives." The waitress headed for the door, where she stepped aside to let a returning Fern enter first.

"This baby is so different from my other two." Fern leveraged herself into her chair by propping both hands on the table. "Maybe it's 'cause I'm older, but I never had morning sickness with Sophie and Isabella. My feet didn't swell to the size of watermelons. I had much more stamina back then, too. I was still playing weekly tennis matches when I went into labor with Isabella. With this one, though, I'd rather take a nap."

"Growing a baby does take tremendous energy," Diane said. "And remember, you weren't chasing two young girls around all day back then, either."

"It's perfectly normal to need a nap once in a while," Kim assured the pregnant woman. The age gap between Josh and Nat was a little closer than with Isabella and Sophie, but she remembered how tired she'd been those first few months of her second pregnancy. "Don't tell anyone, but once I fell asleep on the couch while Josh was playing with building blocks. I didn't wake up until he tried to stick one in my ear."

"That makes me feel a little bit better." Fern's face colored lightly. "Last night I nodded off in the middle of a conversation with Scott."

"Who hasn't fallen asleep when Brother Dearest is talking?" Diane asked. "That's how he wins so many cases—he simply lulls the jury into a trance. Then they come up with whatever verdict he wants."

"Spoken as only a sister can," Fern said, laughing.

"We should eat those pancakes before they get cold." Margaret picked up her bread plate and held it out. "Kim, could you give me one?"

"Of course." Kim hustled to serve her aunt.

Fern looked longingly at the crunchy treats. "Do you think they have onions in them? Onions give the baby the hiccups."

Kim chewed thoughtfully on a small bite of pancake. The flavor was surprisingly bland. "Nope. No onions," she assured her cousin's pregnant wife.

"Good. Then I'll have one." Fern reached for her fork.

"Take a couple," Kim said, transferring the crispy rounds onto Fern's plate. "They're small, and you're eating for two."

By the time they'd polished off the appetizer, the rest of the group crowded into the room carrying brightly colored shopping bags and wrapped packages, which they stacked at one end of the long table. After enjoying a leisurely lunch—a mix of freshly prepared salads and oversize sandwiches—Vandy wheeled in the cake Amy had had delivered from her bakery. White-on-white icing offered best wishes to the bride-to-be on one side of the round cake, while the other half welcomed the newest member of the Dane clan in strawberry pink. In no time at all, they'd demolished the moist layers of vanilla sponge separated by tasty mascarpone whipped cream.

When it came time to open their gifts, Kim and Fern took turns taking one from the piles the others had placed in front of them.

"That ought to get his motor running," declared Margaret when Kim held up a "barely there" black negligee that bore a label from one of Belle's favorite designers.

While Kim, her cheeks burning, thanked her cousin, Fern opened a box from Diane and immediately burst into tears. "I can't believe you made this," she cried. She clutched the crocheted pink blanket with its white trim to her chest. "Sorry. Baby hormones," she said, dabbing at her damp eyes with a napkin.

"No apologies necessary," Diane assured her sister-in-law. "I'm glad you like it." She peered at the still crying woman. "You do like it, don't you?"

"I love it!" Fern declared. "We'll bring her home from the hospital swaddled in a pink blanket from her Aunt Diane."

"I don't know how to thank you all," Kim said a half hour later as she stared at a collection of gift cards from nail and hair salons in Sebastian that promised to pamper brides on their special day, the new bathing suit Nat had insisted on buying after Kim had balked at the hefty price tag, and an adorable pair of bedroom slippers adorned with puffy white feathers.

"We're twins," Kim said, holding her scuffs aloft when Fern opened a box that held plush terrycloth zories.

"Ahhhhh," Fern sighed, whipping off her too-tight sandals and sliding her feet into the flip-flops. "My feet thank you. I may never take these off." She stuffed her old shoes into the carry bag that came with the slippers and stared past the stack of receiving blankets, frilly dresses, and onesies to a couple of large gift bags in shades of bright purple. "What are those?"

"Those are gifts for Isabella and Sophie," Kim explained as she exchanged a glance with Diane. With so much attention focused on their new baby sister's arrival, they'd wanted to make sure the older girls felt included. Each bag contained enough craft kits and other art supplies to keep each of them busy for hours.

Fern's eyes watered a bit more. Pressing a hand to her chest, she said, "This has been the absolute best day," she declared. "Thank you. Thank you all." Still clutching the blanket Diane had made in one hand, she hauled herself to her feet. "And now, I must make yet another of my thousand daily trips to the restroom."

"You go ahead, Aunt Fern," said Nat. "We'll clean up here, and then we can get ready to go to the outlet mall."

Fern turned a pained expression on Kim's daughter. "I think I've had as much exercise as I can handle for one day. Would you mind if I called Scott to come pick me up? He and the girls are probably ready for a little break anyway."

Thirty minutes later, the women exchanged hugs before Scott helped his wife awkwardly climb onto the passenger seat of their shiny SUV. Amy settled a box of cupcakes decorated with pink-and-white frosting between her nieces. Kissing each of their cheeks, she made each promise not to open the box in the car.

As she waved goodbye to Isabella and Sophie through the rear window, Kim pulled out her cell phone. After sending Craig a brief text about the plans she'd made for them on Sunday afternoon, she pocketed her phone. The device buzzed with a reply before she had a chance to join the others in their continued shopping spree. Staring down at Craig's thumbs-up emoji, she smiled. Her Aunt Margaret had been right. She had, indeed, picked herself a winner.

Ten

Jen

"Hey. Look at these pretty little flowers." Jen dropped the hoe she'd been using to weed between the bushes and knelt to take a closer look. Dozens of tiny purple blossoms had sprouted on each of the bean plants overnight. The itty-bitty buds reminded her of the bracelets and necklaces she and Kim had spent hours making out of the wildflowers that grew around the inn. She plucked one of the blossoms and rubbed the stem between her fingers. Deciding these would be much easier to braid than the Creeping Charlie they'd used when they were kids, she gathered a handful.

"Whoa. Don't pick those." Caleb practically leapt over the row of low bushes to get to her side.

"Why not? They'll make a pretty crown." Weaving the stems together, she produced a colorful strand.

"Each one of those flowers turns into a bean. The more you pick, the less green beans we'll have."

Jen stared down at the blossoms that looked nothing like green beans. "I had no idea." She shook her head in disbelief. The amount she *didn't* know about tending a garden would fill an encyclopedia. "I'm so sorry."

"That's okay. How were you supposed to know?" Caleb squatted down beside her. Almost reverently, he singled out one of the remaining blossoms and held it between his calloused fingers. "The flowers only last a day or two. When the petals dry, a bean grows out beneath them."

A thrill she'd never expected passed through her. Something she'd planted with her own two hands would soon produce food. "How much longer?"

"It takes about two weeks for the beans to mature. By tomorrow, we'll see them begin to take shape. After that, we'll need to start checking them every day. Once they get about this long, we'll want to pick them." He held out one hand, his thumb and forefinger forming a four-inch gap.

"That's not very big." The fresh beans she bought at the grocery store were quite a bit bigger.

"Commercial growers—like the ones who supply the grocery stores and canneries—choose varieties based on their shelf life. Ours will be super tender. Tastier, too," he promised.

Looking over the neat, straight lines, she noted that only two of the six rows of bushes had sprouted flowers. She pointed to the other four rows. "Those don't have blossoms. Does that mean they aren't any good?"

"We planted these earlier." Caleb motioned toward the low bushes on either side of them. "We waited a couple of weeks before we put in the next two rows. And a couple more before we planted the last two." He aimed a thumb toward the flowerless plants. "They'll bloom in stages. That way, we aren't overwhelmed by having all the green beans ripen at the same time."

Her brows knitted. Thousands of blossoms danced at the end of the stems, but she'd helped Kim in the kitchen often enough to know that she could fill an entire pot with raw green beans, and they'd shrink to a bowlful after they cooked. "Seems like a lot of work for, what, four or five bowls of beans?"

"Oh, no." Caleb chortled. "Beans aren't one-and-done like corn. As long as we keep picking, they'll keep producing. We'll have fresh beans right up until the first frost."

Her heart sank. Once her Aunt Margaret stuck a For Sale sign at the end of the driveway, she'd load all her meager belongings into her car and hit the road. Not long after the first harvest, certainly well before the second crop ripened and months before the air turned chilly, she'd leave Emerald Bay. She had to. She had to go soon, before the feelings that grew between her and Caleb had a chance to put down roots. Leaving was the only way to protect his heart—or her own—from breaking, though she strongly suspected it might already be too late for hers.

"...'course, we won't get any beans at all if we let the weeds take over."

We did this. *We* need to do that.

His use of the word wasn't lost on her. She sucked in a breath. She should be putting some distance between her and Caleb. Should be preparing both of them for the not-too-distant future when she'd leave Emerald Bay. Yet she couldn't help the way her chest warmed every time he said *we*.

Suddenly irritated, she sprang to her feet, snatched her hoe from the ground where it had fallen and began chopping at a clump of crabgrass. "What are you sitting around for?" she demanded. "These weeds aren't going to hoe themselves."

Confusion furrowed Caleb's brow at her sharp tone, but he propped his hands on his knees. Pushing himself to his feet, he said, "Guess I'd better get back to work, then."

Salt stung her eyes, but she refused to watch him walk away when Caleb returned to the small plot of herbs at the far end of the garden. Instead, she kept her head down and took her misery out on the interlopers that had grown between the bean bushes. Beans she wouldn't be around to pick, she reminded herself. Angered at the thought, even though it was her own plan, she chopped furiously at a spindly plant with raggedly edged leaves.

"Whoa! Whoa! Whoa, now! What are you doing?" Caleb's hand clamped down over hers.

"I'm working here!" she insisted. She wrenched hard at the hoe, but Caleb held on with a viselike grip.

"Hold up a sec. Those are tomatoes, not weeds. Don't be chopping them down, or our salads are gonna look a little bare." Relinquishing his grip, he lowered a basket of freshly picked herbs to the ground.

"Tomatoes?" Jen took a closer look at the leggy plant that looked nothing like the pictures Caleb had shown her on the seed packets. "No, they aren't," she protested.

Caleb folded his muscular arms across his wide chest. A smile teased his lips. "Just exactly who is the farmer here?"

Bending, he scooped up what was left of the plant she'd attacked. He draped the thin stalk across the middle of his hand and held it out to her. "Smell," he said.

Grudgingly, she took a sniff. The acrid scent that clung to the on-the-vine tomatoes she'd bought from the local grocer filled her nose. An apology rose to her lips. She clamped her mouth shut before the words had a chance to escape. Instead, she struck a saucy pose. "Well," she huffed. "How was I supposed to know?"

"Um, the sign?" Caleb pointed to a picture of a bright red tomato mounted on a small wooden stake between the end of the beans and the start of the tomatoes.

She kicked at a clod of dirt. "I don't guess it can be saved?"

Caleb examined the leaves and the scraggly stalk. "Funny thing about farming—you put seeds in the ground, and when they start to sprout, the first thing they do is put down roots.

You can move that bush or tree or, in this case, tomato plant, wherever you want and it'll do just fine. Continue to grow and flower and, eventually, produce fruit. Just as long as its roots remain attached. Without them, without its roots, the plant withers and dies." He prodded the tiny leaves. "You chopped this one off at the roots. So, nah, it's a goner." He tossed the ruined plant on a pile of debris that was headed for the compost heap and dusted the dirt from his hands.

She silenced a groan. She and Caleb had planted tomato seeds in tiny containers and babied them along for weeks before transplanting them into the garden...only to have her ruin one of them. This was it. If she'd needed proof that any relationship between her and Caleb was doomed to failure, she'd found it. She shoved the hoe in his direction.

"This was a dumb idea," she grumbled. "I don't know why you thought I'd be good at gardening. I'm never gonna get the hang of it. I might as well quit now."

Forcing herself to remain strong, she spun on one heel. If Caleb hadn't gotten the message that they weren't right for each other before, if he hadn't already realized that they had nothing in common, the little scene she'd just pulled ought to convince him she wasn't what he needed.

Fighting tears every step of the way, she struck out for the main house.

Apparently, she hadn't stopped to consider Caleb's particular brand of stubbornness because he caught up to her less than ten seconds later. Striding up the row of beans beside her, he matched her step for step. They marched along in silence until they reached the path that led past the small orange grove to the inn. Only then did he reach for her.

"Hey, now," he said, his big hand landing on her forearm with a touch as light as a butterfly's. "Are you all right?"

"I'm fine," she snapped.

"You don't sound fine. You sound angry. Was it something I did or said?

"I just want to be left alone. Okay?"

"Whatever it was, I didn't mean to upset you."

His assumption that this was all his fault threatened to break her in two. There was nothing wrong with Caleb. He was a good man, a perfect man. He had those roots he was always talking about—to the community, his church, his land. She, on the other hand, had been raised rootless, and like the tomato plant she'd ruined, she was destined for the reject pile.

"It's not you," she insisted. "It's me." *Good*

grief. She couldn't be more trite and condescending if she tried, could she?

Despite herself, she stopped her headlong rush to go anywhere Caleb wasn't and turned to face him. Clearly, picking a fight with the man wasn't going to end things between them. She'd have to resort to the only thing left in her bag of tricks—honesty.

She blew out a breath, forcing her anger out with it. "Care for a drink of water? I know I could use a drink." Walking to the small cooler they'd brought to the garden with them, she pulled two bottles of water from the ice and handed one to Caleb. She took her time unscrewing the lid to hers, marshaling her thoughts as she did while she sank, cross-legged, onto a nearby patch of grass.

The sudden shift in her mood had the intended effect on the big man, because Caleb plopped down beside her, his muscular legs outstretched. Leaning back, he braced himself on one arm while he chugged water from the bottle she'd given him. Watching him, watching his throat work, his chest rise and fall, she felt desire stir within her. To give her fingers something to do—something besides giving them free rein to wander up and down Caleb's arms—she slipped one nail under the label on her bottle and began slowly separating the paper from the plastic.

"I think it's about time for me to be moving on." She refused to look up while she spoke. Her words were sure to hurt him, and she couldn't bear to see his pain. If she did, she might chicken out. Stick around. Which would end up hurting both of them even more in the long run. "I promised Aunt Margaret I'd stay until she sells the inn. After that, I'm outta here." Her hands stilled while she waited to see what he'd do, what he'd say.

"I see," he said slowly. "I'll hate to see you go, but you gotta do what you gotta do."

Wait. He wasn't going to argue? Wasn't going to fight for her? For them? He was just giving in? When the day came, he'd wish her bon voyage and move on with his life...without her?

She shook her head. She'd expected more from him.

She paused. Or maybe the truth hadn't sunk in yet. She resisted the urge to snap her fingers. That had to be it—Caleb hadn't accepted that she really intended to leave. She gathered her wits about her, determined to make him see that they weren't right for each other. That he had to let her go.

"What you said about roots back there." She deliberately glanced toward the debris pile. "I'm like that poor tomato plant. I don't have what it takes to stay put." When Caleb started to protest, she talked straight over him. "It's how I grew up. My mom hauled us from one end of the country to the other, depending on which way the wind was blowing when she got up that morning. Which makes me more like a tumbleweed than anything growing in our...in *this* garden."

"I'm not buying it," he said simply.

This time, she couldn't help but gawk at him. Caleb was one of the smartest men she'd ever known. How could he not understand that the differences between them made them wrong for each other? He was grounded. He had deep ties to the community. All she had were her connections to the members of her family, which would scatter to the four ends of the earth once Aunt Margaret sold the inn.

"But it's true," she protested. "I blow from one place to another just like my mom did."

"Nah," he scoffed. "Everybody has roots. Even your mom."

At that, she had no choice. She had to argue. "You didn't know her. I did. I'm telling you, the woman never stayed in one place more than a few months. I lost count of the times she rousted me and Kim from bed, told us to pack our things, and loaded us in the car. The next thing we knew, she'd slam on the brakes in front of the inn, toss a couple of garbage bags full of our clothes and stuffed animals to the curb and order us to march up the driveway to the front door. Before we reached it, she'd be off on some grand adventure."

"I'm sorry you grew up like that. That had to be hard, never knowing where you were going to be from one year to the next."

Caleb's sympathy plucked a chord in her chest. "Don't get me wrong. It was just how we lived. I thought it was normal. I was nearly in my teens before I realized the other kids in my class stayed put. I thought, whenever I came back to Emerald Bay, that they'd just come back from traveling around the country, too."

Caleb chuckled. "Funny thing, the way a kid's mind works. When I was a little tyke, I thought everyone was born speaking English and had to learn all those 'foreign' languages like Spanish or French."

She laughed softly and sobered just as quickly. It was important to make him under-stand. "The thing is, growing up the way I did, the longest I've ever stayed in one place was when Mom got cancer. We came back here, and after she died, we had no place else to go."

"Hmm." Caleb tossed a strand of the long, dark hair she longed to run her fingers through over his shoulder. "You don't think it's possible that your mom saw Emerald Bay, saw the inn, as her home? As the one place she was rooted to? Maybe she wanted you to develop that same connection she had to this place. It would explain why she'd bring you and your sister here, time after time." He gestured beyond the garden to the house that had been in her family for generations. "It would also make sense that she'd come back here, bring you and your sister back here, when she got sick."

"I just told you, she didn't have any ro—"

Jen's mind went blank as her world turned upside down and all the pieces rearranged themselves, like in a kaleidoscope. She would have sworn her mother hadn't had strong feelings for any particular place. Yet she couldn't deny that in her hour of need, when she knew she couldn't beat the cancer that had already spread throughout her body by the time the doctors identified it, her mom had returned to the place where people loved her.

She'd come home.

She hadn't gone to a hospital in whatever city they'd been living in at the time. Not to a treatment facility where some well-meaning social worker would separate her from her children. Not to a clinic or university that might use her as a guinea pig to test the latest, greatest cancer drugs.

But home.

Not only that, but thanks to all those previous visits, she'd brought her daughters to a place that was familiar to them. Where people weren't paid by the state to look after them. Where their aunts doted on them and their cousins played with them and, all too soon, grieved with them.

Her gaze swept over the garden, past the grove, and traveled the path toward the main house as far as it could go. The inn was out of sight, but she pictured the stately two-story house that had once been hailed as "the jewel of Florida's Treasure Coast," the six cabins her uncle had built, the sweeping lawn that led to the dunes and the beach beyond it. She would have sworn she'd never belonged anywhere in particular, but the inn had been the one constant in her life.

Had she been wrong all along? Did she, in fact, belong somewhere? Was she, despite all the many places she'd lived, rooted to Emerald Bay?

In which case, could she stay?

Before she could sort things out completely, she heard Caleb clear his throat. She looked toward the man who'd given her so much to think about. "Yes?" she asked.

"I guess, as long as we're getting things out in the open, there's something I should tell you."

That didn't sound ominous at all, she thought. Was he breaking up with her just when she was beginning to think they might have a future together after all? "What is it?"

"The truth is, I'm not looking for a lifelong commitment. Not from you. Not from anybody. I thought me and Wilma had that, that we'd be together forever." He took a breath. "But when she died, I realized no one can promise forever."

Jen's head filled with conflicting thoughts. Caleb had once referred to her as "the one who got away." Now he was saying he didn't want a long-term relationship with her. Confusion filled her head with cotton balls. "Exactly what are you trying to tell me?"

"Nothing." Warmth filled the depths of Caleb's eyes. "Just that, well, if you decide to stick around, you don't have to worry about me trying to pressure you into making it permanent. All I can promise you is today. Today, I'll be faithful. Today, I'm yours. That's all I have to give. It's all I'd ever want in return."

"Today, huh? No promise to love, honor and obey for the rest of their lives?" She searched his broad face for any sign of deception but found only openness and honesty written in his features.

"Yeah."

"I can give you that much." It didn't seem like too much to ask. Standing, she extended a hand to help him to his feet. "As long as we're here *today*," she said, emphasizing the word, "we might as well finish hoeing this garden."

"Sure. Then, as long as we're at it, maybe we can catch a movie tonight. That action flick is still playing down in Vero."

Jen nodded. She could do that. She could go to the movies with Caleb. Especially since tonight was still part of today.

Wasn't it?

Eleven

Kim

e made it.

Kim couldn't get the thought out of her head as her gaze flitted among the women gathered around the long table in the dining room. Though she'd never dared voice her doubts aloud, she'd worried that they had far too many queens and not enough worker bees to get the job done when Aunt Margaret had asked them to plan one last Dane Family Reunion. After all, each of them had—in their own way— achieved a place of importance in their chosen profession. Certainly no one in this room would deny that Belle had reached the pinnacle of success in her career as a pop artist. Or that Amy had parlayed the tiny sandwich and cookie business she'd started in her own kitchen into the best bakery in the county. Jen's knack for customer service had earned her a spot behind the velvet ropes in the high-roller section of one of the country's largest casinos. Diane had climbed the corporate ladder to Executive Row in one of the largest accounting firms in the state. Not to toot her own horn, Kim thought, but before Connors had restructured, she'd been in management, too.

With all these leaders gathered in one place, was it any wonder she'd questioned their ability to work together? But they had because they were family. They'd put aside their individual power trips to work toward one goal—granting their aunt's final wish.

Grabbing a napkin from a stack on the table, Kim dabbed at her eyes. She knew she was going to miss this, when all was said and done. The camaraderie, the laughter and the tears—she was going to miss it all when Margaret fulfilled the other part of the bargain she'd made and put the inn on the market. When Belle and The Emeralds catapulted to the top in Christian music and Diane dove headlong into the accounting business she'd started. When, with Aunt Margaret squared away in Emerald Oaks and the inn in the hands of new owners, Amy devoted her full attention to running not one, but two bakeries.

When Jen left without warning—as she so often did. As for herself, even though she loved Craig more than she'd ever thought she'd love any man, even though she'd found her calling in Royal Meals, her own future looked far too bleak without daily visits with her sister and her cousins.

"Hey. You look like you could use a drink." Amy lifted a tall glass of tangerine-colored liquid from the tray she carried.

"Yeah, sure." Tucking the napkin into her pocket, Kim gave the room a final sweep. Her daughter still hadn't joined them, despite the text message she'd left on her phone. Kim shrugged. She'd give Nat five more minutes. If she hadn't shown up by then, they'd have to start without her.

While Amy made the rounds, handing out beverages, Kim studied the notes spread out in front of her. Wondering again how she'd ended up in charge of the reunion, she ran a finger down the schedule. Delegate and designate had been her twin watchwords, and each person in the room was responsible for at least one item on her list. Tonight's review would ensure they had all their ducks in a row. Satisfied that she was ready to get started, she took a swig from the glass of fruity sangria.

"Yum." She smacked her lips. Turning to the petite brunette who'd slipped into the chair beside her, she addressed her cousin. "This is wonderful. What's in it? Papaya?"

Amy tucked a strand of dark hair behind her left ear. "One of my customers brought a huge basketful into Sweet Cakes this morning. I thought you might want to cut them up for breakfast one morning this weekend." Her blue eyes glinted. "I did steal one for the sangria, though. Along with a bunch of other tropical fruit—guava, mango, even some passion fruit juice. And, of course, white wine. I already emailed the recipe to you."

"Thanks. It's delish. I'd like to add it to the afternoon rotation." At four each day, they put out freshly baked cookies and sangria or wine for the inn's guests.

Kim took another sip. Over the rim of her glass, she spied her daughter. Nat must have snuck into the room when she wasn't looking, she thought, and wondered why her normally exuberant second child looked so glum. Making a note to ask about that later, she rapped her knuckles sharply on the tabletop. The noise drew the attention of the others, and the usual chatter died down.

Kim cleared her throat. "I can hardly believe Memorial Day weekend is staring us in the face. A little less than eight months ago, Aunt Margaret asked us to plan one last family reunion here at the inn." She sent her aunt a winning smile. "There were times when I didn't think we'd make it."

"You weren't alone. I had my doubts." Margaret's voice cracked.

Belle slipped one hand over her mother's. Smiling brightly, she asked, "Like when we had to wash down every wall and cupboard after the workmen refinished the floors?"

"Some of them twice." Amy pointed a finger at Jen.

Kim chortled. The accident with the Shop-Vac wasn't their only misstep, but it had been a doozy. "We had a few setbacks," she acknowledged. "But we kept at it until we whipped the inn into the best shape it's ever been in."

"I'll vouch for that." A joyous smile wreathed the lines in Margaret's face. "You all did an amazing job." She sipped the tea she preferred over the sangria.

Kim lifted her glass. "Here's to all we've accomplished."

Around the table, glasses and cups clinked as

each of them raised their beverages in a toast to bringing new life back to the inn. When the noise settled down some, Kim continued.

"In a few short days, we'll throw open the doors, spread our arms wide and welcome the entire Dane family home one last time." She held her glass aloft again. "Let's make this the best reunion ever…for Aunt Margaret."

"To Aunt Margaret," someone said, and they tipped their glasses once more.

When they finished, Kim asked each person for updates on their assigned tasks.

"We have sleeping arrangements for everyone who RSVP'd," Diane reported. "There aren't enough beds, so we rented roll-away cots for the overflow. Those have been set up in all the sitting rooms." As for arrivals and departures, volunteers had been lined up to provide transportation to and from the various airports, train stations and bus depots. "Tim will handle pickups from the Orlando airport, and Craig offered to get anyone who's flying into Melbourne. One of Edward's grandsons is a student at Florida State. He's catching a Greyhound bus to Vero, due to arrive at two on Friday. Caleb said he'd give him a lift to the inn."

"Sounds like you've got everything under control," Kim said. She'd expected nothing less from the woman who thought numbers were fun. Bending over her papers, she started to put a checkmark by Diane's name.

"There's just one thing."

"Yeah?" Kim's pen hovered.

"I'm worried that someone might show up unannounced. We have exactly one extra space, a roll-away cot in Jade, but if more than one person forgot to RSVP, I don't know where we'll put them. I'd offer to let them stay with me, but my place is a construction zone." After he'd finished renovating Sweet Cakes 2, Max had begun converting the mother-in-law suite at Diane's house into office space.

"They can stay at my house as long as they aren't allergic to cats," Amy volunteered.

Diane nodded. "If they are, we'll shift room assignments and pray that everyone is flexible."

"I think that's going to be the key for the weekend—flexibility," Kim noted. There were bound to be snafus. In her previous life as a program manager, she'd learned no one pulled off a flawless conference. There were always a few hiccups. Being flexible enough to resolve those issues without making a huge fuss about them often determined the event's success or failure. She crossed lodging and transportation off her list and moved on to the next item.

"Jen, how about the bonfire and the activities for Friday night?"

"Got it covered," her sister announced.

"Um. Do you think you could provide a few details?"

"What? And spoil the surprise?"

Amy nodded. "It's fine to surprise our guests, but if you come down with food poisoning and can't get out of bed, the rest of us need to know what you had planned."

"I hardly think Kim is going to give me food poisoning," Jen huffed. "But point taken. When they check in on Friday, each person will receive an agenda for the weekend, along with their room assignment and a little bag of items provided by some of the local businesses in town."

"Goodie bags?" Amy asked. "What a great idea."

"Thanks. I'd like to take all the credit, but it was Nat's idea." Jen shot her niece a thumbs-up sign. "Each bag contains a tube of sunblock from Long Boards Surf Shop, a fifty percent off coupon from A Likely Story, a toothbrush and toothpaste from Gentle Dentistry, a bottle of water and a granola bar." Her nose scrunched. "We would have asked for something from Sweet Cakes, but Amy's done more than enough already." In addition to supplying all the breads and desserts for the reunion, their cousin was making the cake for Kim and Craig's wedding.

Jen continued. "The first thing on the schedule is the welcome barbecue at six. The guys already set up the tents, tables and chairs. Island Smokehouse will be here with the meat at five thirty, right?"

"Right," Kim answered when Jen pinned her with an inquiring look. She knew her limits. Slow-smoking enough chicken, pork and ribs for upwards of a hundred people definitely exceeded her abilities. She could, and would, handle the side dishes, though. "I'll have mountains of potato salad, coleslaw and mac 'n' cheese to go with the meat."

"The bakery is providing garlic bread," Amy added.

"There'll be no shortage of food," Jen declared. "As soon as it gets dark, we'll set up the projector and screen on the deck and play the video Nat put together." Using the photos and information she'd been given, the graphic designer had assembled a montage that told a little bit about each member of the Dane family.

Kim smiled proudly at her daughter. Her conviction that something was really bothering Nat grew when the petite blonde's head remained bowed, her eyes downcast. Kim hiked one eyebrow while she aimed a questioning look at Jen, but from her sister's answering shrug, she didn't have any idea what was troubling the girl. Determined to dig into the matter as soon as she could, Kim prodded the meeting forward.

"That takes care of Friday," she announced. "Amy, you're up next." She tilted her head toward her cousin. "What's on tap for Saturday?"

"All kinds of good fun," Amy said with a grin. "I dug the croquet set out of storage in the attic. I had to replace the hoops—the old ones were bent beyond use—but everything else was fine. We'll set that up on the front yard, right where it was in previous reunions. Max and I added more sand to the horseshoe pit, so that's all ready. We'll erect the volleyball net on the beach that morning. For those who simply want to lie back and relax, there are plenty of beach towels and blankets for sunbathing. Plus, I ran off a bunch of copies of the treasure maps we used for Scott and Fern's gender reveal party. This time, instead of colored stones, I filled the chests with all sorts of trinkets—beads and light-up necklaces, plastic coins, whistles and yo-yos." A frown crossed her lips. "Everyone keep your fingers crossed for good weather, okay?"

"I've been watching the reports," Diane said. "Except for a shower Friday morning, we should have bright sunshine and cool breezes all weekend."

Looking up from her notes for the first time since she'd snuck into the room, Nat let out a breath. "That's a relief. The last thing we need is a hurricane to ruin everything."

Nat's glum attitude deepened when quiet laughter rippled around the table. "What?" she demanded.

"It's the wrong season for hurricanes," Belle hurried to explain. "We don't have to worry about those until much later in the summer. That's one reason we've always held the reunion over the Memorial Day weekend."

"Oh. I did not know that." Nat's head and shoulders drooped.

"It's okay," Kim soothed. When her daughter's moodiness threatened to draw attention away from the purpose of their meeting, she quickly moved the conversation on to the next topic.

"Saturday morning, we'll have the usual assortment of sweet rolls and croissants for breakfast, along with fruit salad, thanks to Amy," Kim announced. "I'll also serve a couple of egg casseroles. Lunch will include chips and cookies, along with sandwiches made with Aunt Liz's special sauce." She grinned. The simple mix of mayonnaise, ketchup and pickle relish had been a staple at every family reunion. "We're having Italian that night—salad and garlic bread, baked ziti and vegetable lasagna. The pasta dishes are already prepared and in the freezer."

"Mama and I borrowed a dozen hand-crank ice cream makers from all her friends so we can make homemade ice cream for dessert, just like we did when we were kids," Belle put in. "That'll be a lot of fun."

Diane made a face. Rubbing her shoulder, she said, "Oh, my poor arm."

"Don't worry. We'll leave the actual making of the ice cream to the youngsters," Belle assured her.

"Sounds good so far. That brings us to Sunday." Kim ran her pen down her list. "Church is at eleven, so I thought we'd serve breakfast from eight to ten. Pancakes and waffles. Fruit and cereal. Is that okay with everyone?" When no one objected, Kim marked the item off on her list. Her gaze sought Belle's, and she turned the floor over to her cousin.

"Okay." Belle clapped her hands. "We thought Sunday would be a good day for just visiting and getting to know one another a little better. By mutual consent, we didn't plan any new activities that day. Of course, we'll still have the croquet and horseshoes and the volleyball net for those who want to do that. But the big event is the talent show and family sing-along that night. I have portable screens that will turn the back deck into a stage."

"Thank goodness," Amy exclaimed. "I'm too old to have to climb trees."

Memories of the years when they'd draped sheets from ropes they'd tied to tree trunks sent a fresh wave of chuckles through the room.

Belle waited until the laughter faded. "I was surprised that so many people have already signed up for the talent show. So far, we have twenty acts. I'm sure we'll get a few more at the last minute."

Ever the competitor, Diane asked, "What about trophies?"

"We have ribbons." Belle held one up for everyone to see. *Dane Family Talent Show* read the gold lettering that had been stamped on wide streamers attached to a bright green rosette.

"I want one." Jen reached for the ribbon.

Belle clutched the award to her chest. "Sorry, you'll have to sign up for the talent show. Everyone who participates will get one."

"I'll just have to dazzle everyone with my card tricks, then," Jen joked in good-natured humor.

"You do that," Belle encouraged. She tucked the ribbon out of sight. "Whenever we finish with the talent show, we can either move to the firepit for the sing-along or stay where we are. We'll just have to see what everyone wants. Daclan and Jason will be there with their guitars to accompany us. Anyone else who plays is welcome to join in."

"What about The Emeralds? Aren't they going to perform?" asked Amy.

Belle shook her head. "This isn't about The Emeralds...or me. It's about family." She waited a beat for everyone to realize she was serious before she tilted her head.

Kim concentrated on not turning as red as a beet when Belle said, "But the next day is all about Kim, beginning with a sunrise wedding on the beach."

Diane, who'd volunteered to serve as the officiant, rubbed her eyes. "Tell me again why we're doing this at six thirty in the morning?"

"Because it's romantic," Kim said softly. "And because I can't wait another minute to be Mrs. Craig Morgan."

"I think it's sweet," Nat said, looking up.

"Thanks, honey," Kim said.

Diane pretended to yawn. "I guess I'll be there," she grumbled.

"Mama and I will be there." Belle nudged her mother. "Won't we?"

"I wouldn't miss it," Margaret declared.

"We're keeping it simple since it's a second marriage for both of us," Kim explained. "Nat and Craig's nephew will stand up with us. After we exchange our vows and take a few pictures, we'll come back to the inn for a wedding breakfast which, in keeping with the theme, will be simple. Just mimosas, fresh fruit and wedding cake."

"It's the perfect ending for the reunion," Margaret declared.

"People will be packing up and leaving right after breakfast," Diane acknowledged. "Tim and Caleb will return their people to the airport and the bus terminal. Max offered to take Craig's place on the Melbourne airport run so our newlyweds can have some time to themselves."

"For those who are heading out a little later, I'm sure there'll be plenty of leftovers and sandwich fixings."

"Well, it certainly sounds as if you girls have outdone yourselves." Margaret pushed away from the table. "I can't tell you all how much I appreciate the hard work that went into planning the reunion."

"And getting the inn fixed up," Belle reminded her mom.

"That, too."

Kim gathered her papers together, determined to catch her daughter before Nat slipped off to her room. She needn't have bothered. The girl stayed put.

Without giving anyone a chance to stand, Nat cleared her throat. "There's, uh, one more thing. Hmmm." Normally a person who dove headlong into the deep end, she hesitated. "I have a problem. I was kind of hoping I could get some advice?"

Her hands in her lap, Kim held her breath. Months earlier, she'd assured her daughter that if she ever needed help, her aunts would be all too happy to listen and offer guidance. Would they come through for her this time?

She expelled a relieved sigh when the doubt and unease in her youngest's voice called an immediate halt to any plans to leave the room. As if responding to a clarion call, every single woman settled back into her seat, her attention acutely focused on Nat.

"What's up?" Jen asked softly.

"You're sure you don't mind? I know everyone has a lot going on, but…"

"It's okay," Belle assured the young woman. "We're here for you. So what's going on?"

"The thing is, I kind of need to know where I go from here. I've received a couple of offers.

One in New York, one in Denver. Both of them need answers pretty quick, and, well, I just don't know which one to accept."

"You're leaving?" Kim stiffened despite her determination to remain supportive. "This doesn't have anything to do with me getting married, does it?"

"Relax, Mom." In spite of whatever troubled her daughter, Nat laughed. "No, my problems have absolutely nothing to do with you and Craig. I'm glad you're getting married. You're perfect for each other. You both deserve happiness."

Kim inhaled a thready breath. "Then why would you leave?"

"I can't afford to stay here," Nat said slowly. "I mean, after this weekend, Aunt Margaret's going to put the inn on the market. Once it sells, I'll need to get an apartment or something." Sorrow filled her eyes when she looked at Belle. "Don't get me wrong, Aunt Belle. I love working with you and Daclan. But you don't pay me enough to cover rent and utilities."

To her credit, the onetime superstar winced. "If it was up to me, I'd give you a huge raise. You certainly deserve it for all you do for The Emeralds. At this point, though, we're lucky if we make enough to cover gas and expenses when we perform in churches in Jacksonville or Miami. If we sign with a record company, that could change tomorrow. Or it could take us ten years to get to the point where we could afford to pay you—or ourselves—a living wage."

"That's what I thought." Nat accepted the disappointing news with an unflappable calm. "That's why I've come to the conclusion that staying in Emerald Bay won't work for me."

"I could hire you." Aunt Margaret's voice shook the tiniest bit. "After the auction, I'll have more money than I could spend in ten lifetimes. You could work for me, and I'd pay you to keep doing whatever it is you're doing."

Nat's features softened around a sympathetic smile. "That's a wonderful offer, Aunt Margaret, and I appreciate it. I really do. But I won't take advantage of you. Uncle Scott said that money's yours to keep. It wouldn't be right for me to take it."

Kim's heart filled with so much pride, she felt sure it would leak out of her eyes. After she divorced Frank, Nat and her brother had chosen to live with their fun-loving, free-spending dad. A man who would have jumped at the chance to separate Aunt Margaret from her last dime. Yet somehow, somewhere along the way, their daughter had acquired an entirely different set of values. Values that were the polar opposite of her father's.

"I'd have to talk it over with Deborah, but we could probably hire you at Sweet Cakes. At least part-time," Amy offered.

"Much as I love the bakery, Aunt Amy, I'm trying to think long-term. Unless Sweet Cakes needs a graphic designer or a PR person, I'm afraid I wouldn't be much use to you."

"But Denver? Or New York? They're too far!" Jen protested. "Why those cities?"

As if she knew the kind of reception her next words would receive, Nat hunched her shoulders protectively. "Dayglo reached out to me earlier today."

Kim went perfectly still as a profound silence filled the room. Dayglo and Sasha had been America's sweethearts until the TV star cheated on the movie actress. The video her daughter had posted about their spectacular breakup had nearly cost the actor his lead role on one of television's most popular shows. Only a staged reunion had saved his job from the chopping block. But someone had had to take the blame, and both celebrities had pointed their fingers at Nat in a move that had destroyed her credibility in social media.

"Why on earth…" Kim began.

"He apologized," Nat said quickly. "Sasha did, too. They said my video ignited a firestorm of press, and they want me to develop an entire publicity campaign for them."

Belle tsked. "Sounds like they read too much Oscar Wilde. 'There's only one thing in the world worse than being talked about, and that is not being talked about,'" she quoted.

"You're actually considering going to work for them?" Amy asked.

"As horrible as they were to you?" Jen wondered aloud. "I wanted to rip Sasha's hair out by the roots." Her eyes narrowed. "I still do."

"The money is crazy good." Nat's lips formed a thin, straight line. Seconds later, her expression crumpled. "But you're right. I can't trust them, can I?"

"I wouldn't." Diane idly drew boxes in the margins of the paper in front of her. "Who's to say the next time they need someone to take the fall, they won't throw you under the bus again?"

"You're right." Nat seemed to shrink into her chair. "In my heart, I knew it was the wrong move. I guess I just needed to hear someone else say it."

"Well, I, for one, am mighty glad to hear that. I always thought you were a smart girl, but you had me worried there for a minute." Clapping her hands together, Margaret applauded her great-niece.

"So that's a big *N-O* to New York?" Kim asked, just to be sure.

When Nat replied with a firm denial, it took a concentrated effort, but Kim managed not to frown. With New York out of the running, that left her daughter's other option—Colorado— which was even farther away from Emerald Bay. "Then Denver?" she asked.

Nat ducked the question by asking one of her own. "You guys know Samuel and I have been seeing each other a lot, right?"

Kim's chest quivered as questions filled her head. *Had Samuel popped the question?* Was her daughter engaged? She blinked back tears that weren't entirely happy. Ever since she'd first held her baby daughter in her arms, she'd imagined how excited she'd be when Nat and the man she loved announced their plans to get married. Now that the moment had arrived, however, she felt awash in trepidation and doubt. Why couldn't she be happy for the couple, she wondered.

Her gaze dropped to the bare fingers of Nat's left hand, and she pushed back against the doubts that rose like an incoming tide. There were any number of reasons why her daughter wasn't wearing an engagement ring. Maybe the one Samuel had purchased was too big and needed to be resized. Maybe he wanted them to shop for a ring together. Or, considering how little a youth pastor earned, perhaps the couple had decided to break with tradition and save for a nice set of matching wedding bands instead.

"Samuel is moving to Denver. He's asked me to go with him," Nat announced.

Murmured protests whispered about the room.

"That's so far away."

"This is awfully sudden."

"I didn't hear anything about a wedding."

At last, Amy's voice cut through the fog. "Why Denver?"

Nat toyed with her ink pen. "Samuel always knew his assignment in Emerald Bay was only temporary. About a month after he got here, he applied for a position as the youth pastor in a bigger church in Colorado. A few days ago, he found out he got the job."

Margaret crossed her arms and tucked her hands out of sight. Clearly not pleased at the news, she spoke through pinched lips. "This is the first I'm hearing about any transfer to Denver. Why is that?" she demanded.

"I don't know," Nat confessed. "I only learned about it last night. I guess he didn't want word to get around before he knew for sure that he was leaving."

"Back up a second," Diane cautioned. Worry lines appeared on her face. "He didn't tell *you*? Didn't discuss it with you? Pray over it with you?"

"No." Nat delivered the one-word response in a matter-of-fact tone.

"But he expects you to support this decision?" Diane's gaze held Nat captive.

"It's his calling. Doesn't he have to follow it?" Nat looked perplexed.

"Nobody's arguing with that. We get that this is the right move for him," said Amy. "But he's not our concern. Or at least, not our main concern. You're the one we're worried about. We need to find out what's right for you." Running her finger down the side of her glass, she moistened the tip and drew a circle on the tabletop. "I will say this...it seems, um, selfish of Samuel to spring this on you when he's known about it for months. When does he want an answer?"

"Right away." In the first sign that anything about the move troubled her, Nat's mouth slanted to one side. "He has to be in Denver next week. He's asked me to be there when the pastor introduces him to the congregation."

"As his what?" Diane leaned forward, clearly unable to keep silent. "As a friend? His fiancée?"

"Is he going to support you? Will you live together?" Shock tinged Margaret's voice.

Nat studied the rapidly darkening sky beyond the panes of glass that overlooked the front lawn. "We haven't really talked about it. I suppose I'll need to get a job. From what I hear, lots of places are hiring out there."

"So, no promise. No commitment on his part. But he wants you to up and move to another state with him." Amy threw her hands up in the air. Her gaze sought Belle's. "What do you think, Belle?"

"Sorry. I can't weigh in on this one." Bright red curls rippled when Belle shook her head. "Any advice I might give could be tainted by what's best for me." She cocked her head in Nat's direction. "Just so you know, what's best for me is for you to stay right here in Emerald Bay."

"That means a lot to me, Aunt Belle." Nat's chest swelled for a moment. It just as quickly deflated. "But what am I going to do about Samuel? He'll be destroyed if I don't go with him."

Kim cleared her throat. She'd listened to her sister and her cousins ask their questions. It was her turn. "Samuel wants you to move with him to Denver. He has a valid reason for going. But in all of this talk, there's one thing I haven't heard. I haven't heard you say you love him. Or that he loves you. Do you? Love each other?" Kim held her breath. The answer would make all the difference in the world.

Nat studied the walls, the windows, the tabletop. Without meeting her mother's gaze, she finally said, "I think he loves me. And I like him...a lot. He's a—a good friend. Someday, I might grow to love him. But right now?" She shook her head. "I can't say that I do."

On the other side of the table, Jen huffed. "You've known Samuel, what, five months? In all that time, there's been no spark?"

Nat's color deepened. She fidgeted in her chair. "There's more to a relationship than sex. We have the same interests, the same beliefs. I think we could be a good fit. Besides, there might be a spark if we...when we...you know."

"Uh-uh. Girl, if it ain't happened by now, it ain't gonna happen." Jen shook a finger at Nat before crossing her arms over her ample chest. "Trust me on this. You don't go traipsing halfway across the country for a relationship that *might* deepen. Marriage—not that you've said anything about marriage—but even a marriage between two people who are deeply in love with each other can fall apart." She eyed Diane, who raised her eyebrows but nodded. From Diane, Jen's gaze traveled around the table. "Just ask anyone in this room. Except for Belle, we've all been married. Most of us have been divorced. Some of us more than once. Marriage is hard, hard work. I can't imagine trying to build a future with someone I only *like*."

Nat picked at a hangnail. "I don't want to let Samuel down. It'll break his heart if I don't go with him."

"It'll break yours if you get all the way out there and he falls for the first cowgirl he sees," Amy said. She didn't have to say she was speaking with the voice of experience. They'd all been there for her the day she'd discovered her husband with another woman.

Kim had heard and seen enough. She might not have liked it, but she would have stood idly by if Nat had said she loved Samuel, if she was in love with Samuel. But she hadn't. That being the case, as a mother, she could not, would not hold her tongue while her daughter stood on the railroad tracks, a freight train barreling toward her. And that was just what this situation was…a train wreck in the making. She knew it. Her sister knew it. Her cousins and her aunt knew it. She was willing to bet that, on some level, Nat knew it, too. Why else would she seek their advice?

Steadying herself, she did what she had to do to protect her child. "Honey, much as we all love Samuel, and we do—" Kim looked around the room for confirmation.

"He's a very nice young man," Aunt Margaret said.

"No one could have done a better job with the lock-in at New Year's," Belle acknowledged. The night had marked a turning point in her life.

Kim nodded. "Much as we love him, he's not the right man for you. You deserve the kind of love I share with Craig."

"Someone who makes your heart sing, like Jason makes my heart sing," Belle said.

"A man who gives you tingles." Amy's eyes sparkled.

"Forget tingles. You want a man who gets your motor running." Jen pretended to rev the engine of a motorcycle. "Vroom. Vroom."

"One who's there for you, through thick and thin." Diane patted hips that, thanks to her new diet and exercise regimen, were much slimmer than they'd been eight months earlier.

Margaret leaned across the table, her arm resting on the wooden surface. Her voice firm, she took her grandniece's hand in hers and said,

"You want a partner, a teammate. Someone you can build a life with. Someone you love enough to have children with. Someone who enjoys sitting on the porch with you and, Lord willing, will grow old with you." Though her voice grew strained, she continued. "Someone you can't imagine living without. That's what you deserve, what you want. Please don't settle for anything less."

Kim wiped her eyes as she noted the tears that ran down both of her daughter's cheeks. And theirs weren't the only damp cheeks in the room.

"Thank you, Aunt Margaret," Nat whispered while, around her, women sniffled and blotted their eyes. "You're right." She gave the rest of the women a quick glance. "You're all right. I don't have that kind of relationship with Samuel." She heaved a sigh. "And I never will. I need to tell him I can't go with him to Denver." She stood then and, without another word, ducked out of the room.

"Whew," Jen whispered once they heard Nat's footsteps reach the top of the staircase. "That's one crisis averted."

Amy focused a pointed look on Kim. "Do you think she really needed us to tell her?"

"I think, deep down, she knew it was never

going to work out with Samuel. Whether she did or didn't, though, I'm glad we were all here for her today."

They spoke in hushed tones for a few minutes longer. Finally, Aunt Margaret struggled to her feet. Grabbing her cane from the back of her chair, she announced that it was past her bedtime. Once they'd bid her goodnight, the rest trickled out behind her, leaving Kim alone in the dining room.

She really was going to miss this, she thought with a deeper appreciation for the close ties her family shared. This—coming together to solve each other's problems—was what family was all about. Not Zooming in on a phone call or chiming in on a group chat but sitting down in the same room, hashing things out, giving and receiving advice from those who'd been there, done that, and loved each other enough to be open and honest about it.

She refused to fool herself. The inn was as much a part of their family as each person who'd sat at the table tonight. When they were just kids, she and Jen and the others had forged strong bonds while they cleaned up the kitchen after dinner each night. Those connections had deepened while they changed the linens and cleaned the rooms and toted their guests' luggage up and down the stairs. They'd learned to work as a team on treasure hunts, had relied on one another while they explored the twenty acres surrounding the inn. Later, after they'd grown up and most of them had moved away, the inn had played an integral role in pulling them all back together again. This past year, as they'd worked to restore and preserve the home their grandfather had built, they'd also restored the bonds of their childhood.

What they had as a family, what they had here at the inn was precious. Why would they let it slip through their fingers? Especially now that Diane and Nat had discovered a treasure trove of gold and precious gems. When she sold it, her aunt would have all the money she needed to keep the inn afloat for the rest of her lifetime. Perhaps even longer.

Her thoughts spun in circles until they centered on the reason she'd returned to Emerald Bay in the first place: Aunt Margaret couldn't run the inn on her own anymore. Could one of them take her place? One by one, she studied the empty chairs her sisters-in-arms had occupied only minutes earlier. They all led busy lives, with jobs and businesses none of them would willingly walk away from.

With a resigned sigh, she gathered her notes and headed upstairs where, between her daughter, her responsibilities with the reunion and the imminent loss of the one place her family called *home*, she doubted she'd get a moment's sleep.

Twelve

Diane

For the first time since she'd joined Nat and Jen at the reception desk nearly two hours ago, the flood of arrivals had slowed to a trickle. With most of their expected guests checked in, the noise of children running up and down the halls, the clatter of dishes coming from the kitchen, the occasional bursts of loud conversation brought a smile to Diane's lips. Watching for the last of their seldom-seen relatives to arrive, she spotted an SUV with Texas plates pull up in front of the inn. Whoever it was, they lingered in the vehicle. Taking advantage of the chance to talk to her niece without one distant cousin or another listening in, she whispered, "How did things go with you and Samuel the other night?"

Nat double-checked that it was just the three of them before she answered, "Better than I thought it would. He didn't break down in tears. He didn't beg me to change my mind, either." She frowned. "I expected him to do at least that much."

From her spot on Nat's other side, Jen said, "If he can move on that easily, it just goes to show that you guys weren't right for each other."

"I know," Nat said. "It still hurt a little. I mean, one minute he wanted me to move across the country with him. The next, he was like, 'Ciao, baby.'"

"Will he be here tonight?" Before they'd learned of his impending transfer, they'd asked Samuel to kick off tonight's festivities with a blessing.

No longer streaked with the blue dye that had colored it upon her arrival in Emerald Bay, Nat's soft blond curls bounced when she shook her head. "He said to tell everyone he's sorry but, as long as I wasn't going with him, he wanted to strike out for Denver a couple of days early. He broke the news to the kids at the youth meeting, and he left this morning."

Checking on the car, which still sat, its doors closed, Diane kept her disapproval to herself.

Instead, she wondered aloud, "Any idea who we can get to say grace tonight?"

"You can do it," suggested Jen. "If you can marry Kim and Craig, you can certainly pray over the food."

"Hmmm." Diane mulled the idea over. "I think we should ask Aunt Margaret. Or, if she won't do it, then Scott."

Jen groaned. "He'll go on forever. We'll never get to eat."

The sound of slamming car doors accompanied Nat's quiet laughter.

"I'll warn him to keep it short," Diane said.

Jen pointed at the trio who were slowly making their way up the stairs to the front porch. "Looks like they decided to come inside after all. I was starting to think they were going to turn around and go back to Texas. Anyone know who they are?" A decade's worth of changes made it hard to recognize some distant cousins. For others, this was their first—and last—reunion as adults.

Nat gave the barrel-chested man a cursory glance. Nearly everyone who planned on attending the reunion had complied with her request for photos and a short bio. "If I'm not mistaken, that's your Uncle Edward's son, Harry. The dark-haired woman must be his wife, Aggie."

She squinted. "But who's the other woman? There's nothing in my files about her. She looks about Aunt Margaret's age, doesn't she?"

Diane felt a frisson of concern. She ran a finger down the list of reservations until she came to Harry and Aggie's names. Since they hadn't given any indication that they'd be bringing someone with them, she'd assigned them to La Popa. The one-bedroom cottage had a king-size bed.

"Wait a second." Jen snapped her fingers. "Is that Uncle Edward's wife, Opal? I've never met her, but I've seen pictures." Their Aunt Margaret's brother, Edward, had married a girl from Texas shortly after he went to work at the Space Center in Houston. Their children, Harry and Heather, had been in grade school when Edward died of a sudden heart attack.

"Gosh. I haven't seen her in…" Diane stopped to think. "I must have been four or five?" Once Opal remarried, she and the children had stopped attending the Dane reunions. If the woman who leaned heavily on Harry's arm indeed proved to be her uncle's widow, more than forty years had passed since she'd last visited the inn.

Rising, Diane stepped out from behind the desk. A sudden rush of excitement lent an uncharacteristic squeal to her voice. "Harry? Harry, is that really you?"

"Yes, ma'am. And you are?"

"Diane, Diane Keenan. I'm your Aunt Liz's daughter. It's so good to see you." She extended a hand in greeting.

"Diane." Harry's voice boomed through the small reception area. "It surely is a pleasure."

Diane barely kept from grunting when the man whose accent was as deep and wide as the Rio Grande enveloped her in a rib-crushing hug.

"Well," she laughed as she extricated herself. "And who's this with you?"

"This here bluebonnet is my wife, Aggie." Harry slipped one arm around the tall brunette who stood at his side.

"Howdy, Diane. I'm so happy to meet y'all. We've been looking forward to this weekend forever." Her drawl even more pronounced than her husband's, Aggie gave Diane a warm handshake. "Oh, and thanks to whoever put the balloons out front. We would have driven straight on past without them." A cluster of bright green balloons danced in the breeze on both sides of the entrance to the Dane Crown Inn. Welcome signs guided new arrivals down the long driveway, which ended under a huge Dane Family Reunion banner.

Harry looked around for the woman who'd relinquished her hold on his arm and now stood off to one side. Blue eyes that reminded Diane of her Aunt Margaret's twinkled as a toothy grin spread across his deeply tanned face. "We brought a surprise with us. This here's my momma, Opal. Y'all remember her, don't ya?"

"Now, honey," chided the scrap of a woman, whose turquoise necklace probably weighed more than she did. Opal grabbed Harry by the sleeve. "I told you, Margaret's 'bout the only one who'll recognize me. Diane was barely out of diapers the last time I saw her."

"I can't say as I remember you, but you're more than welcome," Diane assured the older woman. Reminding herself that she didn't have a bed, much less a room, for their unexpected guest, she summoned the other women at the reception table with a wave of her hand.

"Hey!" Chortling merrily, Jen hurried to take Diane's place. "I'm Jen, one of your Aunt Shirley's girls. And this is Nat, my sister Kim's youngest."

While Jen and Nat introduced themselves and made the round of hugs and handshakes, Diane scooted back to her chair, where she studied the rooms that were still available and did her best to figure out where she could place their surprise guest. The extra cot in Jade was out—she couldn't in good conscience ask a woman in her eighties to rough it for three or four nights. Chewing on one nail, she was considering taking Amy up on her offer to house the overflow when she became aware of a figure standing on the other side of the reception desk. She looked up to find Opal peering at her list of room assignments.

"I sent Harry and Aggie to get our luggage so's you and I could chat. I told him it was a mistake to bring me along without lettin' y'all know ahead of time. That boy always was a stubborn one. Did you know when my second husband—God rest his soul—wanted to adopt him and Heather, Harry pitched an absolute hissy fit? Course not. How could you know?" she said, answering one question with another one.

Diane looked up from her lists. "We are thrilled to have you here," she said earnestly. "I'm going to find the best possible place for you to stay," she assured the older woman. "I had put Harry and Aggie in one of our cottages—La Popa. If they wouldn't mind staying at my sister's in town, I can give you the cottage instead."

"Pfft. Now, honey, we are *not* going to put you to any trouble," Opal insisted. "We already got it all worked out. No reason the three of us can't stay in La Popa together. Me an' Aggie'll share the bed. Harry brought a sleeping bag. He can throw it on the floor somewhere."

Harry had a few years and about fifty pounds on her, and the thought of him sleeping on the floor made Diane's hips ache. "I think we can do a little bit better than that. We have an extra cot. I'll have someone set it up in La Popa for him."

"Problem solved." Opal dusted a pair of wrinkled hands together. "Now wasn't that easy?" She turned as Harry and Aggie bustled through the door carrying several suitcases and one very large plastic bin.

"Oh, good. You brought in the cookies." Despite her small stature, Opal took the box from her son's hands and swung it up onto the reception table. "I don't want to brag, but my Cowboy Cookies have won a blue ribbon at the county fair ten years running." She pried up one corner of the lid.

Diane's mouth watered when the heavenly scent of chocolate, coconut, cinnamon and butter filled the air. "Those are going to wreak havoc with my diet," she moaned.

Opal snapped the lid closed before anyone could steal a cookie. "I brought enough to share with everybody. Could somebody take them to the kitchen for me?"

"I'll do it." Jen darted forward. "You can trust me. They won't end up in my room. No ma'am," she said with a sly grin.

"You'd better not eat all those." Diane nudged her cousin in the ribs.

"Spoilsport," Jen complained. With a little more effort than Opal had shown, she hefted the box. "I'll drop these off with Kim and get someone to take the cot down to La Popa. Back in a flash." And off she went.

Diane turned to Harry and Aggie, who waited patiently for their room assignment. "Okay, then," she said brightly. "As you heard, you'll be staying in La Popa. To get there, go straight down the hall and out the French doors that lead onto the deck. Your cabin will be on the right."

Opal tilted her head to look up at her son. "Why don't you and Aggie get us settled in. I want to visit with Margaret. She and I have some catching up to do." As if the matter were settled, she pinned Diane with a look. "Show me the way, will you, darlin'?"

"Yes, ma'am." Diane smothered a smile at Opal's charming way of bossing people around. Leaving Nat to give Harry and Aggie their goodie bags and such, she lent her arm to her uncle's widow. Moments later, they moved past the stairs that led to the second-floor suites.

"Everything here is just how I remembered it," Opal remarked as she walked in slow, halting footsteps. "It's remarkable how well you've preserved the old place. It's like it hasn't changed a bit."

"I can't tell you how good that is to hear." Diane squeezed the hand that clung to her arm. "We just finished giving the inn a massive facelift." Hearing that all the blood, sweat and tears they'd poured into the project had been worthwhile made her heart skip a beat.

"Would you excuse me for just a sec?" Diane asked a moment later as they passed the game room. She summoned Caitlyn and her friend Stacey. After hurried introductions, the teens loped off in the direction of the lobby, where Diane had no doubt they'd insist on carrying the new arrivals' luggage to their cottage.

"That blonde was yours?" Opal asked once she and Diane had resumed their walk to the living room.

"Yes, ma'am. That's Caitlyn. The other girl is a friend from her soccer team. They'll both be sophomores in high school next year." As she said the words, Diane shook her head in wonder. Where had the years gone? It seemed like only yesterday, she'd been pushing a baby carriage.

"She's just as pretty as you are. Got your bone structure, too." Opal sighed. "She's lucky to be so tall. I always wished I was taller."

"She gets her height from her dad," Diane admitted when they'd reached the arch that led into the room where Aunt Margaret and various cousins and aunts had claimed the couches and chairs. Her pace slowed as she retrieved her cell phone from her back pocket and opened the camera app. "Are you ready?" she asked Opal.

"I am." Abandoning Diane's arm, the older woman steadied herself. Though she wobbled slightly from side to side, she walked into the living room under her own steam, her feet aimed straight for the figure seated in the Queen Anne chair.

"Margaret?" Opal's Texas twang softened the harder consonants in her sister-in-law's name. "Good gracious, woman. You've grown old."

"You're one to speak, Opal Dane," Margaret said without skipping a beat. "Your hair is whiter than mine."

Quicker than Diane thought possible, Margaret sprang to her feet. In seconds, the two elderly women held one another in a fierce hug. Though her tears blurred the images she saw through the camera lens, Diane snapped picture after picture, not stopping until, still holding hands, her two aunts drew back to get a better look at each other.

"Shame on you, Opal," Margaret chided without a trace of rancor. "Springing a surprise on me. Why, you could have given me a heart attack, showing up like this." Taller by a foot, she easily looked over her sister-in-law's shoulder. "You didn't come by yourself, did you?"

"Me? Drive all this way? I might take the truck to the little grocery on the corner, but that's as far as I go these days. Harry and Aggie brought me. They're getting checked in, but I couldn't wait another minute to see you."

Margaret's face filled with compassion. "I was so sorry to hear about Jacob. I would have come for the funeral, but I was in the hospital myself at the time." Opal's second husband had succumbed to cancer while Margaret was recuperating from the accident that had taken her sister's life.

"Lord, I hated to hear the news about Liz." Opal sighed. "We've had our share of losses, haven't we?"

"No one gets through life unscathed, I guess." Margaret's wavering smile firmed as she spoke. "We have so much to be thankful for, though. Starting with having you here this weekend."

As if realizing that she and Opal weren't

alone, Margaret faced the room. "This is my brother Edward's widow, Opal Dane Anderson." She pointed. "That's Lila. She's married to my cousin Randy's son, Bruce. Next to her is Connie. She's my cousin Alice's daughter. Then there's..." She didn't get a chance to introduce anyone else because, as soon as she'd said their names, the women rushed to exchange warm greetings, hugs and handshakes with the newest arrival.

Noticing that Fern didn't join the others who clustered around Opal and Margaret, Diane headed for the back of the room, where her brother's wife had settled onto a love seat with her fingers folded atop her belly.

"You think anyone will mind if I don't get up?" Fern asked.

"There have to be some perks to being eight months pregnant." Diane sank onto the next cushion.

"False labor is not one of them." Fern's lips pulled taut. She leaned forward, her fingers splaying across her belly. "Ooof," she gasped.

Aware that the Braxton-Hicks contractions Fern had experienced previously hadn't lasted very long, Diane counted off the sixty seconds it took for this one to ease. "Have you been having these often?" she asked when some of the tension faded from Fern's face.

Fern took a deep, cleansing breath. "I thought I was over them. I haven't had any since the day of the shower. But I had a terrible backache this morning, and then they started up again." She clucked her tongue. "I probably overdid it getting ready for the weekend. I'm hoping that if I just sit here and rest, they'll go away."

"Did you try walking them off?" Though things had no doubt changed in the sixteen years since she'd had Caitlyn, her doctor back then had recommended light exercise as a method for stopping false labor in its tracks.

Fern nodded. "Walking. Toe touches—not that I can actually touch my toes." She laughed. "I did some yoga right before we left the house. Nothing worked. They just keep getting stronger."

Diane swallowed. Strong, regular contractions were the hallmarks of real labor. Hoping that wasn't the case this time, she shifted the conversation. "Do you like the way the nursery turned out?" Leery of the paint fumes, Fern and the girls had spent the day at her mother's while Scott had overseen the work party that assembled the crib and transformed the guest room into a nursery. "I liked the sage green you chose. It's soothing."

"The room turned out so well," Fern gushed. "I can't believe you did it all in one day." Tracing a circle on her belly, she said, "Someone even washed, folded and put away all the baby clothes. All I had left to do was open a pack of diapers." Her brows knitted. "Oh, for pity's sake."

Diane checked the time when Fern's features tightened around another contraction. Five minutes, she noted, not loving the fact that the pains were so close together.

Trying to distract Fern, she asked, "I love the booties. Did your mom make those?" Though Diane deeply admired people who had mastered the art of knitting, she had an altogether different reason for posing the question. When Fern only shook her head, unable to concentrate on anything beyond the tightening of the muscles around her belly, her concern leapfrogged forward.

"Whoo!" Fern said slightly more than a minute later. "What were you saying?"

"Oh, it wasn't important." Diane grabbed several tissues from a box on the end table and handed them to Fern.

On the other side of the room, the beehive of activity around Margaret and Opal began to break up. As the various relatives drifted back to their seats and Fern blotted sweat from her brow, Diane kept her voice deliberately nonchalant.

"Did you talk to your doctor about the Braxton-Hicks? What'd she say?"

Fern nodded. "I saw her this week. She was very reassuring. Said everything was right on track." Noting Diane's concern despite her efforts to hide it, Fern insisted, "This is not real labor. It can't be. The baby's not due for another month yet."

Diane wasn't sure which one of them Fern was trying to convince, but she didn't like her sister-in-law's pale, drawn complexion or the light sheen of sweat that broke out across her forehead with each new contraction. Not wanting to alarm anyone, especially if her suspicions were wrong, she kept the conversation light while she watched the seconds tick by. Sure enough, barely five minutes had passed before Fern nearly doubled over with another contraction.

"Um, where are the girls?" Diane asked when the worst had passed.

Fern panted lightly. "Scott took them outside. They needed to run off some energy."

Ignoring the curious glances from some of the other women in the room, Diane thumbed buttons on her phone. "Just a sec, Fern. Let me check with Jen and Nat to see if anyone else has checked in."

Lord, forgive me for lying, she prayed while she texted Nat to find her Uncle Scott and tell him his wife needed him in the living room pronto. Looking up from her phone once her niece assured her that the job was as good as done, she smiled warmly at Fern. "You know, with everything else going on, I never asked you if you'd picked out a name for this little one."

"Funny you should ask," Fern said while she arched enough to rub her lower back. "Scott and I agreed on Isabella and Sophie's names almost immediately. But with this one..." She traced another circle over her belly. "We haven't had any luck at all."

"I have no doubt in the world that the perfect name will come to you as soon as you see her," Diane said with all the assurance she could muster.

"You're probably right." Fern held up a finger. "Here comes another one."

Diane thought her niece must have read between the lines of her text because, before Fern's contraction ended, Scott stood in the doorway to the living room. While others might not notice, Diane knew her brother well enough to read his concern in his slightly disheveled appearance. It took all of two seconds for his gaze to zero in on his wife and two more for him to move from across the room to the love seat. As he neared, Diane moved out of the way, giving her brother plenty of space to kneel at his wife's side.

"What seems to be going on?" His normally sonorous voice was devoid of its usual confident, all-knowing air.

"Nothing to worry about," Fern panted as the contraction lost its grip. "I'm sure it's more false labor."

"Yeah?" Scott's tone announced that he wasn't convinced. "How long has this been going on?" he asked gently.

Fern studied her fingers. "Since early this morning."

"And are the contractions getting stronger?"

Fern bowed her head. Her voice muffled, she confessed, "A little."

"How about timing? Would you say they were coming at regular intervals?"

When Fern glanced up with questions in her eyes, Diane answered, "Five minutes apart for the last twenty minutes or so."

"You don't say."

Diane whispered a silent prayer when a dazed expression replaced the unflappable calm that served her brother so well in the courtroom. In less time than it had taken him to cross the room, however, his jaw set exactly the way she remembered it doing when he was eight or nine and had made up his mind about something.

Fern's breathing slowly returned to normal. "It's early yet. The baby's not due for another month."

"True. But it wouldn't hurt to take a little trip to the hospital. Simply as a precaution," Scott said in his most persuasive voice.

"Nonsense. Let me just call Dr. Salena. I'm sure she'll say it's false labor."

As stubborn as he was decisive, Scott stood. "We can call her from the car…on the way to the hospital. Diane?"

From her spot nearby, Diane assured her brother. "I'm here."

Digging in his pocket, Scott pulled out a set of keys. "Will you bring the car around front?"

"Sure." She didn't waste a second but high-tailed it out of the room. Passing the registration desk, she signaled Jen. "Fern might be in labor," she informed her cousin. "I'm going to get the car. Can you grab some towels, blankets?"

By the time Diane backed out of the parking spot and braked to a stop in front of the steps, Scott waited for her with an obviously miserable Fern at his side. Jen lingered beneath the welcome banner, her arms laden with linens.

Moments later, Scott lifted his wife onto the thick towel Jen had spread over her seat. His motions steady, he snapped her seat belt in place while he asked, "Honey, where's your hospital bag?"

"It's in the back," Fern admitted in a small voice. "I put it in there this morning, just in case."

A glimmer of humor momentarily softened Scott's jawline. "Good," he said. "We probably won't need it, but it's good to have it with us...just in case."

Diane looked away when, in a loving gesture, her brother pressed his forehead against his wife's. A tear rolled down her cheek when she heard him say, "Why don't you call Dr. Salena while I get us to the hospital in record time."

Thirteen

Amy

"I think things went well today, don't you?" Max stood, his feet splayed, bare forearms resting on the top rail that circled the deck. Beyond the river, the sun slowly sank toward the horizon, the last of its rays sending long shadows across the green grass.

"Better than I could have hoped." Enjoying the feel of Max's elbow pressed against her own, Amy listened to the shouts that drifted from the front yard, where yet another croquet match was underway.

Taking in the view, she noted Margaret and Opal holding court on the upholstered cushions of rattan chairs beneath one of the tents. Belle and Opal's daughter Heather sat nearby, ready to fetch anything their mothers needed, while various aunts and cousins entertained the family matriarchs with stories and plied them with sweets. Beyond them, at the edge of the path that wound through a patch of neatly landscaped trees and flowering bushes, Nick, Josh and Nat taught Isabella and Sophie how to play horseshoes.

Amy had to give Nat credit—from the moment Scott had whisked Fern off to the hospital, the young woman hadn't let her two cousins out of her sight. Not only that, but she'd made it her mission to keep the girls so busy playing games and working on craft projects that they didn't have time to miss their parents.

Nor was Nat the only one who'd gone out of her way to make the reunion a success. Caitlyn had surprised them all by inviting members of her high school soccer team to spend the afternoon at the inn, where the teens had held an impromptu soccer camp. Amy didn't know who'd enjoyed the scrimmage at the end the most—the parents or the players. Both had walked away from the makeshift field wearing wide grins. Afterwards, Caitlyn, her cousins and friends had taken over the game room. The last time Amy had walked by, a rousing Wii tournament had been underway at one end of the room, while at the other, several board games were in session.

"What's next?" Max popped a bubble that drifted in the still air from the spot where a group of toddlers were engaged in a bubble-blowing contest under the watchful eyes of their parents.

"I'm thinking about getting another one of those cookies Aunt Opal brought. They're incredibly good." Loaded with chopped pecans and shredded coconut, the oat cookie was a sweet and cinnamony treat.

"Mmm. I think you're too late. The last of those disappeared right after lunch."

"Rats," Amy complained. Not that she needed anything else to eat. She'd managed to snag a second helping of Kim's veggie lasagna earlier. Still, she liked to polish off a good meal with a taste of something sweet. Considering her options, she listened to the clinking of dishes and pots and pans as Kim and her crew of volunteers cleaned the kitchen after supper.

As the shadows grew longer, the last of the beachgoers rounded the corner of the house carrying towels and pulling a beach wagon loaded with boogie boards and umbrellas.

"Amy," called Steve, a second cousin once removed who hailed from the other side of the state. "Where do you want us to put all this stuff?" He hefted a lawn chair from the cart.

"Just leave it at the end of the deck." It made no sense to stow the gear in the storage shed when they'd just be getting it all out again the next day. "Be sure to wash the sand off your feet. I left a fresh stack of towels on the shelf by the outdoor shower." Putting away the play equipment was one thing; tracking sand across the inn's freshly refinished floors was something else again.

"You got it!" Steve called. Seconds later, giggles and screams filled the air as he herded his youngsters under the cold spray.

"Have you heard any more from Scott or Fern?" Max asked while a smile played around his mouth. "You must be over the moon—a new baby." Scott had called to let everyone know that the newest member of the family had put in an appearance shortly after they'd arrived at the hospital.

Thinking of all the fun she'd have teaching her new niece how to bake, Amy grinned. Isabella and Sophie loved wearing the Sweet Cakes aprons she'd made especially for them. Before too long, she'd add another tiny apron to the ones that hung from hooks near the back door. At least once a month, she and the girls would take over the bakery on a quiet Sunday. They'd fill the kitchen with giggles and laughter while they pressed cookie cutters into dough, slid the shapes into the ovens and then decorated them, and Amy could hardly wait for the newest addition to the family to join them.

Max let out a long, slow breath. "That took everyone by surprise, didn't it?"

"I'll say," she agreed. No one, not even Fern's doctors, had anticipated this baby's early arrival. Especially since Isabella had been born a day after her due date and Sophie a day before. "I was afraid she'd give birth before they made it to the hospital, but according to Scott, the delivery was textbook-perfect. And so's the baby. Ten perfect little fingers, ten perfect little toes."

"And she's okay? The baby, I mean."

Amy couldn't blame him for the note of concern his voice carried. His brother and sister-in-law had suffered several losses before Max's nephews had been born.

"She's a little on the small side," Amy admitted. "Five pounds, two ounces."

Max whistled. "That's not much more than a sack of sugar."

The slightest frown tugged at Amy's brows. At the thought of how it would feel to hold someone so tiny, so fragile in her arms, a fierce protectiveness surged through her. She might not have children of her own, but she'd do anything for Nick and Caitlyn, Isabella and Sophie, and for this new baby, too.

"Have they named her yet?"

"Not that I know of." She ran a hand over her ponytail. Had she imagined it, or had her brother acted a little cagey when she'd asked him the baby's name? Or was he simply wrung out after the rush delivery? She'd let him rest a day before she asked again.

"Are you going to the hospital to see them tonight? I'll be glad to take you," Max offered.

"I don't think so," she said slowly. "Fern needs her rest. She's going to have her hands full once she gets home." Not that she'd have to juggle two preteens and a newborn on her own. Scott had hastily rearranged his caseload so he could spend a few weeks at home with his wife and daughters. Not only that, but Nat had volunteered to watch Sophie and Isabella for several hours each day. Kim had already planned to stock the family's freezer with simple heat-and-serve meals. In addition, Amy, Belle and Jen would take turns helping out as much as they were needed. "I'll wait to visit until they get home. They should be discharged first thing Monday morning."

"Sounds good. Let me know if there's anything I can do, too. You know I'm willing to pitch in."

Amy pressed a tiny bit closer to Max. Not many men would give up an entire holiday weekend to spend time erecting tents, setting out chairs, helping to man the grill or just sitting around and visiting with their girlfriend's family. But Max wasn't like any other man she'd ever known, and she counted herself lucky, indeed, to have him at her side.

Content to linger at the railing, they spoke in low voices until movement along the tree line caught Max's attention. He pointed to a couple of men and young boys who emerged from the trail that led to the river. "Looks like somebody's been fishing."

A young boy of five or six dropped his fishing rod in the dirt and raced across the yard yelling, "Mama! I catched a fish!" The youngster plowed into the legs of a distant cousin who lived somewhere in the Midwest.

"That brings back memories." Amy watched the boy excitedly spread his arms wide as he described the *monster* he'd pulled out of the water. She laughed when the dad shook his head and held his fingers about six inches apart.

"My own dad taught me to fish when I was about his age," she murmured.

"That's what reunions are all about, isn't it? Making new memories, recalling the old ones?"

"Yeah, I guess it is," Amy acknowledged, even as tears threatened. So far, the weekend had exceeded everyone's expectations, but she couldn't deny that every event, every meal she shared with her far-flung family members carried with it the bittersweet knowledge that this was the last reunion they'd ever hold at the Dane Crown Inn.

As if he sensed how she felt, Max draped a comforting arm over her shoulders. He leaned down to whisper in her ear, but she drew back in surprise at his next words.

"Didn't you say you wanted something sweet?" he murmured. "Let's walk out to my truck. I have just the thing to cheer you up."

"Ma-ax." Amy gently punched his arm. As much as she loved the moments when she and Max held one another in their arms, she was pretty sure sneaking off to steal a few kisses in the middle of her family's reunion was not a good idea.

Max's hearty laugh filled the air. "Don't worry. I'll be on my best behavior. Scout's honor." Tucking his little finger under his thumb, he saluted.

And, in yet another surprise in a weekend that was rapidly filling with them, he remained the perfect gentlemen as he pulled a large cooler and a basket of supplies from the bed of his truck.

Max had been right, Amy admitted a short while later. Being sad was impossible with a mouthful of chocolate, melted marshmallow and crunchy graham cracker. Enjoying the sweet taste, she handed another yummy s'more to one of the children who'd gathered around the firepit.

Fourteen

Belle

"Remind me to never eat again." Belle placed a hand on her abdomen as the car whizzed past palm trees and scrub oak. She'd had to suck in her breath in order to zip up the dress she wanted to wear to church today. "I used to think Kim's cooking would make me fat. It won't. It's all the desserts people brought to the reunion that will do me in." Practically every female relative and some of the men had shown up with a homemade cake, pie or tin of cookies.

"What was your favorite?" Jason asked as he signaled his intent to pull into the church's parking lot. Behind him, a long line of cars loaded with family members followed his example. "Mine were the cookies your Aunt Opal brought from Texas. Do you think we could put in a standing order for those each year?"

Belle slumped the tiniest bit when the request sent regret winging through her chest. She hated to disappoint Jason—or anyone else, for that matter—but this would be their last reunion. At least, it would be the last one in Emerald Bay. By this time next year, the Dane Crown Inn would belong to someone else. Another, stronger wave of regret washed over her.

"Maybe you could get the recipe, Belle." In the back seat of the car, Daclan leaned around the guitar case he'd propped between his legs.

Sitting beside the teen, Jen laughed.

"Hey! You aren't laughing at me, are you? 'Cause I can make a mean hard-boiled egg." Belle's stern look dissolved into giggles. Jen was right; she wasn't much of a cook.

"You fixed tea and toast for me when I needed it," Jason said, coming to her defense with a reminder of the weekend he'd gotten food poisoning from a breakfast burrito. "I certainly wasn't in any shape to shift for myself. Not that I'm a whiz in the kitchen. My parents were always on the road, so I grew up on takeout and pasta. I can grill a pretty good steak, though."

"I like steak," Belle said. Chicken, turkey and burgers, too. Which was a good thing because the moment the reunion ended, she'd resume her usual low-carb diet.

The car bumped over the rough surface of the church's parking lot. Jason pulled into the first available space and shut off the engine. While the others in their caravan did the same, he leaned over to take Belle's hand in his.

"Since neither of us cook, I guess we'll be the couple who orders a big meal at a restaurant and lives off leftovers for the rest of the weekend," he said.

"I could get on board with that. Risotto and shrimp from Uncle Georgio's. Fried green tomatoes and fish dip from Waldo's." She named two of their favorite restaurants.

"Sounds perfect."

The squeeze Jason gave her hand spread warmth from the roots of Belle's hair to the tips of her toes. Although it'd be an understatement to say their relationship had gotten off to a rocky start—he'd fired her, after all—she'd quickly come to see that a heart of gold beat beneath the starched white shirt Jason wore to his office on the top floor of the Noble Records building. It hadn't taken long for her to fall for him, utterly and completely. Lately, she'd even caught herself daydreaming about their future together.

"Hey, Belle?" Daclan's voice rose from the

back seat. "Before I forget, there's something I've been meaning to ask. Did you write Sammy Fasta's latest hit?"

"Since when do you listen to R&B?" Belle didn't know which shocked her more—that her young protégé was expanding his musical library or that he'd recognized her handiwork.

"Since you told me to." Daclan flipped open one of the latches on his guitar case and closed it again. "So did you?"

"I did." Sammy's contract had arrived by email the day after she'd sent him the demo tape. A healthy check for the advance had landed in her bank account soon after. "What'd you think?"

"I liked it. You should write more like it."

"Thanks. I might just do that." She exchanged a knowing glance with Jason.

"Hey, you two, get moving. We have a show to put on." Jen popped her door open and stepped out of the car while, on the other side, Daclan did the same.

Belle lingered, her hand in Jason's while family members began to spill from the other vehicles that had followed them from the inn. At last, he pressed a chaste kiss to the back of her hand.

"To be continued," he promised before

relinquishing his hold. "I'll save you a seat inside."

"You'd better." After giving him her best smile, she joined Daclan and Jen for the short walk to the back of the church, where The Emeralds would wait with the pastor while the organist played the prelude.

As the sky darkened that evening, Belle, dressed in jeans and a simple top, her masses of red curls pulled into a casual knot, stood on the deck. Looking out over the audience of family and friends, she cleared her throat. "Welcome," she said, speaking into the microphone Jen had set up on the makeshift stage. "Welcome to the Dane Family Reunion Talent Show!"

A smattering of claps rose from the crowd, and she grinned. "Is that the best you can do?" she challenged. She was rewarded with a slightly heartier round of applause.

"That's a *little* better." She let doubt creep into her voice. "I'd ask you to try again, but I want you to save your energy for all the wonderful acts we have for you tonight. First, though, for those of you who are new, let's go over a few ground rules." The move was necessary, considering it had been ten years since the last reunion.

Consulting the slip of paper in her hand, she quickly ran down the guidelines that included five-minute time limits and preserving the family-friendly atmosphere. She concluded with a rule her uncles had added the year a rowdy teen had reduced her second cousin Frank's five-year-old to a puddle of tears. "Positive comments only. Break this rule, and you *will* be asked to leave." She swept the crowd with a look that showed she meant business.

"Whew," she said, lowering the paper. "Now that that's over, let me introduce our first act." Like a circus ringleader, she let her voice rise. "La-dies and gentle-men. Hailing from the great state of Texas, home to bluebonnets and those awesome Cowboy Cookies, please welcome Aggie and Haar-ryy Da-ane!"

At their cue, the couple stepped from behind the black, trifold screens that formed the stage's backdrop. In matching Stetsons, white shirts with black piping, and jeans, they walked across the deck while the heels of their cowboy boots tapped hollowly against the wooden boards.

They aren't going to launch into a rousing rendition of a Reba McEntire song, are they?

The question brought the fiasco in Nashville

surging to the surface, and Belle stiffened. Wasn't she over that already? Sure, she'd struggled, but she'd forgiven Teddy Baynard for tripping her up that night. She'd moved on, hadn't she?

Not if the mere sight of her cousin and his wife dressed in country-western attire stirred up so many memories, she hadn't. She swallowed. Perhaps she had a wee bit more soul-searching to do. Later. After the talent show. Maybe after the reunion. Still not sure she wanted to hear their answer, she managed to ask Harry what he and Aggie were going to perform.

Her cousin grinned widely and said, "A little boot-scootin'."

"Well, then, take it away!" Belle said. Immensely relieved that their act had nothing to do with her dismal appearance in a distant honky-tonk, she hurried down the steps to her seat beside Jason, who waited for her on the front row of the picnic benches, lawn and folding chairs that had been lined up in front of the deck.

As the twangy notes of a popular country-western song rose from a pair of speakers Jen had positioned on either side of the deck, Harry and Aggie danced up a storm. The beat was infectious, and by the time they finished, most of the youngsters and quite a few of the adults had filled the aisles, where they tried, with varying degrees of success, to mimic the steps of the line dance.

After the dancing duo had taken their final bows, Belle grabbed two ribbons from the box of awards she'd created. She presented them and spent the next two hours racing back and forth from her seat to the deck where, one after another, family members entertained each other with a variety of musical instruments, knock-knock jokes and several surprisingly tuneless songs. She was watching a ventriloquist "talk" with a large doll when Sophie tugged insistently on her sleeve.

"Yes, sweetheart?" Belle's gaze bounced from the little girl into the crowd. Had Sophie wandered off on her own, she wondered. But no, Nat stood, not two rows away, holding Isabella's hand while keeping one eye on her sister. Belle's attention refocused on the younger girl.

"Mama and me always sing 'Are You Sleeping?' before I go to bed. I want to sing it for my baby sister. Will you sing it with me?"

"Right now?" Belle prepared to pull the little girl onto her lap and croon the lullaby.

"No. Up there." Sophie pointed to the stage.

Belle hesitated. She'd sworn she wouldn't participate in the talent show, but how could she resist the plea she saw in Sophie's blue eyes? There was only one answer—she couldn't, of course.

On stage, a cousin she'd only gotten to know this weekend was wrapping up her ventriloquist act. Behind the screens, the final pair of performers waited. Belle turned to Sophie. "Are you sure? 'Cause we'll have to go on stage this minute."

Sophie slipped her hand in Belle's. "I'm sure," she said, her voice trembling only slightly.

Remembering how nervous she was the first time she ever stood before a crowd, Belle whispered in Sophie's ear. "When we get up there, I'll get the microphone. You sit on the top step and wait for me."

Sophie did as she'd been told while Belle mounted the stairs and presented her cousin—and a floppy doll named Ursula—with participation ribbons. The mic thunked loudly as Belle removed it from the stand. She waited until the noise subsided.

"Before I introduce our final act of the evening…" She paused to make sure the couple waiting behind the screen understood there'd been a slight change of plans. Relieved when no one sprang from behind the curtain, she continued. "I'm sure you've all heard that my cousin Scott and his wife, Fern, welcomed a new member into our family on Friday. Their daughter Sophie has asked me to help her sing a lullaby for the baby." She glanced down. "Are you ready, Sophie?"

"Yes, but…" Sophie shuffled her feet on the wooden boards.

Belle smiled down at the child, a little more than half-expecting the girl to change her mind entirely now that she looked out over the large crowd. "What is it, sweetheart?"

"It's not a lull-bye," she insisted. "It's a song. We sing it three times." Sophie held up three fingers.

The child's earnest conviction made Belle want to throw her head back and laugh out loud. Sensing that might ruin the little girl's moment in the spotlight, she stifled the urge. Instead, she sank down on the step beside her niece and held the mic between them.

"Do you want to start? Or do you want me to?" she asked.

Rather than answer, Sophie's clear, lilting voice rang out. "Are you sleeping?"

Feeling the tiniest bit upstaged, Belle hurried to come in on the next line. As promised, they ran through the song the requisite three times. When they reached the end, Sophie gave a huge yawn. Her head dropped to her chest and, in seconds, her eyes drifted shut.

Awww, she fell asleep.

Belle's heart positively melted. Pressing one finger to her lips, she searched the audience for someone she trusted to carry the sleeping tyke inside. The effort was wasted, it turned out. Less than thirty seconds later, Sophie's eyes popped open. She tipped her face to Belle's.

"Did I fool you, Aunt Belle?" Sophie's chest puffed out. "I fool Mommy every night."

The audience responded with hoots of laughter and a huge round of applause. Belle held her breath, hoping her niece wouldn't burst into tears, but Sophie jumped to her feet and took a bow as if she'd been performing her entire life. Laughing and feeling very much like she'd been played by a six-year-old, Belle scrambled to her own feet. Inordinately proud of the little girl for creating her moment in the sun, she waited until things had quieted before she stepped forward.

"You did a wonderful job, Sophie," she said, meaning every word. "It is my absolute honor to give you this award." Taking one from the dwindling supply of green ribbons in a nearby box, she handed it to her niece.

Sophie eyed the prize like many of Belle's fellow performers had looked at the trophies handed out at the Grammys. Crushing it to her chest, she wrapped one of her thin arms around Belle's thighs. "Thanks, Aunt Belle," she cried. Then, holding her ribbon aloft, she trotted down the steps.

"Well." Belle took a second to regroup while Nat led Sophie back to her seat beside Isabella. Slipping back into her role as the master of ceremonies, she announced the final act of the evening before she returned to her own seat.

Five minutes later, sitting with Jason's arm around her shoulders, Belle laughed along with the crowd at the antics of a black-clad brother-and-sister team who pretended to toss beams of light back and forth between them. She, along with everyone else who'd gathered to watch the talent show, had been mystified at first. It had taken her a moment to realize the pair had tucked tiny flashlights into the palms of their hands. With impeccable timing, they turned the lights off and on with each 'toss' and 'catch'. Reaching their act's finale, the teens threw faster and faster without missing a single beat. As the pair took their bows to the thunderous applause of family and friends, Belle reluctantly slipped out from beneath Jason's arm and hustled up the steps to the stage one last time.

"And there you have it, folks, our final act of

the evening. Weren't they all wonderful!" she announced. "Let's give them another round of applause." She took the last two participation ribbons from her box, handed one to each of the teens and gave them each a warm hug.

When the noise died down, she said, "I don't know about the rest of you, but the talent show is a highlight of the reunion for me. The first time I ever sang in front of a group was right here on this deck when I was six years old." Looking out at all the smiling parents who just knew their little Susie or Sam was destined for greatness, she took another breath.

"We're going to take a short break to clear the stage before we start the sing-along," she continued. "Meantime, help yourselves to another slice of pie, a piece of cake or a cookie. We'll meet back here in fifteen minutes." As family members and a few invited guests began to stir, another thought occurred to her. "Oh! One more thing," Belle called. "Jason and Daclan have offered to accompany us on their guitars tonight. If anyone else would like to join in, we'd love to have you. Please feel free to bring your instruments and sit on the stairs."

Though she could practically hear a slice of pound cake calling her name from the kitchen, Belle resolutely ignored the urge to rush inside and grab dessert. Instead, she scurried about, helping Jen put away the mic and amps while Josh and Nick removed the tri-fold screens they'd used as a backdrop for the stage. Once they'd safely stored the equipment, she recruited several of the younger cousins to hand out copies of the lyrics for some old, familiar songs. And, in no time at all, it seemed, she was sitting on the steps with Isabella on one side and Sophie on the other, while Jason, Daclan, Nick and Josh fanned out behind her with their guitars.

Time ceased to exist for Belle when the first notes of the music began to fill the air. At one point, she looked out over the crowd, seeking the faces of those she knew best. Her mom, of course, sat on the front row alongside Opal, who couldn't seem to find the right key to save her soul. Kim and Craig sat several rows behind them, their voices blending in perfect harmony with the rest of the family's. Max, who claimed he couldn't carry a tune in a shopping bag, stood, his arms wrapped around Amy, who was clearly enjoying both his presence and the music. The harvest didn't stop for holiday weekends or family reunions, and Belle had been sorry that Caleb missed the talent show. The farmer had arrived in time for the sing-along, still dressed in his overalls, and immediately sought out Jen.

The two of them exchanged tender glances between songs. Caitlyn's teammates had departed before dinner, but she didn't seem to mind. She and several teenage cousins had claimed the back row of chairs for themselves. Though they jostled one another and joked around a bit, they joined in on all the songs. Meanwhile, Tim, who'd confessed earlier that he was looking forward to the sing-along most of all, looked positively blissful seated next to Diane.

Sophie, who'd fallen asleep for real this time, pressed uncomfortably into Belle's side. She shifted the girl onto her lap as the final notes of "He's Got The Whole World In His Hands" faded. After stealing a quick look at her watch, she called out, "Last song!"

Though the announcement was met with a few grumbles, Belle remained firm. "Last song," she repeated. Much as she knew everyone would like to, they couldn't spend the entire night singing. Not if they were going to be ready for a wedding by sunrise, they couldn't.

She shot the happy couple a smile before, taking Isabella's hand in hers, she began "Will The Circle Be Unbroken," the song that traditionally capped the sing-along. Across the yard, voices rose in unison. Belle's voice hitched.

This, she thought, was the last sing-along at the last reunion they'd ever hold. Though she prided herself on being a professional and knew from experience that she could make it through all three verses of Collin Ray's "Love Me" without crying, she couldn't deny the tears that dampened her cheeks when they reached the final verse.

Fifteen

Kim

Sitting at the makeup table in Belle's bedroom, Kim stared into the black void beyond the windowpane. Reassured that the sun wouldn't pop over the horizon in the next five minutes, she drained the last sip of coffee from a heavy white mug. Though she wanted a second cup in the worst way, too much caffeine would make her jittery. Today, of all days, she wanted to keep her wits about her. Setting the mug on the table beside Belle's immense makeup kit, she stifled a yawn.

"Tell me again why we're up in the middle of the night?" she complained.

"Because you just *had* to get married at sunrise." Jen carefully released a strand of Kim's hair from the curling wand she was using to transform her sister's normally straight hair into a headful of soft curls.

"Any sign of Craig yet?" Kim bit lightly on the nail of her index finger while she wished, not for the first time, that she'd managed to squeeze a manicure into her schedule. But with all the hubbub of the reunion, plus the unexpected arrival of Scott and Fern's baby, she hadn't had a minute to spare, much less the half day it would have required to drive to the nail salon and let the technicians work their magic. And why waste the time when not even the best manicure could last through all the chopping, sautéing and dishwashing she'd done over the past few days? Keeping a hundred people fed over a holiday weekend was hard work.

"And whose brilliant idea was it to get married at the end of the reunion, when we're all so exhausted? I feel like I could sleep for a week."

"Again, yours. And that man of yours." Belle gently tugged Kim's hand away from her mouth. "Don't bite your nails," she chided. "You'll ruin your polish."

Kim dropped her hand into her lap. Tears stung her eyes. Unable to sleep, she'd cajoled her sister into painting her nails at 3 a.m. Smudging the polish—or, worse, ripping a nail—was the last thing she needed to do.

"No one's going to be looking at your nails. They'll be looking at your hair. Which is gorgeous, if I don't mind saying so myself." A slight hiss rose from the strand Jen had wrapped around the curling wand.

"Or your face. Your makeup is sheer perfection." Belle feathered a brush over Kim's cheeks.

"You guys are beyond amazing." Kim flexed her fingers. "Who else would get up at oh dark thirty to do my hair and makeup?"

"Diane and Nat," Jen said in a matter-of-fact tone. "They took the floral arrangements down to the beach an hour ago." Max had constructed a simple arch especially for the occasion. Diane and Nat had insisted on dressing it up with greenery and flowers.

"Amy's in the kitchen. She wanted to fill the coffee urns so everyone can grab a to-go cup before they head on down to the beach." Belle returned her powder brush to its assigned spot in the makeup case.

"Oh, and wait until you see what Josh and Nick did." Jen tugged a curl into place.

"What?" Kim's gut softened. Her son's emotional distance had completely dissolved in the three days since he'd stepped off the airport shuttle. She had Nat to thank for that. Over the last six months, her daughter had kept up a steady stream of communication with Josh. Nat was the one who'd convinced him to come to the reunion, where he'd surprised himself by having a good time. Of course, it helped that Nat and Josh, along with Diane's son, Nick, had been thick as thieves throughout the long weekend.

"You know how we've all been concerned about Margaret and Opal making it to the beach?" Both in their eighties, the two aunts had enough trouble walking on solid ground.

"That soft sand is treacherous for anyone who uses a cane," Belle mused. Using the golf cart was out. No motorized vehicles were allowed on the beach during turtle nesting season.

"Right. Max and Caleb planned to escort them, but Nick and Josh came up with a better plan. Yesterday, they commandeered two of the beach wagons." With their canvas sides and wide wheels, the wagons were great for hauling umbrellas, chairs and blankets to and from the water's edge. "They spent hours cleaning them. Then Nat and Isabella and Sophie decorated them with flowers and streamers. Margaret and Opal will ride to your wedding in style."

"I can just see it now." Belle bowed with a flourish. "Madame, your chariot awaits."

Picturing the two elderly women seated in the bright red wagons, Kim chuckled.

"I think you're done. You want to take a look?" Belle reached for a mirror.

"Wait," Jen cautioned. "Let me finish this last curl."

Without showing the slightest sign of impatience, Belle puttered about while Jen arranged Kim's hair using the pointy end of a styling comb. "Okay," she said when she was satisfied. "What do you think?"

"Oh, it's perfect." Kim sighed. Belle's mix of potions and lotions had taken ten years off her face. As for her hair, it hadn't looked so soft and shiny since the last time she'd spent four hours and a small fortune in a salon.

But as she set the mirror aside, she stole another glance out the window. Was it her imagination, or was the sky beginning to lighten?

A rush of nervous energy made her hands tremble. "Has anyone heard from Craig? Or any of the guys?" The men had thrown an impromptu bachelor party at Craig's last night. She worried that they'd be late for the wedding. Or—perish the thought—too hung over to show up at all.

"Relax," Belle soothed. "It's an hour till sunrise. Besides, Jason texted. He said they spent a very tame evening playing cards and smoking cigars. Craig made them all turn in at midnight. They've already had coffee and doughnuts and are on their way. They'll be here in plenty of time."

"Oh, good," Kim breathed. There had to be worse things than not seeing a groom waiting for her when she walked down the aisle, but at the moment, she couldn't think of one.

Wielding a can of hairspray, Jen lamented, "With so much going on, we didn't get to throw a bachelorette party for you."

"Oh, I don't know," Kim said. "I think the day we went shopping counts. That was pretty special." Despite her insistence that she and Craig didn't need a thing, her sister and cousins had showered her with gifts.

The faint sounds of family members greeting one another, getting their morning coffee and heading out to the beach drifted through Belle's closed bedroom door. "I think it's time to put on your dress," she announced.

Kim eyed the Oscar de La Renta suspended on a padded hanger on the back of the closet door. By far the most beautiful dress she'd ever seen, the gown was a confection of blue chiffon covered in pink hibiscus flowers and green leaves. She couldn't even begin to imagine how much Belle had paid for such an elegant creation. She knew only one thing for certain—she'd never be able to afford it herself.

Kim frowned. "Are you sure I can't wear the print I wore for New Year's?"

Belle scoffed. "Craig's already seen you in that dress. This is your wedding. You need something with a real *wow* factor."

The dress her cousin had chosen had enough *wow* for a lifetime, Kim thought. She drew Belle into a tight hug. "I can't thank you enough," she gushed.

Her head buried in Kim's shoulder, Belle issued a muffled protest. "Please. We're family," she said when Kim relinquished her grip. "Besides, every bride deserves to feel special on their wedding day."

A fresh rush of tears threatened. Fighting them back, Kim warned, "You're going to make me cry."

Wiping her own eyes, Belle plucked several tissues from a box on the table while she gruffly ordered, "Don't you dare ruin your makeup!"

Careful not to smear her mascara, Kim dabbed the skin beneath her lashes with the tissues. Once Belle had approved her efforts, she nodded to her sister, who unzipped the dress and removed it from the hanger. Jen pooled the gown on the floor at Kim's feet.

While butterflies beat their wings against her ribs, she stepped into the opening. The silk lining whispered over her thighs and hips when Jen and Belle pulled the dress to her waist. She slid her arms into transparent sleeves woven from threads as fine and wispy as a spider's web.

"Don't worry about tearing it. The fabric is sturdier than it looks."

As if she'd read her mind, Belle's admonition eased Kim's fears. She stood, her back to the mirror, while Jen zipped up the back and Belle fluffed layers of organza that made up the skirt.

"Here, slip these on." Belle placed a pair of sparkly sandals on the floor in front of her.

Kim eyed the shoes she'd bought especially for the occasion. As much as she hadn't wanted to wear flats, tromping through sand in three-inch heels was an excellent way to break an ankle. She slid her feet into the sandals and stood perfectly still while Belle adjusted the straps.

"Oh, my word. You look like a princess," Jen proclaimed.

Stepping back, Belle nodded. "Sheer perfection."

Anxious to see for herself, Kim slowly spun toward the floor-length mirror. Her breath caught as she took in the makeup that turned her complexion dewy soft, the blond curls that trailed onto her shoulders and the gown—sheer blue organza covered in leafy vines that sprouted fluffy pink hibiscus blossoms. It was all practically guaranteed to take Craig's breath away, just as it had stolen hers.

"Oh!" she gasped. Fighting the urge to cry, she bit the knuckle of her index finger.

"Is that a good 'oh' or a bad one?" Jen demanded.

"It's good," Kim assured her sister and her cousin. "Very, very good. I never imagined..." Her voice trailed off. She drew in several thready breaths while she steadied. "Thank you," she whispered. "Thank you."

Belle retrieved a light shawl from the foot of her bed. She cleared her throat. "We could stand here gawking all day, but if you want to say your vows at sunrise, we'd better get moving." Adding a touch of elegance to her jeans and T-shirt, she casually draped the shawl around her shoulders.

"I'll make sure the way is clear." Jen started for the door. "It's bad luck for the bride and groom to see each other before the wedding."

"Wait," Kim called. "Where's Nat?" She'd asked her daughter to serve as her maid of honor.

"She said to tell you she'll be waiting for you on the beach. She had to get two sleepy little flower girls ready."

Amy and Diane waited for them in the kitchen. "Everyone else has already headed down to the beach," Amy said. "They cleared out of here about five minutes ago."

"Aunt Margaret and Aunt Opal?" Kim asked.

Diane chortled merrily. "I wish you could have seen their faces when Nick and Josh hoisted them into their carriages. It was a sight to see." She waited a beat. "Do you have everything? Something old, something new, something borrowed, something blue?"

Kim swished her skirts. "My dress is borrowed and blue. My shoes are brand new. Something old?" Her brow furrowed.

"I have just the thing." Diane stepped forward. "Tuck this in your bra. You're supposed to wear it in your shoe, but that doesn't work with sandals."

Kim stared down at the small silver coin her cousin had pressed into the palm of her hand. "Is this what I think it is?" She gulped. Glancing over her shoulder, she reassured herself that they had the kitchen to themselves. Nonetheless, her voice dropped to a whisper. "Is this from the treasure?"

"It is." Diane grinned. "Aunt Margaret had me take it from the collection. It is certifiably old. Hurry up." She lifted Kim's elbow. "You don't want to be late to your own wedding."

The metal felt cool between her breasts when Kim dropped the quarter-size disk into her bra.

And then, they lined up just as they'd done so many times when they were young girls, embarking on whatever adventure the day held in store. Kim took her usual place in the middle. With Amy and Jen flanking her on the left while Belle and Diane took the right, the five women linked arms and set off.

At the beach, gentle waves lapped the shore while the rising sun painted the horizon with pinks and purples. As Kim and her entourage approached the crowd of friends and family who stood in clumps on either side of a white carpet runner that led to a wooden arch, she beamed at Josh, who stepped forward to take his place at her side. Jen and Belle offered hurried hugs and kisses before they moved to a nearby table, where Jen began tinkering with the music system and Belle picked up a microphone. Diane and Amy peeled off right after them, each skirting around to the front, where Amy would take charge of Isabella and Sophie once they completed their role as flower girls and Diane would lead the short service.

Kim's heart rate kicked up a notch when Nat, with two little girls in matching sundresses in tow, appeared as if out of nowhere. Taking two baskets from a long white florist box that lay open on a folding chair, her daughter handed one each to Sophie and Isabella.

"Stand right here," Nat told them, positioning the girls beside each other at the edge of the runner. "You're going to follow me down the aisle, just like we practiced. Stay on the carpet. Drop the flowers, and then stand with Aunt Amy." She pointed to the arch Max had erected at the water's edge.

Isabella nodded solemnly. "Just like we practiced in the hall."

Sophie sifted rose petals through her fingers. "They're so soft," she declared.

Kim hiked a brow when the youngster stuck a handful of petals in the pocket of her dress. "She's a riot, that one," she said, nodding at Sophie as Nat turned to face her.

"Tell me about it. She's been up for hours. I already feel sorry for the man she'll marry one day." Retrieving two bouquets from the box, Nat held the larger one out to Kim.

Kim lifted the flowers to her nose. As she

inhaled their sweet scent, she glanced at the crowd of family members who'd rolled out of bed before daybreak to celebrate the occasion with her and Craig. Her gaze fell to Isabella and Sophie, and regret pricked her like a thorn. Scott and Fern's girls would never know what it was like to share such a special day with their entire family. For that matter, neither would Nat or Josh. By the time her son and daughter found their special someone, the last Dane Family Reunion would only be a memory, the inn where they'd shared so much love and laughter no longer a daily part of their lives.

"Mom? Are you okay? You're looking a little lost. You're not having second thoughts, are you?"

Kim started, suddenly aware that Nat was staring at her with concern etched on her fine features. "About Craig?" She shook her head. "No, not at all. I was just thinking how lucky I am to spend this day surrounded by the people I love." And, resolutely pushing her own concerns about the future aside, she smiled and held her bouquet a little higher.

"Good. 'Cause you look stunning, Mom," Nat said after a split second.

"She's right," Josh echoed. He threaded her arm through his. "I've never seen you look so radiant. Craig is a lucky man." He inclined his head. "I like him," he added, his voice low and serious over the sound of the waves.

Kim suppressed a giddy laugh. Having her son and daughter's blessing meant the world to her. "I like him, too," she whispered.

Catching them all by surprise, the first notes of the processional blared from the speakers. Kim felt an instant thrill when Nat hurried to her place at the head of the short line. Moments later, she watched as her daughter moved gracefully down the aisle, followed by Isabella and Sophie, who race-walked from one end of the carpet to the other while they tossed flowers by the handfuls.

Then it was her turn.

Her gaze locked on Craig, who stood resplendent in a cream-colored suit over a shirt the same shade as her dress. The love she saw reflected in his eyes nearly took her breath away. Reminding herself that she did, indeed, need to breathe, Kim tucked her arm more firmly into her son's and, with her head held high, walked down the aisle to marry the man of her dreams.

"Daddy's here! Daddy's here!" Sophie raced through the house, yelling at the top of her lungs. "Isabella, Daddy's here!"

"Hush," Kim scolded gently. "We don't want to wake Aunt Margaret." Exhausted after all the excitement of the reunion, her aunt was napping. Other than the faint hum of the vacuum wielded by either Irene or Eunice in an upstairs bedroom, the inn had fallen silent after the last batch of family members had bid fond farewells and issued promises to return for the next reunion.

As for the rest of them, they'd scattered. The last she'd checked, Diane sat in the office, looking over the inn's accounts. Amy and Jen were going from room to room, returning books to shelves and replacing throw pillows on sofas while they collected a few odds and ends for the Lost and Found box. Belle had texted a half hour ago to let everyone know she was headed back from dropping Jason off at the airport in Orlando, while Nat had insisted on taking Josh and Nick to the one in Melbourne. In the backyard, Craig, Max, Caleb and Tim were breaking down the tents, returning lawn chairs to their usual spots and picking up what little trash had been scattered about the grounds. With Isabella and Sophie's help, Kim had straightened the kitchen after a scrumptious wedding breakfast. After that, she'd taken the girls upstairs, where they'd finished emptying her closet and packing her bags for her move to the house she'd share with Craig for the rest of her life.

An insistent hand tugged on hers. "Daddy's here," whispered Sophie.

"Yes, sweetheart." Kim knelt until she was eye-to-eye with her niece. "Why don't you go give him a big hug?"

Screaming, "Dad-deee!" Sophie charged toward her father.

Watching the tiny girl slam into her dad, Kim chuckled. She should have known better than to expect a six-year-old to remain quiet. Shaking her head, she stood, ran a hand over the simple white dress she'd changed into after the ceremony and glanced toward the front door, where her cousin had lifted his daughter into his arms. Despite the happiness that filled his eyes, Scott looked a little worse for wear in rumpled clothes and with unshaven cheeks. She hurried to greet him as he shifted Sophie to one hip.

"Congratulations, Daddy." Kim wrapped him in a warm hug. Standing back to get a better look at him, she tsked. The man was positively dead on his feet. "I hate to say this, but you look like you could use a good night's sleep. Why don't you leave the girls here for another night so you and Fern can have some peace and quiet?"

Scott practically swayed on his feet, but he shook his head. "We couldn't wait another minute to see our girls." Despite his fatigue, he squeezed Sophie closer. He leaned down to her. "Why don't you go get your sister, and I'll take you to see Mommy. She's in the car."

"Mommy is?" Sophie slid to the floor with all the grace of a cat. "Isabella!" Her shout rang through the house. "Isabella, Mommy's here!"

"With the baby?" Kim's shock was quickly replaced by elation. "Can I see her?"

A look that was part good humor mixed with pride softened Scott's expression. "Let me take Sophie and Isabella out first. Give us ten minutes. Then you and anyone else can come meet our new...baby."

"Of course, of course," Kim assured her cousin. It would take at least that much time to round up the girls' things. Not to mention grabbing everyone else within earshot. They'd all want to welcome the newest member of the Dane family.

A clatter of footsteps on the stairs signaled Sophie's return with her sister.

"Daddy!" Isabella called. "Where's Mommy? And the baby?" She raced across the room.

"There's my big girl." Scott sank into a crouch, his arms open wide.

Kim blinked back tears while her cousin reunited with his oldest child. In minutes, he'd herded the girls outside and down the steps. When they rounded the front bumper of Scott's big SUV and disappeared from sight, she spun, eager to alert the others.

Amy and Jen were in the game room and offered to get Diane while she called the men in from the backyard. Kim left them to it and hurried down the hall and through the kitchen to the French doors that opened onto the deck. Seconds later, she beckoned Craig and the others from the railing.

"Scott's here," she called, mindful of her aunt, who'd somehow managed to sleep through all of Sophie's shouting.

Or maybe not, Kim corrected when the door to the family quarters creaked open. Margaret peered out with owlish eyes.

"Did I hear Scott's voice?" she asked in a raspy voice.

"Yes, ma'am. He and Fern and the baby are waiting out front. Want to greet your newest grand-niece?"

"I wouldn't miss it for the world," Margaret declared. "Let me get my glasses."

Ten minutes later, Kim and Craig helped Aunt Margaret negotiate the front porch steps. Slowly, they moved across a small patch of grass to the spot where Scott's imposing SUV sat, the engine idling. They surged toward the front passenger window, but instead of finding Fern and the baby there, Isabella occupied the spot.

"I get to sit up front now 'cause I'm the big sister." The preteen proudly buckled and unbuckled her seat belt.

Once Isabella had been roundly congratulated on her promotion, Kim helped her aunt circle around the open passenger door. Just beyond it, Fern leaned against the fender.

Everyone, it seemed, spoke at once.

"Oh, my goodness. How are you?" Margaret asked.

"Shouldn't you be sitting down?" Jen demanded.

"Can we get you anything?" Diane wanted to know.

Fern shoved a hand through her hair. "I'm sorry. I must look an absolute fright."

Kim eyed the woman who'd given birth less than three days earlier and wished she'd looked half as good a month after she had Nat.

"Good grief," blurted Jen with her typical bluntness. "No one expects you to parade down the red carpet hours after you've had a baby." She looked her cousin-in-law up and down. "But if anyone could do it, you could. You look amazing."

Fern's shoulders straightened, and a smile played across her lips. "You're lying, but I appreciate it." She clapped her hands together. "Enough about me. You want to see the baby?"

"I do!" Margaret declared. Leaning heavily on her cane, she took a step forward.

"Scott?" Fern called.

"Coming." From the spot where the men in their group had been slapping him on the back and offering their own versions of congratulations, Scott eased into the opening between his aunt and the SUV's door. An audible click sounded. Seconds later, her cousin turned to face them holding a tiny infant strapped into an infant carrier and draped in a blanket.

A *blue* blanket.

Diane whispered into Kim's ear. "I thought they were going to use the one I made for her. I know they had it with them at the hospital."

Kim lifted the hand she'd clasped over her mouth the instant Scott had turned to face them. Pitching her voice for Diane's ears only, she said, "I think there's been a change of plans. Check out the color of that blanket."

"Say what?" Diane's head whipped around. She sputtered. "But the ultrasounds. The gender reveal. The…"

"What can I say? We have a very modest son." Scott's face positively glowed.

"Oh, my gracious," Margaret crowed. "Are you saying…?"

Fern leaned in. With a delicate touch, she pushed the decidedly blue blanket away from the baby's face. "Scott and I would like to introduce the newest addition to our family, Paul Dane Sommer."

Margaret inhaled sharply. "A boy," she said on the exhale. She tipped her head to her nephew's. "You named him after your dad. He'd be so honored."

"I hope you don't mind that we chose Dane for his middle name," Scott said tentatively. "We can change it if you don't like it."

"Why would I want you to change his name? It's beautiful. He's beautiful."

With perfect timing, Sophie poked her head through the opening between the seats. "He's better than a kitten!" she declared to the great amusement of everyone who'd gathered around the SUV.

Sixteen

Diane

*D*iane's footsteps dragged along the pavered walkway like those of a man on his way to the gas chamber. Her arms strained beneath the weight of her laptop and files. A monk parakeet hopped across the stones in front of her. Normally, she laughed at the antics of the tiny green birds that roosted in the palms at the edge of the inn's property. Today, she didn't even crack a smile.

Why was that?

She should be happy, she told herself. Should be sitting on top of the world. After all, it wasn't every day she got named as the executor of an estate worth eleven million dollars. More, even. As much as another million more if she counted the money her aunt would make when she sold the inn. Of course, such a position of responsibility didn't come without a catch. This one was a doozy: her role in distributing the assets of the estate wouldn't begin until Aunt Margaret died.

Was that why she felt so sad? So certain they'd taken a wrong turn somewhere along the line? That all the plans she and Margaret and Scott had so carefully outlined during today's marathon meeting in her brother's home office were doomed to failure?

She gave her head a rueful shake. *No, not doomed to failure.*

The plan Margaret had come up with was a good one. Solid. Logical. Practical. There was no reason she and Scott couldn't carry out her wishes when the time came. Which, Diane prayed, wouldn't happen for years and years.

Except, by then, by the time she distributed the money left in her aunt's estate according to her wishes, it would be too late. Too late to save the Dane Crown Inn. Too late to preserve their family's heritage. Too late to keep their family intact.

And that was the real issue, wasn't it?

Though Scott was far too reserved to admit it, she had a sneaking suspicion her brother shared her doubts and fears. Or, at least, some of them.

Hadn't he leaned forward at one point this afternoon, taken Margaret's hand in his and suggested that, in light of the fact that she would soon be a very wealthy woman, she might want to hang on to the only home she'd ever known? Diane had felt hope flare in her chest, but her aunt had only shaken her head.

"No," she'd said, her voice thin and wavering as her gaze flickered between Scott and Diane. "Belle and the rest of the girls are right. It's time for me to retire. Running the inn is too much for me to do on my own anymore."

But what if she didn't have to do it all on her own? What if…?

Diane began to hurry down the walkway. Maybe she was alone in her fight to preserve the inn. Or maybe not. She wouldn't know until she and Amy, Kim and Jen, Nat and Belle had an open, honest discussion about the entire situation. If she was wrong, she'd have no choice—she'd have to abide by Aunt Margaret's wishes, whatever they were. But if she was right, if the others felt the same way she did, maybe they could come up with a plan of their own. One that would save the inn and preserve their family.

Regardless of the result, though, they needed to have that talk soon. Today. Tomorrow at the latest. Because, even now, steps were being taken, events were being set into motion, and once things really got rolling, it would become nearly impossible to stop them.

As she approached the entrance used by employees and family members, Diane heard voices coming from the deck. Her footsteps stumbled to a halt while happiness spread through her. She and the others had been so busy catching up on their busy lives after the reunion that they'd barely spoken all week, but tonight, it sounded as if the whole gang was getting together. Pivoting, she circled around to the back of the house.

"I can't believe it's over," Jen was saying as Diane mounted the steps onto the deck. "It felt like the weekend just flew by. Like I blinked and everybody was headed home."

"I felt the same way." Amy poured herself a glass of something pink and frothy from a pitcher in the center of the glass-topped table. She looked up to greet her sister.

"Oh, hey, Diane. Are you here to pick up Caitlyn? She's in the family quarters with Aunt

Margaret. The two of them are crocheting baby booties."

Diane stacked her laptop and files on an empty chair. "I'll get her after a while. Right now I could use some girl time." Scanning the faces gathered around the table, she stopped when she came to Kim. "I'm surprised to see you here tonight. You need a break from that handsome hubby of yours already?"

"Not hardly." Kim's cheeks pinked while she twisted the shiny platinum band Craig had slipped on her finger only four days ago. "He's at a town council meeting tonight. While he was out, I thought I'd come by and see if I need to do any shopping for Royal Meals." She'd put deliveries on hold for the two weeks leading up to and following the reunion, but bright and early next Monday morning, it'd be back to business as usual.

"I thought you guys were going on a honeymoon." Belle nibbled on a carrot stick.

"We decided to wait until the weather cools off. Late fall, maybe?"

Diane nodded. As far as she was concerned, Florida's combination of high humidity and ninety-degree temperatures made summer a prime time to stay indoors and enjoy the air-conditioning.

"At least we had good weather for the reunion," Amy said. "Could you imagine how miserable it would have been if it had stormed all weekend?"

"Speaking of the reunion..." Belle turned to Kim. "What was your favorite part?"

"Do we really have to do that?" Diane bit her tongue. They'd shared their favorite moments from holidays, movies and trips to theme parks as far back as she could remember, and she usually enjoyed the activity. Tonight, though, she had something far more pressing to discuss.

"We have to," Amy protested. "It's tradition."

Diane opened her mouth to argue. One look at the puzzled expressions on her cousins' faces forced her to reconsider. Instead, she reached for the pitcher and poured herself a drink. Taking a sip, she tasted strawberries and wine. "Carry on," she said, sinking into a chair.

"I'm game." A sweet smile turned Kim's expression positively dreamy. "It was the wedding. I loved everything about it. That dress was sheer perfection." She nodded at Belle. "We said our vows at sunrise, the perfect start to our new lives. And that cake—oh, my word, that cake. Amy, it was amazing."

"I have to agree," Diane said, getting into the spirit of things. Instead of the plain white sheet cake Kim had requested, her sister had gone several extra miles by creating three towering tiers of white chocolate sponge decorated with buttercream hibiscus flowers. One look at her wedding cake had reduced Kim to tears, but not her. No. It was the rich blend of chocolate and sugar that had done her in. She'd had two pieces.

"Mmm. And what about that breakfast?" Jen asked. "That was something else, too, wasn't it?" They'd trouped back to the inn from the beach, where they'd all been surprised to find that Irene and Eunice had turned Kim's simple wedding breakfast of fruit salad and sweet rolls into a feast that included mountains of crispy bacon, an enormous tray of fragrant sausages and huge bowls of fluffy scrambled eggs.

"Eunice said the breakfast was their wedding present for you and Craig," Nat added.

"I tried to tell her they'd been too generous, but Irene told me in no uncertain words that people needed protein to counteract all the sugar in the wedding cake." Kim smiled as she gave her ring another twist. "I did notice there wasn't a scrap of bacon or a single sausage left over." She turned to the redhead who'd been quietly nursing a glass of ice water at the end of the table. "What about you, Belle? What was your favorite part?"

Belle nudged a lemon slice from the rim of her glass. It floated on top of the ice. "Seeing Mama happy. She loved being surrounded by members of the family that she hadn't seen in over a decade, and she was absolutely thrilled to see Opal. I couldn't have planned that part better myself."

"It was good to see her get so much attention," Diane noted. "Every time I looked for your mom, she was at the very center of a crowd."

"I didn't hear a single complaint all weekend," Jen mused aloud. "Not even from Harry. I can't imagine that cot he had to sleep on was very comfortable. He's not a small guy."

"Aggie told Mama he'd ended up raiding one of the linen closets for quilts and made a pallet for himself."

"Maybe we should pick up some air mattresses before the next—"

Jen must have realized her mistake because she paled slightly.

"For times when we need an extra bed," she finished.

"That's not a bad idea," Belle said, choosing to accept the suggestion at face value. She singled Nat out. "What was your favorite part?"

"It's hard to pick out one thing." Nat swirled

the strawberry sangria in her glass while she rattled off a few highlights of the weekend. "Mom's wedding was everything a wedding ought to be. I loved meeting relatives I didn't even know I had. The talent show and the sing-along were awesome. If I have to name one thing, though, I'd have to say my favorite part was when Fern went into labor."

"Oh, my word, yes. That was something else," Jen agreed.

"And to think they had a boy. I have a nephew!" Amy gave a delighted squeal. "I never saw that coming."

"No one did," Diane agreed. She still marveled how, in this day and age, with all the technology available, the baby's sex had taken everyone by surprise.

Kim tilted her head toward her daughter. "Are you still planning to babysit Isabella and Sophie during the week?" Nat had volunteered to help keep the older girls entertained so Fern could have some Mommy-and-me time with baby Paul.

Nat nodded. "I'm actually going to bring the girls here for the afternoon three times a week. I've already discussed it with Scott and Fern. They both agreed that, with Caitlyn working at the inn this summer, it'd be good for them to get to know their older cousin. I have it all planned out. I'm going to give them chores to do. Nothing too strenuous, of course. A little light dusting, fluffing the pillows on the front porch, that kind of thing. When they're done with their work, Caitlyn and I will spend the rest of the afternoon with them. We'll take walks on the beach, go on hunts for buried treasure, have tea parties by the river—the same things you all did when you were growing up here."

Murmured approvals circled around the table until they reached Amy. The baker frowned.

"What's wrong with the idea?" Diane asked her sister. For the life of her, she couldn't think of a single reason why the girls shouldn't take advantage of the opportunity to spend time together.

"Nothing, per se," Amy hedged. "But it does bring up a touchy subject."

Like the tiki torches that attracted moths, the comment drew everyone's attention.

Speaking for all of them, Belle asked, "What subject?"

"It was something Steve's daughter, Joy, said. I guess she and Caitlyn spent quite a bit of time together over the weekend." Seeking confirmation, Amy glanced at her sister.

"Joy's a year younger than Caitlyn, and she

plays soccer." Diane shrugged. "They have a lot in common."

"Whatever the reason, Caitlyn must have told her that she's working at the inn this summer. Steve asked me if Joy could stay on after next year's reunion and help out. Not only that, but his brother-in-law has a girl about the same age. He mentioned having her come with them next year, too."

Diane's heart skipped several beats. Some of her best memories were of the long summer days when she and her brother and sister and their cousins had spent mornings changing linens and doing laundry, sweeping floors and washing windows at the inn. Most days, they'd spent the afternoons at the beach or exploring the twenty-acre spit of land that lay between the river and the ocean. At first blush, the idea of passing those traditions down to a whole new generation of Dane family members thrilled her to the bone. However, there were no plans to hold another reunion next year. Not only that, but if something didn't change, by next summer, the entire property would belong to someone else.

Unless they changed the plan.

"What did you tell him?" Jen asked tentatively.

"I said we needed a few weeks to regroup

after this reunion and that I'd get back to him." Tilting her head to one side, Amy lifted her shoulders while she held out her empty hands. "What could I say?"

Belle ran her fingers up and down the sides of her glass before she wiped her hands on a napkin. "That was smart. In a month or so, Mama can write him and…"

"Uh-hmm." Diane cleared her throat. "Sorry," she apologized, though she really wasn't sorry when the noise cut her cousin off in mid-sentence. "But, uh, that brings up something I wanted to discuss with you all tonight."

"I thought you had something on your mind." Leaning back in her chair, Amy folded her arms across her chest. "You just had that look, you know?"

Not at all surprised that her sister had read her mood, Diane hesitated. Before she sprang her idea on them, there was one critical piece of information she needed. She turned to Belle. "Do you mind if I ask you a personal question?"

Belle held up her cupped, open hands. "You guys know all my secrets. My life's an open book."

Diane took a breath. Without trying to sugar-coat the question, she asked, "How much do you know about your mom's will?"

Belle's green eyes narrowed while her lips tightened the slightest bit. "Not what I was expecting, but like I said, I don't have anything to hide. You mean about the trust?"

When Diane nodded, Belle sighed deeply. "Everything. Mama went over everything with me this week, as a matter of fact. She wanted to make sure I approved of her plan to set up a trust with the money she gets from...from Carmen." With the auction set to take place before the end of the month, Margaret was taking the necessary steps to safeguard the fortune she'd soon receive.

Diane released a breath she hadn't known she'd been holding. Relieved that Margaret had discussed the matter with Belle, she relaxed slightly. She'd been afraid that some aspects of her aunt's estate would come as a shock. Not that she thought Belle would throw a hissy fit over Margaret's plans, but she'd known families that had been torn apart over inheritances that were much smaller.

Belle's gaze flitted about the women at the table while she drummed perfectly manicured fingers on the tabletop. "It's not my place to go into specifics," she said, apparently reaching a decision. "But Mama's not leaving all that money to me when she passes. She'll use some of it—a lot, I hope, because I want her to live forever—to pay her rent at Emerald Oaks and any other expenses. She wants to make a sizable contribution to the church. She's leaving some money for her two favorite charities. The rest will be divided equally between her heirs."

"What heirs?" Amy's eyebrows slammed together, creating a wedge in the center of her forehead. "Don't tell me our Aunt Margaret has a love child no one knows about."

"Yeah, what's that all about?" Jen propped her elbows on the tabletop and stared at her cousin. "You're her only child, aren't you?"

"Well, yeah." Belle answered Jen's imploring gaze with a small, self-conscious laugh. "But as Liz's and Shirley's children, you and Kim, Scott, Amy and Diane are Mama's heirs, too."

Diane swore the ocean stopped its ceaseless roar, the breeze blowing off the water died and the frogs in the distant river stopped their croaking when her sister's mouth gaped open. On the other side of the table, Jen hooked her pinky finger around Kim's and gave it a tug.

Nat swallowed. "Not Edward's children? Not Harry and…"

"No." Belle gave her head an emphatic shake that sent her red curls flying. "When Edward moved to Houston, he insisted on getting *his share*." She enclosed the last two words in finger quotes. "That forced Grampa Dane to put the inn up as collateral on a loan. Mama says he never forgave Edward for leaving like he did."

"Huh!" Nat slumped back in her chair. "The things you learn…"

"Well, you might as well learn this—I don't want any of Aunt Margaret's money." Amy's firm voice hinted at the drive and dedication it had taken for her to build a successful business in their small town. "Or the headaches that go with it. I don't have any children, and I already make a good living from Sweet Cakes."

"I'd like to make sure Nat and Josh are taken care of, but if it was up to me, I wouldn't take a dime from the treasure," Kim insisted.

"Good. Y'all can give your shares to me." Jen smiled widely. When everyone stared at her, she threw up her hands. "Just kidding. Geez. Can't you take a joke? I'm not saying I'd turn down enough to get by on, but I'm talking ten or twenty grand. Not millions. Like Amy said, who needs those kinds of headaches?"

"Look. Don't be so quick to turn this down," Belle said, her voice growing a touch strident. "You don't know how easy this much money can make your life, the lives of your children."

"I'm pretty sure Josh and I are on the same page. We don't want easy." Nat straightened.

"We want to make our own way. Stand on our own two feet. We've watched our dad chase the almighty dollar our entire lives. And what did it get him? Three divorces. Two kids who don't want anything to do with him. He doesn't have a friend in the world because everyone who's spent any time around him at all knows he's just in it for himself. That's not the kind of life I want to lead. And I know, if Josh was here, he'd say the same thing." She turned a pair of watery blue eyes on Kim. "So, no, Mom. Don't take any of that money for my sake 'cause..." Nat's voice broke. "'Cause I don't want it."

While Diane and the others sat in dumbstruck admiration of their niece, Kim wrapped her arms tightly around her sobbing daughter and pulled her close. She waited until Nat's tears slowed before, turning to the rest of them, she said, "You heard her. Aunt Margaret will have to figure out something else to do with her money."

"Oh, no!" Belle protested. "You're not sticking me with this entire fortune. I know everyone says they don't want the money, but there'll come a day when you'll resent me for having it all."

Shock and indignation played across Amy's face. "You didn't feel like we resented you before, did you?" she demanded.

Belle's cheeks turned nearly as red as her hair. "No. Never. If I implied that you did, I'm sorry. The people sitting at this table are the *only* ones I can be myself with."

"Not even Jason?"

Belle's entire expression softened. "Maybe one day. Not yet." She sat up a tiny bit straighter. "The thing is, I want you to think long and hard before you turn down this gift."

For a few moments, they sat, listening to the breakers rolling against the sand a quarter mile away. Kim's seat creaked when a bull alligator bellowed in the distance. His throaty roar was quickly drowned out by the frogs that croaked cheerily along the riverbank. The monk parakeets rustled among the palm fronds in response to the hoot of an owl from somewhere nearby.

Sensing the time was ripe, Diane cleared her throat again. "Here's the thing," she said earnestly. "My biggest concern isn't the money. It's this place and what it means to our family. Aunt Margaret still plans to sell the inn. She still plans to move to Emerald Oaks. Quite frankly, that worries me, too, but I'm even more afraid of what will happen to us as a family without this place as our touchstone."

Jen blinked. "I don't get it. Why should things change?"

"It's already starting. For the past, what—eight months or so?—we've seen each other practically every day. Yet, as soon as the reunion was over, we scattered." She held up a hand to stop their protests. "I'm as guilty as anyone—Caitlyn and I have our own home now, and I've been busier than you know these last few days. Kim is making a home with her new hubby. As she should," she added in case anyone thought she meant the statement as a criticism. "The more success Belle and The Emeralds have, the more they'll be on the road. Nat's already gotten one job offer that would take her away from Emerald Bay. And you, Jen, we're all aware that this is the longest you've stayed in one place in years. I'm just afraid that, once we aren't involved with the inn on a day-to-day basis, we'll drift apart."

Amy, who knew her better than anyone else in the world, followed Diane's train of thought and hopped right on board. "We'll start meeting weekly for dinner at the diner. Only, before you know it, I'll have a rush order and have to miss a night. Belle will be out of town on a gig."

Kim nodded. As if thinking out loud, she said, "Once the new owners take over, I'll have to relocate Royal Meals. To do that, I'll need to expand my customer base, which means I won't have nearly as much free time. I'll want to spend as much of that as possible with Craig, so I could only meet when he has town council meetings."

"And, as we all know, those occasionally get canceled," Diane added.

"The next thing you know, we won't see each other for a month. Without anything to hold her here, Nat will take a job in Atlanta or California. Jen will—"

"Let me stop you right there." Jen rapped her knuckles on the table. "I'm not going anywhere."

"And we're all glad to hear it." Diane was glad to see heads bobbing up and down. "But that doesn't change the fact that we'll drift apart. Maybe I'm the only one who feels this way, but that's not the kind of relationship I want with the people who mean the most to me."

"You're not alone." Belle used her napkin to blot her eyes. "I feel the same way, too."

"I think we all do." Kim's gaze searched the faces of those gathered around the table and found unanimous agreement.

"You mentioned Mama." Belle's breath hiccupped. "I'm worried about her, too. She says she's excited about moving to Emerald Oaks, but I'm afraid once she sells the only home she's ever known, once she moves into a tiny two-bedroom apartment, she'll end up watching the paint dry and regretting the biggest mistake of her life."

"We'll visit," Amy promised.

"Yes. I know." Belle stretched a hand across the table and squeezed her cousin's. "But it won't be like it is here. You won't be dropping in to check on her every morning at the crack of dawn. Kim won't be bustling around in the kitchen, whipping up something tasty and nutritious. She won't have the stimulation she gets from our guests." She sighed. "And our guests. Some of them—Helen March, for instance—have been coming here for decades. They're more like friends than they are strangers."

"She'll be here on Monday, by the way," Nat piped up. "She's reserved Rosario for two weeks."

"Oooh, you know what that means—a new Helen March book!" Slipping out from under Belle's grip, Amy pressed her hand over her heart. The author sought the peace and solitude of the inn whenever she was on deadline.

"What about kids like Steve's daughter? The next generation of Danes?" Kim asked. "Do we really want them to look back when they're in their fifties and say, 'I remember that one year when we had this huge family reunion. It was a blast. I don't know why we never had another one.'"

"But what can we do?" Usually so certain and sure, Belle appeared to be adrift. "Mama has made up her mind. She's going to sell the inn. She knows she can't run it on her own anymore. And there is no one else. We talked about this weeks ago. No one else wants to shoulder that much responsibility. That hasn't changed." A spark of faint hope brightened her eyes. "Has it?

Belle's gaze swept over her cousin's faces. One by one, they shook their heads.

Diane recognized that they all had valid reasons for not stepping in to run the inn. Amy couldn't very well give up Sweet Cakes. Kim finally had Royal Meals on firm footing, but she had to meet her delivery deadlines or her business would fail. Belle and Daclan—or rather, Daclan's parents—had signed a record deal just this week. Her calendar was full. Though they both were willing to help, Jen didn't have the background or Nat the maturity to run the inn on their own. As for herself, her new accounting firm was barely off the ground.

Belle's shoulders rounded. "So we're back at Square One. Mama can't run the inn on her own anymore, and no one else is able to take it on."

"True." Diane refused to argue with the obvious. "But I was thinking…" And, her heart thumping to beat the band, Diane leaned forward and sketched details of a plan that just might save both the inn and their family.

Seventeen

Margaret

Carrying her coffee in a travel mug rather than risk having it slosh over the sides of a cup, Margaret picked her way through the inn to the door. She stepped out onto the front porch and drank in the cool morning air. No doubt, the day would turn hot and muggy later. It was June, after all. In Florida. By late afternoon, moving from the air-conditioning into the heat would feel like stepping into a sauna. For now, though, golden hues clung to the horizon beneath azure-blue skies, and the thermometer mounted on one of the porch's white columns read a comfortable seventy-seven degrees. Setting her cup on the rattan coffee table, she eased herself onto a cushioned chair, determined to enjoy watching the seagrass sway in the cool breeze and the birds hopping about in the grass searching for their breakfast. The ocean's roar faded into the background like the static on her parents' old television.

Lord only knew how many more mornings she'd be able to do this. She was surprised, actually, that she had this one. Kim must have slept in, she mused. Now that her niece had married Craig and moved to his house on the other side of town, she sometimes didn't get to the inn before seven.

As for Belle and the rest of them, they must have stayed on the back deck later than usual last night. She laughed softly. They didn't think she could hear them, but she did. Oh, not the words, maybe, but she'd grown used to falling asleep to the quiet buzz of their familiar voices.

She wondered what they'd been discussing last night. Whatever it had been, it must have been serious. She hadn't heard a single burst of the laughter that usually punctuated their conversations.

Had they been talking about her? Planning what to do if she refused to keep her end of the deal? If so, they didn't need to worry about that. Her daughter and her nieces had carried through with their promise to host one last Dane Family Reunion at the inn. And she'd fulfill her part of the bargain, too. She'd put the old homestead on the market and move to Emerald Oaks.

Even if it did break her heart.

Her eyes filled, and she sniffled. Digging around in the pocket of her slacks, she pulled out a handful of tissues and took care of business.

Why would the girls think she'd renege on her part of the bargain, anyway? She hadn't slipped up. Not even once. Hadn't breathed a word about how much she hated the idea of moving to the assisted living facility. Even two days ago, when she and Belle had taken the new-resident tour, she'd stayed upbeat and positive despite the fact that her heart was breaking inside.

Why was that, though? She'd known what she was getting herself into from the beginning. She had friends who lived at Emerald Oaks. Whenever she visited them, she was always impressed by the cleanliness of the place, the friendliness of the staff, the many food options in the dining room. But visiting the retirement home and living there were two entirely different things, as she'd quickly learned. On this trip, the institutional green walls made her nauseous. The smiles of the caretakers seemed condescending. And the food—good grief. Maybe eating Kim's cooking for the better part of a year had spoiled her, but she hadn't seen one thing she liked on that menu.

As for her suite, if you could call it that, it wasn't even half the size of Beryl, and that was the smallest of the Dane Crown Inn's rooms. Why, the tiny bedroom they expected her to sleep in wasn't much bigger than a jail cell and had all the ambience of one, too. Oh, Belle had flitted about like a butterfly, going on about how the right curtains and the right color of paint would dress up the place. But that was just a bunch of hooey. She might as well try to turn a sow's ear into a silk purse for all the good it would do. It'd take more than paint and curtains to turn those rooms at Emerald Oaks into a home.

Her hand fluttered to her chest.

Still, she'd made a deal. Belle and Kim and the others had kept their end of the bargain. It was too late for her to back out. And after all, it could be worse. At least she had people who loved her. A daughter, a nephew, several nieces and grand-nieces. Some of her friends didn't have close ties to their family and had ended up in nursing homes. She should count her blessings, she told herself.

And, doing her best to ignore a growing sense of melancholy, she sipped her coffee and listened for signs of people stirring in the house while she mentally prepared herself for the move to Emerald Oaks.

"But we had a deal," Margaret protested. She scanned the faces of those who'd gathered behind the family quarters' closed doors. She recited the terms. "You girls would host one last Dane Family Reunion. When it was over, I'd put the inn on the market and retire. Now you don't want me to move to Emerald Oaks?"

"Yes, ma'am. That was the deal." Diane recounted the night aloud, as if anyone in the room had forgotten. Nearly nine months had passed since, with her arm in a cast and bruises dotting her nearly translucent skin, their aunt had made one last request in exchange for selling the inn her parents had built.

"But a lot has changed since then," Belle said from her seat on the couch beside her mother.

"This old place never has looked better," Margaret noted. "That's for sure. You girls did a marvelous job sprucing things up. The floors alone made a huge improvement."

"Remember all those scatter rugs everywhere?"

Kim asked. "You don't need to worry about tripping over them anymore because the holes they were covering up are all gone." Having the floors throughout the inn repaired and refinished had been an expensive undertaking. One they'd never have been able to afford if Amy hadn't sold her longtime employee a stake in Sweet Cakes.

"Or the carpets, either." Belle had sold a pricey piece of art to cover those costs.

"You know, I hated to throw those old runners out, but I can admit it when I'm wrong. The inn looks so much better without them." Margaret rubbed her forearm. Though everyone told her the break had healed cleanly, it still ached from time to time. But that was something she didn't have to admit.

"And we painted. Inside and out," Kim pointed out. "Did anyone count how many painting parties we held?"

"I didn't, but I swear I still have paint under my nails." Nat wiggled her fingers.

"My hands are still sticky from hanging all that wallpaper." Jen rubbed her palms together.

"Remember how overgrown everything was? Weeds choked all the paths. The hedges hadn't been trimmed in years. Daddy's roses had gone wild."

Margaret squeezed her daughter's hand. "Those flowers were your father's pride and joy. He'd be so happy to see them now." The fragrant scent from the vase of roses Belle had picked that morning perfumed the air of the living room.

"Manuel and his crew have done a wonderful job of getting things back in shape." Belle nodded.

"Now that we've refurbished the place, it's easier for Irene and Eunice to keep things spic and span." When Kim first arrived in Emerald Bay, the maids—at Margaret's insistence— hadn't cleaned the upstairs in ages.

The thin wail of a newborn drifted from beyond the closed door of the family quarters.

"Little Paul is fussy." Margaret grabbed her cane. "I'd better go and rock him."

From his seat flanking Margaret's other side, Scott laid a restraining hand on her thigh. "You don't have what he wants, Aunt Margaret. That's his hungry cry. Fern will take care of him." Sure enough, Paul's cries ceased abruptly a few seconds later.

"What about the girls? Don't we need to check on them?" Margaret moved restlessly.

"It's okay, Mama. Caitlyn and Stacey are watching a movie with Isabella and Sophie in the game room. The girls are going to have ice cream sundaes later."

"Great." Scott stretched. "Then you're going to send me home with two little girls hyped up on sugar."

"You used to run around in circles when you ate too many sweets." Margaret smiled fondly at her nephew before her face pinched. "So." She thumped the rubber tip of her cane on the floor. "The girls are fine. The baby is fine. The inn is fine. We had a wonderful reunion. Is anyone going to tell me why you're all here?" So far, no one had explained why her entire family had insisted on holding a meeting. Was this some kind of intervention? For the life of her, she couldn't think of anything she'd done to raise their concerns.

Unless...

Margaret bowed her head. Silently, she prayed. *Oh, dear Lord, please don't let them stick me in a nursing home. I'm not that old and feeble.*

True, she rarely ventured into the kitchen anymore. She no longer struggled to fill the coffee carafes in the dining room. But why would she? Most days, Kim had a pot of hot coffee and a fresh sweet roll waiting for her when she wandered out of her bedroom. On the rare occasions when Kim didn't show up before daybreak, she made up the coffeepots the night before. Those days, all Margaret had to do was flip a switch and—voilà!

Nor was that the only job the others had taken over. She used to spend hours struggling with the reservations. Not anymore. She hadn't had to do that since Nat had updated their computer system. Now if she wanted to see which rooms were available or prepare someone's bill, all she had to do was push a button. She still greeted their guests from time to time, but it was Jen or Nat who showed them to their rooms, pulled back the curtains and checked to make sure they had plenty of fresh towels. Why, half the time, when she walked out onto the front porch, someone else had already swept it and plumped the cushions on the rattan furniture.

Maybe she was that old and feeble—or they thought she was—after all. A tear trickled down her cheek. She brushed it away and hoped no one had noticed.

"Mama?" Worry pooled in Belle's green eyes.

Margaret clutched her daughter's hands. "Please, don't send me to the nursing home," she whispered.

"The nursing home!" Scott's shocked protest echoed through the room.

"Mama, no one said anything about a— Why on earth would you think we'd do that?"

Margaret's lip wobbled. "You said you didn't

want me to move to Emerald Oaks. What other choice is there?" Tears gathered in her eyes. Any second, they'd spill down her cheeks. Which wouldn't help her convince her family not to put her away. Not at all.

"Aunt Margaret." Sounding cool and dispassionate, Diane knelt in front of her. "I can promise you this—no one is sending you anywhere. In fact, we'd like for you to stay right where you are. Here, at the inn. We want you to live out the rest of a very long and healthy life right here in your own home."

"Pshaw!" Margaret exhaled forcefully. "I can't do that. You know how hard it's going to be to find a buyer for the inn? No one's going to want this place with an eighty-year-old tenant."

"That's the thing, Mama." Belle cupped Margaret's hands in hers. "We were thinking maybe you wouldn't sell the place after all."

"Not sell?" Margaret battled down an urge to leap at the chance to keep her family home. None of this was making any sense. She shook her head. "We've been over this. It's too expensive. What with insurance and upkeep and whatnot, the inn loses money every month."

"That's true," Diane agreed. "But if you make certain improvements—put in a swimming pool, turn one of the cottages into a spa, buy a boat

and hire a fishing guide or offer nature tours—
you can appeal to a more upscale market."

"Which is my sister's glorified way of saying
you could charge more." Amy grinned.

"I've worked at several high-end resorts," Jen
said from the spot where she sat, cross-legged,
on the floor. "People practically break down the
doors to get in the better places. Not only will
these changes pay for themselves, they'll put the
inn in the black."

"That all sounds rather grand." Margaret
closed her eyes, envisioning the hotel bursting at
the seams like it had back when it was called the
Jewel of Florida's Treasure Coast. It only took a
minute, though, before reality snuck in and filled
all the cracks and crevices of her chest like fine
beach sand. Her eyes popped open. "What
you've proposed is an expensive undertaking.
We barely scraped together enough money to
refinish the floors and replace the carpeting.
How am I supposed to pay for any of this?"

"You're forgetting the treasure, Mama," Belle
said. "Once those coins and gems sell at
auction—which will happen by the end of the
month—you're going to have more money than
you'd be able to spend in a dozen lifetimes. You
could use some of it to transform the inn into a
resort."

"That money is your inheritance," Margaret huffed. "Yours, and theirs." With a wave of one hand, she indicated the others in the room.

"We had an idea about that, Mama," Belle said softly.

"Yeah, Aunt Margaret." Diane peered earnestly into Margaret's eyes. "We all talked it over and, well, instead of splitting the money between us, we think we've come up with a better plan."

Scott's deep voice rumbled. "What you'd do is set up a trust and fund it with the proceeds from the auction. Going forward, the administrator of the trust would ensure that all the expenses of running the inn—including these plans for expansion—were paid out of that money."

"That way, you could continue living here, Mama. And you'd never have to worry about taxes or maintenance bills. Even the salaries for the gardeners and housekeeping staff would all come out of the trust."

"And then, when you're gone…" Jen winced. "I mean, when you…"

"Just go ahead and say it, honey. I know I'm not going to live forever. When I die," Margaret prompted.

Tears filled Jen's eyes. Unable to speak, she sent her big sister a pleading look.

"After you've been called home," Kim said, "the trust will continue to ensure that the Dane Crown Inn lives on for future generations."

"As long as there's someone in the Dane family to administer it," Scott finished.

Margaret blinked. "This is what you want? You'd rather make sure the inn stays in the family than take the money for yourselves?" She could hardly believe what she was hearing.

"Yes, Mama. That's what we're saying. I never knew what it was like to be an only child because I grew up surrounded by my cousins. I will forever be grateful for the memories we share, for the closeness we have with one another. You and Daddy and Uncle Paul and Aunt Liz gave me that. Aunt Shirley, too, in her own way. But none of it would have been possible without the inn. It's the glue, the touchstone, that holds our family together. And I want that to continue. We all do. Not just for our generation but for generations to come."

"Oh, honey." Belle's words stirred a deep and abiding need in her very center. With a sigh, Margaret pressed her soggy tissues to her eyes.

"Geez, Belle." Jen leapt to her feet, grabbed a tissue box from the counter and made her way around the room passing out tissues to whoever needed them. And they all did.

"I can't think of anything better to do with that buried treasure," Diane said after she blotted her eyes. Having said her piece, she moved to a nearby chair.

Margaret took a steadying breath. "Amy," she said, singling out the baker. "You haven't said much. You agree with them?" She pointed to Belle and Diane.

"Yes, ma'am. I do." Amy gave a lopsided smile. "I wouldn't have the faintest clue what to do with that much money."

She'd probably figure it out, Margaret thought as her gaze shifted to Scott. "Scott, you and Fern have those two precious girls and a newborn baby to think about. You're saying you'd turn down the chance to see that they never wanted for a single thing in their lives?"

Scott chuckled. "Believe me, Aunt Margaret, we have a tough enough time not spoiling them rotten as it is. More money would only present a bigger challenge to us as parents." He sobered. "Besides, I have to stop and ask myself, 'What would Mom and Dad do?' I think they'd want to keep the inn in the family for as long as possible."

"Your mom did love this place," Margaret acknowledged. For an instant, she pictured her sister standing at the counter, singing along with the radio while she chopped vegetables for her family's dinner. Liz had never been happier than when she was in the inn's large and airy kitchen.

Movement out of the corner of her eye caught Margaret's attention. She glanced toward the table in time to see a rose petal fall onto the polished wooden surface. When she turned back, her sister's image had disappeared. She whispered wordlessly.

Soon, sis. We'll see each other again one of these days.

After clearing her throat, Margaret focused on Nat. "You're young. You have your whole life in front of you. Why would you turn down millions of dollars?"

"We'll talk one day soon, and I'll tell you all about it, Aunt Margaret. For now, though, just know that I don't believe you should sell the inn. And neither does Josh."

"Well." Margaret blew out a breath. "It certainly sounds like you're all in agreement." She scrubbed a damp hand along the crease of her slacks. "There's just one problem. Who's going to run this new and improved inn? I can't. You've all been pretty insistent that it's high time for me to retire."

"We all will." Diane pointed out the others one by one. "Jen and Nat will take charge of guest relations. Kim will continue to run Royal Meals from the kitchen. In exchange for free use of the facilities, she'll provide our guests with a complimentary hot breakfast."

"As well as boxed lunches for those who sign up for one of our excursion packages," Kim added. "Eventually, I'd like to add a dinner service, but that's on down the road."

"I'll handle all the finances," Diane promised. "Scott will make sure we comply with all the local and state requirements. Amy and Sweet Cakes will supply all our bakery products."

"She and I will pitch in wherever we're needed," Belle said. "We'll fill in whenever someone goes on vacation or takes a honeymoon." She shot a knowing look at Kim.

"Someone will have to give you cooking lessons." The bride's comment sent a ripple of laughter through the room.

"What about the reunions?" Margaret felt hope swirl in her chest. "Would we still hold them?"

"Yes." Belle's curls bounced when her head bobbed up and down.

"Definitely," Scott echoed. "I want my children and, hopefully, their children to experience the kind of childhood I had. I want them to go on treasure hunts and catch fish from the riverbank."

"I want to take my grandchildren on walks along the beach. To roast marshmallows at the firepit," Kim added.

"In just a few years, Caitlyn will graduate and head off to college. Before she does, I want her to spend time with her cousins, to establish the same connections with Nat and Isabella and Sophie, and now little Paul, that I have with all of you." Diane indicated her sister and brother and cousins with a sweep of her hand.

Margaret's heart swelled. To live out the rest of her life surrounded by the people she loved and who loved her in return? To remain in the house her parents built, to wake up each morning to the sound of the ocean's roar, to watch the monk parakeets flit among the branches of the palm trees whenever she wanted. It sounded like heaven. It sounded like home.

And so she agreed on a Saturday evening in the middle of June that the Dane Crown Inn would live on because sometimes family wasn't simply *more* important than money. At times like these, family was the *only* thing that mattered.

Epilogue

Nat

Her hand on Rosario's doorknob, Nat paused to take a breath. Another successful Dane Family Reunion had drawn to a close. She'd been running hither and yon all day, exchanging hugs and best wishes with members of her far-flung family as they piled into cars or caught rides to airports or bus stations. Most had already circled next year's Memorial Day weekend on their calendars and would return for the event she and her mom and her aunts would begin planning as soon as the dust settled on this one.

She hoped the next reunion would be as successful. Of course, there'd be changes. There always were. Take the pool they'd added three years ago, for example. Guests and relatives alike had raved about it. As they had about the six spacious cottages Max's newly minted construction company had erected. Those made accommodating everyone so much easier. An excursion to the outlet mall in Vero Beach, however, hadn't been received nearly as well. She had no doubt they'd scratch it off the list for future reunions.

Right now, though, she needed to check on her newest charges—the assorted cousins who'd signed up to spend the summer working at the inn. The motley crew of kids who barely knew each other's names was sure to grow closer as they helped make the stays of the inn's guests a little more pleasant over the next three months. And wasn't that the point? To extend the inn's legacy to another generation?

Nat rapped sharply on the door to the cottage. Without waiting for an answer, she stepped inside.

"Are you all settled?" Her gaze swept the interior. Through the open doors of the bed-rooms, she spied suitcases lying on beds and scattered belongings. Typical teenagers, she thought. Her focus shifted, and she scanned the eager faces of the six teens who would work at the inn until school started in the fall. The first-timers—those who'd waved goodbye to their parents only hours earlier—blinked back tears even as they nodded. The others, who'd spent prior summers doing laundry, changing linens and helping guests with their luggage, answered with more enthusiasm.

"I'll be your house mom, as well as your supervisor while you're here." Nat deliberately softened her voice. "Let me know if you need anything or if you run into any problems." As she did every summer, she'd move into the tiny, third bedroom they'd added to Rosario so she could watch over the youngsters like a mother hen and her chicks.

Nat rubbed the ring Troy had slipped on her finger last month. Plans were already well underway for their Christmas wedding. Which begged the question, who would supervise next summer's crew? It was one she'd have to answer over the coming year.

Setting that concern aside to deal with later, she slipped a piece of paper from the slim binder that held everything she needed for the day-to-day management of the inn. As co-manager, Jen carried a similar notebook. They rarely went anywhere without them.

"You all have a copy of the rules," she reminded the teens. "But let's hit the highlights to make sure we're all on the same page." She launched into the spiel she'd honed to perfection over several seasons. When she'd finished, she singled out the two boys.

"Mattox and Tyler are Team A. You have laundry duty tomorrow." Nat aimed her sternest look at the teens to show she meant business. "That means no playing video games into the wee hours tonight. Lights out at eleven. Got it?"

"Yes, ma'am." A redhead like his father, Tyler gave his assent. This was his third summer at the inn. He knew the drill.

"Laundry. All right!" Mattox reached into one of the deep pockets of his cargo shorts and pulled a handheld gaming device out just far enough to give his partner a glimpse. No doubt he imagined sitting on top of one of the dryers while he played games between loads.

"Nuh-uh. There'll be none of that." Nat shook a finger at the dark-haired boy who was spending his first summer at the inn. "When you aren't folding towels or starting the next load of sheets, I expect both of you to be sweeping the front and back porches and walkways. I don't want to see a single leaf or a speck of dirt on those sidewalks by the time our guests start arriving. Tyler, you know what to do. I expect you to show Mattox how we do things here."

"I will." After years of following orders from

an older cousin, Tyler beamed at the chance to be in charge.

Nat turned to the four girls who, except for Isabella, were glued to their cell phones. She smiled fondly at the young woman who'd surprised everyone on her sixteenth birthday by announcing that "Isabella" was too old-fashioned and, in the future, she wanted to be called by her nickname.

"Izzy, we're glad to have you back again this year." Scott's oldest girl had spent the last two summers at the inn. Her sister, Sophie, was still too young to stay on the grounds, but she picked up a little spending money by fluffing the pillows and watering the house plants on weekends.

Nat addressed the others. "Emma, Reese and Avery, remember what we said about cell phones. You'll be docked five dollars every time I catch you talking or texting on one when you're supposed to be working or when you're with me." She circled a finger in the air to indicate the meeting they were having right now.

Emma and Reese tucked their mobile devices out of sight. When Avery did not follow suit, Nat mimicked her own mother and tsked. She held out her hand to the girl who hadn't gotten the message the first time. "That'll be five dollars,

Avery. And I'll hold on to your phone until we're finished here."

"Five? Uh!" Avery's dark eyes widened in shocked protest.

"She's the boss." Izzy spoke from experience. She knew what it meant to break a rule and pay the consequences.

Plucking Avery's device from the girl's outstretched hands, Nat silenced the phone before she set it on the table in the cottage's breakfast nook. As for the fine she'd deduct from Avery's paycheck, it would help pay for the kids' farewell party at the end of the season.

Nat picked up the thread of her little talk. "So the boys are Team A. They'll have laundry duty tomorrow. Team B will work in the main house, where you'll replace the linens, dust and dry-mop the floors in all the suites. Team C will do the same thing in the cottages." Led by Irene and Eunice, their crew of housekeepers would handle all the rest.

Nat singled out Izzy with a look. "As the oldest, you get to choose your partner."

"I'll take Avery," Izzy said without hesitation.

"Okay, then. You're Team B." Nat nodded approvingly. Izzy would help the younger girl learn the ropes in no time. And wasn't that a large part of what this was all about—teaching another generation of Danes to care for the inn as much as their aunts and uncles did?

It was, and she moved on to Emma and Reese. "That means you two are Team C. You'll start on the cottages in the morning." Her focus widened to take in the entire group. "Each team will rotate from the laundry to the suites to the cottages. If you start out doing laundry on Monday, then on Tuesday, you'll be in…" She let the sentence hang while she waited for an answer.

"The main house," Tyler said.

"Right." Nat grinned. "I don't expect you to remember everything off the bat. Check the chart on the cupboard each night until you get the routine down." She pointed to the kitchenette, where a schedule had been taped to one of the cabinets.

"When do we eat?" Mattox wanted to know.

"Good question." Nat couldn't fault the boy for asking, but these teens definitely wouldn't go hungry during their stay at the inn. In addition to the meals served in the main house, the cottage's cupboards were fairly bursting with snacks of all kinds. Fresh fruit and yogurt filled the small fridge. "Breakfast is at six thirty, lunch at noon and dinner at six. Work starts at seven each morning."

An indulgent smile played across her lips when a collective groan rose from the group. "I know. It's early, but you'll get used to it," she promised. "Since the reunion just ended, all the suites and cottages are empty. But they'll fill up fast tomorrow. Check-in starts at three thirty. Once the guests start arriving, they'd appreciate your help with their luggage." Holding her hand up, she rubbed two fingers against her thumb.

"What's that mean?" Avery asked.

"Tips." Emma's blue eyes sparkled. She was saving for college. The extra money she'd earn hauling suitcases up and down the stairs would come in handy.

Nat heard something creak behind her and glanced toward the cottage's front door. Sure enough, Troy had let himself in and now leaned against the doorframe. One glimpse of the man's sun-bronzed arms and the long legs that peeked out from beneath the khaki shorts and shirt that were his working uniform, and she felt her heart go pit-a-pat just like it had the first time she'd spied him climbing onto their dock from his boat. With a lazy smile that always sent her pulse racing, he hiked a questioning eyebrow. He needn't have bothered. He was right on time, as always.

"Okay." Nat rubbed her hands together.

"That's about all I have, except to remind you that this evening, dinner is a potluck." Ordinarily, they held the informal family dinners on Sundays, but they'd postponed this one due to the long holiday weekend. "Weather permitting, we'll meet in the kitchen at six." She beckoned her fiancé forward. "I think Troy has something he wants to talk to you about."

The fishing guide stepped further into the cottage. "I heard the reds are running a little bit north of us." Red drum, also known as redfish, were a sport fish that were prized for their sweet, mild taste. "I'm going to try my luck. If any of you would like to come, you're welcome to join me."

"I'm in." Tyler, who'd taken every opportunity to fish with the guide in the past, immediately raised his hand. "Mattox, how about you?"

"Nah, man." The younger boy patted his pocket. "I got a tournament this afternoon." He aimed a thumb at the room he and Tyler would share for the summer. "I'm gonna hang out here."

"Suit yourself, but you're missing out." Tyler shrugged before he hustled into the bedroom. He emerged seconds later carrying a pair of wading shoes.

"How about you girls? Any of you want to

come?" Encouragement laced Troy's deep voice.

"I've never fished before, but I'd like to go," Reese said hesitantly.

"Never?" Troy's aw-shucks grin widened in mock disbelief. "No problem," he assured the girl. "I'll teach ya." He liked nothing better than to introduce newcomers to his favorite sport.

"Make sure you're back by six," Nat reminded her fiancé.

"Is Craig bringing chicken?" Troy looked hopeful.

"Doesn't he always?" Her mother's second husband supplied fried chicken from the Pirate's Gold Diner for every potluck.

"Then we'll be here. Cross your fingers for us." Leading the teens out the door, Troy waved. "If we land a couple of big ones, I'll blacken them for supper tonight."

"Don't even think about cooking in Mom's kitchen," Nat said, managing to sound shocked at the very idea of such a thing. The Dane Crown Inn's kitchen was her mother's domain. She'd have Troy's head if he stunk up the place with the smell of fish and spice. Not that Nat had to worry. Her fiancé often prepared the day's catch for his clients in the outdoor kitchen he and Max had constructed.

"Miss Nat?"

The curious note in Avery's voice caught her attention. "Yes, hon?"

"What are we supposed to do until dinner?"

"Anything you want." Nat swept an arm through the air. "The game room and the library are available. You and Emma and Izzy might want to go for a walk on the beach." She let her voice drop to conspiratorial levels. "But you know what I would do?"

"What?" Clearly intrigued, Avery looked up.

"I'd swim in the pool." During the week, staff weren't allowed to use the pool on the other side of the main house. Sundays and days like today, when the inn had no guests, were an exception.

Brightening, Avery swung toward the other girls. "Want to go swimming?"

Emma gave the younger girl a warm smile. "I could lay out for a bit. My tan needs some work." She examined arms that already bore the rosy glow of someone who'd spent the weekend at the beach.

"Don't forget sunblock. No one wants to get burned." Tucking her binder under one arm, Nat turned to Izzy. Scott's eldest had completed a rigorous lifeguard training course earlier this year. "You'll watch out for them?"

"Sure. Lemme grab my phone and sunglasses, and I'm good to go."

Satisfied that the girls were in good hands and that Mattox had his own plans for the afternoon, Nat headed out the door. After the long holiday weekend, she wanted to walk the grounds. While she did, she'd make note of any issues their gardening or maintenance crews needed to address. With any luck, she'd finish up just in time for dinner.

Nat's hike from one end of the property to the other didn't take quite as long as she thought it might. Along the way, she retrieved a croquet hoop someone had left on the front lawn and sent Miguel a text about a broken sprinkler head. Other than that, she noted very little wear and tear despite the fact that relatives from far and wide had filled the inn to overflowing during the reunion. Finishing her trek with a quick check on Izzy and the others, Nat cut across the lawn behind the main house after she spied one of her aunts sitting beneath the umbrella that shaded a glass-topped table. The soles of her sandals tapping against the boards, she mounted the steps onto the deck.

"Hey, Jen," she called. Taking in the knives,

forks and spoons that sprouted from glass canning jars on a nearby cabinet, she asked, "Are we eating outside tonight?" They usually crowded around the dining room table.

"Yeah. Belle said she and Aunt Margaret thought it'd be nice to enjoy the sun while we have it." The forecast called for intermittent thunderstorms throughout the week ahead, which was typical for summers on Florida's east coast.

Jen cleared her throat. "Since we're the first ones here, do you mind if we go over the plans for your wedding?" As if she'd been waiting for Nat, she hauled out a thick, three-ring notebook and spread it open on the table.

"Sure." Letting her smile widen, Nat plopped onto a chair. These days, talking about her upcoming wedding was one of her favorite subjects. Besides, her aunt had become quite the event coordinator over the years and loved nothing more than planning a wedding.

While Jen flipped past pages that held fabric swatches and photos of greenery, Nat stole a peek at her engagement ring. Who would ever have thought she'd fall so hard and so fast for a guy like Troy Madden? But she had. The day he'd answered the inn's ad for a fishing guide, she'd taken one look at him and whispered, "I'm going to marry that man someday." Later, he'd confessed that he'd fallen head over heels in love with her the moment they met. Not that their relationship had been all smooth sailing. They'd had their fair share of issues. In many ways, they were polar opposites. But working on their differences had only strengthened their relationship. And soon—three years to the day from the day they'd met, in fact—they'd start their lives as husband and wife. She could hardly wait.

"Hu-hum." Jen cleared her throat again. "Earth to Nat. Come in, Nat."

"Oh. Sorry. I was just thinking of..." Nat felt her cheeks grow warm.

"No apologies necessary. Believe me, I understand." Jen flashed the simple wedding ring Caleb had slipped on her finger in front of a Justice of the Peace four years ago. "This shouldn't take too long." She tapped a page. "I emailed the Save-The-Date notices." Jen grinned. "Everyone has replied. They're all planning to make it."

"Wonderful." To keep their wedding as green as possible, Nat and Troy had opted to email their invitations, rather than having them printed on heavy card stock that would, in all likelihood, end up in a landfill. They'd also limited the guest list to immediate family and a handful of very close friends.

Page by page, they stepped through all the items in Jen's binder until they both agreed that they'd covered every detail. By the time they finished, Troy, Tyler and Reese had emerged from the trail that led down to the boat ramp. The small group moved to the outdoor kitchen, where they started cleaning the fish they'd caught. Soon, the smell of spice drifted in the air while Troy demonstrated the art of preparing blackened redfish. Probably drawn by the aroma, Izzy, Emma and Avery quickly joined them, along with Mattox, who'd apparently decided that hanging out with the others was more interesting than his video game.

Not long after that, the sound of slamming car trunks and doors echoed from the parking area as, one after another, the rest of the family began to arrive. Amy was the first appear.

"Hey! That was some reunion, wasn't it? I swear, they get better every year." A few gray strands among the dark curls that framed her face, Amy carefully balanced an oblong cake box in her hands while she climbed the steps onto the deck. Meanwhile, cradling an enormous wooden salad bowl in one arm, with a cloth grocery bag swinging from his other, Max followed his wife.

"Do you need some help with that?" Nat sprang to her feet. Rushing to the French doors, she held them open. "Did you see Diane and Tim on your way in?"

"No." Amy's answer floated out of the house as she moved toward the kitchen counter. "She texted. They'll be here soon. They'd just finished talking with Caitlyn. She made it back to Tallahassee safe and sound." As a starter on Florida State's soccer team, the junior had begun the long drive to the college right after breakfast.

"You want the salad in the fridge or on the counter?" Max asked.

"Put it on the island," Jen called from the back porch. "We'll eat as soon as everyone gets here." She waited a beat. "I made a batch of iced tea. Grab some when you come back out, will you?"

"I've got it." Nat retrieved one of several pitchers from the top shelf of the fridge. She placed it on the table in front of her aunt just in time to see her mom come around the end of the hedge that lined the parking area. The wheels of a red-and-white chest bounced over the pavered walkway behind Kim.

"I wonder what she brought? Please tell me it's not potato salad." Jen patted her stomach. The dish was the single most requested item at every family reunion. "I ate so much of it this weekend, I may not want any more for a year."

Nat laughed. "It is too good to pass up, isn't it?" She'd eaten more than she wanted to admit. Thinking of the mermaid-style gown she needed to fit into on her wedding day, she vowed to stick to her diet for the next six months. Starting tomorrow, she added when she saw Craig step onto the path, his arms loaded down with not one, but two immense steel trays. Her mouth watered while she imagined the crispy fried chicken in the pans he carried.

Rather than use the stairs, Kim pulled her wagon up the ramp they'd installed to comply with ADA requirements once the new cottages were ready for occupancy. Remaining seated, Jen gave her sister a speculative look.

"Whatcha got in there?" she asked.

"Broccoli casserole and rice pilaf." After loosening the straps, Kim removed an insulated tote from the top of the carrier. "And these are sliced tomatoes."

"Mom, I can't believe you spent your day off cooking," Nat chided while she hurried to help her mom ferry the food into the kitchen.

"I didn't. Honest. I made the casserole and the rice last week and stuck them in the freezer. All I had to do today was heat them up."

"And slice all these tomatoes," Nat said, studying the large platter piled high with thick slices.

"Don't I get some credit?" Craig slowed his long strides to brush a quick kiss on his wife's cheek.

"Oh, you." Kim gave him a gentle nudge. "You deserve a medal." Turning to Nat, she explained. "He did all the peeling. I did all the slicing."

"Well, however the job got done, these are the best tomatoes I've seen all year."

"They ought to be. They came from Moss Meadows." Craig tipped his head to Jen. "Speaking of, where is that husband of yours? I want to talk to him about our next Habitat for Humanity house." Now that term limits had forced Craig to resign from the town council, he'd turned his attention to other community service projects.

"You'll have to call him, I'm afraid. He said to go ahead and eat without him. This time of year, he rarely leaves the fields until it's full dark." Jen shrugged. "I'll take a plate home to him tonight."

"Hey! You going to keep that chicken all to yourself?" Diane stepped into the doorway that led to the kitchen. "We have hungry people in here."

"Aunt Diane, when did you get here?" Nat gave her aunt a one-armed hug on her way inside.

"Tim and I parked out front. We brought baked potatoes and all the fixings. It was too much to lug in from the parking area. Scott and Fern are here, too."

"Are Paul and Sophie with them?" Eager to see the five-year-old she'd rocked as an infant, Nat shoved aside a bowl of green beans to make room for the platter of tomatoes, then helped her mom create enough space on the wide granite island for her other dishes.

"He's here," Fern said, emerging from the hall with a bowl of fruit salad. "But I'm afraid your favorite nephew had a meltdown in the car on the way over here. He's in time out."

"And Sophie?" Nat eyed Fern, who looked as fit and trim as ever.

"She went off to find Isa—Izzy."

Nat smiled. The girls remained close despite their different interests. She dusted her hands.

"Is this everything?" she asked, surveying the island, which had grown crowded. At one end, Diane had arranged bowls of bacon bits and cheese, containers of sour cream, and chopped scallions around a cookie sheet that held at least ten pounds of foil-wrapped potatoes. At the other, a selection of dressings circled Max's salad bowl. Humming the theme song from *Wicked*, Tim bustled about adding more dishes until brimming bowls and platters covered every inch of the granite surface.

"It sure looks like it." Craig slid the restaurant-size pans onto the Aga range. After washing his hands, he loosened one of the lids. Immediately, the aroma of fried chicken filled the air.

With the impeccable timing of youth, Tyler, Izzy and the other teens began spilling into the kitchen. They fanned out among the adults to make way for Troy.

"Hot stuff, coming through."

Warmth spread through Nat's chest when Troy aimed a teasing glance her way. Laughing, she hustled to the stove as smoke and the scent of hot spices wafted from the still-sizzling cast-iron frying pan he carried. Taking hot pads from a nearby kitchen drawer, she tossed them on the counter closest to the trays of fried chicken and showed her fiancé where to place the pan. Mindful of the ribbing her aunts would give her, as well as the example they needed to set for the younger group, she cupped her fingers over the welcome weight of Troy's hand on her shoulder.

"Now all we need is Aunt Margaret to say the blessing," Diane said.

The words had no sooner left her lips than Margaret shuffled out of the bedroom wearing pale pink slacks and a top adorned with pink hearts. Beside her, Belle watched carefully as her mother negotiated the few steps into the kitchen. Jason, who'd moved into the family quarters after he and Belle exchanged vows in a ceremony attended by some of the top movers and shakers in the music industry, brought up the rear.

"Did I hear someone call my name?" Looking not a day older than she had when Nat arrived in Emerald Bay, Margaret propped her cane in front of her and leaned on it.

"Hey, Aunt Margaret." Scott's deep voice quieted the family members who'd gathered in the kitchen. "We were hoping you'd bless the food before these hungry hordes eat everything in sight."

"I won't waste any time, then." Her voice as firm as ever, Margaret delivered a short but heartfelt prayer.

Once the last "Amen" had echoed through the room, Diane clapped her hands. "All right, everybody. Plates, napkins and silverware are over there." She pointed to one end of the sturdy kitchen table that held stacks of paper products and plasticware, along with thirty or forty cups filled with iced tea. "After you fill your plate, grab a glass of tea and find a place to sit outside."

Content to stand right where she was for the moment, Nat tipped her head to Troy. "How was fishing?" she asked while she waited for the crowd around the island to thin.

"Good. Reese didn't catch a red, but she landed two trout and a catfish. I think she enjoyed it."

"You didn't make her bait her own hook, did you?" Nat shivered. Though Troy had taken her on countless fishing trips, she still couldn't bring herself to stick her hand in the bait well and grab one of the wiggly shrimp.

Troy's deep chuckle rumbled in his chest. "That girl only has one speed—full steam ahead. She let me show her what to do once. From then on, she insisted on doing everything herself." He nodded in admiration. "She's pretty good at it, too."

"And Tyler?"

"He actually caught two big reds that we had to throw back." Troy was a big supporter of slot limits. Fishermen who kept reds that were either too big or too small faced stiff penalties. "He did the happy dance when he finally landed one he could keep."

Picturing the gangly teen whooping it up on the boat, Nat stifled a laugh. "Are you ready to eat?" she asked when nearly everyone had worked their way through the food line and before people started coming back for seconds.

"Yeah. I better. I'm going to have to bounce right after. I have an early charter tomorrow." As one of the premier fishing guides in the area, Troy often met clients at the dock long before sunrise.

"We'd better fix our plates then." Though she enjoyed nothing more than spending the evening with her fiancé, Nat understood that he had to leave. Her own days started early. Between her responsibilities at the inn and working on the graphic design projects she freelanced, she stayed incredibly busy, though she had to admit, her schedule had lightened quite a bit once Jason resigned his position at Noble Records to manage The Emeralds.

With Troy at her side, she worked her way through the line. Taking a dab of this and a spoonful of that, she filled a plate nearly to overflowing. She managed to top it all off with a crunchy chicken breast and a fair-size piece of spicy fish. Troy did the same, and soon they joined the others, who sat at tables scattered about the grounds. For the next hour, they caught up on the latest news while they ate.

Later, after they'd eaten their fill and snuck away from the others long enough to share a steamy kiss that left them both rethinking the wisdom of waiting seven more months to get married, Nat joined her Aunt Margaret on the deck. Light filtered through the trees, casting long shadows on the grass. Below them on the lawn, Tim and Max tossed horseshoes at metal spikes, while Nat's charges grabbed bags of marshmallows and headed for the firepit. Scott, holding tightly to his five-year-old's hand, followed. From the kitchen came the sounds of her aunts' singing while they cleaned up after dinner and chatted among themselves.

"That was a pretty good meal, wasn't it?" Nat patted her full tummy and repeated her vow to stick to her diet beginning first thing in the morning.

"It always is, honey. Your mom is an excellent cook." Margaret leaned closer. "Don't tell her, but she's a better cook than Liz was."

"Really?" Nat felt her eyes widen in surprise. For most of her life, she'd heard people rave about the meals her Aunt Liz used to fix.

"My sister could handle simple dishes—her turkey soup was my favorite. But your mom?" Margaret brought her fingers to her lips and tossed a chef's kiss into the air. "That broccoli casserole she brought tonight was the best." She paused the way people did when they had second thoughts about what they wanted to say.

"What?" Nat prompted.

"I don't want to speak ill of your father, but I've never seen your mother look happier."

"Oh, Aunt Margaret, that's the sweetest thing." Nat's heart fluttered in her chest. She pressed a hand over it. "I have to agree—Mom's never been happier. She and Craig—they're so good for each other. Now that she sold Royal Meals, they spend a lot more time together." She knew her mom had thought long and hard about the decision to sell the catering business. In the end, she'd decided that the benefits of spending time with her family and the man she loved outweighed any pleasure she got from owning her own business.

Margaret sighed softly. "We're all pretty lucky, aren't we? Diane and Tim struggled for a while there, but they weathered that storm."

"Moving to Emerald Bay has been good for them, hasn't it?" Nat asked, though the answer was obvious. Diane's accounting firm was thriving, but she still had the freedom to accompany Tim to several of Caitlyn's soccer matches each season and join him on his annual trip for Dentists Without Borders.

Margaret pointed toward the far end of the yard, where Paul, his little legs pumping for all he was worth, raced across the grass with Sophie in hot pursuit. "Talk about surprises—he was a good one, wasn't he?" she asked as Sophie herded her brother back toward the others who were gathered around the firepit.

"Did you know he starts T-ball next week?" The spitting image of his father, the little boy was growing up far too quickly. Every time Nat saw him, it brought back memories of the summer she'd spent entertaining Izzy and Sophie and helping out with the tiny newborn. "Scott's one of the coaches."

Margaret clapped her hands. "Oh, that's wonderful! We'll have to go to all his games."

Behind them, a door swung open. Carrying glasses of iced tea, Nat's mom and her aunts joined them on the deck.

"You doing okay, Mama?" Belle asked while the others sank onto cushioned chairs. "Can I get you a blanket or anything?"

"I'm fine, sweetheart." Margaret stroked her daughter's arm with an age-spotted hand. "Nat's been keeping me company. Did you know Scott's going to coach Paul's T-Ball team this summer?"

"I did." Amy stopped wrapping a napkin around the bottom of her glass long enough to wave. "He and Max have been to the batting cages in Vero a couple of times." She mimicked taking a swing.

"I'd pay good money to see a video of that." Diane grinned. "Did you go with them?"

"Nah. These days, if I'm not at work, I'm sleeping." Amy yawned widely. "I miss Deborah."

"We miss you!" Nat said as she curled her legs onto the seat beside her. After Deborah's husband, Don, led Emerald Bay High to the state football championship last year, he'd accepted a coaching position at Mississippi State. Amy had bought back her partner's share in Sweet Cakes and had been juggling both the original bakery and the one in Sebastian ever since. Though her aunts still got together at least one evening a week, Amy hadn't shared a glass of wine or sangria with any of them in the months leading up to the reunion.

From her seat beside Jen, Fern asked, "Have you heard from her? From Deborah, I mean? How do they like Mississippi?"

Amy shrugged. "She says it's hot. Humid."

"Just like home, then." Jen sipped her tea.

"I know, right?" Fern brightened.

Margaret tsked at Amy. "You work too hard, child."

"I know, Aunt Margaret. All work and no play, yada yada. But it won't be for much longer." Amy shot the group a pleading look. "Keep your fingers crossed, will you? The girl I hired last month has been running both locations all weekend so I could be here for the reunion. She's done such a great job that I'm going to put her in charge of Sweet Cakes 2. Hopefully, my sixty-hour workweeks will soon be a thing of the past."

"From your lips..." Leaning forward, Diane clinked her glass against her sister's, and they all drank to Amy's success.

"I missed seeing Opal this year," Margaret blurted suddenly. Her hands moving restlessly, she fretted, "I hope she's all right." Her brother's widow had broken a hip in a fall this spring and was still recovering.

"Harry promised to fly her out for a visit as soon as she's able to travel, Mama," Belle reminded her mother. "That's something to look forward to."

"I suppose," Margaret sighed, though she didn't sound convinced.

Nat glanced across the deck. Reading a desire to lighten the mood in her mom's expression, she tossed out the first question that came to mind. "What was your favorite part of the reunion?"

"The food," Amy said, right off the bat.

"I had a nice long talk with Harry's son, Emmit. Did you know he runs a dude ranch near San Antonio?" Kim asked. "He invited us to come out whenever we want."

Ever the accountant, Diane said, "I liked that we broke even this year."

"That's the best you can come up with?" Amy nudged her sister's foot.

Looking sheepish, Diane laughed. "Okay," she added finally. "I enjoyed the nature hike Troy took us on. I think we should ask him to lead those every year."

"Except for the part with the alligators." Kim gave an exaggerated shiver. "I could have done without those."

"Don't worry, Mom." Nat did her best to soothe her mother's phobia. "Troy won't let the gators get you."

"Caleb and I had a great time talking about organic farming with that couple from California. What were their names?" Jen ran her fingers through her hair.

"That's a good question," Belle admitted when no one responded.

"Dolly and Cooper," Margaret supplied,

coming up with the names no one else could remember. "Their father was my mother's cousin."

"Two points for Aunt Margaret," Jen said with a nod. "Anyway, they gave us some tips on converting the Bucher land." Caleb, who—much to Jen's surprise—owned several lucrative patents that were currently being used in the space program, had purchased the adjoining farm as soon as the estate cleared probate.

"My favorite part was the talent show. As always," Belle chimed. She aimed a look at Fern. "Especially Sophie's solo. That girl has talent."

"She loves spending time with you. I never have to nag her to practice her scales." Fern's voice filled with a mix of gratefulness for the singing lessons Belle gave her daughter whenever The Emeralds were in town.

Wanting to make sure she felt included, Nat turned to Margaret. "What about you, Aunt Margaret?" she asked softly. "What was your favorite part of the reunion?"

"Hmm. Let me think." Margaret rested her head on the back of her chair for a long minute while laughter from the teenagers and family members at the firepit drifted across the yard. She didn't stir when a pair of monk parakeets, part of the flock that had made its home on the grounds, landed on the porch railing.

After a few minutes, Nat wondered if the ever-present roar of the ocean had lulled her aunt to sleep. But no. Just when she was about to suggest to the others that they call it a night, Margaret's blue eyes blinked open.

With a slight cough, she picked up the conversation right where she'd left off. "I think it's right now. This, right here." Margaret motioned to the group gathered on the deck. "It's knowing that all the people I love the most are living their best lives. And that no matter what happens, the inn—our legacy—will remain in our family for generations to come. To me, that's the best part of the reunion."

Watching the green birds hop along the railing and listening to their cheerful chirps, Nat admitted that she felt the same way, and examining the ring on her finger, she looked forward to seeing the future unfold.

Thank you for reading
Treasure Coast Legacy!

Sign up for Leigh's newsletter to get
the latest news about upcoming releases,
excerpts, and more!
https://leighduncan.com/newsletter/

Books by Leigh Duncan

EMERALD BAY SERIES

Treasure Coast Homecoming
Treasure Coast Promise
Treasure Coast Christmas
Treasure Coast Revival
Treasure Coast Discovery
Treasure Coast Legacy

SUGAR SAND BEACH SERIES

The Gift at Sugar Sand Inn
The Secret at Sugar Sand Inn
The Cafe at Sugar Sand Inn
The Reunion at Sugar Sand Inn
Christmas at Sugar Sand Inn

HEART'S LANDING SERIES

Cut The Cake
Save The Dance
Kiss The Bride

ORANGE BLOSSOM SERIES

Butterfly Kisses
Sweet Dreams

Treasure Coast Legacy

Hometown Heroes Series

Mitch

Luke

Brett

Dan

Travis

Colt

Hank

Garrett

The Hometown Heroes Collection, Vol. 1 & Vol. 2

Single Title Books

A Country Wedding

Journey Back to Christmas

The Growing Season

Pattern of Deceit

Novellas

The Billionaire's Convenient Secret

A Reason to Remember

Find all Leigh's books at:
leighduncan.com/books

Acknowledgements

Every book takes a team effort. I want to give special thanks to those who made *Treasure Coast Legacy* possible.

Cover design
Chris Kridler at
Sky Diary Productions

Editing Services
Chris Kridler at
Sky Diary Productions

Proofs
Raina Toomey

Interior formatting
Amy Atwell and Team
Author E.M.S.

About the Author

Leigh Duncan is the award-winning author of more than three dozen novels, novellas and short stories. She sold her very first novel to Harlequin American Romance and was selected as the company's lead author when Hallmark Publishing introduced its new line of romances and cozy mysteries. A National Readers' Choice Award winner and *Publisher's Weekly* National Best-Selling author, Leigh lives on Florida's East Coast where she writes heartwarming women's fiction with a dash of Southern sass. When she isn't busy writing, Leigh enjoys cooking, crocheting and spending time with family and friends.

Want to get in touch with Leigh? She loves to hear from readers and fans. Visit leighduncan.com to send her a note. Join Leigh on Facebook, and don't forget to sign up for her newsletter so you get the latest news about fun giveaways, special offers or her next book!

Made in the USA
Monee, IL
21 March 2025

14328070R00270